AWOKE

THE **WANT** SERIES

K. T. CONTE

D1293036

Printed in the United States of America

First Printing, 2017

Cover Design: Ana Grigoriu
Interior Design: Kristina Liburd
Publisher: SugarCane Publishing, a SugarCane Media Company
Editor: Brenda Peregrine

Library of Congress Catalog Number: 2017953910

ISBN 978-0-9992259-0-5

SugarCane Publishing
244 Fifth Avenue
New York, NY 10001

www.sugarcanebooks.com

CONTENTS

To Grandma Charlotte,
I will forever love you and miss you.

1

I intended to have a normal, run-of-the-mill, no-vision-having night.

The kind of night that after hours of dancing, you end up holding your pumps because your feet hurt like crazy, but you can't stop grinning through the pinched toes because you had such a great time with friends. The kind of night where you make memories that will stick with you and make you chuckle when you think back on them.

I wanted that kind of night. I really did.

Before I left my house, I even gave myself a good talking to in the mirror. "Katya, you will not mess this up tonight. You will be a normal—no you *are* a normal person tonight. There is nothing weird about you. You will not have strange faraway looks in your eyes. You will not see odd things out of the corner of your eye. The only thing you will see is the bottom of a beer mug that you will convince a flirty college guy to get for you. You are going to dance, laugh, and have fun. Because that's what normal eighteen-year-olds do."

I thought I'd listened to myself. At the very least, I'd tried. And everything seemed okay at first. I made my grand entrance at Jillian's Bowling and Bar for my friend Amie's birthday party, said hello to my best friend Cynthia and Amie herself, and made my way to the ladies' room.

I had just sat down in the stall when I started to feel an unfortunate but now familiar creepy-crawly feeling. My stomach did that odd drop it does when you're on a rollercoaster, about to go down a hill. The hairs on my arms raised up, and I started to feel my skin warm up to alarming heat levels. Someone unfamiliar with my condition would think that I was erupting from the inside out. When my vision started to get small and dark, I understood then what my mother had been complaining about all these years about menopause.

Man, I really don't listen.

I felt myself sigh as I began to see things and people I had never seen before. Places I had never been.

A huddled group of sweaty, burly men, laughing together and pointing at me.
Lukewarm water lapping over my feet as I stood on a large rock in the middle of lake.
A dimly glowing orb in a room covered in silks overlooking a castle courtyard.
Blue eyes, glowing brighter and brighter, that had me frightened and mesmerized—

The scenes always flashed by so quickly that I could never get a clear sense of whether I was experiencing someone else's vision, or God forbid, that I was remembering my own experiences that I'd put out of my mind. It sounds crazy for me to even think that I could forget something so completely that I'd not know whether it had been there in the first place, but my life has forever been complicated. Not remembering something that then returned violently into my psyche without provocation would be just one more complication on a very long list.

"Katya! Where the hell are you?"

I'd never wanted to strangle and hug someone at the same time before. Cynthia's shrill voice interrupting me brought me surprisingly close to that impulse. The visions were quickly disappearing. As the tingling started to lessen, the last vision of the bright blue eyes lingered. I wanted to desperately to hold on. But the longer I tried, the faster it seemed to erase from my head. Then it was gone.

I couldn't even remember what I had just seen. The only thing that remained was the nauseous feeling in my stomach, the impossible heat coming from me, and the sense that I had lost something.

Every single time. It was the same every time.

I heard, "Kat? Katya Stevens, what the heck is taking you so long?"

A green pair heels clicked against the bathroom tiles toward my stall and the sound helped to center me. I needed a minute to keep my dinner from coming up and cool off. The abrupt knocking at the stall door startled me and I could feel my stomach churn again from the adrenaline. Sighing, I made myself presentable and slammed the door open.

"Cynthia, could you be any louder?" I sucked in my teeth loudly. "I was in the middle of something!"

With the sweat pouring down my forehead and the groggy look I had on my face, Cynthia recognized my symptoms and immediately become concerned. "Are you okay? Did you just have another episode?" She reached out to me, but I dodged her touch; I hated her touching me when I was sweaty like this.

"Yeah, I just finished. I think I was about to hold on to something when your high-pitched voice scared the crap of me."

Rolling her eyes, Cynthia smirked. "Literally or figuratively? Doesn't smell too bad in here." I gave her the finger. She had at least the decency to grab a few paper towels and pat down my face. "I'm only trying to make you smile, Kat. Sorry about the yelling, but you were taking too long. I don't want to miss a second of this party. Of all the times to have visions on the can!"

"Shh! What if someone heard you?" I quickly checked the two other bathroom stalls to ensure that we were alone. I headed to the sink to freshen up and wash my hands. "You are acting like I enjoy these visions or flashes or whatever you want to call them that come out of nowhere." My shoulders sagged in annoyance and confusion. "I'm just so done with this. This last month has been a nightmare, and I wish they would just stop."

My best friend studied me. "Do you remember anything this time?"

"If I did, you know you'd be the first to hear about it."

"Maybe you should talk to your mom about—"

I shot her a stern look. "Are you crazy? Do you enjoy me having my freedom? To come and go as I please? If she gets wind of this, she's going to think I'm having another psychotic episode and have me back in therapy sessions like when we were kids. I'm not going back to that time, Cyn. I'm not going back to pills and sessions and people looking at me like I'm nuts or possessed. She has enough to worry about with work, not to mention leaving me alone at home with the shakes."

She looked at me sympathetically, aware of the anxiety that showed in my eyes. "I'm sorry I brought it up. We'll leave it alone. Everything is normal, right?"

I strengthened my trembling smile for her. "Right." I turned to the mirror and wiped the remaining sweat off my arms and my neck. My halter dress fortunately gave me the opportunity to air out the heat I was still feeling.

"Man, I wish I had some deodorant."

Cyn giggled and began to fish inside of her clutch. "Don't ask me why I brought this with me. It was a totally random thought, but something told me to bring this." And she pulled out a travel-sized deodorant.

And I burst out laughing. "Are you serious?"

"Kat, I swear. I have no idea why I brought it."

I applied it, looking at her through the mirror. "Your twin senses were probably tingling. See? It's these instances like this that make me think people should be best friends with someone who shares their birthday."

Rolling her eyes, Cynthia handed me a towel to dry my hands and leaned over my shoulder to gaze into my mirror. "Just say I'm the best," she whispered.

I gave her a happy look and blew her a kiss. "You are the best, Cyn."

Cynthia winked at me and began to ruffle her curly red locks, adjusting her green halter dress and makeup. My best friend had looks that were out of this world. Pert nose, flawless complexion, not one blemish. She came out of the womb with looks that any model would pay for. She knew it, and so did everyone else.

People thought that she was stuck up, but that wasn't the entire truth. Cynthia also had a heart of gold and had always protected me at every chance, ever since we were kids. She always had this sense of just being there when I needed her. I did the same for her. We called it our "twin sense."

As we preened and fixed our makeup, she threw me a sideways look from the mirror. "Don't drive yourself crazy over this. Just let it go, Kitty Kat."

I nudged her out of my mirror. "You know I don't like being called that."

Cynthia giggled. "Whatever, K.K. Look, tonight is about having fun. We only have six weeks left of our last high-school summer. The birthday girl is waiting for us by the pool tables and is having a mini freak out. You both can't be freaking out at the same time. I can only handle so much. Have pity on me, please?"

Sighing but smirking, I nodded. "I guess I do have to be the stronger one here, seeing as I'm the oldest."

"A technicality. You're only like a few hours older."

I grabbed her by the shoulders and pushed her towards the door. "Yes, yes. Now give me a second. I'll meet you outside." Cynthia gave me one last look before her heels were clicking out the door.

Smirking, I shook my head, attempting to clear my thoughts. Cynthia was right. I couldn't let this mess up Amie's night. When

Cynthia and I turned eighteen last month, Amie was one of the few people who came by our neighborhood and just spent time with us. She didn't expect anything, or want anything in return, which was rare for most of the girls in our class.

Because Cynthia and I were popular at school, it meant that someone was always looking for something—either a way to become popular or to increase their own status by bringing us down with some malicious gossip. Amie, neither popular or malicious, just wanted to hang out with us because she liked us. Cyn and I decided that we would do everything we could to make sure Amie Espinosa's eighteenth birthday party was a complete success in return.

And it almost hadn't gotten off the ground due to the tremors.

Six months ago, small tremors started shaking up the eastern region of the United States, and they'd become more frequent since then. There have been more here, in Boston, than anywhere else. While a few of Boston's iconic buildings have suffered some damage and a few individuals have been injured, people were mostly freaking out about having this many earthquakes here in the Northeast in the first place.

Especially Amie's mom, Mrs. Espinosa. She wanted to cancel Amie's party all together because she was afraid that "the big one" might happen while we were downtown. Cyn and I had convinced Cynthia's mom, Mrs. Maroney, to speak to Mrs. Espinosa and remind her that if something big was to come, then the emergency alarms would sound and we would have the chance to seek shelter. Besides, Mrs. Espinosa left her home every day. Couldn't the big one happen at any time? At least that's what Cyn and I told Mrs. Maroney to say. Whether she said that or not, it doesn't matter, because the party wasn't cancelled and we were just glad to have it happen.

I sighed, adjusted my halter dress, threw my clutch underneath my arm, and stepped out of the bathroom to find Amie and Cynthia waiting for me not far from the door. Seeing their faces reminded that I had only one goal tonight.

I was going to have fun, dammit.

2

"Katya!" Amie sounded relieved and motioned for me to come over.

For her birthday, we'd convinced Amie to take off her larger-than-life glasses and replace them with contacts. Her usually curly nest of hair had been transformed into a sleek look around her thin face. Her normally pale cheeks looked alive with blush and color. She'd even swapped her dull plaid clothes and high-knee socks for a fashionable dress out of my closet.

All in all, Amie Espinosa turned into an even prettier hot chick when the effort was put in. But instead of being on cloud nine, the birthday girl looked ready to blow chunks.

"Amie, are you okay? You look a little sick there."

Amie put a hand to her flat stomach to hold down the rising food. "Cynthia is trying to convince me to find a guy and get his number. It's crazy, right?"

My best friend's mischievous grin confirmed her plan. And they say I'm the troublemaker... But I couldn't help but smile too. "Yeah girl! Let's do it! We are finally around men instead of those immature asses at school. Besides, we do need to get Amie a birthday present—perhaps that first kiss, right, Cyn?" I looked around carefully. "Doesn't hurt to look for ourselves either," I muttered to myself.

Amie unfortunately heard me and her mouth flubbed like a fish. "Katya Stevens, what are you saying? You're already dating the hottest basketball player in school. Why do *you* need to look?"

Amie was right—I did have a boyfriend. Mr. Basketball Hotshot Roger Simmons. I liked him, at least before we got popular. Then he started doing well on the basketball team and it kinda went downhill from there. The better he did, the more obnoxious people became. For some reason, people thought it was cute to call us the Choco-Vanilla Couple of Benson High. Or Ying and Yang. Or other interracial couple names I really hated. No matter how many times I told Roger that I hated those names, he would just brush it off, telling me to calm down. "It's not that big of a deal, babe," he would say. "You don't see me making a big deal of it." The times I almost smacked him...

For two years, I'd thought maybe he would get a clue that his black girlfriend didn't want to be reminded that she was part of an Oreo. He was as thick as cement. You would think I would have dumped him by now. I asked myself why I hadn't, and I always felt the answer was... complicated. Roger was an emotional mess that I didn't want to deal with. So, just like with my visions, I went along, business as usual.

However, I didn't want to get into why I would exchange him for someone else at that very moment. No need to get messy now.

"Don't listen to me, girl. We are getting you a kiss tonight! Or at least finding someone you would like to talk to and then maybe kiss after finding out you guys have something in common... You know what I'm trying to say. But if you don't feel comfortable and want to stay where you are," I gave her a meaningful look, "you can stick around the table with your mom and family members."

Amie took a glance to the left to see her mother, a frumpy woman wearing a very loud and colorful dress that looked like it belonged in the disco era. Mrs. Espinosa had also been drinking cocktails in quick succession, and she was talking and cackling quite loudly into her cell phone. Amie's family was a mix of much older cousins, aunts, and uncles who looked like they either had no interest in staying at the table, were completely bored, or had just decided to nurse a cocktail or two themselves.

With a determined look, Amie said, "No punking out now, right?"

I beamed. "That's my girl! We are grown women now, and grown women don't punk out!" We guided Amie away from the set party area into a larger room that had several pool tables and a large bar. The lighting was poor; there were a few strobe lights flashing colors, just enough so that people could get around, mingle, and watch the countless sporting events on the TV screens surrounding the room. The red and blue strobe lights in the pool room were making everyone look otherworldly. Like they were nocturnal creatures skulking around to find a new activity since the moon had made an appearance. It was weird to me that they'd want to be in a room like that but I guess that's what adults did—get in a dark room with alcohol in their system and throw their inhibitions to the wind.

I watched a group of people yell and argue their heads off over a game of pool in a room adjoining the main bar. The competitiveness never failed to get people aggressive and unresponsive to reason. They were so pissed that it looked like their eyes flashed red in anger. Which was silly, obviously. It must have been the strange lighting reflecting off their eyes.

As the fight unfolded, a man sat behind the group watching the argument. His dark, greasy hair fell over his face, but his wide grin showed his enjoyment of the spectacle. I could tell, from the nervous energy that had him clenching his seat and the bouncing of his knee, that he wanted to participate but couldn't.

Another look to the left of the fight revealed three guys, not much older than us, whose attention had strayed away from their pool game. They began to nudge each other, overtly pointing in our direction and attempting to make eye contact with us.

Meh, it's a place to start. Flipping my dark, coiled hair over my shoulder, I asked, "Girls, there are some cute guys over there. Why don't step a little closer?" Neither one said a word. Looking in the opposite direction, both Cynthia and Amie had odd looks on their faces. Their jaws were slightly open, their eyes were glazed over, and they were frozen in place. They were mesmerized. Looking for the distraction, I said, "Hey! What are we looking at?"

I found it, and I completely understood.

In the opposite direction of the pool tables was a small dining table area by the room's entrance. A man stood tall next to the table in the corner and was staring intently in our direction. His short-cropped brown hair crowned a chiseled face with a pert nose. His frown only accentuated his full, masculine lips. Even with the dim lighting, you could make out the lines that defined his built chest, strong arms and legs, and his muscular back. His chin donned a slight shadow that only added to the allure of his physique.

One could have taken him as a model but, for some reason, he struck me as a fighter instead. The way his hand gripped his glass of beer and how his knees were slightly bent—he was ready to move at a moment's notice. As if he knew something could happen at any second. I was taken aback by my sudden need to get a better look, but also felt that I needed to stay clear away from him.

An odd pulse rattled through me as I studied him and the desire to stare at him disappeared. As soon as the shiver ended, a slight tremor shook the room. With bated breath, everyone stopped moving and waited for the shaking to cease or increase.

"Oh God, do you think this is it?" I overheard a waitress say to a coworker. "My sister said she was watching a talk show and they were teaching everybody what to do if the 'big one' comes."

The coworker shook his head. "No, it's not gonna be the shakes. The big one is about the water. All the water that we have is gonna dry up and this whole country is gonna turn into a desert. See California's drought? Just the beginning, sweetheart."

I rolled my eyes. These doomsday people were just feeding into the paranoia and fear. There was a lot of mention of the "big one" but no one could say what the "big one" was supposed to be or how it was supposed to feel. Was it supposed to be a massive earth-splitting earthquake? Was it gonna be one of those tsunamis? No one really understood what was going on. As much as they had their brave theories, the concerned and nervous expressions on everyone's faces betrayed their thoughts; they were looking for any clue that they should bolt from the room. The hot guy, however, continued to stare intently at the opposite corner, unfazed by the tremors.

The tremors only lasted for a minute though, and everyone returned to their activities, maybe a bit less at ease. The shaking effectively broke the hypnosis on the girls as well. "He. Is. Gorgeous. What do you think? Twenty-three? Twenty-four?"

Cynthia said breathlessly. "If I already didn't have Steve, I'd go talk to him."

"Y-y-yeah," I stuttered.

"Amie! Go talk to him!" Cynthia exclaimed.

Amie immediately paled and started to back out of the room. "Chica, are you crazy?" she screeched. "I'm not talking to him! I can't. I'm not like you, the Redheaded Bombshell or Katya, the Nubian Princess. Or the neighborly hot sisters from other misters or whatever stupid names everyone else calls you! Why did I think I could do this again? You know what? I'm not a grown woman—I'm a punk.   I'm just going to go back to our table and—"

Cyn grabbed the scared silly girl before she could leave the room. "Amie, stop! Just breathe!" Amie still looked ready to bolt as her eyes started to gloss with tears.

"Hey, hey," I said, rubbing her shoulder. "Come on now. Talk to us."

I watched as she took several calming breaths and said, "I don't want to make a fool of myself. I've told you that I've never done this before, and maybe this isn't meant for me."

I drew her in my arms and gave her a tight hug, "Babes, we want you to be happy. Remember all those talks that we've had about you wanting to live freely and not be shackled by everyone's expectations of you? Remember we promised ourselves to not be held by what happened in the past? Ames, just live for a second! We want you to have a great time tonight. And have you even seen yourself tonight? You are gorgeous, and any guy would love to have you. You are smart, sweet, and witty when you want to be. Just believe in yourself."

Cynthia nodded. "Look, if we think you can do this, then you can do this. He doesn't look like he's with anyone. What's the worst he can say? 'No, I'm sorry?'"

Amie looked at the both of us before sighing deeply. "All right. I'll try."

Cynthia squealed. "Okay. Remember what we talked about. Just introduce yourself, make eye contact to exude confidence, and be curious! He seems friendly enough. Remember, we live for today!" Amie took another calming breath before walking slowly to the table. With every step she shook, a slight shiver could be seen running up her spine.

"Cyn, is this a good idea? Maybe she isn't ready for this yet," I said, gnawing at my bottom lip. We kept back a few paces behind our trembling friend to hear the exchange.

"Oh, sure she is. Wasn't the entire point of this adventure to convince her mom to have the party here so that Amie could experience something more than her house, our houses, and school? She cannot go to college like this!" Cynthia tossed her fire red hair over her shoulder and looked me in the eye. "Why?" she asked, her eyebrows arched. "You don't want him, do you?"

"What? Girl, please!" I scoffed but felt the heat rise in my cheeks. I would never admit that I found Corner Guy ridiculously attractive and was a bit jealous that Amie was getting a chance to speak to him.

Cynthia wasn't fooled and smirked at me. "Okay. If you say so. Now be quiet." Unfortunately, we had taken too long to pay attention because Amie had already approached the man. She wasn't saying much, but he was saying quite a bit. Not sure what to make of it, I quickly stepped closer to listen.

With a brogue, he said, "Why can't a man be left alone without having some chit, a poorly dressed one at that, come up to him and ask him such stupid questions? High school, lass? Really? Can't people just stand around and enjoy themselves without having some bird act ridiculously dull?" At this point, his voice rose in volume and a number of people and staff members were now staring at them. Corner Guy took a look around and seemed to swell with more anger because people were staring.

"Why don't you do me a favor?" he lowered his voice, giving Amie the dirtiest look he could muster. "Take your timid, haggard, cardboard-shaped, lumpy body out of my sight and allow me some peace and quiet!" He slammed his glass down on the table, splashing Amie completely, ruining her dress. Without another look, the man stalked out of the room.

Unable to hold in her embarrassment, Amie turned around and vaulted into my arms, sobbing loudly.

Wow. I did NOT see that happening. What a jerk! Furious, I wiped away Amie's tears and had her look straight at me. "Don't cry, sweetie. You do not listen to him. You are beautiful and no one can say anything to change that. I'm going to make him pay for that. Don't cry anymore. I got this." I turned to Cynthia, shifting my clutch underneath my arm. "Take care of Amie. Tell her mom that she dirtied her dress and needs to go home. Grab a cab and make sure no one else sees her. I'll catch up with you later."

I turned for the exit only to have Cynthia grab my arm, "Wait, where the hell do you think you are going? You don't know who that guy is! He could be a complete psycho."

"Cyn, I know you are usually the one who flies off the handle, but I cannot sit here and not get that asswipe. You don't talk to people like that! It took Amie everything she had to go up to him, and he treats her like this? I'm going to tell that bastard off and he's gonna apologize!" Not giving Cynthia a chance to talk me down, I quickly walked out the door, down the stairs, and out of Jillian's.

3

Man, what a jerk! I was pissed at myself for convincing my poor friend to go out on a limb, but mainly I was really pissed at that guy. I found his tall form stalking down the street; he was moving further into downtown Boston's cement maze.

"Hey, asshole! Stop right there!" I shouted over the honks and beeps of the taxis passing by, searching for fares. The jerk either didn't hear me or he ignored me. Either way, it only ticked me off more. I began to run after him, dancing around the large cracks in the broken cement sidewalks. "Stop!" Pushing through the crowds of people, I focused on cornering that rude Scottish guy and chewing his ear off.

The tapping of my heels against the pavement filled the air as I blindly ran after him, not realizing he'd entered an alley several feet ahead of me. I turned the corner, getting ready to yell again when he stopped in the middle of the alley with a man kneeling in front of him. It was the same man who had been staring at the arguing group of people back at Jillian's. It was only then that I realized that I had been blindly following a guy who could actually be a psycho. *Not a smart move, Kat.* I was just about to run in the other direction when I heard the kneeling man cry out.

"Please," the kneeling man pleaded. "Please, Kyrios. I'm not ready to go yet. There's too much I want to do still!"

Another tremor started shaking the ground again, much stronger than the one earlier. I could hear the surprised shrieks of people running away from older buildings in case rubble fell below. Then I heard an unearthly sound, like grating nails running against a chalkboard, that only amplified the chaos of the moment tenfold. It brought a painful ache to my core that I never knew I could feel. I covered my ears, hoping to lessen the noise and the pain.

"Do you hear that?" the Scot said, over the chaos. "It's already searching for you, tearing up the ground and people in its quest. All because it wants to devour you. At least you had the decency to leave that crowded bar. How thoughtful of you," he sneered.

"Thoughtful? Of those assholes, who couldn't give a damn that I'm gone? I couldn't care less if every Wanter devoured them," he yelled. "I only left because I was trying to escape from you," the man sniffled.

"You know the rules," the Scot said harshly. "You've had your time. You need to leave now, before you become more of a liability. The Craver is around the corner." The ground continued to shake with intensity, as if the tremors were coming closer to us. In the corner of my eye, several feet away from the entrance of the alley, I saw a shadow. The shadow had the shape of a nine-foot-tall, incredibly fat person, but with spikes covering it head to toe. The shadow took another earth-shattering step towards the alley and gave another soul-shaking scream.

"No, please! I'm not ready. I haven't gotten back at those who deserted me. Those who made me what I am now!" His pleas fell on deaf ears as the Scot raised his open palm over the man's face.

A bright blue light appeared from his hand, engulfing the man. The man continued to scream in protest before he vanished.

The Scot whirled around to face the shadow. His eyes glowed dangerously bright blue, intensified by his anger and determination. It was only then that he noticed me, staring at him and then at the shadow.

The shadow must have sensed that the man was gone because it repeatedly stomped, like a child having a massive tantrum. The shadow's form swelled, making each spike grow to a size as large as a jackhammer. The more it swelled, the more its form clarified, and the more afraid I became. The nine-foot giant was now twelve feet tall, excluding its mammoth spikes. With blood-red eyes and a noticeable hole in its left shoulder, the dark figure's intentions were clear: destroy the Scot. And I was in the middle of the battle with no way out of the alley. With each stomp it took, the foundations of the buildings that surrounded us began to crumble. Which meant the brick building was getting ready to flatten me.

Before I could register his movment, the Scot was in front of me, shielding me from the shadow. "Run to the other side of the alley now," he yelled. "You don't want to be here when it starts attacking. Go!"

But I couldn't move. I was petrified. *I'm going to die. I don't want to die.*

Then my vision symptoms came back. My stomach dropped and goosebumps rose on every part of my body. Every hair stood on end. I fought to keep the nausea away and focus on the danger in front of me.

Suddenly a gust of unnatural wind swirled in the middle of the alley, spinning into a huge cyclone of dirt and debris. The dirty cyclone spun faster, growing as tall as the giant. The whirlwind's body then transformed from a dirty brown gust of wind to a glistening silver swirl, similar to the shiny chrome on a brand-new car.

Before I could study it any further, the cyclone rocketed towards the shadow, like a bullet exiting the chamber of a gun. The dark figure never even had a chance to react as the chrome wind ran straight through it, effectively cleaving it into two equal pieces. It gave one last scream as its right and left limbs went in opposite directions. I stood in disbelief and watched the dark figure's body pieces crash to the ground and disintegrate into red, glowing particles.

Where the hell did that come from?

Then the same odd pulse that gave me the shivers earlier came back stronger and rattled my core even more than the chalkboard scream. It suddenly became hard to breathe. My heart pounded painfully fast. I broke into a sweat and then felt freezing cold a moment later. Every inch of my body vibrated like it was ripping itself apart and coming back together. I stumbled back into the wall of the alley, desperately gripping my chest and head.

Someone help me.

I shut my eyes, trying to control the pain, but it was too much. I heard a woman's blood-curdling scream only to realize that the scream was my own. My lungs felt constricted, and I was left gasping for air. In the midst of my pain and my panic, I felt something tear open, right between my heart and my lungs. It was an intense, hot sensation—as if a new organ was coming into existence. The organ felt new, but also felt like it had always been there. Something I didn't remember, but I did at the same time. A feeling that scared me, but I understood it completely. I looked down at my hands and noticed my palms glowed blue. My whole body glowed, and I continued to glow brighter and brighter with every second.

Then it was over, taking all my energy with it. My body returned to normal, my knees buckled underneath me, and I went straight to the ground. As my head hit the pavement and my eyes unconsciously started to close, I remembered seeing the Scot approach me. Out of the whole experience, the look he had then freaked me out the most. His eyebrows met in the middle of his forehead and his lips formed a pout. His eyes no longer glowed, but he looked at me as if I were the strangest thing he had ever seen.

4

I woke to the smell of lavender. It smelled like home. A pair of down pillows cradled my throbbing head. Pillows that looked exactly like the pillows that I had at home. Ivory cotton sheets pooled around my body as I looked around.

Wait, I am home. How did I get here?

The pictures of my mother and father were on the tall oak dresser, just as I remembered. My closet door was slightly ajar from the amount of clothes stuffed inside. My wall mirror atop my vanity stared back at me, reflecting my confusion and wonder. I looked okay—my long, black coiled hair looked like a rats' nest, but nothing marred my dark skin. My dress had some stains, but everything was basically intact. I was really in my room. However, I'd failed to notice the pair of blue eyes watching me from the corner of my room on the first scan. I found them soon enough.

Jumping out of bed and clutching the wall, I said in a panic, "What are you doing here? How did I get back here?"

The Scot remained silent, watching me carefully. Now in good lighting, I could do the same. Fair-skinned, a few freckles dotted his face along the bridge of his nose. His frown deepened as he crossed his arms, and a strand of his dark hair fell into his eyes. He never lost his focus on me as he quickly ran his hand through his hair. He still displayed that nervous energy—ready to pounce on me if necessary.

Better lighting only confirmed what I had seen at Jillian's. His long black jacket did nothing to hide the strong arms encased in its sleeves or his muscular chest. Even his long legs in his black jeans looked sculpted. His square jaw was clenched; a muscle pulsed by his ear. The most arresting part of him was his eyes: they were the bluest eyes I had ever seen in my life. This man could have easily fallen out of my dreams. But this wasn't a dream; it was reality. He was a stranger, sitting on my vanity chair, watching me and waiting expectantly. Him being hot meant nothing.

Annoyed, I said, "I know you have a clear command of the English language because you verbally chewed out my friend. So answer me. What are you doing here, and how did I get here?"

For a moment, I thought he would ignore me again. He suddenly leaned back into the chair, his gaze never leaving me. "I brought you here."

My eyes widened. "How did you know where I live? Did you break into my house?" I looked around for my purse and couldn't find it anywhere. "Where's my purse? Did you steal it? I'm barely eighteen. I don't have anything valuable."

The Scot rolled his eyes in amusement. "Peace, lass. I hardly need keys to enter anywhere, thank you. As for your purse, it's probably back at the alley."

Crap. Well, there goes my money. I pulled the sheets closer to my body. "You still haven't answered my question. How did you know where I lived?"

The Scot smiled a smile I found gorgeous and annoying all at the same time. "I looked around. Now, if you are done asking your questions, I have a couple of questions for you."

My eyebrows disappeared into my hair. I crossed my arms over my chest. "I don't think you are in any position to give me any orders, seeing as you are trespassing and were a complete jackass to my friend. Okay, maybe you weren't interested in her, but the name calling? The yelling?" I could myself getting riled up again, remembering Amie's tears. "I mean, do you have any idea how much it took her to go up and talk to you? I mean, what kind of person—"

"You know, lass," he interrupted, annoyed, "the least you could do is be grateful that I protected you and even brought you here. A true jackass would have left you lying there, fainted and all."

The bravado I felt left quickly. "I fainted?" A small tremor shook the house, and I closed my eyes, trying to not to panic. I hated being home during the shaking. I felt them more at home than anywhere else. Being home alone with semi-constant earthquakes made a horrible combination. Again, the Scot didn't seem to be bothered by it. His attention was on me. But any easiness the Scot displayed before had disappeared, and he resumed his leaning stance.

"Don't you remember what happened?"

My eyebrows furrowed, trying to remember. What exactly did happen? Images flashed through my mind: me running after the Scot into the alley, the kneeling man, the shadow, the Scot's burning eyes. I bolted out of the bed, putting a clear distance between us. "Whoa! What the hell happened? What was that dark big thing?" I clutched my chest, remembering the tightening. "What did you do to me? What did you do to that man? Where is he?"

The Scot's eyes showed the same intensity as they had before in the alley. "You don't remember what you did?"

"What I did? I didn't do anything. Look, my guy, all I saw was that massive shadow thing, you saying for me to run away—thanks for that by the way—and then that tornado taking it out. I mean, how the hell does a tornado form in the middle of downtown Boston and then take a shadow monster out? How the hell did the shadow monster get there in the first place?"

The Scot shook his head incredulously. "She doesn't know. How is this possible?" he whispered to himself. He looked at me. "You did something. Remember."

I looked at him, not sure what to think. I just stood there behind him. *What the hell did I do?*

Remember.

Chills fell over my body as I felt something building up in the middle of my body, right behind my heart. My heart clenched, causing me to grab my chest. I started to panic and clamped my eyes shut, trying to figure out how to make it stop. As I started to concentrate on it more, the feeling sent a pulse through my body and the goosebumps raised all over again. Like it was caressing me as a greeting. **Hello**, the voice from inside me said. My eyes snapped open to find the Scot, no longer sitting on the chair, but on my bed, much closer to me than before.

"W-w-what are you doing? Did you do that?"

The Scot shook his head, inspecting me like some fascinating science experiment. "No, that's all you. And I want to know how. What power is that inside of you? I mean, you are definitely a human. But I've never seen a living human exhibit that type of power. You're not one of those spiritual clairvoyants, are you? With the TV commercials who can talk to the dead? I always thought those stories were rubbish."

I slunk closer to my bedroom wall, shaking my head. "Why wouldn't I be human? And what the heck are you talking about?" I inched closer to my closet, hoping I still had that baseball bat from pee wee in there—just in case. "Look, this is all new for me, and I'm not a fan of strange things happening to me without an explanation. I just want to know what happened in the alley. Who are you? What was that dark figure? And what happened to that man?"

The Scot studied me slowly, assessing me from head to toe. Feeling uncomfortable, I crossed my arms to cover my heaving chest. "All right, lass," he said after a few moments. "I will tell you what happened. But are you sure you want to hear this? There are things that once you hear them, you can't run away from them." I felt that his warning went a bit deeper than just the incident in the alley.

In the back of my mind, something said, *He's right, you know. If we step out into this, we could be stepping back into a world we swore we wouldn't talk about anymore. We have to think about Mom. We can't put her through that chaos again. We swore to be a normal teenager.* I wanted to tell the Scot that I'd changed my mind, that I would decline the information because I didn't want to leave my realm of normal. Because everything about him would pull me away from the careful world I had created for myself. But I couldn't say it. I even tried to, but my mouth and tongue remained shut.

Instead, that small voice from inside of me said, **It's time.** Time for what, I wasn't sure. But before I knew it, the words I wasn't sure I wanted to say spilled out of my mouth.

"Yes, I want to know."

The Scot sighed and motioned for me to sit. I chose the forgotten vanity chair, pulling it back towards my bedroom door. Easy exit, just in case. He rolled his eyes, crossed his arms, and sighed. "I have a working theory as to what happened tonight," he started.

"So, you don't know what you did tonight?" I asked, already frustrated.

"No, I know what I did. I'm talking about you."

"I want to know what you did first, before we get into what I did. The way I see it, you did it first. You explain yourself first."

The Scot clenched his teeth. "Fine. We'll go in order. But before I say what I did, I need your solemn oath that whatever is said in this room shall go no further. Not that anyone would believe you, but I want to know whether you can keep a secret."

I looked at him skeptically. But with his eyes bearing down on me, I finally said, "All right, you have my word."

The Scot continued to stare me down, and I looked back at him unflinchingly. "Shake on it?" he finally asked. I nodded and reached for his hand. His hand closed over it, and mine instantly went warm. No, scratch that. My hand was on fire!

I wrenched it out of his grasp, yelling, "What the hell are you doing to my hand?" My hand, now impossibly hot, had an odd mark branded into the middle of my palm. "Did you just brand me?" I asked incredulously.

The Scot smirked. "Just a little insurance."

I could feel myself losing whatever patience I had with the stranger. "What the hell does insurance—"

"Don't worry, lass. Your hand already is better, right?"

I frowned and looked down again. My hand looked and felt normal—as if the branding was an illusion. But was it? I distinctly felt the burning. I opened my mouth to say something but couldn't find the words to express what just happened. Satisfied, he returned to his explanation. "I had been tracking someone at the pub when your friend interrupted me."

"The man from the pool table?"

"Yes. I was curt with her because her awful attempts at flirting gave the man the opportunity to run. I cornered him in the alley. What you saw in the alley wasn't murder. The man was already dead."

I snorted. "Right, because dead people hang out at bowling bars and beg to be spared from murder all the time."

He smirked. "You'd be surprised at what the dead will do to get what they want."

"Hey, I thought we were going to be honest with each other here."

"I am. It's up to you whether you believe it or not."

I sighed and crossed my legs. "Okay, fine. I'll play. Let's say the man in the alley was already dead. Where did he go?"

"A human spirit that doesn't cross over causes an imbalance here in this plane, which we call the Live Realm. To right this imbalance, I sent him over to another plane, which we call the Room of Apofasi, for judgment. Had he stayed in the Live Realm any longer, he would have become a liability. When they don't cross over, that energy acts like a beacon for some pretty ugly stuff."

"Wait, so you sent a dead spirit to this place, the Room of Apofasi, to be judged?"
The Scot nodded, studying me again. "Yes. Spirits like him, and unfortunately there are many more like him, are the reason behind these tremors and the unearthly screams you heard. That massive shadow beast was from another plane—a much more dangerous plane. The screams were from the beast. The tremors were from the beast walking around the Live Realm looking for the human spirit to devour and absorb any remaining power they may have. In a sentence, the beast was hungry."

His face remained very serious though there was a slight glimmer of amusement in his eyes as he watched me process his words.

"So, you are saying you sent a dead man to be judged to keep a giant shadow from finding him. And you have this ability because...?"

"I am a Kyrios." I remembered the man in the alley: *"Please, Kyrios. I'm not ready to go yet. There's too much I want to do still."*

I eyed the Scot suspiciously. "The man did call you Kyrios. What exactly is a Kyrios? Sounds like cereal."

He smiled eerily and leaned slightly forward. "I've been called many things over the years. The Ankou in Celtic. Hades. The

Shinigami in Japanese. Angel of the Dark, though angel is a misconception. Far from it, actually."

My eyebrows rose. "What are you saying? You're…"

"The Grim Reaper? Death? Yes, all of the above."

5

"You're kidding, right?" I snorted. "You're Death?"

The Scot shrugged, leaning back, getting comfortable on my bed. "Eh, I'm not much of a fan of the name Death. Kind of a misnomer, but when you deal with dead spirits and monsters, people jump to names they know. Most of us just call ourselves Kyrios."

Right. Of course. Whatever else would you call yourselves?

This was starting to get too real for me. The Scot couldn't tell but I was inwardly freaking out. Because on some level I could understand him. And I did not want to understand, not one bit. "You know what, I think I've heard enough for today. Wow, look at the time. You must be busy with…you know, Death stuff… So why don't I just show you the door and—" Another small tremor shook the house, but this time I could hear another chalkboard scream not too far away that made my hair stand on end. "What was that?"

A cell phone started to buzz. The Scot pulled it out of his pocket, took a quick look at the screen, and made a phone call.

"Samuel, send two men down to the Quincy-Weymouth quadrant. We've got two Shatterers running rampant. Repeat: level one Wreckers. I'm dealing with the anomaly still."

With a quick flick of a button, his attention was back to me. "Got two more of those shadow beasts you saw earlier emerging nearby. They probably sense that jittery energy you're giving off and think you're a human spirit. You may want to calm down there. You're attracting the wrong attention. I had to redirect my men to deal with the incoming problem. Like we don't have enough to do already."

My eye began to twitch. "What did you mean by 'your men'?"

The Scot grinned, clearly enjoying himself. "You don't really think there is one person sending all the deceased to judgment? There are quite a number of us Kyrios stationed all over the Live Realm. I happen to be in charge of the Boston/New York spirit area. It's been keeping me pretty busy as of late, which is a bit out of the norm. But then, the entire world is going through this right now—increased tremors, odd energies affecting the weather, the increase in unexplainable phenomenon. People are not acting 'people.' I haven't been this overworked in a very long time."

I held up my hands for him to stop—this was starting to feel like Alice falling down the rabbit hole. "Nope. No more. Unable to can. This can't be real. You can't be real. This is probably a vision! Yes, this is a vision that has lasted a bit too long. Please, Katya, please snap out it."

The Scot smirked, studying his hand. "Visions, huh? I thought we were going to be honest here." He mimicked me from earlier. "Put everything out there for everyone to see."

"What the hell are you talking about?"

The Scot resumed his intense stance from earlier. "What I am talking about, lass, is that secret you are hiding in that pretty little head of yours."

"What do you mean?" I lifted my head with more bravado than I was feeling. "I don't have any secrets. Besides, how the hell would you know?"

"How do you think I got you back here? How I knew where you lived?" He pointed to my head. "Call it another one of my gifts, but I know that there's an interesting little world in there. Your father passed away when you were six years old. Your mom's a pretty busy sports lawyer who goes on many trips and is not home most of the time. You stay at home by yourself alone or with your best friend, Cynthia Maroney, the person who you call your 'twin.' You are a senior in high school. You are at the top of your class and are considered a popular girl, though you don't like it. You want to be a dancer. But you are rather clumsy though, aren't you? Saw a couple of spills you took in the past week that would've broken a burly man in half."

I was stunned. "Are you telling me you invaded my privacy and went through my mind? I have every right to call the police for this! Would you please just get out of my house?"

My shouts didn't move the Scot. He waved his hand nonchalantly and got even more comfortable. "It was a quick read, simply to get your information. I promise you I didn't delve any further. And we both know you are not calling anyone. I am not going anywhere. I am your only chance of figuring out what in the world you are." He paused, looking for some disagreement from me.

"What do you mean, what I am? I am human!"

"A human with an extra pinch of weird, am I correct?"

Weird.

Oh, that word brought out so many feelings and memories from me. None of them were warm and fuzzy. Just feelings of loneliness, shame, anxiety, and fear. Of days being stuck inside of a room and having people question me over and over. Telling me that I was making things up. "Stop lying, Ms. Stevens. You didn't see that." Of my classmates whispering things they heard from their parents. "Oh, that's the weird black girl from down the street." Of my seeking refuge in our family room and sitting on the window bench where I could stare out at the street and sidewalk and watch people and cars go by. Where I could pretend I knew where they were going and what they were thinking.

Because it was always safer to pretend than to find out the real and ugly truths about the world.

My face must have gone a bit ashen because the Scot had the decency to look abashed. "Oh, sorry, you don't like that word, right? Apologies, but we need to get to talking about tonight. You saw things tonight that most humans would not, lass. You can't deny that."

"Get out!" I walked briskly out of the room and bounded down the stairs, with the Scot hot on my heels. Normally, I loved my house; it was the safest place in the world to me. On the first floor, the open grand foyer welcomed visitors into my beloved family room, filled with cushions and comfortable couches. The Scot behind me demolished any sense of safety I normally felt. He kept close to me as I made for the next room: the kitchen.

"For the love of God, you are infuriating!" the Scot growled. "You want further proof?" He turned on the television on the kitchen counter. Instead of the usual late-night talk show, a breaking news report interrupted with the headline "ERUPTION AT MOUNT SAINT HELENS." Several pictures and videos of Mount Saint Helens, near Portland, Oregon, showed a fearsome volcano erupting steam, rock, and ash into the Washington air.

"Mount Saint Helens released a ferocious roar about two hours ago, without much warning," the male newscaster explained. "Scientists are baffled at how the quiet volcano suddenly erupted without its usual buildup prior to eruption. Typically, dangerous seismic activity builds up slowly, and any potential eruptions are closely monitored. Since 2008, Mount Saint Helens had been relatively quiet, according to geologists. But that all changed just an hour ago when the volcano went from an unprecedented one to four point five on the Richter scale, blowing its top, and burying about forty people within its ash cloud who weren't able to get off the mountain in time. We have not been able to determine the property damage quite yet."

What surprised me were creatures surrounding the volcano. Large white creatures with grotesque figures—either with spikes, holes, or boils covering their bodies. They were clear as day, helping the volcano, throwing more ash into the air and destroying homes. But no one reacted, screamed, or pointed at them. They were invisible. Except the Scot could see them. And he could see that I could as well. I didn't dare say a word.

"These creatures are the same monsters you saw in the alley tonight. They are called the Want or the Wanters. You think this volcano is bad? This is just the tip of the iceberg. And that feeling in you that's scaring you? Your visions? It's all playing a part. Something is brewing underneath the surface. Because the Want don't normally do such things on a grand scale. Accidents, yes. Loss of life, definitely. Any disaster creates more human spirits to eat. But this? This is more. You are reacting to this. Or at least something inside of you is reacting."

The Scot approached me slowly, probably fearing that I would bolt. "Now, as I was browsing through your mind index, I did see something locked away, like a vault within a vault." I simply looked at him as he continued his explanation. "You see, the mind is quite similar to a house with many doors. Some doors are readily available to open, like your name, where you live, or your family. Others are locked away, like precious memories or hurtful things. You have a particular dusty door that looks like it's been neglected for years. A prison door. But something's behind that door, lass. Something is bursting at the seams with that same power you displayed earlier. And it's only getting stronger by the hour. So I'll ask you again. What secret are you hiding in that head of yours?"

The room suddenly felt too small. Memories of Mom crying… A coffin being lowered at a gravesite… Broken bricks all over the sidewalk and the street.

"I can't be mistaken, lass. I know what I saw."

I said nothing as I rummaged through the food in the fridge, finally finding the chocolate syrup. I dipped my head back, squirting the cool, sweet liquid into my mouth and savoring its deliciousness. I felt the Scot watch me inhale the syrup and suddenly I felt rude. "Would you like something to drink?" I suddenly asked.

The Scot startled. "What?"

"Sorry, I needed a hit of chocolate. Would you like something?" I looked at the fridge door. "Or do Kyrios not need food or water?"

Eyebrows arched, the Scot shook his head in amusement. "I

can drink and eat just fine. I don't need it, but that doesn't mean I can't enjoy it."

"Well, you can't have the chocolate. House rule. Even my mom knows not to touch it. What would you like?"

"Water is fine." I grabbed a glass out of the cupboard, filled it from the tap, and handed it to the Scot. He looked down at his glass and said, "Back where I come from, we salute each other first before taking a drink."

I shrugged and sucked on more chocolate. "I didn't realize Kyrios had drinking traditions."

"They don't. Cheers, lass."

"Cheers." We both took a swig of our liquid. I felt a bit better, but unsure of where to go from here. Could I really let someone else know? It didn't feel safe. When I'd told people in the past, they always had this look on their face that flashed the same message: liar. For years, I told myself I wouldn't have to go through this again, but it seems like I had lied again, only to myself this time.

The Scot must have sensed the turmoil within me because he said, looking uncomfortable, "Look, I know you have no reason to trust me, lass—"

"Katya. My name is Katya."

He gave me a soft smile. "Pardon me, Katya. The only way we are going to make sense of what happened earlier is if you talk. That tornado didn't come from me. But it was powerful enough to cleave through a powerful creature like cheese."

"But it wasn't *me*," I said exasperated. "I didn't even know what that thing was called until now."

"But you've seen it before, right?" The Scot sighed. "The only way we can figure it out is if you tell me about that door."

I studied my nail beds. "Why should I tell you anything? If it's locked away, maybe it should stay that way."

He said softly, "Because it's my job to know. I haven't given you much reason to trust me. Other than that alley, we might not have ever gotten here. But we did, and I believe that there's a reason for it. I was supposed to meet you. And that news report proves that you see much more than you let on. You've probably have noticed already, in the past couple of years, that there have been more unexplainable things happening—extreme weather all over the world. The typhoons and the tsunamis in the East, and the super storms destroying lives here in the Northeast. The droughts and extreme heat peppered everywhere. Not to mention people themselves are turning colder, more pessimistic, and more hateful with each day."

The Kyrios was right about that. I thought it was me being too sensitive to people's emotions, but even Cynthia had made a comment, just the other day, about how people were acting odd. More and more people were shutting themselves away, becoming superficial, greedier in every sense of the word. At first I noticed the behavior on the internet, but now it was manifesting in person.

"I tell you, these are not isolated incidents. I have a feeling you sense more than you want to admit because you don't want to call attention to yourself. You are afraid. But no one can help you if you don't speak up. You've got to tell me your story, lass. Please."

I suddenly felt the weight of years of secrecy bearing down on me. The burden of my mother's warnings, delivered since I was eight. The stress of Cynthia being the only other person I could run crying to about all of the looks of concern, fear, and worry. The quiet phone conversations coming to an end as I came into a room. Kids laughing and pointing at me, parents keeping their children away, and most of all, my feelings of shame.

Apparently, all of it had been buried behind a door in my head. I looked at the Scot, who was looking at me earnestly. "If I tell you," I said quietly. "Would you be able to tell me what's wrong with me?"

The Scot's eyebrows wrinkled together. "I don't think there's anything wrong with you. You just have something more than other people. I may not understand it, but if I don't know it, then I am sure I know someone who will."

"I don't think there's anything wrong with you." The pit in my stomach started to unfurl and some of the anxiety started to melt. The final push came when that small inside voice gave me a nudge. **It's okay, Katya. Tell him.**

6

I worried my bottom lip, praying for strength, and took a seat at the kitchen table, rubbing my arms for warmth. "The earliest memory I have was from when I was five. Mom took me out to the playground, and there was a girl. A girl named Sara. Blond-haired, big green eyes, wearing a solid purple romper and white tennis shoes.

"Sara always wore the same thing every day, and she was there every time I came to the playground. The first time that I met Sara, she had been crying for her mother. My mom always told me to be kind to people when they cried, so I went up to her and asked her what was wrong and told her not to cry. Sara told me that she was lonely. I promised that I would see her every day and play with her. And for the most part, at some point during the day, I was able to convince my mother, father, or babysitter to take me to the park. And Sara was always there waiting for me. And we would talk and play. Sometimes we would sing songs together.

"I thought Sara was special like me because Sara could always see things that only I could see. Like the young guy in the white shirt and black jeans that walked by every day with his Walkman.

We always wondered why he had a ketchup all over the front of his chest. Or the pregnant lady who sat on the same park bench near the entrance of the park and how she massaged her purple neck and stared out like she was looking for someone. I tried to ask my mom about those random people but Mom told me to stop playing around. She used to say that I had such an active imagination."

I shrugged, still clutching at my arms. "At least Sara could understand. Sara could see it. We played for several weeks together, every day without fail. Then, one day my mom couldn't take me because she got called into the office. I told her that I needed to see my friend and had a meltdown because I couldn't go. When my dad came home from work and saw me sniffling, he asked about my friend. Mom insisted that there was rarely anyone at the playground and that I played alone with an imaginary friend. I remember being furious and told her that Sara was not fake.

"When I described what Sara looked like," I angrily swiped away the tears that had formed, "my father realized that I was describing a girl that had died not far from playground several weeks before. She had been strangled by her stepfather. I've never forgotten my parents' looks of horror, trying to figure out how I knew this child. They refused to take me to the playground again. I had another fit the next day when they told me I couldn't go. I begged them to take me because I heard Sara calling out for me, asking where I was. My parents put me in my room for the rest of day."

"Later on that day, I heard Sara, screaming in pain, screaming for help. I never saw her again." I quickly took a look at the Scot, who just continued to stare at me intently. He nodded for me to continue. I exhaled a shaky breath and took a new swig of chocolate syrup.

"Sara wasn't the last dead person I saw. And those monsters? I've seen them create the worst accidents and disasters ever known. Most of the time, when I did see them, something horrible happened or was about to happen. Someone was about to get hurt or die. Anytime my parents turned on the TV, I would see them just like I did today. People fighting, fires ripping homes apart, causing cars to crash, destroying something in sight.

"They weren't always that big, like that one from tonight. What did you call it, a Wanter?" He nodded again. "Sometimes they were smaller, no bigger than a small dog, but they were always around trouble. People would be screaming in pain, wondering why, why would this happen? And here I was, just a little kid, and I was the only one who could see them. The only one who could see the cause of their pain.

"I tried to tell my parents. I would beg them to see the monsters. To warn people that something bad was going to happen. At first, they just chalked it up to an active imagination and too many cartoons. Then it was psych evaluations, ADHD medication, banned from watching television, and forbidden from telling lies. I had to stay inside because other parents found out about my stories, so I had to stay away from everyone else's kid because they didn't want the freaky black girl to scare them. Cynthia's parents were the only ones who didn't care. Cynthia was the only person I could play with, until I was about eight years old."

I felt tears swell up in my eyes. "Then one day, after my dad died in an accident, it just stopped. I really don't remember too much about how it stopped. I just remember hating seeing those things, and I wanted to protect my mom. The next morning I woke up and it was like I'd never seen anything. Peace, quiet, just no more. Mom was relieved and she moved me to another school. Cyn's parents moved Cynthia too, and the two of us were able rebuild our reputations, I guess."

I chuckled darkly. "For years, I thought it was something I'd just made up. Just like my mother told me. That it was just a nightmare that haunted me. Then the visions started to come a few days after my birthday last month. And now this... If this entire thing about you is true, apparently I can see them again, and they are very much real. Ready to ruin my life again. Ready to ruin whatever peace I was able get. So much for being normal, right!" I laughed mockingly, fighting back the tears.

I cleared my throat, staring at my hands. "I haven't said this out loud in years, and somehow you just squeezed it out of me." I sucked down another gulp of chocolate, watching the Kyrios process my words. "That's it. That's my secret. So tell me, am I crazy? A nut job? Am I 'weird'?"

The Scot closed the gap between us and bent down to look me in the eyes. "No, Katya. I know exactly what you are talking about. I know what you were seeing. I just don't understand why."

"But you believe me? You believe that what I saw was real?"

He nodded.

Someone believes me. The dam broke, and I couldn't hold back the tears and relief I felt. Years of denying myself because no one would believe. Even Cynthia hadn't ever fully admitted that she believed it—she just said that she loved me no matter what. All those times of being told I was a liar, and I'd almost believed it. And now, someone believed me, believed in me. The Scot remained silent as I regained control.

"But wait, how do I know that you are real? That you aren't a spirit talking to me? That you aren't going to disappear when I try to prove that you are real?"

The Scot softly laughed. "Your friends saw me, didn't they?"

Oh yeah. "But are you dead?"

He hesitated. "It's complicated." He leaned closer, taking my hand into his. It wasn't completely warm as I would've expected, but there was flesh in my hand. "I may bring the dead over to the other side, but I am as real as anything in this room. Just as real as the spirits you saw when you were a child."

Unable to hold on, I drowned in his eyes, feeling immense gratitude. "Kyrios…"

"Gregor."

"What?"

"Kyrios is what I am. My name is Gregor."

With his name, an unspoken shift happened between us. Sharing a deep dark secret about yourself can do that—create a bond that is unfathomable, but fitting. We silently stood there for a moment, until Gregor cleared his throat and stepped away from me. "You have an odd gift, Katya. One that is more powerful than I've ever encountered before. From what I've seen, you have something more inside you than just the ability to see Wanters and human spirits. I don't know how, but you were able to cut down the Hungry in the alley."

"The Hungry?"

He nodded. "It's a second-level Craver. It's a type of Wanter. There are seven different types of Wanters: Wreckers, Cravers, Posers, the Thirsty, Wishers, and Stuffers. The strongest are Generals—the Want leaders. Level one is the weakest, while level three is already deadly dangerous. Anything stronger than a level three is something you want to get away from as quickly as possible. And if it's a General..." Gregor trailed off, clearly unwilling to follow that train of thought.

"Anyway, the Cravers are always hungry, so they sit in between the Live Realm as a shadow to pounce on any potential energy source. It probably sensed the energy from the man and probably from you too. But the most amazing thing you did was to cut it down. We've had some living humans feel things from time to time, but nothing like this. I am certain that it was your energy that created the cyclone, and by God it was intense. With the way you are leaking energy off of you now, I should have noticed you before. There was something off in that pub, but I thought it was the dead man hiding from me. It's as if your power has just woken up from a deep sleep. Your energy rivals that of an experienced Kyrios."

Not sure what to make of it, I shrugged and said, "I think I felt something when I first saw you."

The Scot looked sharply at me. "You did?"

I nodded. "My friends saw you first and pointed you out to me. I didn't think of it then, but I felt something flicker inside. Like an on switch or something." I felt the heat rising in my cheeks, clearing my throat. "I just thought it was because my friends thought you looked hot. By the way, they had this funny look on them like they were completely mesmerized. Did you do something to them?"

He grinned so sheepishly that something twisted inside of me. "We call it 'Walk into the Light' syndrome. There are some people who look at us and just feel compelled to follow us. Or bed us. That whole brush-with-death feeling. It can be a sticky situation for us if we come out to the Live Realm, so we try to limit our interactions with live humans."

"It still doesn't excuse your attitude towards my friend. It was her birthday and it took a lot of courage to speak to you."

He looked as if he was about to say something, but sensing that I was rearing for an argument, he bowed his head and said, "If I ever have the opportunity, I will seek her forgiveness. On my honor as a Scot."

I felt the corners of my mouth lift. "Good to know at least Scots are self-aware of their asshole ways. Thank you."

Gregor met my eyes for a moment and then turned around to step out of the kitchen. "I need to get going."

"Wait!" I followed him out of the kitchen into my living room. "You can't just leave like this! Where are you going? What am I supposed to do?"

Gregor rolled his shoulders and stretched his arms over his head. "I have to get back to headquarters to give a report. I'll be looking into your power with the Generals. Until then, continue to live your life."

I looked at him and said in a flat tone, "Continue to live my life? I pour out my secret, and you just head out?"

He shrugged. "Why? Do you want to end your life now?"

I rolled my eyes. "If that is Death humor, it sucks."

Gregor laughed heartily; his deep chuckle soothed my anxious nerves. "Katya, just keep low. I'll be back soon." He turned and raised his right hand. A bright light erupted from the middle of his palm. The bright bead of light flew into the air, growing larger until it effectively split the room in two. Like a bright blue tear in time and space. As he was about to step into the rip, he turned back to me. "Oh, one more thing."

The brightness and the power coming from his eyes arrested me. "What is it?"

"Don't get too agitated. Control your emotions. You don't want to be a beacon for anything."

With that, he stepped into the rip and was gone.

7

I woke up with a start, completely disoriented. Cursing the sun for shining through my window and instigating a splitting headache, I curled further into my sheets, praying to God to make the headache magically go away.

Unfortunately, the ringing of my cell phone kept me from falling blissfully back to sleep.

"Hello?"

"Katya Elizabeth Stevens!" I fell out of my bed at the sharp tone.

"Cynthia?" I asked as I fumbled around with the sheets.

"I've been calling you since last night! If you hadn't answered this morning, I would've thought someone kidnaped you! What the hell happened to you?"

"Cyn, wait—"

"You scared the crap out of me! You never called or texted! Do twin sisters do that? Abandon each other? What's worse is you left me with Amie sobbing! And not just tears, but the kind of sobbing that leaves you hiccupping and snot running down your nose. It was bad enough with just her, but then her mom had to jump in and start crying too. You try dealing with a grown woman crying about her daughter crying!"

"Cynthia!" I yelled. "Give me a second. I just woke up, okay?" Silence answered me on the other line. Taking a deep breath, I tried to remember. What happened? I couldn't remember taking a cab home last night. How did I get home? A look around my room didn't prove anything out of place. If anything, it looked normal. But my clutch was on my nightstand. That didn't feel right either.

"Excuse me? Can I speak now?"

I shook my head, not realizing she couldn't see me. "Yeah, sorry about that. I... You woke me up, and I was lost for a minute there."

Cynthia sighed. "It's fine, Katya. Please just tell me you are okay."

"Yes, sis. I'm fine. I'm just a bit hazy right now."

"Don't disappear like that again! I was just going to come over, but Amie did not want to be left alone at all. And you not picking up your phone just freaked me out. If you were wondering, I brought Amie back to my house for a sleepover. I told her we would hang out today."

I wiped my face, still trying to shake the sleep away. "Sure, whatever. How is she doing?"

Cyn sighed. "Not gonna lie, Kat. Her confidence took a beating. What happened with that guy?"

"What guy?"

She paused. "What do you mean, "what guy"? The guy you left us to chase after! The guy you wanted to yell at! That guy! Did you lose him?"

Blue eyes. The alley. The shadow. Gregor. It came back with such force that it hurt, increasing my headache tenfold. "Ow!"

"Are you okay?"

I rubbed my temples, attempting to massage the throbbing away. "Ugh, yeah. I just have a headache. The visions, Cyn—"

"Leave those alone for now. Talking about them always put you in a bad mood remember? We'll talk later. Amie's waking up, and I don't want her to hear us talking about this. I'm going to take her to her house to change, and then we'll meet you at Downtown Crossing around 11:30. Okay? Gotta go. Love you!"

I closed the phone, still massaging my pulsing temples. What the hell happened last night? Did I have a vision again last night? The entire conversation with Gregor came back, and I had to laugh out loud. There was NO way I would have told a complete stranger my secret. And all that blue eyes, blue light crap. I must have had a dream vision. Although it would have been the first one I could remember.

As I shuffled through my closet to find something to change into, my cell phone began vibrating again. A quick look at my desk clock showed 9:30 a.m. Not bothering to look at the caller ID, I answered it, saying, "Hi, Mom. Right on time."

"Of course. When would I have missed a phone call with my

pumpkin?" I rolled my eyes, smiling. Some nicknames never get old. "Is everything okay? What you are doing today?"

I continued to rifle through my closet. "The tremors haven't been too bad since you left. Though last night was odd—there were a lot more shakes than the previous couple of nights. But the party wasn't canceled, thank God! Cyn and I are heading out to Downtown with a friend. After that, I'm not sure."

"You would think you'd be more concerned about the world breaking apart with these tremors, and here you are worried about a party," Mom said, exasperated. I could sense my mother shaking her head. "Promise me you guys will stay safe. How are you doing for money?"

"We'll be fine, Mom. I haven't spent much since you left."

"Are you eating?"

I snorted. "Do you think Cynthia would let me go without eating? She's as bad as you are."

"Just checking. I'm your mother. I need to ask these things."

"Yes, Mom."

On the other side, I could hear my mother clear her throat three times. *Uh oh.* She only did that if she felt uncomfortable telling me something. "Katya, I'm not going to be home like I initially planned. Dallas is experiencing some bizarre hail, and we had to push back the negotiations quite a bit. It looks like I'm going to be home next month instead, probably right before school starts."

This wasn't the first time Mom's return home would come much later than expected. Being a law partner at Boston's premier sports and entertainment law firm, Mom felt a greater responsibility to prove herself because she was an African-American woman. Earlier on, she volunteered to take trips to meet with potential sports clients, which meant she was traveling all over the country to meet all kinds of sports athletes. But she never complained, even when she was away from home for weeks on end. It was also the reason why she made partner—because she took her role as the silent, diligent worker seriously and made the firm tons of money.

"It's okay, Mom. I know you'd be here if you could."

My mother sighed. "Are you sure? I know I promised to take you to Miami for your birthday, but the way this deal is going, it's driving me absolutely crazy. Men always complain about women being emotional. Give me a break. Professional football players are the worst."

I said brightly, "It's totally fine, Mom. And yes, you've said that before. The way I see it, you will just have to take me during the school year, right? I'm thinking for Christmas break but instead of two weeks, it will be three weeks. And that means I can get more bathing suits, right? Shopping spree!"

It was several seconds before my mother chuckled. "Okay, I'll take your proposal under consideration. Remember, no Roger alone, no parties—"

"Really, Mom? Give me a break!"

Mom chuckled. "Okay, Kitty-Kat. I gotta run. Have a good day and be good."

I got off the phone quickly so my mother could not hear the disappointment in my goodbye to her. My eyes traveled to a family photo taken on a trip to Myrtle Beach. I was six years old, clutching my father's leg, and grinning. Both my parents were smiling down at me, completely at peace. What I remembered the most about Dad was how much he used to smile. And it wasn't an obnoxious smile, but he genuinely just liked to smile and joke around. He loved seeing people happy. Which is probably why I purposely jumped into his arms whenever he'd get home, even knowing that tickling was in store for me.

That particular Myrtle Beach trip I just remember that he just clung to me and Mom, telling us how much he loved us. That we were his best gift. Shortly after we returned home, the monster sightings had become more frequent, and nothing was ever the same. Less than two years later, Dad died a hero, saving me and a coworker from a drunk driver incident.

The memory of how it all happened was fuzzy; I just remember feeling helpless and guilty. I rubbed the only scar that I'd received from the incident—a long, crooked scar on my left arm. It always itched whenever I thought of that day. Since Dad died, Mom had entangled herself with work, becoming partner and volunteering to travel. Without me. She said she does the long hours to provide me with the life she thinks I deserve. I know the truth. She does it so she doesn't have to remember Dad. I do not blame my mother for running. I don't want to remember either.

My phone buzzed again. It was Roger texting me.

"Hey Kat, you up?"

"Hey, morning."

"Morning. How was the party last night? You get into anything crazy?"

I hesitated. So many things flitted through my mind, with the Kyrios taking a prominent role. I wished that Roger was the kind of boyfriend that I could have confided in. But the longer I stayed in this relationship, the longer I questioned my own motivations. Yes, Roger was hot. Sandy-haired, amber eyes, great body due to basketball, and sometimes he was actually a decent, caring human being. But those moments were becoming fewer and fewer.

"Nothing special. Amie had a bit of an accident but she's good now."

"That sucks. Hey, there's a party tonight over at Devin Chirico's. I told him we'd go."

A twinge of annoyance hit me. "This is the first time I'm hearing about these plans."

"Well, you know. The guys were talking about it since last week and I wasn't really sure if I wanted to go, but then I heard that Devin's dad is going to be there. He's the assistant coach for the Huskies. And you know I wanna make that team. So it works for me, you know?"

I sighed. Of course it had to do with basketball. Of course it had to do with him getting on a team. And he knew that I hated not being included in making plans. Trying to sound a bit more supportive, I texted back "I hear you about that coach. You should definitely go. I'm not sure about tonight for me, but I'll get back to you. I'm heading out to meet up with Cyn. I'll hit you up later." I ignored all the other texts from him, knowing my limit.

My thoughts wandered back to the Kyrios as I showered and got dressed for the day. I couldn't stop making comparisons to him and Roger.

Roger and I had been together since our sophomore year. The day he asked me out, he approached me at my locker as I was packing my book bag. I could remember our conversation like it was yesterday.

Decked in his basketball jersey, he swallowed hard. "Hey Katya."

I gave him a small smile. "Hey Roger. Heading to practice?"

His eyes never left my face. "Yeah," he said breathlessly.

After he didn't say another word, I shrugged and closed my locker with a slam. "Okay, well I gotta get to ballet class. See you later," I said, brushing my hand against his shoulder.

He let out shuddering sigh and stared after me as I put my bag on my shoulder. After a few seconds, I heard behind me, "Katya, would you like to go out with me Saturday?"

I turned around, smiling. "Sure, why not?" And the smile he gave me was electric.

I continued to my next class with a huge smile, only realizing later that we didn't exchange numbers. When we did the next day, he swore he'd give me a call that night. And he did. I used to get phone calls every day for almost a year. He used to be so sweet, asking me how I was, and calling me just to stay on the phone.

And we did spend hours together, to the point where my mom gave me an unnecessary "birds and the bees" talk. (*I know you said you'd wait but you just never know.*) But never in all that time did I ever feel comfortable telling him about my complicated life before I became "normal." Maybe my instincts told me that I would never have a safe place to do so with him.

As our popularity grew, so did his ego. Being with the guys was more important. Basketball was more important. Being popular was more important. And I became more of a prop on his arm than the object of his affection—eye candy and the status of him being a "baller." I let it happen because it was the normal thing to do. Who didn't want to be popular? Who didn't want to be pretty and wanted?

I shook my head. I didn't. Not anymore. I didn't want to finish my last year of high school as a toy on a pedestal, but just as Katya. Just Kat.

I thought about it as I took a bus downtown. As I tried to find a seat, a man in a black bowler hat bumped me from behind, effectively knocking me to my knees as he exited the bus from the rear. "Hey, do you mind, buddy?" I yelled at the man's back. I brushed my knees off and adjusted my clothes, never realizing that the man had stopped in his tracks beside the bus and turned around to stare at me. Nor would I realize that his eyes continued to seek me even after the bus left him behind.

As the bus door moved forward, I felt a tingling behind my heart like something was stirring. It was the feeling from my vision. I shook my head, starting to panic. *It's a dream, Kat. Your vision, remember?*

A now-familiar, but still unnerving, earthquake rattled the street, effectively stopping all traffic, which waited for the tremors to pass. The tingling inside of me continued to buzz, almost in tandem with the shakes that had frozen all human activity. With sweat beading down my neck, I took a deep breath to calm down. After a couple of cleansing breaths, the tingling stopped and the shakes shortly after. The bus continued its route into the heart of Downtown Crossing.

8

In my opinion, downtown Boston was underrated solely because it wasn't a huge metropolis like New York City. There were plenty of skyscrapers for the bankers and the investors who worked downtown, and there were all the colleges and universities that Boston was known for, even if it wasn't one of the largest cities in America.

My favorite thing to do was to take the bus to the edge of the Boston Commons, a huge park and garden of trees and flowers, where you could find couples, children, and everyday people walking, strolling, or traveling through to their next destination. I loved meandering through and watching people, like I did at my living room window. Imagining where they were going. Who they were talking to.

The largest path in the middle of the Commons led straight to Downtown Crossing. The simplicity of the intersecting walkways and cobblestones of this area of the city showcased a rich history; the walkway, originally paved with brick, originated from the city's Pilgrim beginnings, winding in between buildings for a mile, with cars zipping on concrete pavement as its bookends. Buildings as old as our country housed stores that sold the latest electronics and clothing. Even without a building to conduct business, street vendors of all ethnicities could be seen pushing their carts, selling their wares, or enticing potential customers with the smell of the food they made.

All walks of life ventured through Downtown Crossing, from the hustling businessman walking through the shopping district to their next meeting, to the lowliest worker getting a bite to eat before their next job. Downtown Crossing had been a hub for passerby walkers and intentional shoppers for hundreds of years. It just reminded me that on one profound level, our necessities were all the same. That our past, present, and future would always share one thing—the need to congregate and to be around other human beings.

As I arrived at the bus stop, Cynthia texted me to say that she and Amie were at the Underground Food Court. I frowned. The Underground was a usual hangout for some of the popular crew, who always seemed to take offense that Cyn and I were friends with Amie. One girl in particular who did the absolute most: Andrea Pana. A pretty girl who also was rich—a winning combination.

We were never really cool with Andrea; we simply tolerated each other. I particularly didn't care for her since Roger told me she tried to make a pass at him a couple of months into our relationship. But, again, I tolerated her. Until she saw Amie was sitting with us and that we were spending time together.

As she put it to us when she first saw us sitting together, "Did the world enter the twilight zone or did someone forget their place? Math nerds sit in the opposite corner, away from here. Or did Ugly Glasses forget?" It took everything in me not dump my food on top of her expensive Brazilian hair extensions. Cynthia cussed her out something fierce that day, and she left.

But Andrea did not stop there. At every chance she got, she continually made comments about Amie's clothes, her hair, or just the fact that Amie was friends with us. She could not let it go.

Cynthia was more of the guard dog type, but I definitely had words with the spoiled brat a couple of times. Amie had been hurt at first, but once she saw that Cyn and I were not wavering at all, her spine got stronger and she became more confident in herself and our friendship. Seeing that her barbs weren't hitting as they used to, Pana had been paying less attention to us. I just hoped that Amie was in better spirits today and that Pana was still in her mansion cave terrorizing someone else.

As I entered the doors, I quietly I prayed, "Please don't let her be there." Unfortunately for me, God must have been busy because Pana and her group had surrounded Cynthia and Amie at a table in the middle of the food court. From the sounds of the jeers and laughs, I could tell my friends were not having a good time. The closer I got, the better I could see, and I immediately noticed tears running down Amie's cheeks and smoke coming out of Cynthia's ears. I swore under my breath and quickly made my way to the table.

"Well, if it isn't the chick of the hour!" Andrea called out, calling attention to my arrival. I tried to make eye contact with Cynthia to figure out what was going on, but her eyes remained fixed on Andrea.

"Shouldn't you be buying some silicon or extensions or something?" I said tersely. "Go bother someone else who gives a damn."

Unfazed, Andrea smirked back at me. "I am surprised you are even out of bed, Stevens. Shouldn't you be a little sore from your escapades last night?"

"Excuse me?"

The posse began to giggle. A bunch of twats. I wanted to smack their faces. Andrea simply leaned forward and placed her head in between Cynthia and Amie. "I was just telling these two how I saw you last night. In the arms of a guy that wasn't your hot boyfriend."

I could feel all the blood leave my face. "Wh-what?"

Andrea cackled. "Oh, come on Stevens! Stop acting so innocent. I saw you with him. You didn't do half bad either. He was hot, carrying you around Boston like he couldn't wait for you two to be alone!" She pulled out her cellphone and on her screen was a dark but relatively clear picture of Gregor carrying me out of the alleyway and turning a corner.

My heart leapt into my throat. *Oh, dear God, they know. They know about me. They saw me glow blue.*

"I just happened to be parking my car near that alley after that shake, and here comes hottie with your black ass in his arms. I wanted to get your attention, but he just seemed to be in such a hurry," she purred. Pana then placed a hand on Amie's shoulder, giving her a light massage. "I was just trying to figure out who he was when sugarplum here tells me you were supposed to be defending her last night—from the hottie!" She crossed her arms, looking very smug. "All this time and I was right. Looks like friendship with a freak only goes skin deep. Especially if there's guy involved, huh?"

Before I could respond, Cynthia shot out of her seat, nose to nose with the offending bully. "Pana, say one more word," she said, gritting her teeth, "and I swear I will tear the plastic off your body that you call your nose and boobs!" She grabbed a quiet Amie and me by the arm and dragged us outside.

Heaving, Cynthia stopped a few feet outside of the Court with her back towards me. Finally finding my tongue, I cleared my throat, "Guys, it's not what it sounds like. She's making it seem like something it's not. Amie, I never would do something like that to you. I was furious when I left, and I went after him to make him pay for what he said to you."

Amie didn't say a word. To say she looked miserable would be an understatement. Her hair was in a messy, static-y bun at the top of her head and she'd abandoned her contacts for a set of larger-than-life glasses again. Probably to hide her red eyes underneath. She looked at me like I'd grown two more heads. "Katya, there's a picture. You're in his arms. Unless that's a new way to fight someone, it looks like you're enjoying his company a bit too much."

Cynthia softly grabbed my arm and pulled me aside from Amie. "Listen, I'm not saying you had some rendezvous with the man, but the picture doesn't look good. Not to mention you were making comments about getting a new boyfriend, and I saw how you were looking at him." She raised her hand to stop me from interrupting. "I know you wouldn't do it on purpose. But you disappeared. What happened to you last night?"

I shook my head, refusing to get into my whole run-in with Death and spirits in public. "I will not talk about it right now."

"Why not? Kat, will you talk to me?"

I shrugged her off, turning back to Amie, who had taken to hugging herself. "Ames, I swear I didn't do anything. I passed out—"

Amie pulled a moist tissue from her pocket and blew her nose loudly. "It's okay, Katya. I underst—actually, no I don't fully understand. I know you, or at least I thought I did. Part of me knows that you wouldn't lie to me about this. That you would've tried to defend me. But the other part…I know what you said last night. That picture is real because you haven't denied it. So maybe you saw him, he liked you better, I don't know. I don't want to think like that but… You don't think I've noticed, but you're not as open you think you are. You put walls up, Katya. I thought maybe I was getting through those walls. But I honestly don't know. Maybe this, this guy, is another secret, another part of you you're keeping away."

I felt the morning's frustration begin to build up behind my eyes. "No, Amie. Listen to me. That's not what happened. I would never—"

Amie shook her head and wrapped her arms around herself tighter. "Katya, just give me time. I just need some time to think. Now if you excuse me, I think I'll go home." My jaw brushed the ground as she kept her head high and walked away.

At least our time together had taught her some pride and not to take crap from anyone, including her friends. I ran after Amie, skirting around the midday shoppers. "Amie, wait!" I called after her retreating figure. "You don't understand. Please let me explain. I swear that nothing—"

"Katya the Nubian Princess strikes again," Pana yelled out behind me.

I stopped and slowly turned around to find Pana alone, stalking up to me with a huge smirk on her face. "Newsflash! Katya isn't the all-holy saint she pretends to be! I always knew you got down and dirty. And for some reason you've been holding out on your boyfriend too? Two years and no sex? Be careful, Stevens." She licked her lips like a lion licking their chops. "You might find yourself without a boyfriend if you stay a tease."

"Would you shut up, Pana? I didn't do anything last night!"

The smirk on her face only grew. "Then he did all the night's work? You sure you didn't twerk for him a little bit?"

I felt the heat flare in my cheeks, and I snapped. I stalked up to Pana and yelled at the top of my lungs in her face. "NOTHING HAPPENED!"

Instantly the tingling returned and pulsed throughout my entire body. Like an echo, it reverberated through the ground and shook the block. Or at least I felt the shaking. The Downtown Crossing shoppers looked unaffected, moving on with their business. My lungs contracted, and a wave of fatigue left me clutching my chest. With that one stomp, I felt like I had run a marathon and was gasping for air.

Cynthia immediately moved in and pushed me away from Pana, fearing a fight. Pana calmly wiped her cheek of any spittle, still smirking. "Just remember who has that picture, Stevens. I think my job is done for today. I look forward to your next breakdown."

With that, she walked away.

Realizing I'd missed Amie, who was now long gone, I stumbled to the nearest bus stop a few feet away and sat on the bench to regain my breath with Cynthia in tow. Less than twenty-four hours from dishing my secret and my life was already spiraling out of control.

"No," I whispered. "No, I don't want this. This can't be happening again."

"Katya." I whirled around to find Cynthia looking at me

worriedly. "Are you okay?" She took a seat beside me. She gave me a small smile. "I haven't seen you do that since we were kids and you tried to convince your parents about what you saw."

I wiped my face, regaining some composure. "I really didn't do anything, Cyn. I swear."

"I know, Kat. I was just concerned about you. We'll talk about it later," Cynthia said softly. She bit her lip, looking guilty. "Oh, um… Before you got here, Roger came around, thinking that you might have been here. He heard about last night from the Queen of Plastic."

I groaned, not looking forward to more drama. "Tell me you didn't say anything."

Cynthia sighed, staring up at the towering buildings around us. "Of course I didn't. But he just thought that I was covering for you. Amie started to tell him about what happened, about the "sexy British guy—"

"He's Scottish," I corrected her absentmindedly.

Her eyebrows cocked. "Sorry, sexy *Scottish* guy, so he kinda went off the deep end, yelling about cheating on him and telling Pana about your sex life. Or your non-existent sex life."

That ass! How could he not trust me? Just as I was about to let Cynthia suffer through the rest of my morning rant, something different distracted me. A strange birdlike creature glided through the air and then disappeared the moment it landed on the side of the building. Cynthia forgotten, I stood from my chair and squinted at the sky to find it again.

"Kat?"

"Hold on, Cyn."

Several more birdlike creatures circled around the Boston skyscrapers, over one hundred feet above the bus stop. Something within me was urging me to do something, but I didn't know what exactly. I couldn't tell what they were. They were seven times bigger than any average bird and much uglier. Large bodies and diamond-shaped heads. Studying them, I came to realize that they all were looking in the same direction. Directly at me.

Run, the voice said. I slowly backed away. The urge to run away got stronger each second. "I gotta go."

Cynthia threw me an odd look. "Kat, what are you talking about? You just got here."

I shook my head. The creatures hadn't moved from their spot, but I could feel their eyes following my every move. "Cyn, I gotta get out of here. I'll call you later!" Without another word, I grabbed my purse and walked briskly down the sidewalk through the busy crowd. I could hear Cynthia yelling my name, but nothing could make me turn back to acknowledge her.

The afternoon shopping crowd swelled, so I stepped off of the sidewalk and walked on the cobbled street. As I walked towards the subway station, my internal tingling continued. It sent out signals like a sensor, looking for strangeness. Distracted by the odd sensation, I failed to stop walking in time to avoid a man standing on the street.

The problem was I walked right through him.

Any apology I might have offered died on my lips. I simply stared at him. He turned to me with a wild look and said, "You're like them. You're like the Kyrios!"

I shook my head, backpedaling slowly. "No, I'm not." I vaguely realized how crazy I must have looked to the shoppers walking around me—a girl talking to the air in front of her.

The man shook his head vehemently. "No, I felt it when you touched me. I want to get out of here. Send me away. I can hear them. They're coming! I don't want to change into one of them!"

Completely freaked, I changed directions, darting around people and headed towards the end of Downtown Crossing towards normal car traffic, sincerely hoping the man wouldn't follow me.

He didn't.

Or at least he couldn't. As I turned to head into the train entrance, I heard the terrible-but-now-familiar chalkboard screech. The scream sent a terrible jolt through my body, paralyzing me from the waist down.

Trembling, I slowly raised my head to find the several bird creatures I saw from the bus stop were now hanging from the building only thirty feet above me. The "birds" were not birds at all. They were pure-white, boney-looking pterodactyls. Their pointy and jagged diamond-shaped heads were stretched horizontally, leaving only slits for a nose and eyes, but their eyes were beady and blood red. Their beaks opened wide to show vicious rows of teeth. Their scream was even worse up close. Their bat-like white wings had a wingspan of at least eight feet long. Claws protruded at every point on their wings. The disgusting creature balanced itself on one foot that looked more like a human hand with claws.

Before either I or the man could react, three of the bird creatures swooped down on the poor spirit, who stood frozen in fear. The three birds hauled him in the air, fifty feet up. Each grabbed a limb and started a tug a war. Ignoring the man's screams of terror, the tug of war eventually ended with each getting a piece and leaving his head and torso to drop to the ground. A man's spirit was just torn to pieces above people's heads, and they never were the wiser. One final bird swooped in and finished the man off. Though I knew the man was dead, seeing him tortured in death was enough for me to believe that I was in serious trouble.

Abandoning all attempts to look normal, I darted through the crowds of people, pushing, shoving to get away. I heard the creatures' shrieks and screams from above, getting closer. Their wings beat so hard that they created winds that pushed people into each other and into the buildings in the vicinity. Bewildered, people screamed out of surprise. The weather hadn't called for anything like wind gusts today.

My immediate thought was that I had to get away from the congestion of people. What if they caused some weird weather pattern to happen with all the wind they were causing? Another cyclone? I ran as fast as I could and ducked into an alley that happened to be a dead end. The wired fence mocked me as I ran into it, desperately wishing for it to magically open. With another loud screech, I turned around to see the five bird creatures floating in front of me, probably enjoying the chase. The biggest one roared and splayed its wings open, getting ready to pounce. I could do nothing but close my eyes, duck down, and wait for the pain.

I only felt the sunlight dim over my face. No pain. A quick check proved that my limbs were still in place. Slowly, I opened my eyes to find a shadow cast over me. The back of a tall man stood before me. He held the creature by its beak as it flailed about, trying to get away.

"I thought I told you," he said with a familiar Scottish brogue, "don't get agitated."

I just stared at his back wordlessly.

He looked slightly over his shoulder to address me. "Just sit tight, lamb, while I take care of this." A sudden flash of a blue light flared at the top of his head, and a slight animalistic growl came from this throat. The same blue light from the rip in my living room swirled around the Scot, and his arms and legs seemed to swell with power. His back, already muscular, grew larger, and as much as I tried to get a glimpse of his face, his powerful body never gave me a chance.

With one hand throwing the creature into the air, Gregor ran forward towards the others and released a growl that shook everything around him, including me. The sound elicited a fear so deep I didn't even know it was possible. I knew that if I even attempted to take Gregor on, it would be the last thing that I would do. Two of the creatures probably felt that same deep fear because they immediately flew away, while three others, feeling emboldened themselves (probably from the spirit's limbs they'd just devoured) charged forward in search of the Kyrios's limbs and blood.

All of the combatants rocketed to the sky, and they flew so high up into the air that I couldn't keep track of them. My ears perked up just to hear anything I could. There were clashes of metal and loud angry growls but I couldn't decipher who they came from. I clutched at the chain-link fence behind me, holding my breath, praying for a good outcome, for the Scot to return and for me to be safe.

I couldn't tell how long the battle was. It could have been an hour or several seconds, with the fear and adrenaline. But then it was over. After loud screeches, white leathery wings and bones fell to the ground with a resounding thud. Lastly, one boney head fell from the sky, disintegrating into a plume of red dust before hitting the ground.

Another look around revealed that the wings and bones had disintegrated as well. It was clear who had won this battle.

I could hear footsteps coming from the other end of the alley, moving towards me. I raised my head to see a man at a distance. He took his time returning—a quiet power radiated from him. My body started to heat up like the night before, my pulse raced, and it became harder to keep my eyes open, to stay conscious. As the man got closer, I noticed that half of his face was distorted. One side showed a handsome face I recognized with blue pupils. The other side was stretched and leathery, with the similar blood-red pupils of the creatures he'd just destroyed. The man's facial appearance was half human, half monster. But with every step he took closer to me, the leathery skin and red eyes shifted into the fair skin, dark stubble, and blue eyes associated with the Kyrios I knew.

The blood rushed to my head, the adrenaline and the chaos becoming too much. I barely heard Gregor ask me, "Are you all right, lass?" Even his voice had lost its soft timbre, shifting to an unearthly low sound.

Everything became too much to handle and spots blurred my vision once again. The last thing I remembered was the feeling of my body hitting the pavement and Gregor's arms around me.

9

For the second time in less than twenty-four hours, I awoke in my bed with no recollection of how I'd ended up there. And I was getting real tired of it. I slowly rose, taking in the familiarity of my bedroom when I heard, "Welcome back, lass. You were a bit touch and go for a while there."

I jumped to the other side of my bed, away from the Kyrios sitting on its edge. I yanked the sheets around and looked around wildly for some weapon. "Why are you here? What are you?"

Gregor rolled his eyes. "I thought we already went through this. I'm a Kyrios."

"Damn it, I already know that. I'm talking about t-t-that thing you turned into back in the alley."

Gregor got up and ran a hand through his hair. "That was just my body armor when I fight. There is nothing for you to be scared of. No need to freak out," he said, refusing to look me in the eye, turning his back on me.

My hackles rose in anger. I jumped out of bed and began

poking the Scot in the back. "No need to freak out? I… You've got to be kidding! This whole thing is a friggin' trip! Who the hell do you think you are, coming into my life, turning it completely upside down and then having the balls to tell me not to freak out?"

Gregor rounded on me, coming only a few inches away from my face. His lips thinned and a slight color came to his fair cheeks. He looked like he was about to let out a stream of angry words but caught himself. He took a step back. "Look," he said quietly. "I understand that this is all jarring. But I am not your enemy, chit. Remember? I came to help you when I didn't have to help you at all. I could have left you in the alley last night and I could've let the Cravers absorb you or destroy you today. But I've saved you twice now. And I let you know some information that no living person should ever know. We are both in some uncharted territory, lass. So I think a bit of trust is in order here, don't you?"

My eyes warred with his, searching for some reason to find him untrustworthy. But he was right. He had been helpful since the alley and I really didn't want to alienate the one person who could help me understand…myself. I slowly nodded my head in agreement. Wordlessly, I exited my bedroom and made for my kitchen. I made a beeline for the Hershey's and dipped my head back, sucking in the sweet cocoa syrup. Gregor followed me and was leaning against the doorframe, silently watching me.

Feeling slightly uncomfortable under his gaze, I crossed my arms and cleared my throat. "What happened today?"

Gregor shrugged, his eyes never leaving me. "You didn't listen to me."

My eyes narrowed at his accusation. "What do you mean?"

"I told you before I left last night not to get agitated. What did you go and do? Get agitated. So agitated that anything with any soul energy reached out, searching for the source. The Cravers were the first ones to find you."

"Those bird ugly things were Cravers? They looked so different from the one we saw yesterday."

"Remember that there are three levels of Cravers. Those were level one. They are actually the most common in the Live Realm and typically cause the most trouble because of their frequency. Like blasted pigeons. Like someone else here."

My thoughts went to the spirit I'd run into. "I met a spirit. Right before the Cravers got him, he was saying that I was the same as a Kyrios. What did he mean by that? Am I a Grim Reaper? And that man the Cravers got to, what happened to him? He was already dead, but it felt like he died again."

He sighed. "You are a living human girl—you're no Kyrios. He probably meant your Vis. Everyone is born with Vis in their body. Plants, animals, even the dirt. It's what you might call 'the spark of life,' essentially. Those life sparks are enclosed with your memories, what is more commonly called your soul. When you die, your Vis and your soul is severed from your corporal body. The Want need to absorb Vis in order to survive and get stronger.

"The man wasn't entirely wrong, you know. You have an enormous amount of Vis. It's like a well of power in its purest form, which is very rare for any Kyrios, let alone a living person. The Want are drawn to your Vis because it's like gourmet food to them. It would give them the energy to stay on this plane and evolve and become stronger. The larger forms of the Want seek out and absorb high-Vis creatures, including their own, in search of power to evolve into another form. It truly is survival of the fittest."

Gregor shook his head. "As for that man, he, unfortunately, became food. When a spirit is in the Live Realm after his body dies, it usually means that he didn't want to cross over. That he had some unfinished business. Most of the time it has to do with people that the spirit once loved. Although it could be anything. Money. Fame. Revenge. Addictions. Whatever. But to stay in the Live Realm is a risk. It's a risk to be absorbed, and it's a risk to everyone still living in the Live Realm. That's a Kyrios's job—to make sure spirits cross over like that man last night, and to destroy any Wanters that come over to the Live Realm. All to protect living people."

He released a deep sigh. "Today's spirit...his refusal to cross over cost him dearly. And, yes, it's like he died a second time. His very essence, which is supposed to live on after the body's death, was ripped apart and absorbed. Once absorbed, there's no saving him. His Vis now belongs to the Cravers."

I could only wonder what would've happened to me, and I could feel Gregor's piercing eyes bearing down on me. He was thinking the same thing.

I brushed past him and plopped down on the couch, burying my head in the pillows. "I didn't go out today to be eaten, Gregor. It wasn't my fault! That bitch Pana always gets underneath my skin. What's worse is everyone thought I had slept with you last night." I looked away from him, but still saw his boyish smirk and his blue eyes glittering with mischief.

He said, "Would that have been such a bad thing? I think that you might've enjoyed it."

I threw him a dirty look. "First, you are an ass, and I don't like you. Second, I'm a virgin. And third, a friend from school approached you first, remember? I was supposed to be defending her honor."

"And I am sure if you had given me a piece of your mind, you would have done it soundly."

Rolling my eyes, I said, "I don't need your sarcasm."

Gregor left the doorway and fully entered the room. "I'm not being sarcastic. I've heard enough from you to know your tongue is not one to be trifled with."

Ignoring the sudden fantasy of him warring with my tongue, I said, "I think you are just trying to make me feel better."

He gave me a small smile in return. "Is it working?"

"Maybe." I sighed. "I can't go on like this. I want my life to be normal. Before the world got all crazy with me at the center of it. What am I going to do?"

Before Gregor could answer, I heard the doorbell. I glanced out the window to find a tall, sandy-haired boy wearing a varsity basketball jersey and looking pretty annoyed.

"Aw, crap!" I squeaked. "It's Roger!"

"Roger?" Gregor asked, puzzled. "Who the daft is that?"

"He's my boyfriend. Look, go hide! You can't be here! He cannot see you!"

Gregor crossed his arms and assumed his position against the doorpost. "I will do no such thing. I don't hide."

"Please, Gregor! Just go!" I pleaded. But the Scot wouldn't move.

"Kat? Are you in there, babe?" a voice called out from behind the door.

I closed my eyes, praying for strength. I ran to the door and opened it with a huge smile on my face. "Hey! What are you doing here?"

Roger didn't wait to be invited in. He barged into the foyer. His footsteps came to a halt as he came to Gregor's back in the middle of the way. Gregor quietly moved and allowed Roger to enter the living room. Roger eyed Gregor suspiciously and held me by his side, kissing me on the cheek. "Kat! I've been worried sick about you! Cynthia told me that you ran from Downtown Crossing this afternoon and haven't called her since. What's going on? Who the hell is this?"

I plastered a smile on my face and patted Roger's hand, which was now wrapped around my own. "I'm fine. A lot was going on at the Underground and I just wanted to get away. This is my friend, Gregor."

Gregor grinned and offered his hand to Roger. "Pleasure."

Roger accepted the handshake suspiciously but then pulled his hand quickly away. "Wait a minute. Pana told me that some Scottish guy was hanging around you." He rounded on me. "Are you kidding me? It's true? You did not cheat on me with some foreigner, did you?"

I cringed but kept the smile on my face. "Yeah, I heard what Pana was saying, and no it's not true. Do I really seem like the type to do that?"

Roger opened his mouth to retort but said nothing.

"Besides, you should be thanking Gregor. I passed out in an alley and he was helping me out last night. He's been a perfect gentleman. He even stopped by today to see how I was feeling. Gregor is a foreign medical exchange student from Scotland." I lied smoothly. I gave Gregor a look, indicating that I needed some backup.

"Yes, while we didn't meet up in the best way, exactly, I felt it was part of my duty to make sure that my patient was feeling better. I just came over to check her vitals and to make sure she was getting plenty of rest and staying calm. From what she tells me, she was pretty agitated today, after some girl made some wild accusations about her. Who would believe such a shrew?" He added a broad grin to his last remark.

Roger's cheeks flushed red with embarrassment and anger.

I fought the urge to roll my eyes and returned my attention to Roger. "Thanks for checking up on me. I'm sure everything Pana said must have freaked you out. As it would anyone," I said. "But I'm still kinda pissed that you would believe that witch so easily."

Roger threw his arm around my shoulder, bringing me closer to him. "I... I didn't know what to think. Andrea was showing me pictures of the two of you and I just kinda lost it. I'm sorry. Andrea just has this way... Never mind. It doesn't matter."

Not particularly liking his intimate use of Pana's first name, I replied, "You do trust me, right? I mean, I heard stuff about you too. Like really damning stuff that I couldn't forgive you for if it was true, but I always give you the benefit of the doubt. Because I trust that you wouldn't do that to me."

Roger just pulled me closer, burying his face into my side of my neck. "Of course I trust you. I was just worried about you, Kat." He lifted his head slightly, eyes down. "No more about trust stuff, okay? I'm here because I wanted to make sure that my Kat was all right," he said, with a slight pout.

I rolled my eyes but begrudgingly gave him a smile. Whenever he made that face, it reminded me of the guy I started to date and nostalgia won out. "I'm fine, Roger. Really."

"Perfect!" He abruptly pulled me along with him towards the front door. "Then you can come out with me to the party we talked about earlier. You know, Devin Chirico's party. This might be my best chance to show off for his dad. I want to have them as a backup for basketball next fall."

Gregor quickly stepped forward. "Sorry, Rodney—"

"It's Roger."

Gregor flashed him a phony apologetic smile. "I'm sorry. Roger. Katya is not up for any plans tonight, and I still haven't finished my checkup with her."

Catching on, I nodded and stepped out of Roger's arms and stepped closer to Gregor. "Yes, that's right! I'm not really up to going out tonight."

Roger's jaw clenched as he eyed me. "But I need you tonight, Katya. How is it going to look like with me showing up without my girlfriend?"

"Look, I'm sorry," I said curtly. "But I'm not going with you tonight. I never said I was going out, and I'm not feeling up to it."

Roger looked at Gregor and me before saying, "Katya, can I see you in the kitchen for a moment?" Not giving me a chance to answer, Roger grabbed me by the elbow and propelled me into the kitchen.

I wrenched my arm away and growled, "What is your problem?"

"My problem? My problem is that you are sleeping with him!" Roger hissed.

"Oh my god! Didn't we just go over this? I'm not sleeping with anyone!"

"Yeah, well you know what? I don't buy this story. I don't buy you being sick. I think you want to 'stay home' because you've been screwing him since last night. Andrea was right—the picture doesn't lie, Kat!"

"You have got to be kidding me. I haven't been with anyone, you idiot! Gregor has been helping me because I don't feel well! He is a just male friend. Just because I have a male friend does not mean I'm sleeping with him. By your own logic, you sleep with all your female friends! And I am tired of hearing about Pana! You want to believe her over me, then go talk to her."

Roger raised his arms in front of him as to if to shield himself from my blows. "You know what? Fine. Ditch me, your boyfriend of two years, to go out with some foreigner. I mean, why the hell would my girlfriend be concerned about my dreams or my college plans!"

Exasperated, I asked, "Roger, how many parties have I been to? How many games have I gone to? How many times have I gone out spreading the word about you to my mom's sports clients? I am asking you to give me one night to rest. Because I do not feel well. Is that so much to ask? Besides, I wouldn't be touting 'two years' too quickly. Your boyfriend track record isn't that great, okay? Name the last thing we did together because it was my idea, not yours. I can't think of one either, so guess what? I think I deserve a night off from being your little doll that you tout around as a trophy. I am not the one."

Roger dropped his arms in resignation. "Fine Katya. Have it your way. I'll see you later." Without another word, he left the kitchen, passed Gregor, who had been listening, and walked out the front door with a slam.

I leaned against the kitchen counter and allowed my head to fall back on my shoulders. Gone were the days of endless calls, of wanting to be nearby just because. The Roger I fell in love with back during sophomore year would have offered to stay with me. To bring me back some soup or just understand that I needed some time to relax.

A year into our relationship, when he'd started to get better at basketball and he'd moved up to team captain, there was less time to be there. Less time to care. Just a few weeks ago, for our final dance class project, I had choreographed a dance and was to perform it solo. I reminded Roger for months, so he could make sure that he could attend. As I waited backstage, warming up and chatting excitedly with my co-dancers, I received a text message: "Sorry Kat. I can't make it. I'm going out with my cousin. He got us Celtics tickets! Maybe I'll get on the Jumbotron!"

Crushed couldn't begin to describe how I felt. I knew that he had missed plenty of dinners with friends for basketball. He had missed dates lately because of basketball. But I didn't think he'd miss the one thing I was passionate about and talked about as much as he talked about basketball—my dancing. The one thing where I could lose myself and just feel the music. Where I felt light and unburdened. Dance was my basketball.

After the countless games I'd attended over the last two years,

I never thought he would miss my event. That night, I held it together and gave a stellar performance like I was meant to. But I went home and sobbed into my pillow for a good hour. And since then I've been asking myself: "Why did my boyfriend have to be a selfish, pompous ass?"

Gregor entered the kitchen just as I hit my head against the cupboard doors. "I take it that hasn't been the first time your lover has acted like that."

I avoided eye contact with Gregor as I swept past him and entered the family room again. "Everyone fights. He's just really anxious about getting on a college basketball team. And don't say lover. It's creepy."

Gregor looked puzzled. "Do you not love him?"

Again that question. I hated the fact that after one encounter with Roger, Gregor could see the same questions that I was wrestling with myself. I didn't want to look indecisive in front of Gregor so I said, "I wouldn't have been with him for two years if I didn't."

Gregor arched an eyebrow, smirking. "Being with someone doesn't mean you like them. It just means that you have a habit you can't break."

I scowled at him. "So, doctor, what are our plans for tonight?" I asked, changing the subject.

"Your Vis reserve is still growing, and you have little control over it. It is reacting to your emotions. The stronger the feeling, the greater the power will flare. More powerful the flare, the more dangerous it becomes for you."

"So when I got pissed off downtown—"

"It sent off a signal to every Vis creature up and down the Northeastern corridor. The small Cravers got there first. Who knows what else could have answered that call?"

A chill ran up my spine as I thought about the things I had seen. "What do we do now? How do I control my Vis? Why do I have so much of it? Your explanations only increase the number of questions I have."

Gregor smiled crookedly. "I assumed they would. That's why we are leaving."

"Leaving? Where are we going?"

Gregor raised his right hand and concentrated on the center of his hand. A bright blue portal, similar to the one he'd entered the night before, opened.

"We are leaving the Live Realm and going to the other side."

10

I stepped back in shock at his announcement. "The other side? Wait, does that mean I have to die? Are you are going to kill me? Oh no thanks. I'm good."

Gregor rolled his eyes and offered his hand. "Don't be stupid, woman. No one is going to die. They know you are coming and are allowing you passage without death."

"Who are they?"

"The Department. They will explain everything to you. But you need to come with me."

I nervously studied the portal ripping space and time apart in the middle of my living room. "I don't know about this," I said, licking my lips, feeling uncertain. Crossing over dimensions to the realm of the dead didn't see like a very smart idea or a safe one. What would happen if I couldn't leave? What would then happen to Mom?

"Katya."

The soft timbers of the Kyrios's voice broke through my anxious thoughts, causing a spike in my heart rate. I was transfixed, unable to turn away from his face, his glowing eyes. "You need to trust me. No harm will come to you. I promise." After a few moments, I extended my hand and allowed Gregor to pull me into the portal. I thought we would have to travel within the portal itself to get to our destination, but we simply stepped through to the other side.

Initially, we were met with mist, fog, and clouds. I could barely see three feet in front of me. But Gregor seemed to know where exactly to go. We'd walked for several minutes when the mist began to clear and a large shadow in the distance became clearer. The closer we got, the larger the shadow appeared. Finally, as if we flipped a switch, all the fog and mist cleared to show the Great Wall of China. Or something that looked amazingly like the Great Wall of China. A white brick wall stretched for miles and miles on either end until it touched the horizon.

However magnificent the wall appeared was nothing compared to the towers beyond the wall. Five blazing white towers created a castle beyond the wall's entrance, and it looked large enough to fit thousands of people. The pointed caps of the towers reminded me of a trident piercing the cloudy sky, boldly displaying its strength and intimidating onlookers.

"Is this the Room of Apofasi?" I asked breathlessly.

"No. The Room of Apofasi is solely for the judgment of dead souls. This place is Ager, the Department's headquarters." We headed for the immense wall's entrance, guarded by two tall men. The men were dressed similarly to Gregor—black jacket, black pants, black boots. And they were both incredibly handsome. They could be featured on the cover of a fashion magazine that would just be called "Handsome." I wondered if being gorgeous was a requirement to be a Kyrios.

One of the men stepped forward—a blond man with brown eyes—and said, "State your name and business."

Gregor didn't miss a beat. "Kyrios Gregor escorting the living Katya Stevens to the Generals."

The two men's eyes fell on me, and I tried very hard not to squirm underneath their inspection. "You may enter," the blond guard answered and the large gate shot up high in the sky. Gregor nodded curtly, took my arm, and marched forward.

What was beyond the wall was just as imposing as the wall itself. The massive towers, centered in the middle of the main compound, were pristinely clean and new, though they looked impossibly old. Surrounding the center towers were many smaller buildings that were much less imposing and a lot less scary. The entire "town" looked like it came out of a history book on sixteenth-century England. I half expected peasants to stream out of the smaller buildings wearing dirt-stained rags or the rich to saunter down the streets with powdered wigs and white stockings.

Instead of peasants, there were Kyrios everywhere. Men and women from different races and ethnicities from all over the world, all similarly dressed to Gregor. Some Kyrios were running in packs, doing drills. Some were transporting large packs that resembled industrial-sized potato sacks. Others were lounging around, laughing and talking to each other, but still on alert for any alarm. It felt like I'd entered a military base, and I told Gregor so. He slightly smirked but kept his eyes forward. "You could say that we are a form of military," he said quietly.

"But I thought you guys were Death. Why would you need to be militant?"

"Your questions will be answered later. Let's keep it moving." Some of the Kyrios stared at us as if sensing that my presence in Ager was unusual. I ducked a bit closer to Gregor and followed him quickly. We headed towards the tallest tower, stationed in the middle of the four other large towers surrounding it. But when we entered through the main door, there was no way to get anywhere. No stairs, no elevator. And the only platform I could see was at the very top of the tower.

"How are we supposed to get up there?" Gregor hoisted me up into his arms, bridal style. I was immediately struck by how easily he pulled me into arms and the strength that I felt emanating from him; I felt like I could sink further into him and be cocooned in safety. Realizing that I was on the verge of possibly doing something embarrassing, I half-heartedly attempted to leap out of his arms but gripped his neck in the process. I shrieked, "What are you doing?"

"Just hold on tight," he answered and jumped up. The rush of jumping several hundred feet high got the best of me, and I screamed the entire way up. As soon as we hit the platform, I released my kung-fu grip on his face, leapt down from his arms, and adjusted my clothes. "That wasn't so bad," I said, refusing to make eye contact with him.

Gregor gave me a sideways glance. "Really? I think my ears disagree with you."

Still refusing to look at him, I brushed the imaginary dirt off me. "Well, who are we meeting here?"

"We are right here," a voice said from behind.

My head shot up, and I subconsciously inched a bit closer to Gregor. Four men and one woman stood before me, all wearing the familiar all-black Kyrios uniform, with one exception: a long medallion necklace hung around each person's neck. There was a different presence about them that clearly indicated they were in charge. Without effort, power radiated from them. My tingling within felt lighter with them, enjoying their energy.

Gregor dropped down to one knee and placed his hand on his chest. "Generals."

A relatively young-looking tall man came forward. He had dark hair cropped low to his brow, olive skin, and piercing light brown eyes. The best artisans out of Rome must have sculpted his body. There was no way that a physique like that could've come naturally. From the energy I felt from him alone, he seemed to be the strongest. The man smiled down at Gregor. "Relax, Gregor. No need for protocol around us." His accent sounded Middle Eastern.

Gregor straightened and smiled, "I'll always stand on ceremony when it concerns you, mentor."

The man's laugh boomed against the walls. "You always did, my boy. A Scot isn't a Scot without his traditions." He then turned to me and bowed slightly. "You needn't be afraid, child. You are amongst friends here. My name is Nabil." He motioned to the other Generals behind him. "That is General Lamar, and these are Generals Victor, Raf, and Michiko, and together we are the leaders of the Department. We oversee all operations regarding the Kyrios and spirit transfers from the World of the Living to the Room of Apofasi."

I frowned, hardly remembering the names even a moment later. "I'm sorry, but you don't look that much older than me. Isn't calling me a child a bit patronizing?"

Nabil smirked. "I like to think I have aged pretty gracefully. Not bad for sixty-five hundred, huh?"

"Six thousand and five hundred years old?" Embarrassment burned my cheeks. "Oh wow, uh, sorry. I just… I'm a bit lost, you know."

Nabil smiled at me serenely. "No need for the apologies. It is all unknown to you, and you have many questions, yes?"

Not trusting myself to speak, I nodded.

"Very well, let's adjourn to the next room while we explain it to you. Gregor, you may continue with your duties. You are dismissed."

I cleared my throat loudly and edged back to stand directly in front of Gregor. "Um, Nabil, again, don't wanna be a pain, but I would consider it a personal favor if you kept the only man I know here around. I'd feel better about this situation if he was here to help me process everything."

Gregor didn't speak a word. He simply lowered his head, waiting for his leader's decision. Nabil looked at the other Generals, who shrugged and turned around to enter another room. Nabil smiled, though not as widely as before. "Fine. Gregor, you may stay. Follow me." Without waiting for my thanks, Nabil and the other Generals entered the next room.

Gregor relaxed from his stance and begin to walk slowly forward with me in tow. "You know nothing would have happened to you," he said quietly. "I really don't need to be here."

I shook my head. "Cut me some slack. I don't know anyone else here. I trust you more than the entire Kyrios force combined. I won't talk to them unless you are with me."

Gregor looked over his shoulder at me with a mixture of

exasperation and amusement. I simply arched one of my eyebrows and crossed my arms. "Don't look at me like that. You think I'm being childish. Think of it as me self-preserving myself, hmm? Plus, I bet you want to know what they know too."

He turned back around, with his own smirk shining on his face. "Enough with the cheek, lass. You're getting your wish."

11

We stepped into the next room with a large oval table in the center. The Generals were already seated, waiting for us to take our seats in turn. Nabil sat at the head of the table. "Ms. Katya, what do you know about the Kyrios?"

I shrugged. "Not too much. Gregor has told me about Vis and that the Kyrios are like Soul Police, that you bring souls to judgment. Although I may a bit confused about this entire operation. Why are you guys so militant?"

Nabil sighed deeply. "As you may know, the Live Realm is made up of positive Vis. When you die, your soul and your personal Vis leave your body. The Vis is supposed to return to the Live Realm, and the soul needs to enter the Room of Apofasi to cross over. Some souls go immediately without help. Most, however, do not and require the Kyrios to lead them. However, there are times when a soul is so tied to the Live Realm that their anger about dying or having to move on changes them. They hold on to their Vis, and it physically changes until they are the beasts that chased after you today. Unfortunately, as the world has gotten more self-absorbed and more consumed with what they have in the Living Realm, there's been an increase of souls changing into Want creatures."

"Wait, so you're telling me that the bird Cravers that tore apart a human soul were once humans?" I asked, horrified. What could hold someone so much that they changed into those things?

Nabil nodded. "I see Gregor has been teaching you some of our terminology. Unfortunately, that's just the beginning." He leaned in closer across the table. "You see, the Want mainly desire one thing—they are angry that they are dead and want to live in the Live Realm again. It's unnatural for the dead to stay in the Live Realm, so they need Vis to sustain them. They absorb the Vis from other dead souls, effectively destroying the soul as well. Continuous destruction. Outside of the Live Realm, there are two places for deceased souls. Paradiso is for those have passed judgment and The Abyss is for those who failed judgment or have turned themselves into the Want. It's meant to be their prison, their hell for eternity, though they continually break out."

"Wait, I don't understand. How do they get out if the Abyss is supposed to be their prison? Aren't they under lock and key?"

Nabil smiled ruefully. "If only the system was designed that way. The Abyss is another plane—the poorest mirror image of the Live Realm, but with no Vis to sustain them. Once a Want creature is put into the Abyss, they have three choices. First, they can wither away and die. A rare choice for a creature who is hell bent on returning to the life they once had or getting the revenge they want.

"Second, they can survive and absorb. To survive is to get stronger. Which means a Want creature with some Vis must feast on other Want creatures and take their Vis for strength. That's why there are different levels of strength within the Want. The highest rank is called a General, just like we do here. I'd like to think it's a flattering thing, having them name themselves after us.

Third, they can use whatever Vis they do have to pierce the veil that separates the Abyss and the Living Realm and enter the Living Realm in search for more Vis to sustain themselves. Every time they enter the Live Realm, they are causing themselves harm. But they are only looking to the end result—more Vis and the ultimate destruction of the realm they can't enjoy anymore.

"The Want generally employ a combination of choice two and three because they hate everything about the Live Realm, and they hate those who keep them in The Abyss. They desire nothing more than to destroy the world they cannot live in anymore and destroy their wardens."

"Don't they just make you all warm and fuzzy inside," I muttered. "Also, I have to say, this seems like a sucky system. Why don't you just put them in cells like normal prisons rather than having them break out all the time and having to chase after them every single time? Who created this system?"

Gregor cleared his throat. "God, Katya."

God. *God?*

I would never be the one to say that I was an atheist but throughout my life, with all of the craziness and heartache I'd experienced, I did think every now and then that I must have pissed God off. Because...well, my life speaks for itself. My relationship with God was mainly what Mom had told me and what she had been taught by her parents. She would always ensure that we'd go to church when she was home. More so I think because she didn't want our white neighbors to think that she was too good to attend the local black church. That even though she was a law firm partner, she was not too good for the likes of them now. That she had ties with them, like my grandparents did until the day they died.

I just hated the way the church congregation was so passive aggressive. Even when we would make it to church for consecutive weeks, there would always be one or two people who would stop by our seats to say, with the least amount of concern in their voice, "Great seeing you. We missed you these past couple of weeks. Everything all right at home?" You could tell they were only looking for the next bit of gossip to pass on at the next fellowship meeting. Or if they had been a part of the church for a long time from since when I was a child, asking whether I still needed some prayers about casting out any "unsavory spirits." Those people I truly despised.

But it wasn't that I hated God because of those people. I just never understood why he would let them use his name as means for their own ends.

Hearing Gregor say that God made this system brought some questions. "God created this system as punishment for the Want? Did he create you guys too?"

Nabil leaned back in his chair, satisfied with my rapt attention. "All souls, whole or damaged, have a place to be. The Abyss, Paradiso, the Living Realm—they all serve a function to preserve a balance. To maintain equilibrium for this universe. The Abyss was never meant to be punishment—the Want turned it into one themselves, by harboring their hatred. As for us, we Kyrios chose this life. We chose to function in this hybrid world of living and dead as wardens but to also serve a function for maintaining this balance. To lead unchanged souls all over the world to judgment and to keep the Want in The Abyss.

"Because the Want constantly break out to cause trouble, when we mobilize to send them back, or in many instances, destroy them, it becomes a battle. Many battles bleed into the Live Realm and, unfortunately, cause more chaos. It's one of the reasons why there's dangerous weather and unexplained activity. It's due to the shift in Vis in the Live Realm.

"The most horrible disasters are the fruit of the Want's revenge," Nabil continued. "If they sense that there is a soul passing around the Live Realm, they'll enter the Live Realm to retrieve it. Whenever the Want enter into the Live Ream, the shift in the realm's Vis balance disrupts normal life. Wanters trying to absorb Vis to sustain themselves can cause calamity, famine, and earthquakes; whatever chaos there could be, it is more than likely caused by them."

"If that is the case, why can't you just destroy them all? Aren't you supposed to be protecting the humans?"

Nabil's eyebrows rose. "That is not our role. We are keepers only. We only destroy Wanters if they enter the Live Realm. We can't stop the creation of Wanters—all we can do is contain them in the Abyss. But as of late, something is off in the Abyss, and we have no idea what it is. The Want are tearing into the Live Realm at a higher-than-normal rate. And we believe it is not just because of you."

"Speaking of Ms. Katya," the female General called, "let's discuss her current situation."

"Yes. I'm sorry, General…?"

The female smiled softly. She was quite beautiful, with almond shaped eyes, high cheekbones, long midnight hair, and heart-shaped lips. "It is General Michiko. I am the head of Scouting and Intelligence. I had Gregor bring you here so we could talk about the extraordinary well of Vis you have."

I looked eagerly at the soft-spoken woman. "General Michiko, do you know what is wrong with me?"

Michiko shared a look with the other Generals and said, "I'm sorry, but we are not completely sure yet. As far we know, we have never encountered a living human with such immense Vis reserves. We've been charting you since you've entered, and your reserve has only grown exponentially in the past hour that we have been together."

Alarmed, I asked, "Is that a bad thing? Will something happen to me?"

She sighed. "I am unable to answer this question until we've had some more time to study you. Tell me, has anything in particular been different for you? Gregor told us that you had the ability to see spirits when you were a child but that it stopped ten years ago, only to return now. Has anything happened?"

"After my eighteenth birthday, I started to experience some flashes, or visions. I could never really remember them. The last vision I had was the night I met Gregor." I almost added, "And there's an odd voice in my head that talks to me when it's really quiet and/or I feel extremely confused about what to do" but decided against it. I mean I understood that I was in another dimension talking to spirit wardens, but I was very sure hearing voices in your head was not a good sign in any dimension.

Michiko was writing furiously in a pad of paper that had appeared out of thin air. "The visions seem to coincide with when the abnormal activity in the Abyss started. Gregor did say that he felt a small abnormality when he initially met you. Perhaps the Wanters might have noticed it too and may have been looking for you, mistaking you for a recently passed soul. But since meeting Gregor and that incident in the alley, your Vis reserve has almost awakened from a deep slumber. It's why the Wanters have been actively looking for you in particular these last thirty-six hours."

"If they were able to consume you, then they could move up the food chain quite readily. I reckon any Wanter that did devour you would become a General instantaneously," Nabil piped in.

I furiously thrust a hand through my hair, fighting back the fear and anger that was starting to build. "So now what? What do we do?" I asked tersely. "All you have done is thoroughly scare me and blow my mind about God and then tell me that I'm strange, that I'm Wanter food, and could effectively bring more destruction if I get eaten." I let out a sigh and said a bit louder, with growing frustration, "What is the point of this if you can't tell me what I am or how I fix myself?" Warmth expanded and engulfed me from all sides. After several seconds, the feeling stopped, and it got cold again.

The room filled with silence for several moments before one of the Generals spoke up. With a Russian accent, he said, "The main point of our meeting is for you to learn to control yourself." I looked at the General who'd just spoken. A silver-haired man, though still young looking, raked his eyes over me with slight annoyance. "We have enough to worry about with Wanters constantly causing trouble. We have another situation in the Abyss that is causing more Wanters to break into the Live Realm and we can't figure it out yet—"

"Why don't you just pop into the Abyss and take a look?" I interrupted fiercely. "For God's sake, it can't be that difficult—"

"Because it is forbidden!" Raf said sharply. "We cannot go in as we please, like the Archs and Phims. We have to play by the rules and do what must be done in our capacity. However we can hardly get a control over the Abyss situation because your tantrums continue to be a risk to the Live Realm. Your job now is learn to calm down and not act like a toddler. Multitudes of the Want will continue to cross over and cause more destruction to look solely for you!" The last bit was hissed out from his tight lips.

Kind of pissed, I crossed my arms, looking anywhere but at the Russian. Gregor reached underneath the table to squeeze my knee as a warning.

Nabil threw the silver-haired General a warning look. "What General Raf is trying to say is that we brought you here because we wanted to you to be informed. We also wanted to discuss your role in this conflict and hope that we can perhaps help each other. While we are trying to maintain the balance, you might find it helpful to receive some Kyrios training for protection. Your Vis reserve is very similar to the Vis that we Kyrios have. If you're able to control your Vis, then you'll less likely be a threat to others around you. And perhaps you'd be an asset to the Live Realm."

Not trusting myself to speak, I nodded.

Nabil nodded as well. "Raf is in charge of training here, and he will be supervising your progress." The Russian man nodded. He then pointed to a dark-skinned, impressive General that reminded me of someone. "General Lamar is in charge of security here at Ager. He will ensure you remain safe both here and in the Live Realm." Lamar gave a soft smile that I returned.

Nabil then gestured to the red-haired General, who was grinning in my direction. "And Victor is in charge of hospitality and energy consumption. He makes sure everyone is taken care of here and that things are running smoothly. You will not have too much time with him. Michiko will continue her research, and I will be checking on your progress periodically."

"And your position, sir? What do you do?" I asked quietly.

Nabil smirked. "I, my dear, am the head General, and I oversee everything." He looked at Gregor. "I believe that your work here is done here, Gregor. Ms. Katya, you will begin your training immediately."

I did a double take. "Wait, you mean right now? How long is this going to take?"

Raf shrugged. "As long as it takes for you to grasp basic principles. Could be a few days."

"Oh, that's not too bad."

Gregor said softly, "For full disclosure, one full day here is three days in the Live Realm. So four days here could be two weeks back at home."

I felt my eyebrows disappearing in my hair. "I can't disappear like that! I may be eighteen, but I'm still in high school. My mother will freak out if she comes home from work and I'm not there. People I care about will worry."

Michiko spoke up, "Ms. Katya, do you understand that we don't completely understand how bad it will get? You could be a threat to yourself and to the people you care about. What about your entire community?"

I knew Michiko had a valid point; I knew I was an accident waiting to happen. That poor man's soul back at Downtown Crossing was a perfect example. But at that moment I could only remember my mother's anguish right after my dad died. After the casket was lowered into the ground, my mother desperately tried to stay strong. I did as well, but I couldn't help but grasp her hand as we took several steps away and said to her softly,

"We'll be okay, Mommy." Suddenly overwhelmed with grief, I remember almost falling under my mother's weight as she clung to me, falling to her knees sobbing into my hair, "My baby. I'm so sorry, my baby. I'm so sorry."

"Generals, please. Give me a week first. I only have my mother, and I don't want to put her through stress if we can avoid it. I promise to keep my temper in order until I can come back here for training. Or is there something we can do to curb my power in the meantime?"

Nabil sucked in his teeth and motioned to Lamar. "What do you think?"

General Lamar shrugged. "I think we can trust her to be good. From Ager, we could monitor her. If her Vis levels surge out of control, we can bring her in immediately." He looked at me sternly with a hint of a smile. "As long as the young lady remembers to stay calm, I don't think it should be a problem."

I nodded earnestly. "Yes, sir. I promise."

Nabil sighed. "It is only because you are still of the Living that I am even considering this. But we will allow you time to get your affairs in order. We will have a Kyrios stationed by your home for additional protection. Everyone, return to your posts."

"Um," I called. The Generals paused in their departure and looked at me. "I'm sorry, but I have one more request."

Nabil looked at me unflinchingly. "What is it?"

I swallowed, got up from my chair slowly and slightly gulped. "Can Gregor be the one who watches me until my training begins?" I asked quickly.

"Katya!" Gregor hissed. "What are you doing?"

I refused to look at him, still speaking quickly. "Look, I'm very grateful that you have been educating me about this whole mess. And it's not that I don't believe that any other Kyrios wouldn't be able to protect me. They all look pretty badass, as do all of you. I mean my Vis immediately responded to your strength. It's just that…I already feel comfortable with Gregor, and he has already helped me understand quite a bit about Ager and all of you. I could be much more use to you if I am at ease and not agitated about having another stranger look at me, expecting me to explode." I bit my lip, trying to get control of my nervous energy. "Please allow him to stay with me. He is the only person I know."

Gregor finally moved in front of me and knelt before the Generals. "Generals, my first duty is oversee the Northeast quadrant. Yes, I understand I have set up a repertoire with Ms. Katya. I do believe anyone could oversee her protection. While I am flattered, I believe she simply is feeling gratitude towards me and feeling a bit uneasy about the ordeal. I request that I remain at my post." He never looked up from the floor.

The Generals looked at each other, silently communicating. Nabil sighed and said, "Gregor, we of course have full faith in your abilities to oversee the Northeast. However, this will take precedent until we have a better understand of the child. Nor do we want start this relationship on a bad foot, yes?" He smiled at me widely, but I could see that it was forced. I guessed I wouldn't be trading pillow talk with him anytime soon. "Gregor, you are now ordered to remain as Ms. Katya's guard until further notice. Your duties will be passed on to your second in command. You shall guard her with your life and not allow anything to absorb her Vis. The last thing we need is the Want getting their claws into her."

"Thank you, Generals," I said softly, watching Gregor remain unmoving on the floor.

With a slight flourish of his coat, Nabil left the room.

12

Michiko and Victor slowly followed Nabil, muttering goodbyes. Raf and Lamar remained behind. With a stare fixated on me, Raf said, "You must return here in a week's time. You will get your affairs in order, and you will return here with Gregor. Then you are mine."

Fantastic. "Will this really only take a few Ager days, General Raf?"

"It will take as long you need to get control of your energy."

"But that could take months, years."

Raf shrugged. "What is time when you are dead?"

"But I'm not dead."

"You will be if you don't control your Vis." He left the room, not waiting for a response. "I will see you in a week's time, Ms. Katya," he called over his shoulder.

I massaged my face, feeling annoyed. "It's going to be just fantastic training with him, huh?" I muttered to myself.

I looked to General Lamar, who was still showing the kind smile from earlier. "This is a lot to take in, isn't it?" he asked softly. The soft, soothing timbre of his voice seeped into me and threatened to unleash the tears I was surprised I was even holding. I nodded. "Things will come easier with time. I'm sure you will surpass all of our expectations," he said softly. I gave my new favorite General a tremulous smile.

General Lamar snapped his fingers, opening a small blue sliver in the middle of the room. He reached in and pulled out a silver bracelet. The incision in the air closed instantly. "In the meantime, I want you to wear this bracelet. This will allow us to keep track of you and get readings of your energy level. I'm sure Gregor will do just fine in keeping you safe. But safety and security is my job, and keeping you safe is a priority." With a snap, the metal bracelet, inscribed with odd hieroglyphic-like markings, infused together and was officially stuck on my wrist. Taking it off for showers didn't seem to be likely.

"What are the markings on the bracelet?" I asked, turning my wrist around to inspect it further.

Lamar chuckled. "A language older than the universe itself. Let's just say it says, 'Send information to the intelligent and handsome man in charge of the Security Tower.' Perhaps I will give you a chance to learn more once you return here."

"And this really will keep me safe?"

"You are a precious commodity, dear. All of us will be keeping an eye on you," he said with a wink.

"General Lamar, thank you for your kindness," I smiled,

though a bit uneasy about all of the scrutiny. "It's truly appreciated." With a nod, the General was out the door. Then it clicked why he seemed familiar—he reminded me of my father. Especially the way his crow's feet around his eyes crinkled together. Like he was excited and happy just to see and help me. And his easy smile… If my Dad were here and he was a General of a Grim Reaper militaristic league, I'd like to think he'd be General Lamar.

I turned around to find Gregor looking at me, very displeased. "What's the matter?" I asked innocently.

He closed the gap between us and whispered in my ear, "Not here. Let's go." He took my arm and led me hastily out of the Center Tower. He barely said a word as we walked back through Ager, out the main gate, and back into my family room. A quick look at the clock told me that it was midnight. It had only felt like an hour in Ager, but we really were gone for three!

The moment the portal closed, he led me to the couch. "We need to talk," he said tersely.

I bit my lip, again nervous about my request for him to stay with me. "What do you mean?"

"I almost don't know where to begin. First, you can't be disrespectful to Nabil, the head of the Kyrios. Second, you lost your cool until quiet Raf, who never speaks unless spoken to, was sharp with you. And after all that, you ask for one of their Majors to abandon his post to babysit?

"Hey, I resent the babysitting!"

He ignored the interruption. "It's just not done that way. The Department, Ager…they are very old and set in their ways. There are protocols and manners to follow—spoken and unspoken. I understand that this your first time with them and I probably should have explained this to you before we left. And perhaps the Generals understood and took pity on you. But in the future, you must watch your tongue. It is a miracle that the Generals were in a good mood, or they could have turned you down flat and locked you up!"

I was about to interrupt him again about the babysitting when his last sentence hit me. "Wait, what?"

Gregor ran a hand through his tousled hair, looking less frazzled than he had just a few minutes before. "You are an unknown. An enigma. Something that could upset the balance within the realm, like the Want. If they had willed it, they could've taken you into protective custody."

I closed my eyes, letting my head fall back on my shoulders. "I've heard that phrase way too many times. Police taking you in 'for your protection.' That's absolute crap. Just say what you mean. You mean prison."

"Something like that." Gregor kneeled down before me, bracing his arms on either side of me. "Katya, take this from someone who knows. Don't be the reason for your loss of freedom. If you cannot control your Vis, they will not hesitate to contain you."

I searched his eyes, looking for an answer. Does that mean he was imprisoned? "Would they kill me?"

He hesitated but shook his head. "The Kyrios do not kill the living. We simply bring souls over. However, the Generals could have gotten the okay from the higher ups to place you somewhere within Ager for safe keeping."

"Who are the higher ups? What does that even mean?"

Gregor sat on the couch beside me, hunched over and balancing himself on his elbows over his knees. "Katya, there is an order to everything. We are the Department, but we are not in charge. There are others in the chain of command, like the Archs or the Phims, that could overrule us. If they're convinced that it's for the benefit of maintaining control, something they treasure, they will do whatever is necessary."

"Archs? Phims?"

"Archangels and the Seraphim."

"Angels? Like real-life angels? Big fluffy wings? Chubby-looking things?"

"Yes on the wings, though not as fluffy. And an absolute no on the chubby. Think deadly warriors with wings and very strong weapons."

My mind instantly pictured Gregor with nothing but wings on his back, bare chested with a cloth covering his bottom half. I shook my head to clear the arousing thought. "Wait, so angels could order my death? Just like that? They can't do that," I said slowly. "I have the right to live my life too. Where is the justice in that?"

He chuckled darkly and stared at the ceiling. "Justice. If only true justice ever existed. It's a fine idea, but nothing is ever that clear cut, even in death." He turned to meet my eyes. "They can detain you, and they will if you don't learn to control your emotions and your Vis."

I stared into Gregor's eyes and found honesty. I sighed heavily, rubbing my arms for warmth. "All right. I get it. But I'm not doing it because of the threat of angels. But because I just want to go back to my normal life."

Gregor also visibly relaxed as he saw my acceptance of the situation. "Good."

I looked down at my lap, fiddling my hands. "I thought for a moment there you were upset that I asked the Generals about you staying with me."

He seemed genuinely surprised, and he began to laugh heartily. "Whatever gave you that idea?"

I shrugged, not looking up. "I don't know. You didn't say a word on the way back and the way you looked at me when I finally turned around... I thought I overstepped my boundaries with you."

Gregor smirked. "I don't mind staying with you, lass. I had to say all that because I didn't want there to be any implication that we had a closer relationship that would be considered inappropriate. We Kyrios are not to maintain any ties to the Live Realm. If the Generals thought there was any possibility of that happening, then I would have been ordered to release you to someone else. The way you explained yourself could have been understood differently."

"So Kyrios can't have any...friends in the Live Realm."

He shook his head. "Of course not. If we got too attached this ever-passing world, then we would create anchors for ourselves, which could possibly tear us apart if we had to choose."

His words both delighted and disappointed me. I was happy that he was thinking ahead and trying to protect me but that meant that I couldn't get involved with him either. I was expecting too much from him because he saved me. Or maybe because he was the first person to believe me.

I inwardly rolled my eyes at myself. I'd barely known this man for forty-eight hours and I was already thinking romance? I always made fun of girls getting too attached to guys so quickly after getting a little attention. I wasn't about to become a hypocrite. I cleared my throat and asked, "What are you going to do now?"

He arched an eyebrow. "What do you mean?"

I looked around. "I don't know. Do Kyrios sleep, eat?"

"We don't need hours of sleep or really any food, but we can sleep and eat should we choose. We just need to stop by Ager from time to time to get our fill of Vis to sustain ourselves. That's what General Victor is in charge of."

My nose crinkled in confusion. "Is there any Vis in Ager? Where does the Vis come from?"

Something in his manner shifted, and he quickly said, "Everywhere and nowhere."

I shrugged. "Okay then. Where are you staying?"

Gregor stood up and looked around. "This room will do just nicely."

I shot up from my seat. "Excuse me? You are staying here?"

He placed his hands on his hips and smirked. His lazy and careless stance infuriated me even more. "How do you expect me to protect you, lass? I need to be close by, so you don't go off the deep end and have a fit."

Rolling my eyes, I plopped down on my couch, bringing my knees into my chest. "How am I supposed to explain you to my boyfriend or my mother?"

Gregor joined me on the couch, throwing his arms behind his head and stretching his long legs. "I'm sure you'll think of something other than the truth. You certainly did last time." He winked, chuckling softly.

"Yeah, a lot of help you were. I can't tell my mother anything? This whole situation actually might make a lot sense for her if I was just honest about it. I know I haven't spoken about this stuff in years, but I'm sure she'll be able to handle it."

He shook his head. "It has been decreed from the time Ager, the Abyss, and Paradiso were created that the living would not have any understanding of after-death inner workings. Even the Generals telling you what they did would be considered a big infraction. Hence we have to keep this quiet and make sure that we are not making too much noise. That's why I had to mark your hand the night we met—to keep the secrets. Fewer people know, the better."

"Decreed by who?"

He gave me a look. "Who else?"

God again. "You try explaining why you're going to be gone for an unknown amount of time to your mother," I muttered. The rumblings of my stomach reminded me that I hadn't eaten at all. Being at the mall with Cynthia seemed like days ago. I stood again and crossed over Gregor's legs. "I'll make some dinner. Is there anything you are allergic..." I trailed off and looked at him. "Never mind. You are not human. It's not like I can kill you."

I made for the door when Gregor called, "Katya."

I turned around. Gregor hadn't lost his relaxed position on the couch, but his eyes betrayed his easy stance. "While this may be my duty, in the six hundred years that I have been a Kyrios, being here is a whole lot better than dealing with the dead. The Living are a lot more interesting. Present company included." His lips quirked into an easy smile, and I felt a familiar lurch in my stomach.

I returned his smile and exited the living room quickly. As I cooked dinner for myself and "Death" in my living room, my smile refused to be extinguished.

13

The next morning, I awoke to the sound of my alarm blasting several feet away from me.

Groaning, I reached my arm over to hit the snooze button but was unable to reach it. I slowly raised my head from my pillow to see an opaque wall, which was giving off a slight energy. I looked around and found that the wall surrounded my entire bed like a dome. Instantly, I felt my palms sweat and a pounding in the back of my head. I tried to get up but felt another wall only several inches above me. My blood raced through my veins as I began to pound on the invisible walls, searching for a way out.

The panic finally rose from deep within my belly and I began to scream.

"Gregor! Gregor! Help me!"

I furiously pounded on the wall, tears streaming down my face. My throat began to hitch and I started to lose my ability to breathe properly. Just as I was about to let out another scream, the walls suddenly came down and a pair of arms encased me and brought me close to a warm chest.

"It's all right. I've got you. Nothing to be scared of." All of the fear, anxiety, and apprehension I had been harboring from the past couple of days hit me and the floodgates opened. I'm not sure how long I cried, but the warm arms never left me. Calloused hands caressed my hair and head, easing the tension away. Soft words of comfort finally brought my sobs to a low hum. I found my equilibrium again.

As my tears dried up, I became very much aware of the Kyrios holding me. As a matter of fact, it was a shirtless Kyrios holding me. Underneath my cheek, I could feel the patches of dark hair sprinkled about the broad chest. With every movement, the muscles rippled, displaying his great strength and fitness. Without having to look, I knew Gregor was a sight to behold.

I slowly raised my head from my chest, my eyes cast downward. "I... I'm sorry about that. I, um, don't do well in closed places."

Gregor had slightly released his tight hold of me, but still kept me close. "It's my fault. I put up the barrier around you to keep your Vis contained in a smaller area in case you released anything while you slept. I should have made it bigger." His body was calm. However, his eyes betrayed his distress.

I shook my head, wiping my face, "You couldn't have known about my claustrophobia. It's okay."

He looked me over, checking for any injuries. "Are you sure you are all right?"

I nodded, trying to discreetly clean the snot running down my nose. "Not particularly attractive right now, but I'm okay."

Gregor chuckled, tucking a stray hair behind my ear. "I don't know about that. Even with bogeys in your nose, you are still quite the sight."

The unfortunate but familiar lurch in my stomach returned, painfully reminding me that the gorgeous Kyrios was shirtless in my bedroom holding me. *Come on, girl. Look beyond the pretty face. Don't be that girl!* It didn't help that I also wasn't particularly dressed for company. After dinner the night before, I'd only thrown on an extra-long tank top, which didn't leave too much to the imagination.

Knowing that I needed to move before I did anything foolish, I pulled back from Gregor. "I should probably get out of bed."

However, during my panic attack, my feet had gotten impossibly tangled in the sheet, starting my downward descent to the floor head first. Gregor caught me before any physical damage could be done. But his actions only placed my head in his lap and my hands against his chest. The quiet strength I had felt against my cheek doubled against my hands. It was though his strength enveloped my entire body, tightening me like a string on a bow.

Gregor's grip tightened slightly around my shoulders, searching my eyes. "Are you all right, Katya?"

I nodded, not speaking for fear that my mouth would betray me. The Kyrios and I were frozen, waiting for the other to do something. For several long moments, neither one us moved, maintaining our close contact. Gregor broke the silence. "Katya—"

The doorbell rang, bringing us back to reality. "Oh, crud!" I grumbled. I reluctantly pushed against Gregor's chest. "Can you help me up, please? I need to get that."

The Kyrios nodded and picked me up, setting my feet on the

floor. I ran a hand through my kinks, attempting to clear the knots as I grabbed my robe and yanked it over my body. "Can you stay in here? I really don't want to have to explain to other people why you are here, especially if it's Cynthia's mom. She sometimes stops by to check on me."

Gregor stood from my bed and crossed his arms over his chest. I stared at his face, desperately trying not to look at his well-defined physique. "Are you telling me to hide in your bedroom, like some coward?"

I looked at him strangely, "This is not some male ego thing. Put the testosterone away, okay? I am asking you to be discreet. Very few people will understand why a half-naked guy is here in my house." The doorbell rang again. Without waiting for Gregor's response, I ran down the hall to the front door.

"Hold on, I'm coming." I shouted.

I looked through the peephole to see my boyfriend looking a bit peeved behind the door. I sighed deeply, unlocked the door and said, "Roger, what are you doing here this early?"

Without a kiss or even a hello, Roger marched straight into the kitchen and unloaded a bag he was holding. "I wanted to have breakfast with you before you did anything else today. I figured it's the least you could do since you bailed on me last night. Did you see the playoff game last night? You should totally watch the highlights. Amazing."

The spikes of annoyance began to ping in my head as I watched Roger take food out of the paper bag and turn the TV on to SportsCenter. "I didn't bail out on anyone last night. I wasn't feeling well. And again, some warning would've been nice before showing up like this, especially at seven-thirty in the morning. If my mom knew you were here this early, she would kill me."

He turned to me with a lazy, charming smile on his face, wrapping his arm around my waist. "Well, she's not here, is she? Plus, I missed you last night. Didn't you miss me?" He began to pepper kisses on my cheek, which typically would have brought out a smile to my face. However, the kisses felt like sandpaper and continued to irk me. I pushed against him, freeing myself.

"Roger, I really am not in the mood. It's been a crazy couple of days for me. I need to get my mind right, get dressed, and take care of a couple of things today. Can't we just talk later?"

But Roger was not to be deterred. He brought me back into his arms, laying his head against mine. "Aw, come on Kitty-Kat. I brought all your favorite foods. I'm doing this as a favor to you since you didn't come out with me."

I pushed him back with some more force. "I am so sick and tired about hearing about this damn party. And for what? So I can be your token black girlfriend, fawning over you? So you can look cool to the guys and show how you are 'down'? Let's be real, Roger. Who's been taking care of who here? Who has been bending over backward, supporting you for two years, trying to get you into a great college team? After all I put up with, you think you are doing me a favor?" I crossed my arms over my heaving chest, trying to calm down. "Do you see anything wrong with me?"

"Kat, what is up with you—"

"Would you just look at me and tell me if there is anything wrong?" I yelled.

Taken aback, Roger looked me over. *If he asks me about my puffy eyes or the snot on my nose, I'll take pity on him. Just some notice and I'll know he is not that over-absorbed. Give me something, Roger.*

After two years, show me this wasn't a waste of time. But that was too much to ask. His eyes raked over me and tried to slip his arm around my waist again. "Nothing Kitty-Kat! Is this because you're on your period? Aww, Kat, you look your usual gorgeous self."

I closed my eyes and took a deep breath. "I look the same?" I asked quietly.

"Of course. Beautiful as usual."

"And everything I said is because I'm menstruating, right?" Disgusted, I pushed Roger away. He looked at me puzzled as I moved to stand in the middle of the kitchen doorway. "Get out."

"What's the matter with you?"

"I am sick and tired of dealing with your selfishness! Every day, it is always what Kat can do for you. Where you can show me off as a prize to your friends. You even let random people hit on me for their own enjoyment, never protecting me. It has always been about what you can gain! In the two years we've been together, you have never supported me."

Roger made a rude noise. "Oh please. I've supported you plenty of times."

I crossed my arms over my chest. "Oh yeah? You skipped my solo dance exhibit, the one major event I do, for a Celtics game! You never ask me about what I want to do. You never ask me how I am doing. You can't even tell if I've been crying my eyes out. I don't know who you are anymore. Cyn warned me about you. 'Don't fall for the sweet talk,' she said. 'He's gonna disappoint you,' she said. I've been sticking up for you. But I'm done. Da-done done. I want you to leave now!"

"Y-you're joking, right?" Roger sputtered.

"Why would I joke about this? I've been thinking about this for quite a while now, and you're just not worth it anymore." I ruefully shook my head. "I just didn't have the courage to say something. Word of advice for the next time you want to date a black girl and her mom happens to be a sports agent—pay full attention to the girl and maybe you'll get her mom's full attention too. Now, get the hell out of my house." I didn't even wait for another response. I quietly walked to the front door and opened it.

Roger stomped out of the kitchen, finally realizing that I was breaking up with him. "Now wait a damn minute, woman!" He grabbed me by the arm, jerking me forward. "I'm not worth it? Sweetheart, do you know who I am? I am making it to the top. And I thought you were going to go up with me. That we were going to do this like Kobe and Vanessa. But no, you wanna make this difficult, talking about dance, friends, and stupid stuff no one cares about. Do you think I'm just gonna give up now? I have spent too much time and effort on you! And don't get me started on the number of black girl and white guy jokes I had to put up with. I could have listened to Andrea last night and not even bothered with you anymore, but where I am now?"

"Did you just say you were with Andrea Pana last night?" My voice deepened to a menacing tone.

"Yeah, I did. And you know what, I'm glad I spent the night with her rather than with a crybaby tease that has to bring race into everything. God, get over it!"

I could feel myself getting warmer and warmer by the minute. Energy started building up in my fingers and I wanted nothing more than to zap that privileged asshole.

"I think the lady has asked you to leave," a quiet voice said from behind me. Roger turned around to find Gregor, still shirtless, his eyes glittering dangerously.

"What's he doing here?" Roger shouted. He turned back to me furiously. "Did you cheat on me?"

I rolled my eyes, focusing on the Scot rather than my own anger. My fingers were still itching with energy. "I did no such thing. Gregor crashed on the couch for the night. And for the record, you have no right to ask me that, seeing as you spent the night with that self-absorbed twat."

"No! I wanna know what the hell is going on! Why the hell is he coming from your bedroom? God, I knew you were a tease. All that stuff about waiting was all bull!" he sneered.

"He was in my room because he was trying to comfort me!" I shot back. "Like you should've been doing, instead of trying butter me up just so you could use me again. Didn't I say get out of my house?!" My tingling was getting sharper, threatening to react. I need to get him out of here now.

Roger took a menacing step closer to me, his eyes were full of anger. "Katya, I will not have you cheat on me, damn it! I can deal with the tantrums, the pouting, and the complaints, but I will not have you leave me for some wack British guy. You are my girlfriend, and it is not over until I say it is!"

Before I could breathe, let alone react, Roger was forcibly grabbed away from me. Gregor took his right arm and pinned it to his back. The more Roger struggled, the more force Gregor added to the grip.

"I believe," Gregor said quietly in Roger's ear, "that the lady asked you to leave. This relationship is over. So why not hold on to whatever pride you have as a man and go?" The Kyrios then pushed the struggling boy out of the front door.

As I closed the door, I said, "Lose my number. Okay? Bye-bye." The door slammed on his angry face.

14

I stared at the closed door, letting the situation settle in my mind. *I finally did it.* I turned slightly to see the Kyrios watching me carefully. Rolling my shoulders, I turned away from him, clearing my eyes of any offending tears, and entered the kitchen. "You didn't have to come out, you know. I could have handled it."

Gregor gave me a lopsided smile. "Your Vis distress said otherwise. Anyway, a Scotsman never leaves a damsel in distress. I could never let a lady, let alone a lady that I have taken as my ward, go into battle alone."

I unwillingly let out a snort. "Whatever, Kyrios. Looks like we have a free breakfast here. Care to join me for some bacon and eggs?"

Gregor sat the small kitchen table. "Whatever you are offering, I'll take it, lass. I miss the taste of food, and your cooking last night has only reawakened my longing for meat and hash."

As I moved about the kitchen, I could feel Gregor's eyes watching me, surveying my every move. Flustered, I thought of any question I could ask him. "Tell me about Scotland."

A small smile appeared on his face. "Aye, Scotland. There's no other place like it in the world. The Scottish Highlands are the lushest green you'll ever see. It is the one place in the Live Realm that could honestly take your breath away."

I smiled wistfully. "I've always wanted to go abroad. My mom has gone, but she's never had the chance to bring me. School always got in the way."

"If you ever have the chance, you should! The isles of Scotland truly are one in a million. It's like the Princess of the Earth made it her palace. The lush green hills and mountains, the freshest air in the world. It is truly the gem of the entire planet."

I smiled as I continued to cook our breakfast. "I always knew I wanted to go. When was the last time you were up there?"

Gregor got quiet, studying the table. His knuckles turned white, gripping his armrests. "Been too long, really. Too many memories." I couldn't help but notice the far away and forlorn look in his eyes. Not wanting to press the subject, I changed the topic.

"So what are you doing for the rest of the day?" I brought our plates to the kitchen table. Gregor dug into his with the gusto of a man on a fast for months.

"What do you mean? I'll be with you."

I paused and eyed him. "I guess it's fine for today, but I have to visit Amie before I leave with you. I don't want to this incident with you to be a thing before I leave."

He looked up from his plate and smile tightly. "Everywhere you go, I go, remember?"

It was just not my morning. "Gregor, you can't come with me to talk to Amie. How am I going to explain you and apologize? I'm pretty sure she is not going to react well if the man who insulted her on her birthday comes with me as my escort."

"What would you have me do, Katya?" he asked, slightly annoyed. "You're essentially a loose cannon here. I need to be around to make sure you don't send off any signals to Wanters wishing to destroy you. Someone needs to keep the people around you safe."

Eyes narrowing, I said, "I can keep my cool, Kyrios, okay?"

Gregor leaned in and smirked, "Haven't seen much of that control yet."

Food completely forgotten, I huffed and threw down my napkin. "I'm starting to get a little sick of everyone dictating my life. I used to do it by myself, you know. Since I was a kid, I've been by myself because I can handle it all myself. But now all of that is gone. Now, I can't do anything without a shadow following me. I'm trying to keep cool but it seems like the universe and you want to remind me constantly that I'm a ticking time bomb. Who the hell would not react to that, especially when their life has been turned upside down! And for your information, my temper could be excellent if you would just give me a friggin' chance!" I turned on my heel and was out the door. Gregor was hot on my heels.

"Oh, and I suppose this is an example of you keeping your temper? I can't wait to see you perfectly calm!"

"You know what, I've had it up to here with you men! Why must you—" Gregor's hand suddenly clamped down on my mouth, stopping my tirade. I struggled against his grip to only realize that his attention wasn't on me, but on something else that was apparently moving. He brought me closer against his chest.

"Don't say another word," he whispered. "Something is nearby."

My eyes widened and listened. A screech and beating wings could be heard not far from the house. Cravers were nearby. I closed my eyes and focused on the Vis bouncing around inside of me. It took several breaths to calm myself down, the inner energy quieting with each breath. After several minutes, it had quieted down completely, with the Cravers' screams now further away.

Gregor released me shortly after it went quiet. "They are certainly coming out to play more than usual. What are they up to?" He scrutinized me from head to toe. "Have you finally realized that your temper is precariously balanced on a cliff?"

I bit my lip, feeling ashamed. "Look, I'm trying, okay? And I have no desire to fight with you. I've had enough of that this morning. But you have to give me some room to breathe too. I'm just having a hard time with this, and I'm used to being by myself. Can we just agree to start over from here?"

I took a deep breath. "Hi, I'm Katya, I'm a human with some weird abilities. I have only-child syndrome and I don't like not getting my way. I'm a work in progress, and I'm asking for some patience."

The Scot smiled ruefully. "Hi Katya. I'm Gregor and I'm a Grim Reaper who's here to protect you from deformed evil souls looking to devour your soul. I will do my best to give you some space but I want you to know that this is all for your well-being. And you're not alone anymore. You can lean on someone else for a change."

"It'll take some practice." I sighed and said, "But it's still gonna be weird with you being there when I meet up with Amie, Gregor. Unless…remember when we first met and you said you would apologize to her? We can have you do it then and it will also help me apologize to Amie."

Gregor put his hands on his narrow hips and sighed as well. "Fine. It still gives me the chance to be close by."

I beamed, relieved to find a solution. "Thank you. I'll need to contact Amie but maybe we can all meet later on this afternoon?"

He smirked, giving me an all-knowing look. "Whenever you want to, lass. Wouldn't want you not to get your way."

Choosing to ignore him, I stretched my arms over my head and said, "I guess I should probably get in the shower." Gregor didn't reply; he merely stared at me. Puzzled at his gaze, I looked down and saw that my robe had opened in our scuffle and gave him a full view of my tank. Before, I had been still wrapped in the sheets, with my top half concealed. Now, the full view of the tank came into view, showing the Kyrios the top of my breasts, the majority of my thighs and the rest of my legs. His perusal did nothing to calm the goose bumps on my body and I feared he could tell I was off-balanced.

I laughed shakily, closing the robe around me. "You better get back to your breakfast, Scotsman. You don't want it to get cold."

Gregor shook his head and cleared his throat. "Of course. I'll be waiting for you while you get ready." And with that, he returned to the kitchen.

I swallowed as I watched him walk back, his sinewy back and legs putting distance between us. I rolled my eyes as I made for the bathroom. I needed a cold shower.

15

After several begging texts to Amie and a call to Cynthia for help, Amie finally relented and agreed to meet up, but she would only agree to come over to my house that night. When thinking about the threat of Wanters possibly breaking up our circle, Gregor and I thought it was probably best to keep it at home anyway. I really didn't mind because home was one of the best place to be for me. I ordered a couple of pizzas and waited patiently for Amie to come. Cynthia promised to stop by later on to make sure that we were "back to lovey-dovey friends again."

A few minutes before Amie was to arrive, I called Gregor into the family room. "Gregor, I need you to keep watch in other room until Amie is ready. I'm going to talk to her first and then we can bring you in for your apology. And make it a good one, will you? Make it look like you are sincere but that you're also afraid of my wrath."

His eyebrows arched. "I'm supposed to be scared of you, now? You're such a wee thing. Who'd ever be scared of you?"

I put my hands on my hip, trying to look menacing. "Plenty of people, Scotsman. Don't you know the most fearful thing in the world is a woman's wrath? Add a black woman to the mix and you'll be ducking for cover!" Gregor guffawed like I'd said the greatest joke. I was slightly amused as well. "Anyway, go into the kitchen and I'll call for you."

The doorbell rang. I pushed as hard as I could against his retreating back, not that it would've made a difference. "And keep quiet." He wordlessly entered the kitchen. I looked over my reflection in the mirror by the door, ensuring that my high bun was messy enough to look careless but chic at the same time. I opened the door to find Amie looking a lot better than she had the day before. More color had returned to her cheeks, the light had returned to her eyes, which were still covered by her glasses. Her hair was a controlled curly set that framed her face. She had given up her plaid clothes once again, for a t-shirt and shorts this time. She tentatively stepped into the house. "Listen Kat, I—"

I enveloped her in a hug before she could say another word. "You don't have to say anything. I know Pana got in your head." She clung to me as we held each other, realizing that we both needed that human contact for a bit. I released her and was relieved to see that no tears fell. I took her by her elbow and led her to the family room. "How's the last forty-eight hours been?" I asked, sitting on the couch.

Amie let out a sigh and sunk into the couch beside me. "Meh, not too bad. When I got home, my mom was screeching about my eyes and let out a string of Spanish curses that I won't share. I told her I was fine and that my friends were looking out for me. The rest of the day was just her feeding me because that's what Dominicans do when they feel emotional. My dad just asked me if I was okay at the end of the day and was satisfied that I said yes." She gave a crooked smile. "What about you? Are you okay? I know Pana was saying some ugly things about you."

I rolled my eyes but returned her smile. "Yeah she was. I got really upset and apparently I passed out."

"What? Again? Are you okay?"

"Yeah I'm fine, girl. Just all of the stress, you know? Roger came over and we just fought. I realized I was done with him, so we broke up."

Amie grimaced. "I bet it was Pana. This morning she was bragging on Twitter about getting something that belonged to her. I'm assuming it was Roger."

"Whatever. She can have him. I'm actually better off. But I didn't ask you to come over for all that. I wanted to give you a proper explanation of what happened that night."

Amie looked away, studying her nails. "The guy was a jerk. End of story."

I snorted, "Yeah he was. But he did help me out that night. That's why he was holding me. I passed out in the alley after chasing after him. He took me to get checked out. He ended up being a medical student. When I did come to, I had a chance to yell at him for what he did. And we had a chance to talk."

Amie's eyes rounded. "What did he say to you?"

I stood from the couch and smiled down at my friend. "Why doesn't he tell you himself? Gregor?"

Gregor silently filled the room's doorway and Amie's eyes glazed over again, with both surprise and with the utmost feminine interest that could be displayed. *Hmm, must be that walking-into-the-light attraction Gregor had talked about.* The Scot entered the room and sat down on the couch with a healthy distance between them. "Hello Amie. My name is Gregor." He stretched out his hand for hers.

Amie only hesitated for a few seconds before she reached over and slapped the Kyrios in the face. Her hands vaulted to her face, surprised at her own actions. I could only watch, feeling my eyes pop. The room stilled. Gregor looked at Amie for a stunned second before a deep laugh escaped his lips. His laugh was so infectious that we too began to giggle.

Once Gregor calmed, he said, "I guess I deserved that, huh?" His face sobered a bit. "I told Katya the day that we met that if given the chance I would apologize to you. On my honor as a Scotsman, I am deeply sorry that I offended you. I was not in the best of moods that night, and I didn't mean to take it out on you. I hope you can accept my apology."

Amie's eyes filled with that dreamy look again and she didn't immediately reply.

"Amie?" I asked.

She jumped as if she had just awoken. "Yes, I accept your apology."

Gregor beamed. "Thank you. I wouldn't want any ill will between us. Or I'm sure Katya will let me have it."

I pursed my lips and lightly tapped his shoulder. "That's right. The wrath of a black woman."

"Yes, yes. Please allow me to save face in front of the two of you, you mean horrible woman," he teased.

"I've been known to reduce monsters to dust simply because they pissed me off," I joked.

We smiled at each other until I caught Amie watching me with sharp eyes. "Are you sure there's nothing between the two of you?"

I held my hands up. "Nothing! Gregor can't get into any relationships anyway."

Her eyebrows furrowed. "Why?"

"Well…" I fished for something. "Gregor can't get into any relationship with me or any other woman. He's gay."

Amie's eyes reflected understanding while Gregor's eyes flashed with surprise and anger.

"Katya, what—"

I smacked myself in the head. "Oh, I'm so sorry Gregor. I didn't mean to out you. I just didn't want Amie to get the wrong idea about our friendship. I just wanted to be clear that you are essentially off-limits, right?" I gave him a look, daring him to refute my story. And he looked as if he was about to when the front door opened and closed.

"Katya Stevens, why I am just learning that you broke up with that ass Roger—" Cynthia rounded the corner to find all three of staring back at her, showing the same surprise.

"OMG! KATYA!"

"Jesus Christ, Cyn! Stop yelling! We're right here," I hissed.

"What's he doing here?" she hissed back. "I heard online that you and Roger broke up and he's telling everyone that you cheated on him with this...person. Thanks for telling me, by the way!"

Since we'd returned from Ager, I had been dying to call Cynthia and tell her everything, even just to help me process everything that had happened. But each time I'd reached for my phone, I remembered Gregor's warning about not telling anyone else. He clearly didn't understand how best friends worked. Even now, the truth was right on my lips ready to be spit out. But with the threat looming over me, something held me back from saying the truth. There's only so much weirdness one person can take before saying, "This is too much." I didn't want Cynthia to get to that point.

"God, no! As I was just telling Amie here, Gregor is a medical student that was helping me back in the alley, and Roger assumed that we were sleeping with each other. I just broke up with him this morning. I was gonna tell you when you came over, Cyn." I looked her fully in the eye hoping she would just drop it. "Gregor is here now because he wanted to apologize to Amie. Which he did and she accepted."

Cynthia looked me and then gave Gregor an evil look. "Excuse me, Greyson—"

Gregor's eyebrows arched up. "It's Gregor, sweetheart."

My fiery red-haired friend plastered a smile on her face. "Whatever. I'm just going to grab my friend for a little chat in the kitchen. You don't mind, do you? Amie, be a dear and keep the guest entertained." Before anyone else could say a word, Cynthia grabbed me by my hand into the next room.

"What is it, Cyn?"

"Don't you 'Cyn' me!" she hissed. "You are keeping something major from me. I can feel it. He's now a medical student? You know I can tell when you are lying, and you're definitely lying about him. I want the truth, Kat. I can't protect you unless I know what's really going on."

I looked down and studied the sandals on my feet, feeling incredibly helpless and increasingly frustrated with the Kyrios, the Want, and everything in front of me. If I didn't say something that would please Cynthia, it could potentially turn into a massive fight, and I couldn't allow myself to lose my temper. "Cynthia, I love you very much. You are my sister in every sense of the word. I totally understand your confusion, but—"

"Kat, we've been through a lot. I know what you are going through. You know that I'm here for you, right? I can handle it. Just tell me." Her eyes showed all the concern for me that my own mother would have. I nearly broke—maybe she could handle it. Maybe she won't run from the room screaming. I opened up my mouth to spill, only to have my hand heat up considerably, causing me to grab my hand and yelp in pain. *What the hell?* Then I remembered:

"Did you just brand me?" I asked incredulously.

The Scot smirked. "Just a little insurance."

The Kyrios bastard never mentioned that it would burn!

"Katya! What's the matter?" Cynthia grabbed my hand and studied it for some injury. I looked into the family room and shot the Kyrios a dark look. He merely crossed his arms and waited for me to return. "Katya, look at me. What's going on?"

As much as I couldn't stand the Kyrios's tactics, I had to admit I was a bit relieved. I could not willingly give Cynthia a reason to leave. I could not handle having another person in my life reject me because of my "weirdness."

I stared into my best friend's eyes, hoping that she would gain some understanding, that she would see through my actions and not hold it against me for the rest of our lives. I wrenched my hand away, surprising her. "Look Cyn, it's no big deal." I smoothed my hair, making sure it was secure in its bun. "Gregor and I are friends, and he's hanging out with us. Don't be weird about this. He helped me out the other night and he's not so bad. Stop being over protective." Cynthia's face flushed with anger. She stared at my hand as I flexed it to relieve the pain.

"So, you're not going to tell me?"

I gave her a funny look. "There's nothing to tell."

"Is that the way you want it? Fine. I'll play. Gregor's your friend. And that's it."

I shook my head yes.

She looked behind my shoulder, directly at Gregor. Her eyes cooled and she made a beeline for him back in the family room. I rushed after her, asking, "Cyn, what are you going to do? Please don't embarrass me!" Cynthia stopped short several feet in front of Gregor, staring hard at him. It was stormy blue vs. rainforest green and I wasn't sure whether I should intervene.

After several moments, Cynthia finally spoke. "Gregor," she said authoritatively.

Gregor relaxed his arms, never breaking his eye contact with Cynthia. He nodded.

Cynthia paused for another second before saying, "I accept you. You'd better not hurt my friend. Guard her with your life."

Cynthia and Gregor stared at each other hard for several moments before Gregor nodded solemnly.

Amie and I shared a look before Amie giggled. "Cynthia, way to be melodramatic! I don't remember you telling me that when I became friends with Kat."

Cynthia gave her a small smile. "You don't have what he has, sweetie." She looked down at the pizza on the coffee table. "Oh great, you got food. I haven't had lunch yet." And just like that, the tension was gone. For the next hour, my two friends ate with the Kyrios and had a decent conversation. They asked him about Scotland and he regaled them stories about how beautiful his home was and the different places around the world he had traveled to.

I watched over them, feeling a mixture of happiness and wistfulness. I had so few people in my life where I could feel like myself. Amie was quickly become a member of the exclusive circle. And as much as I knew that Gregor could not have any permanent ties here, I was becoming increasingly grateful for his help.

Watching the three of them laugh and talk over pizza reminded me that I was going to have to leave this in less than a week. I still had no idea what I was going to tell Amie, Cynthia, or Mom about why I had to leave, and I knew that there wasn't really any reason that would be enough for them. And I had the strongest feeling that it was going to be a long while before I could get back to this—the simple luxury of simply eating pizza at home with friends.

After Amie and Cyn left, with promises to meet up the

following night, I felt increasingly alone. How could I leave home, my sanctuary? How I could leave my family and friends? I quietly told the Kyrios that I was going to read for a bit in my room.

"Katya," he called.

I stopped at the bottom stairs and looked back at him.

He stepped forward, his blue eyes shining with understanding. "The hardest burden to carry is duty. Even the strongest of us have moments of doubt and worry. But the greatest battle, despite all of these particulars, is whether you can move forward with what must be accomplished. I can feel the swirl of indecision and concern within your spirit." Gregor stepped closer and laid a hand on my shoulder, squeezing it lightly. "Take solace in the fact that what you are feeling is completely human. To not feel this would make you…well, a Wanter. Do not feel guilty for feeling this way. Revel in it, embrace your humanness, and move forward."

My nervous lip-biting returned. "Gregor," I said, looking down. "I know what I have to do. I know I have to protect them. It's just, I have this feeling that something bigger is coming and—"

"Katya, one step at a time. We can only concern ourselves with what today's troubles are. Whatever is set for the future, we'll handle it together. Remember, you are not alone anymore."

Feeling my lower lip tremble, I bit down harder to stop any potential tears. "How could I possibly forget, with your humongous self walking around here?"

The Scot chuckled. "Aye, how else do I remind you that I'm here?" We both laughed at that, clearing any further tension.

"Thank you, Gregor." Before I could even think about why I absolutely should not do it, I closed the gap between us and softly laid a kiss on the Kyrios's cheek. He stayed absolutely still, looking down at me unblinkingly. His eyes showed his complete surprise and something else I couldn't necessarily pinpoint. I cleared my throat, turned, and ran up the stairs to my room. "See you in the morning!"

As soon as I closed my bedroom door, I let out a silent wail. *How could I have done that?* He was probably mortified that a living human just kissed him. He was probably already planning how he would let me down gently with a speech he'd probably used before: "I'm Death and you're alive. This can't work." With my heart beating out of my chest, I prayed all that was holy that he would not bring it up tomorrow and that he would pretend that nothing happened.

As I snuggled underneath my blankets, I thought back on my duty and my resolve to do what was right. We had to leave before my mom got home.

If I see her, any resolve I have now will crumble to nothing, and I just might say to the world, "To Hell with you all."

16

As soon as my eyes closed, I found myself in a dream.

I was at a beautiful lake, surrounded by a vast forest made of the most beautiful fir trees I had ever seen. In the middle of the lake was a large rock about the size of a car. And I was floating over it. Every time I looked around to figure out a way down, a mist covered the entire lake, making it impossible to see anything else. Then I got the sense that someone was watching me through the mist. I called out for several minutes, but I heard only the softest of whispers in return.

And just as I was about to make out what the whisper was saying to me, my alarm clock rang so loud and surprised me so much that I fell straight out of bed. Thankfully, the Kyrios did not rush upstairs to find me sprawled on the floor eating carpet fibers.

Now effectively awake, I made sure I was properly dressed as I made my way downstairs and to the family room. I found Gregor sitting on the couch watching the news—an earthquake had just hit Los Angeles the night before. I got a bowl of cereal and joined him wordlessly on the couch. I was relieved to learn that there had been no deaths. Several buildings had been damaged, but it could have been a lot worse. I avoided watching the wreckage as I didn't want to see Wanters out at play, but their screeches came loud and clear through the reporter's live feed at the scene.

Gregor noticed that I was nose deep in my cereal and said, "You know you really should get used to seeing them. To deny their existence is to reject reality."

"I'm not denying their existence. I just don't enjoy looking at them. They are ugly, and it saddens me that humans are capable of turning into that." I took a bite and wiped the dripping milk from my chin. "I mean what could you hold so much that you turn into...that?"

I missed the flash of pain on Gregor's face as I got up to return to the kitchen. "It could be many things, not just material greed, that could rip a soul apart," he called after me. "Just remember, humans are very complex creatures—now and in death."

I returned to the couch and turned down the TV. "I get that, but it's still a terrifying thing to look at and focus on so early in the morning. I'd rather talk about our night tonight."

"Um, Katya, about that—" Gregor began.

"You will accompany us like we all discussed and act as the big bodyguard that you are and keep all of the icky Wanters away." I arched my eyebrows, daring him to refuse to go and to bring up anything but the plans I was discussing.

Gregor said nothing but shook his head yes. I gave him a solid pat on the back. "Great, it's settled. The girls will be over later on today. I'll be in my room, starting to pack some of my stuff and trying to figure my letter to Cyn and my mother." I stood up, stretching and cracking my fingers. "You can keep yourself occupied, right?

He stood from the couch and pulled out his phone from his pocket. "I'm sure I can, lass. I'm just going to call into my squad to check in."

I edged closer to him and poked him in his rock-hard abs. "Does that mean you're leaving? I thought you had to stay nearby."

"And I will be. Don't fret. I'll just be on the roof for a bit." He snapped his fingers, opening a bright blue rip. "Do keep calm while your minder is away."

"Ha ha," I said drily. He grinned and disappeared.

The rest of the day was a whirl. I was able to start packing some of stuff and started to write an email to Cynthia and my mother, setting the transmission for after I'd left. As I was trying to write it, I realized the gag branding didn't allow me to say too much, so I had to be a bit creative. Hopefully, when I did return, neither one would take my letter to heart and go too crazy. As I put the final touches to my mother's email, my phone buzzed with a text message from Cyn.

"Let's go to Nicky's. Arcades and my boyfriend! Be over in about an hour and half or so."

I sent a quick "OK," finished the email, and quickly got in the shower and dressed. As I started putting the final touches of makeup, I called for Gregor. I didn't hear a sound. Rolling my eyes, I dashed downstairs, calling for him again. I peeked in the living room and didn't see a soul (no pun intended). It wasn't until I noticed that the water was running in the shower that I realized where he was. *He's taking a shower?*

I slowly inched my way to the door, trying to not make a

sound. Straining my ears, I heard the soft musings of his voice. He was singing. The song wasn't exactly in English, but the tone was utterly captivating that I didn't realize that the water had stopped running and that footsteps were right behind the door.

And that's how Gregor found me. Right behind the bathroom door, like a deer caught in the headlights. What really caught me off guard was the masculine, sculpted beauty that stood before me with only a towel wrapped around his waist. Had it not been for my nails cutting into my palms, I'm pretty sure I would have passed out. Again.

The Scot spoke first. "Do you need something in the bathroom, Katya?"

"Yes," I said huskily. I cleared my throat. "I just need to get…something." I licked my lips, my eyes dropped to the floor. "I thought Kyrios don't need to shower."

He shrugged, bringing the towel slightly lower with his movement. "Being in the Live Realm makes you pick up some old habits. Never hurts to be clean." He brushed past me into the living room. Not wanting to make another fool of myself, I pretended to grab something in the bathroom and ran to my bedroom.

I closed my eyes as I leaned against the door. *It is getting harder to be around him. I don't think it's particularly fair to have Kyrios look so ethereal and perfect! Who wouldn't want to die if you could be led off into the sunset with a man like that?* A knocking sound at my door startled me out of my inner thoughts.

"Katya? Let's get this over with. Are you ready?"

I opened the door to find Gregor dressed in the same drab, black-on-black ensemble. My disappointment must have been clear on my face because he asked, "What's the matter? Is there something wrong with my clothes?"

I smoothed my sundress down, refusing to look him in the eye. "Well, can you wear anything other than black? Can you change it a little bit?" I shuffled back into my room and grabbed a magazine. I flipped it open to a male model that I had been admiring few days before. "How about this guy? Do you have anything like that?" The male model wore a gray button-down shirt and blue jeans—trendy but still casual. Gregor took the magazine from it and studied it.

"You want me to look like this?"

"Or something like this. I don't want the girls to start asking questions as to why you wear the same black shirt, pants, and coat every time they see you. I... You know what? It's okay, Gregor. I can make something up." I took the magazine and returned it to my desk. "I'm sure the girls were more focused on your..." The words died in my mouth the moment I turned my attention back to Gregor, who had miraculously changed his clothes to mirror the model's outfit within seconds.

If I had to compare the magazine model with Gregor, the Kyrios would win. Every time.

The Scot smiled and performed a pirouette. "How is this?" The grey button down showcased the strong chest and forearms, elongating his tall frame. His jeans gripped his body but effortlessly fell against his legs. Even his simple boat shoes made me feel a bit jittery.

"How did you do that?"

The Kyrios gave me an all-knowing grin. "Lass, just because it looks like I changed my clothes doesn't mean I did. I just changed the appearance of it. Why do you think we all wear the same thing? So we can change our clothes at will, whatever the situation dictates."

I merely grinned. "You are full of surprises, you know?"

Gregor tapped my nose and returned the grin. "Took the words right out of my mouth. Come on, wouldn't want you to be late."

17

Cynthia arrived promptly. Expecting that she would have to wait for me, she entered through the front door with her set of keys and sat on the couch to wait for me. She was shocked to find me ready, arm in arm with Gregor in the foyer. "Gregor, are you a miracle worker? Who would have thought that Katya could actually finish on time?"

"Hey, I'm not that bad! And you're just as bad as me!" I replied.

"I'm here on time, aren't I?" She looked me over with a calculating eye. "Well, come on, turn around." I nodded and did a pirouette for her, showing off my black sundress that fitted me quite well. Massaging her chin, she nodded. "I approve. Do me now."

Cynthia followed my exact movements while I looked over her outfit. She had on a green sundress with off-white polka dots and wedge shoes. Cute but sassy. I nodded. "Fierce and beat, girl. You may proceed."

Gregor gave us both a look. "What was that about?"

Cynthia clasped her hands behind her back and she began to walk in a circle around Gregor and me. "You see, my dear man, when ladies step out for an evening—"

"OMG! We just check on each other to make sure we don't look like losers." I grabbed my purse off the coffee table. "Geez, Cyn. No one is trying to hear a lecture, damn!"

Cynthia looked at me haughtily. "If you'd been a bit more patient, I would've gotten to that point. Why do you always have to rush me?"

"Why do you have to be such a know-it-all?"

"Why do you have to be such a brat?"

"Takes one to know one!" I took a step closer to her.

"Birds of feather, sweetheart. And looks like your feathers are all over me!" She took another step closer to me, our noses dangerously close.

Gregor looked between us uneasily. "Ladies, let's not let our emotions get—"

He was interrupted by our burst of laughter and giggles. I leaned on my best friend's shoulder and grinned. "That line you used was pretty good. I'll have to remember that for next time."

Cyn winked and patted me on the back. "Kinda just came to me." We let out more giggles as we looked at the dumbfounded expression on Gregor's face. "Oh men," Cynthia said, shaking her head. "They won't ever really get us, will they?"

Another knock at the door announced Amie's arrival, and with a quick, approving look over her lovely romper and hair, we all clamored into Cynthia's car. "Mom and Dad are away for the next two days so we can use the car as much as we want." The ride over to Nelly's was quick—a fifteen-minute drive from our homes. Nelly's Pizza and Arcade was brimming with people by the time we arrived. We headed to our usual corner, dragging Gregor behind me. Apparently Cynthia had prepped our friends before we got there because the corner was set up with several tables with several people friendly with Amie from school waiting for us.

"Better with a crowd, right?" Cynthia said loudly over the music. I smiled. *Thank God it's not anyone from the Plastic Brigade.*

"Guys! Welcome!" Steve shouted gleefully. Cynthia's dark-haired boyfriend came from behind one of the counters and greeted his girlfriend with kisses and a hug. I always did like Steve. He was the type of guy that you could hang out with, tell him some crazy secret stuff, and know he would never tell a soul. Cynthia and I had both met him a year and a half ago when we found out about Nelly's and its famous pizza. Steve was eighteen at the time, and we had just turned seventeen. I noticed how starry-eyed Steve had gotten after meeting Cyn, and knew my friend would be happy with him.

Samantha, a girl I was relatively friendly with, said, "Kat is here! And who is this yummy person behind you?"

Before I could say anything, Gregor threw a hand up to say hello. "I'm Gregor."

Samantha stepped up first. "Hello, hello, hello!"

I pushed her back to her seat. "Stop being thirsty, girl." I turned to include the Kyrios. "Gregor, these are my friends from school. You just met Samantha. The guy behind her is Ben—we go way back to middle school. The tall blond is Don. The ginger is Ally, and of course the guy Cynthia is wrapped around is her boyfriend, Steve."

The crowd gave a rousing "Hey!" to the new visitor.

"Kat, hunny. We've were just talking about you. Roger is telling everyone that you guys have broken up! How we doing, girl? Are you okay?"

I rolled my eyes and flipped my curls over my shoulder. "Girl, please. I'm fine. *I* broke up with Roger. He was an ass, and I'm just glad that it's over."

"I'm just glad you finally saw it. We," she pointed to the others, "were all hoping you were gonna figure it out. We didn't want to push, but we were hoping!" I looked around and all their nods confirmed Samantha's sentiment. "Just took a bit longer than we hoped, but hey, you made it! Not to mention with a sexy man to boot."

Amie took a seat next to Samantha. "Samantha, I thought the same thing too. But she swears up and down that they are just friends."

She and Samantha shared the same disbelieving look.

"Ooh Katya! American boys can't be your friends either?" A dark-skinned guy stepped forward behind Samantha, with a twinkle in his eye.

I smiled, rolling my eyes. "Don't be jealous, Ben," I crooned. "Gregor is just a good-looking friend who would have a better shot at me than you."

Ben barked with laughter. "Oh, Kitty, you wound me!"

I hit him lightly on the arm. "You know I hate that name!" I looked back to Gregor, nudging him to sit down. "Okay, enough. Gregor is just here to hang out with you losers so let's just show him a good time, okay? No more questions about me and him being together."

We crowded around the table while Steve grabbed a couple of pitchers of soda and passed them around the group. "So Gregor," Don said, handing both of us a cup, "how old exactly are you?"

"I'm twenty."

"Do you work or are you in college?"

Crap! We never discussed this. I frantically looked at Gregor, hoping he would make eye contact. But he took a swig of Coke, smiled, and said, "My job is protecting Katya from unwanted predators."

The crew laughed, taking his honesty as a joke.

Ben slapped him on the back. "I can understand that. Our Kitty-Kat has been known to get herself into trouble a time or two."

The Scot gave me a sly look. "I absolutely believe it."

I grimaced, throwing Gregor a look. "Hey, why don't we just have a good time instead of talking about the stupid stuff I do, 'kay?"

The night went remarkably well. The guys talked about sports and guy stuff with Gregor and the girls needled me with constant questions about my new "friend."

"Katya, you lucky hobo! How did you even find him?" Ally asked, her eyes never leaving the Scot.

"Oh, she said he's a medical student that happened to save her in an alley, but we actually met him at a bar on my birthday," Amie said mischievously. She cleared her throat. "Apparently not only is he hot, but he's a knight in shining armor too."

Ally bounced in her seat, tapping my arm. "Well, tell us, how is he?"

Samantha and Ally looked pointedly at me and I suddenly understood what they were asking about. "Oh my God. We are NOT doing that."

Cyn giggled. "You know Kat's innocent! Why bother asking? She's waiting for when the time is right."

Their jaws dropped to the ground. "Are you mad? Are you blind?! How could this time be any less right?" Samantha screeched.

"Keep your voice down!" I hissed. "And no, I'm not blind. We're not like that, okay? What part about friends don't you get?"

"Oh, I get it," Ally said grumpily. "He's gay!"

I rubbed my forehead in slight frustration and shared a look with Amie, who shrugged. "Yes, that's exactly it."

"What!" the girls chorused, clearly disappointed. Except for Cynthia. She had a pensive look on her face and kept studying Gregor.

"That is so unfortunate!" Samantha grumbled. "It's always the good ones! He is so polite, charming, and everything else in between. I mean, that's just…ugh, look at him."

At her insistence, I did. I watched him as he talked with the guys. And the odd thing was that they acted like they had known each other for years. Gregor suddenly turned and looked at me, catching my eye. Completely relaxed, his brilliant gaze softened as he looked me over, checking if I was okay. With a wink, he returned to the boys' conversation. Though the entire exchange took not more than a few seconds, it sent my heart in an upheaval.

Unfortunately, a small tremor rumbled shortly after. Everyone paused, waiting for the weak tremors to stop while I closed my eyes and tried to calm down and keep the excitement out my heart. For a short while, I'd totally forgotten about what was to come and remembering brought some of my mood crashing down.

Once I was able to calm my beating heart, I knew the signals I was giving to the Wanters would stop, effectively stopping the tremors as well. One cleansing breath and I found my control. I looked around to find Cynthia watching me very closely and Gregor giving me another look before returning everyone's attention back to the festivities around us.

After a couple of pizzas, group laughter, and dart contests, I stepped outside to get a breath of fresh air. Ever the protector, Gregor was right behind me, checking me over. He walked over to where I was leaning against Cynthia's car. "I'm fine, you big Scot. It was just so much fun in there. I'm going to miss this when we leave."

Seeing my sad expression, the Kyrios unexpectedly brought me into his arms for a hug. He smiled softly and said, "It's not goodbye forever. Who knows, maybe you'll be back before they miss you."

I let out a sigh, secretly enjoying Gregor's tight hold. "What were you and the guys talking about?"

"Oh, nothing in particular. Just told them about you and my world."

"What!"

Gregor laughed heartily. "Are you daft? Of course not."

I pouted and pushed him away, "That was mean, Gregor. They were so into your stories, they would've believed it."

Gregor returned his arm around my waist. "Don't worry, lass. They mainly teased me about you all night. Talked sports, girls, you know."

I rolled my eyes, but smiled, accepting his embrace. "Fine, you can keep your manly stuff."

Gregor sighed happily. "You know, I'm glad you convinced me to go. Being back in the Live Realm just feels really good. I've missed just being a person."

I turned to face him, feeling particularly giddy. "Oh really? You were a person?"

"Yes, a long time ago. But that was then and this is now. I'm just enjoying the now."

I grinned at him. "And you were worried something was going to happen."

Gregor nudged me and gave me smirk. "I wouldn't be so sure.

There was that very small spike in your power when I looked over at you."

I froze and then became over-animated. "Oh, well, that was just the girls. They wanted me to take a look at you and then they put these ideas in my head, so it's nothing."

Gregor's eyebrows crinkled together. "What did they say to you?"

I bit my lip and studied my hands. "Something like you were pretty much perfect. And it's too bad that you're gay."

I totally expected him to get on me about calling him gay again. But the Scot didn't say a word for several minutes and then he asked, "What did you say?"

I cleared my throat. "Well, I agreed. I mean it's kinda unfair how you Kyrios are put together. You are perfect. You're sweet, kind, and polite, among other things." I stared down at my hands. "But I just did it to humor them. I mean, c'mon. I'm human and you're...not? Besides, I'm pretty sure you wouldn't be interested in me. And that's—"

Gregor's finger on my lips impeded my mouth's movement. I suddenly became very aware of the closeness of our bodies. He had moved so that he had me pinned to the car underneath his body. Our knees could not move without touching.

Gregor slowly moved his finger down, slightly caressing my lips. "Why would you think I wouldn't be interested in you?"

Unable to speak, I shrugged my shoulders, my eyes pulled in by his bottomless blues.

His hand travelled to my face, his thumb caressing the

contours of my cheek. "Let me clear up the miscommunication, then."

18

With bated breath, his lips slowly made his way closer, softly touching mine. When I didn't move away, he touched my lips again with a bit more pressure. It wasn't long before I responded in kind. Earning a slight groan from me, the Scot felt emboldened and flicked his tongue against my lips, gaining entry.

The total amount of pleasure I had ever felt was nothing in comparison to Gregor's kiss. Every single nerve was alive, and every sense was electrified. Even the tingling bubbled over with happiness, fluttering inside of me excitedly. I couldn't help but wrap my arms around his neck and bring him closer. Every lick, every groan, and every caress emboldened Gregor, and I couldn't move an inch. My temperature was on the rise and my hands began their own exploration. Into his hair, massaging his scalp. The Scot's own hands delved into my hair, travelling downward to my hips.

Passion met passion.
However, our passion was also increasing my heart rate and fluctuating my energy so much that it became a pulse that shook the ground underneath us. The forgotten bracelet from General

Lamar began to beep loudly and it sent a zap to my wrist, causing me to cry out and spike my energy further.

Gregor quickly pulled away and swore. "What was I thinking?"

I desperately tried to calm down but couldn't find my equilibrium. Like something kept hitting my internal panic button. "I'm sorry. I didn't—" A loud, heart-stopping screech stopped the both of us and had us staring at the sky above. The pulse had not just attracted your run-of-the-mill Craver this time. Something much larger, uglier, and with much sharper teeth had emerged from a new hole in the sky, similar to the rips that Gregor had created to cross over to the other side.

The new humanoid creature stood at least five stories tall and was covered from head to toe in white, boney scales. Its fingers were elongated claws that could have ripped the street to shreds. One swift kick from its long, webbed feet could have taken four buildings and Nelly's down flatter than a pancake. But it was its head that frightened me the most—it was not between what you would call its shoulders. The familiar, diamond-shaped head was lodged in the middle of its chest, with bone armor protecting it from all sides.

Gregor immediately pulled out his phone and began barking orders. "Patrol fifty-eight, I have one Devastator—Wrecker, level two in the southwestern quadrant of zone thirty-two. Requesting backup to arrive to the southeast. With Precious Cargo. I repeat, with Precious Cargo." The Scot didn't hesitate as he gathered me into his arms and jumped high into the air.

"Gregor, wait! Cynthia and the others!"

He landed on the roof of the building next door and heading the opposite direction of Nelly's. "I know. If we suddenly leave, he'll have a tantrum and possibly cause more destruction. We have to lure him away from the population centers and your friends to someplace more remote so the patrol can either send him back to the Abyss or destroy him. We'll head to the industrial complex." Over his shoulder, the Wrecker could tell that its intended target was moving quickly away from him and it roared in anger. It stomped quickly towards us, but not without taking out electric poles and two homes that were nearby. Screams could be heard from underneath the rubble.

Shortly after, three men ripped through their blue portals and fell in line with Gregor. They ran and jumped from roof to roof with precision and speed. "Sir," a steel-haired man said. "What are your orders?" They stopped on a nearby roof, still in sight of the terror that was chasing after us.

"Precious Cargo must stay within my care. Take Williams and Carey with you three and take it out. Ensure that no human casualty occurs."

"Sir!" the three men chorused, and disappeared into the night. Gregor continued to run until we reached the industrial complex and stopped at the highest rooftop available, with the Wrecker not far behind. The hideous thing seemed to smile, as if savoring the chase of a new power source. It whacked an empty water tower off a nearby apartment building and launched it in our direction. Gregor dodged to the left to avoid the massive missile, but didn't notice the incoming debris that followed the water tower.

"Look out!" My scream came two seconds too late. A large metal girder knocked him back, whipping me out of his arms and into the air.

Free falling doesn't happen as fast as one would think. Not to me anyway. Everything happened in slow motion. My body rocketed first fifty feet higher, twirling like a human cannonball, and then resumed its descent. Somehow I was able to flip myself upright, but I was less than two hundred feet away from the Wrecker. Even with no words, I could tell it was pleased that with just two steps, it would be able to snatch me midair, devour me, and absorb a new source.

And I was terrified. I didn't know which terrified me more: hurtling into the ground or getting captured by the Wrecker. All I could think was, *This can't be the end. I need to do something!*

Within seconds, a white blinding light launched itself at the Wrecker, splitting into four spears and embedding itself into the Wrecker's limbs. The creature let out a terrible screech and came to a halt. The spears disappeared in a white blaze but the attack had created searing holes in the Wrecker's armor, leaving the creature heaving for breath. I didn't know how, but I knew I had attacked it. That white blinding light came from my chest! I was so mesmerized by the attack I briefly forgot about the ground coming towards me. Before I could I scream for help, Gregor flashed underneath me, murmuring softly, "I've got you."

Before the Wrecker could take a furious step forward, five other Kyrios had surrounded it in an odd formation. One stepped forward to taunt the beast while two positioned themselves at the Wrecker's feet and the remaining two at its claws. With a shout, all four raised what looked like glowing swords and slashed away at the beast's limbs. Dismembered, the Wrecker fell on its back to the ground with a surprised roar, leaving its armor open around his face. The remaining Kyrios quickly scaled the large beast and embedded his sword in the middle of the Wrecker's forehead. With one last roar of agony, the creature disintegrated into nothing.

The steel-haired returned to Gregor's side with a salute. "The creature has been destroyed, sir."

Gregor nodded. "Return to your post."

The five saluted with a chorus of "Sir!" and disappeared, once again, into the night.

I hadn't said a word to Gregor since we left Nelly's, and I still couldn't speak. Gregor quietly dashed back to Nelly's to find that the nearby homes that had been partially destroyed had police surrounding them and that the road leading to the residential street was blocked off. Thankfully no one was hurt and people were blaming it all on a gas leak-turned-explosion.

Everyone that had been in Nelly's crowded around the police tape to get a closer look at the destruction. Gregor and I surreptitiously entered the crowd from the back and pretended to be just as shocked as everyone else. Our group could not stop talking about how Nelly's had shook from the reported gas explosion. Gregor remained quiet as I spoke robotically and added, "Wow" or "I know, right?" when necessary.

Cynthia remained quiet in Steve's arms, looking inexplicably exhausted. She watched us both carefully and asked, "So where were you two when all this happened?"

I shifted uncomfortably. "I needed some air when Gregor came out to check on me. We were outside when the shakes started happening so we ducked for cover nearby until it stopped. We figured it wasn't safe to go back inside."

She narrowed her eyes, but shrugged it off. "Right, it wouldn't have been safe in Nelly's, but you could've been killed from the explosion." She gave me a quick peck on the cheek and made for the car, which had somehow remained unscathed. "I just want to go home. Let's get Amie," she said with a particularly scathing look at Gregor.

No one uttered a word the entire ride back. I don't think I could have had a full conversation if I'd wanted to.

My mind was mush, first of all, from that earth-shattering kiss I had shared with Gregor. I mean, even if water were always that electrifying, I would never stop drinking. I couldn't know what possessed him to kiss me or to go that far, but I liked it.

But I also knew the danger—what if I became an anchor for Gregor and he was forced to leave? And what had happened back there? I stared at the bracelet on my wrist. That shock had made me lose a bit more control, not contained it. *Maybe it malfunctioned from my fluctuating levels?* I wondered. I massaged my head, thinking how lucky we were that no one got hurt. It could have been so much worse.

Second, I was still reeling from Cynthia's very clear animosity towards Gregor. I knew my best friend could be protective of me, but she didn't know anything that would make her dislike him so much. There's no way she could.

If only Gregor was a normal guy. If only the Want never existed and I could actually enjoy a normal life.

We dropped Amie off first. I stepped out of the car to give her a proper hug. I knew this would likely be the last time I would see her for a couple of weeks. "Kat, you really scared me and Cyn. We had no idea where you were and—"

"I know, sweetie. I am sorry about that. But we're fine, okay? This is gonna sound really weird for me to say, but I'd never purposely make you worry. You guys matter to me."

"Like family?" she said quietly, her lips raised in a timid smile.

"Like sisters, Ames." I gave her another tight hug and waved goodbye as Cyn drove back to our homes a few blocks away. We pulled into Cynthia's driveway and for several moments no one moved.

I glanced at my best friend. "Hey, listen, Cyn, I'm sorry about worrying you earlier—"

"Love, you have nothing to apologize for." She looked behind her at Gregor in the back seat disdainfully. "It's not as if you had anything to do with tonight."

"Cyn—"

"You are absolutely right, Cynthia. Katya, stop apologizing," Gregor interrupted. "You had nothing to do with this, so let's move on. I'm sure that it won't happen again."

I inwardly groaned, hating that Gregor was already heading in the direction I knew was coming but so desperately wanted to avoid. But before I could even say another word, Gregor had stepped out of the car and waited for me several feet away. I looked at my friend sternly. "Cynthia, I get you were worried earlier, but what's your problem with Gregor? It's as if you are blaming him for what happened tonight!"

Cynthia stared down at her steering wheel. She didn't seem to have even heard me. "Katya," she said seriously.

"What?"

"Be careful, please."

I looked at her oddly. "What, you think we're gonna have another gas leak?"

She shook her head, her eyes stressing the seriousness of her words. "No, it's not about that. Katya, just please promise me you'll be careful. I worry about you, and tonight you scared me half to death when you disappeared and we couldn't find you. Just promise me, okay?" Seeing the tears in her eyes alarmed me. Cynthia was not the crier, I was. She was the one to hold me and comfort me.

I took her into my arms and held her close. "Hey, it's going to be okay. I still don't understand your mixed feelings about Gregor, but don't worry about him. He really is a good guy. I will be fine, I promise."

Cynthia sniffled. "Call me later?"

I gave her an extra squeeze. "You got it." I got out of the car and walked across the lawn with my Kyrios waiting my arrival.

As I unlocked the door, he started, "Katya, we need to talk."

Uh-oh. I opened the door and entered the foyer. "I know. I know we do. We—"

"Major Gregor!" A man in the Kyrios uniform was waiting inside of the living room and stood at attention the moment we entered.

Gregor looked at him, surprised. "Sargent Davies. What brings you here?"

The younger-sounding Kyrios cleared his throat. "General Nabil has sent orders that you and Lady Katya return to Ager at once."

"Did he say why?"

"He simply said they had found something regarding Lady Katya that she might want to know."

Gregor nodded. "We shall return shortly." The younger Kyrios entered the portal without another word. The Scot cleared his throat, not turning around, "Katya, I guess we'll put that talk on hold for now?"

"Yes, I think so. I'm just going to quickly change." I made for my room, hearing Gregor's deep sigh as I walked away. As I changed into a t-shirt and jeans, I began to wonder whether taking him out had been a good idea in the first place. I began to wonder whether anything that happened that night would lead to any good later.

19

The moment we entered Ager, we knew something was off. As we made for the grand gate, the sentry guards, instead of the aloof stares we'd received previously, immediately dropped to one knee, bowed their heads and said, "Welcome Lady Katya and Major Gregor."

I immediately looked at Gregor and whispered, "Lady Who? What's their issue?"

He shrugged and ushered me forward. As we walked through the courtyard toward Central Tower, I noticed that most of the Kyrios stopped their training to watch us. Some of them fell to their knees or just gaped at us. I could hear the whispers: "Is that her? Can't you feel her Vis? Wow, she's really here."

I tugged on Gregor's arm. "What is going on? Why are they staring at us?" I whispered.

Gregor looked around suspiciously. "I have no idea. But we will find out soon." In a loud clipped tone, he said, "Everyone, return to your duties, immediately."

"Yes, sir!" And they did, but not without lingering stares or side glances. We cut through the crowd quickly, ignoring the bows and staring and entered the Central Tower. Gregor scooped me into his arms and I automatically put my arms around his neck to get ready for the high jump. But he didn't move immediately. I found that he was eyeing me with an unfamiliar look in his gaze.

"What's wrong?" My arms unconsciously tightened around his neck.

He continued to look at me wordlessly. Something shifted in his eyes that I could only guess was confusion, suspicion, and perhaps longing. But I didn't dare get my hopes up.

Finally, he shook his head and said, "Nothing. Let's go."

With one leap, we made it to the top of the Tower to find the Generals waiting for us again. Only this time, they slightly bowed their heads. Nabil had a grand but fixed smile. That officially freaked me out.

"Okay, can someone tell me what's going on? Why's everyone acting like this?"

Nabil chuckled softly. "Please, Lady Katya, there is no need for alarm. We found some answers about you, and we're simply treating you with the respect that you deserve."

How big of an answer could it have been for the Generals to act like this towards me? I worried my lip. "Can you please start from the beginning?"

Nabil gestured to the previously used conference room. "Why don't we adjourn to the other room then?"

The General nodded and quietly shuffled inside. Gregor began to turn to leave the tower, but Nabil stopped him. "Gregor, your presence continues to be required. You will remain with Lady Katya."

Gregor nodded curtly. I gave him an annoyed glance. Didn't he know I did not want to be by myself with these people?

We assumed the same seats as before and I patiently waited for someone to begin talking. After five minutes of silence, patience took a time out. "The lieutenant said that you had something to share with me?"

The Generals looked at each other, wordlessly deciding who should explain. Michiko lost the battle of the wills and cleared her throat. "Well, my lady—"

"I'm sorry, but why is everyone calling me that? I am not a lady or a princess or anything like that. General Michiko, please just call me Katya."

Taken aback, Michiko looked to Nabil who nodded his assent. She cleared her throat again. "Katya, as you know, I began my research the moment we left this room. After many hours of searching our libraries, I came across an old tablet sent by Our Lord as a record of creations."

"Our Lord? God, you mean?" I asked, looking around.

Michiko nodded. "Within the record, his Lordship spoke of the First battle with the Want at the beginning of time. The fierce battle had taken many souls on both sides, but Our Lord was victorious in sealing Drachen, the leader of the Want and his creations below the Live Realm in the Abyss."

"And I am assuming Drachen is what we call the devil?"

Michiko nodded again. "However, Our Lord understood that there would be a time when the Want would try to regain power and storm the Live Realm. We Kyrios have been on the front line, protecting the Live Realm along with the Archs—"

"Archangels, right?"

Nabil muttered. "Another department, another story. Continue, Michiko."

"But within the record, He spoke of an entity he would leave within the Live Realm. A power unlike any other, with portions of His own dominate power. One who would be alive, but with the power of the dead, with the ability to call and control Vis from both realms. The one who would be the decider of the Live Realm's existence.

"The record called this power the Balancer."

Michiko took a deep breath. "It was said that the Balancer would be the bridge between the dead and the living, with the ability to see beyond the apparent and look within to determine the true purpose of a soul. A portion of Our Lord's power bestowed to ensure that the peace would be maintained in all realms. Based on the readings that we have done regarding your power, the fact that you've had this ability since you were a child and the fact that a greater part of your power has manifested during a time of unusual activity in the Abyss, we believe this power, the Balancer, is you, Katya."

My entire world completely went off kilter. "No, you got it all wrong. There's no way that I could be that."
The tingling nudged me inside and spoke. **It's true.**

My head continued to shake. "There has to be some mistake. I'm no Balancer. I'm just a..." The phrase "normal, average girl" seemed too ridiculous to even utter. "This can't be true." I looked to Gregor, my eyes pleading for some help. "This is a joke, right?"

His blue eyes bore into mine, his surprise shone clearly. He didn't say a word.

"I'm afraid Michiko is very correct, Lady Katya." Nabil stood from his seat and walked to the other side of the table, his eyes never leaving mine. "It seems that you meeting Gregor came precisely on time. In fact, from what we can tell, it was more than likely foretold. Around the same time Gregor discovered you, we discovered a number of breaches made by Wanters in the veil between the Abyss and the Live Realm in several places throughout the world."

He gestured to the wall and immediately an image came to life, as if there were a projector. Mountains and a large forest surrounded a large city, bustling with activity. However, what was very clear was the tear in the air, towards the back of the city near the tallest mountain. It was similar to a tear Gregor would make to enter Ager. But this tear simply poured out monsters.

"This is just one example, out in Denver, Colorado. It's as if a number of them decided to break through at the same time, creating a hole. Tears like this have been occurring all over the Live Realm. New York, Sydney, Tokyo, you name it. These holes are small enough now that most Wanters leaving are in level one forms. We are managing the small droves, but the breaches do have the potential to grow. But that's not our only concern. The effects of the breaches themselves are being felt everywhere. The negative Vis seeping out of the Abyss is hitting humans like a virus. The immediate effect that we have seen is that humans have become colder, darker, and more selfish.

"We are still trying to figure out why these holes are occurring, but a theory is that this may be Drachen's attempt to breach the Abyss wall and begin gaining a stronghold in the Live Realm."

"But I still don't understand. What's Drachen's end game?"

Nabil shrugged. "In a word—jealously. Just like other Wanters, Drachen wants what he can't have. So he'll destroy it so no one else can have it. But we are not going to let millions of souls be destroyed because of his desire."

He looked pointedly at me. "Before these holes become any larger, you must go to these cities, use your power, and deal with the tears."

"Me?" I squeaked.

"Yes, you. You will start with the largest tear so far, which is in Los Angeles. Our forces are currently maintaining, but they'll need your help sooner than later." A new image of the West Coast city came to life on the wall. Car accidents, small and large, plagued the streets of downtown LA. Drivers rumbled in the streets, brawling over the smallest fender benders. Ambulances and caretakers fought to get to those seriously hurt. Those avoiding troubles ran from the carnage attempting to swallow them up. And perched on almost every human shoulder were small Wanters, whispering in their ears.

I closed my eyes and said through gritted teeth, "Look, I am no savior. I can't even control my Vis. Find yourself someone else."

Raf suddenly stood from his seat, looking very annoyed. "You know what? Perhaps she's right. Our Balancer can't be some spineless girl. This one can barely keep her faculties straight."

Michiko stood as well. "Wait a minute, Raf. You know I'm right! I've shown you all the records!"

Lamar nodded. "Besides, she's young. You can't possibly think that she would take this calmly. A seasoned soldier would be in shock as well."

"But at least a soldier would understand that it is his duty to act. She says she will not. So what good is she to us?" He eyed me with derision. "We have no use to her, and she's already seen too much." Raf looked at Nabil, "Hold the boy down."

Nabil immediately understood and jumped on the table, kicked Gregor out of his chair to the floor and pinned him down.

The Scot immediately began to struggle. "What are you doing?" With a flash, Raf had a large sword in his hand, poised to strike.

"Taking care of this problem." He leapt straight in the air and charged at me with his sword raised over his head. I simply stared as Raf made his descent. Just as he was about to swing his hand down, one thought came to my mind: *Protect*. I looked around to find that I'd placed a opaque shield around me, similar to the one that Gregor had erected around me while I slept. Amazed, I gently touched the covering, feeling a hum within me as the tingling responded, **I will protect you**.

I looked to my left to find Raf standing over me with a smug look on his face. "If you won't accept what we say, perhaps you will heed your own heart. Denying who you are isn't going to make this go away. The sooner you realize this, the sooner you can accept your purpose." His sword disappeared with another flash, and Raf smiled for the first time. "You can relax the shield, girl. No one will harm you."

At that, I felt some of the tension leave me and I nodded. It took me a few tries to relax, but I finally did, taking the shield down. Nabil released Gregor and returned to his chair. "My lady, I am sorry we had to do that. But we had to make you realize that this power you have is real. You are unable to stop this as much as you are unable to stop breathing. This is not a choice."

Nabil smiled again. No matter how attractive he was, seeing his smile gave an icky feeling. Like a kid in a candy store ready to devour a feast. "Your training should begin immediately, and you will be housed here in Ager until you have gained enough training to close the tears. Once the threat has been dealt with, you can return to your Live Realm life. Can we agree on that?"

A sudden chill swept over my body. Something told me my life would never be the same again. But I nodded. "There's no way this is a mistake, huh? Thank God I put things in place before we left." I sighed and tried to rub the tension out of the back of my neck. "I guess I'd better get started."

The Generals were pleased with my response. Nabil nodded. "Wonderful. Raf, begin training tomorrow. Gregor, you will continue as Lady Katya's protector indefinitely, until further notice."

Gregor slowly rose from his chair. "Sir, perhaps another person might be better for the position."

My heart dropped to my stomach. Gregor's demeanor changed and his eyes remained on his superior, who looked over him with a calculating eye. "Has something happened that impairs your ability to protect Lady Katya?"

His eyes shifted minutely over to me and my eyes pleaded with him silently to not compromise himself.

"No, sir."

"Then I see no reason to change my mind. You will do as you

are commanded. Lady Katya will be housed in the Marble Tower. Take residence there as well."

His body went rigid with anger, but he answered, "Yes, sir."

Nabil turned to the other Generals. "I think we are just about done here, Generals. Shall we adjourn?" The Generals nodded and one by one left the conference room. Lamar was the last one to leave. He gave me a wink and said, "This may not have been in your plans for your life, but I am glad you are joining our group."

I appreciated his sympathetic look and felt like I could be honest. "General Lamar, I am scared outta my mind. I don't think I can do this."

He patted me on the back. "My dear, you don't know how important you are. You are exactly what we have been waiting for. Don't forget that." With a slight bow, the kind general left the room, leaving the Scot and me alone.

I slowly stood from my chair and looked at Gregor carefully. "Gregor, look I know we need to talk—"

Gregor stepped away from the table and placed his hands behind his back. "Lady Katya, shall I escort you to your room?"

I sucked in my teeth. "Come on, don't do this. You know I don't want to be called that."

Gregor didn't meet my eyes and said quietly, "Unfortunately, I haven't been given leave to address you otherwise, so you will have to excuse the formalities, my lady." He bowed in a way that I could only take as condescending. "To your room, *Lady* Katya?"

20

I rolled my shoulders, giving the Scot an epic eye roll, and nodded. He led me out of the conference room to the main lobby. Gregor scooped me up and jumped down to the entrance floor below. With noted haste, he put me down after we landed and walked out the door. The Scot moved briskly, looking over his shoulder from time to time to ensure that I was still following him. We walked through the courtyard and made a slight left at the entrance gate toward several smaller towers.

The Scot cleared his throat. "The barracks, where the majority of the Kyrios are housed to rest in between assignments, are set on the other side of the Agee compounds. These towers are for the higher-ranking Kyrios. The Generals are housed in the largest tower here. You will be housed in the second largest," the Scot explained without looking at me.

"Where are you normally housed?" I asked quietly.

"The barracks. As Major, I could be housed at the Marble Tower. It's considered a perk some Kyrios can't wait to have—to be able to have a room to yourself. However, I was raised to prefer family and closeness over solitude. My father always said to me that being alone breeds a selfishness that you don't know is there until you are put to the test. To combat that, you remain close to your kin so you never forget what and who you are fighting for."

My eyebrows furrowed. "Family is really important to you, huh?"

Gregor's cheeks rippled as he clenched his jaw. He simply nodded and did not offer any more information.

We walked the remainder of the way to our destination in silence. The largest tower within the set was a sight to behold. Similar to the Taj Mahal's ambiance, the General's tower was made of simple white brick that shone with the brilliance of a gem. It had large windows that faced out to the courtyard where we stood and that were surrounded with gold engravings, the meaning of which I could not make out. Inside the lowest window I could see a large canopy bed that was plush with pillows. It reminded me of the story my mother had told me about Rapunzel and her long locks of hair. If Rapunzel had been trapped in this tower, I doubt she would have minded it too much.

The second tower was similar in grandeur, of course, just smaller. We entered the second tower through a side door. Thankfully, there were a set of staircases. Again in silence, we made it to the top of the tower to find several rooms. He led me to the last bedroom at the end of the hallway. The room had a large canopy bed, plush with many pillows. The room also had a view of the courtyard and of the main gate. I looked around, pretending to be inspecting the room, but I was really waiting for Gregor to say something.

"Is everything satisfactory, my lady?"

I crossed my arms and gave him my own piercing stare. "Gregor, enough. I get it. We messed up back there."

Gregor's jaw clenched again. "It's not 'we,' my lady. I messed up. That should have never have happened."

I studied my nail beds, avoiding his gaze. "I'm not going to say all that because..." I let the words fade as my courage failed me. "Look, I don't want this to affect our friendship. Can we just go back to before Nicky's?"

"Aye, I think it's best we put some distance between us. You came across a different Gregor. A Gregor that let his human nature get the best of him. A Gregor who temporarily forgot his duties to this organization. A Gregor that could have put everything in jeopardy. He is no more."

My eyes blazed with anger, "Just like that, you're just going to step back and what? We're not friends anymore? I trusted you and came here because our friendship! How are we supposed to—"

"I know my place!" he exploded, his face distorted by his anger, his eyes dangerously flashing. "I am a leader of a group that keeps people safe from dangers every day. Any distraction from that is a liability I cannot afford. And it's about high time you grow up and understand you can't get everything you want, Lady Katya." He stomped to the door. "If you need me, I'll be down the hall." And with that, he slammed the door.

I grabbed the first thing next to me and threw it at the door. Unfortunately, it was simply a pillow that didn't quite make it to the door. But it did make me feel a bit better. For a moment. Then I remembered: the entire world was on my shoulders. I collapsed to the floor, tears rushing down my cheeks. All the frustration, the fear and anxiety broke the dam and the tears couldn't be held back any longer. I never figured out how soft the bed was that night. I didn't make it past the floor. My only bedfellow was the pillow I had thrown on the floor and the floor itself, sodden from my tears.

The next morning, I awoke very confused (which was becoming a common thing) and sore. Sore from the hard floor. Confused because I was in the bed that I had ignored. The sleek silk sheets rolled off my shoulders, pooling on the floor.

How did I get up here? It must have been Gregor. My heart beat painfully at the thought of him. *What is going on?* I would have thought that after last night, things would have changed for us. Perhaps not in the direction that I would have preferred. But I never thought he would have just turned away from me, to divorce himself from...us. I massaged my temples, feeling increasingly frustrated. There were holes in some of the stories I was hearing. Why would the Balancer be needed? Couldn't God just fix this problem? And why did it feel like the Kyrios had some animosity toward the angels, at least Nabil anyway? Shouldn't they be working together? And Gregor's statement the night before—he was raised, as in he had been alive at one point.

What had happened to him?

I wasn't any closer to these answers, and the only person who I had any conversations with at this point had just told me that he needed to distance himself. Sighing, I got out of bed and stretched when I heard knocking at my door. I opened it to find the Scot himself, with a fathomless look in his eyes. "I trust you slept well, my lady."

I snorted, knowing very well he already knew the answer. Instead of the easy retort resting on my tongue, I said, "What are we doing today, Gregor?"

He assumed a position that sadly reminded me of a butler: arms behind his back and nose in the air. "You will be training with General Raf this morning, and we will be starting our meditation exercises in the afternoon. Lieutenant Young Jae will be escorting you to the courtyard and to the training room."

Biting my bottom lip, I said softly, "I thought you were to stay by my side."

My comment only angered him, for he said in a steely voice, "Other matters need my attention. Young Jae will be with you shortly." The last I saw of him was his back, retreating out the door.

Growling, I couldn't help but punch the many pillows on my bed. *Other matters need his attention? What am I, then?* I stopped shortly and thought, *Wait, he is a big deal here. This is a military base. He probably does have other things to do.*

Oh geez! And he's been babysitting me for the past few days. I could only imagine the workload that was probably waiting for him. The last thing I wanted to do was cause Gregor more trouble. Feeling all the anger drain out of me, I pulled a couple of pillows by the window, kneeled down on them, and gazed out the window. I watched the crowds of Kyrios move in and out of the gate for several minutes before I heard a knock on the door.

"Be right there!" I called and started to step away from the window when I heard a female voice call out, loud enough for me to hear, "Gregor! You're here!" Curious, I stuck my head out a bit further to find a blond woman running swiftly toward the towers with a large smile on her face. She made a beeline for a dark-haired man who caught her as she jumped into his arms. Feeling like I was intruding, I began to turn my head when I realized the dark-haired man, who was now traveling through the courtyard, was Gregor. And he was smiling!

Don't get jealous. Don't get jealous. Do NOT get jealous, Katya Elizabeth Stevens! A full-on explosion would've detonated had it not been for another knock at the door. "Sorry!" I shuffled to the door, plastering a smile on my face. I opened the door to only have my jaw drop to the floor.

Before me stood the second best-looking man I had ever seen in my life. Jet black hair swept into a queue. The softest brown almond eyes I had ever seen in my life. He had the tall physique of a model and the brightest smile to boot. *I need to find out who to complain to about this Death being dumb handsome; it really wasn't fair!*

Realizing that I was staring, I backed away from the door, "I'm sorry. Are you Lieutenant Young Jae?"

"Yes, Lady Katya. It is a pleasure to meet you."

I sighed inwardly. *Even his husky voice sounds like music.* I held out my hand. "Please call me Katya. I hate formalities."

Young Jae slightly bowed over my hand and kissed it. "Of course, Miss Katya. Rather than calling me 'the ever-dashing Lieutenant Young Jae,' you may simply call me Jae."

I could help but smile at that. "You're not serious like the others."

"That's because I aim to please, Ms. Katya." He gave me a dashing smile that I returned. "So, before we begin your training, I've been asked to give you this." He snapped his finger, forming a rip portal. He stuck his hand in and pulled out a box. "This holds your attire for training. I hope you find it pleasing."

"I'm sure I will." I took the box, remembering that I'd forgotten the bag I had packed. So much for taking care of my hair!

Still wearing an easy smile, Young Jae nodded. "I'll wait for you outside." He looked around once and closed the door behind him.

I sighed deeply, this time letting the sound fill the room.

I headed to the next room in the suite, where a bowl had been filled with water. I splashed my face and wiped it down with a convenient towel left nearby. With damp hands, I ran a hand through my hair to attempt a finger detangle and pulled what I could into some semblance of a bun. I returned to the bedroom and to the box, which I'd laid down on my bed. Inside the box were a pair of oddly soled shoes and a black bodysuit. I put on the articles without complaint and noticed immediately how much lighter I felt. Like I weighed close to nothing. Like I could run for miles—and I hated to run! Shrugging, I met Young Jae outside my bedroom. I didn't miss the appreciative glance Young Jae slid across my body as I stepped out.

Offering his arm, he said, "Please follow me."

21

We stepped out of the tower and towards the courtyard. I took in my surroundings with a good eye. Young Jae noticed my study. "Is there anything you have questions on that I can answer, Ms. Katya?"

"What is this place? How did this come into being?"

He paused for a second before starting. "It is said that when God created the Live Realm, angry Archs were already plotting to overrun it and rule it as their own kingdom. They were also jealous that God had provided such a place for humans, but wouldn't create anything remotely close for them. So Drachen, a high-ranking Arch at the time, sent his underlings into the Live Realm to wreak havoc."

"So the first Wanters were Archs? Or were they Phims? I don't know the difference."

"Phims are not warriors. It's a bit hard to explain, but their role is more administrative. Like they hear orders from God and they send the orders out. We really don't meet Phims. Our interactions are really with Archs. And yes, the first Wanters were Archs. They are the Want Generals, the strongest Wanters in the Abyss.

"Now, when the first Wanters entered the Live Realm, early humans couldn't see them. They were only aware of the major disasters they were suffering from and the cruelty of their own people. The more powerful Archs-turned-Wanters were able to keep some human form and sowed dissension and chaos among the humans. In the beginning, there were many lives taken in the struggle, and human selfishness caused those souls to fail to cross over. It was a win-win situation for Drachen. He destroyed God's loved creatures and got more to add to his army. The remaining Archs still loyal to God had their hands full. That period was called God's Great Silence because the Phims did not receive any orders for a long period of time."

"But then how do the Kyrios play into this?"

Young Jae smiled at my enthusiasm. "There was a group of souls during that dark time that had particular Vis gifts, and when they died, they sought out God to give them power to fight against those who caused havoc on their fellow man. It was that drop of humanity still in these souls that compelled and moved God to create Ager and to create the Department to house the first responders to chaos in the Live Realm."

"Wow, that's amazing. It's one thing to hear about God at home, but it's another thing to see all of this in person." I said, smiling at his face.

Young Jae chuckled. "Trust me, there is a lot more to this dimension and the powers that be."

We talked amicably as we headed towards the barracks and to the training dome. I had wanted to ask why Nabil had a dislike for the Archs but got distracted by the massive training room we'd just entered. An immensely large dome with not one weapon inside. I glanced around and noticed that no one else was there either. "Is there anyone else joining us for training?"

"General Raf ordered that the training dome this morning be for your use only."

My annoyance flared. "I don't want special treatment. I'm just like everyone else."

Young Jae smiled kindly at me. "How very far from the truth you are, Katya. You are very much special." The soft look in his eyes elicited so many good feelings in me that again I had no choice but to smile in return.

"Ah! I see you made it on time!" We both jumped at the sound of General Raf's appearance. He stood behind us, still looking menacing and scary. "Young Jae, you may return in three Live Realm hours to escort Lady Katya back to her chambers."

"Yes, sir." He bowed slightly, winked at me, and whispered, "Go knock 'em dead!"

As he exited the dome, I turned to Raf and asked, "General, why can't I go back by myself? I'm sure the lieutenant has other duties to accomplish rather than babysit me."

"It is not about babysitting. I have every intention of exhausting you to the point that you might possibly need an escort to carry you back."

General Raf circled around me, studying my physique. I too had a chance to study him. His ice-blue eyes were remarkable additions to his chiseled face. The striking white hair seemed out of place with his relatively young face, but it somehow fit all the same. His attire was similar to mine, but his tunic was sleeveless, which allowed me to admire the built biceps and shoulders he had. What really took me aback was the number of scars he had that I hadn't noticed before. Even his face was marred with scars. But it didn't take anything away from him.

"Sizing me up, are you?"

My eyes snapped back up to his face where a smirk waited for me. I stood a bit straighter. "Maybe I am."

"Good. You should always be aware of what your enemy can do before you act." He stood tall with his arms behind his back; his eyes didn't reveal anything. "The point of our lessons is for you to get a better sense of your Vis and to help you protect yourself. If there is one thing you leave with today, if you are to protect yourself effectively, never underestimate anyone. Including friends. Be aware of everything around you. The better you are at evaluating your situations, the better chance you have at surviving." He snapped his fingers and a rack filled with weapons appeared on the right side of the room. He walked over slowly to the rack, speaking over his shoulder. "What do you know about the Want?"

I crinkled my nose. "Basically that they are souls that didn't cross over and are turned into monsters that you guys whip back into the Abyss or destroy."

Raf's hand rested on a long wooden staff, quietly assessing it. "That's it?"

"I mean, what else is there to know?"

Raf threw me a look. "A lot." He snatched up a staff from the rack and charged at me like he had done the day before. In the air and ready to kill. Realizing his aim, I ran away in time for him to slam into the floor with such force that it created a large crater. My eyes widened. He hadn't stopped himself this time.

In a flash, Raf again jumped up in the air with the staff above his head, poised to strike. His eyes showed no mirth or jest. He was out to kill. The air was acrid from dust and debris. It was thick enough already that I lost sight of Raf.

"General Raf! Wait! Why are we doing this?" I cried out, desperately trying to find his location.

His voice came from the dust, nowhere and everywhere. "I'm asking you the same question. Why are you doing this? Why are any of us doing this?"

I looked around wildly, but I couldn't even find a shadow.

"It is imperative for you to determine your answer to those questions. If you don't know yourself, then you can't use your Vis to its full potential. If you don't know your enemy, then they can easily come up behind you." A poke at my back and a hand on my shoulder gave me the answer I was looking for. "Like this—and then extinguish your life." Raf's breath on my nape gave me goose bumps, and not the good kind.

He released me and I turned around to face him. He moved the staff to his shoulder and gave me a hard stare. "So yes, there is a lot more for you to know."

I nodded. He seemed to relax in my quietness and brought the staff down as a cane and leaned on it. "Lady Katya, what you have to understand is where the Want come from. Death is an untouchable power that comes for everyone. It is supposed to bring peace to the constant pain and discomfort the body suffers from. And it's not only your body that suffers, but also the soul. Death is supposed to be a release that allows the soul to quiet and to be led to the next place. Ghosts, as humans put it, are souls that have left the body without guidance. The longer a soul stays within the Live Realm, the more it becomes bitter and angrier—until the soul collapses within itself and dies a second time, becoming the Want.

"This is the core of any Want's motivation—anger, selfishness, jealousy, and envy. They seek to destroy the place that they can't have any longer. And anyone who keeps them from that goal must be destroyed or absorbed for power. You, a living human, are able to connect to your spirit energy, the energy that sustains your soul, in a similar fashion that we can. Your capacity to do this continues to grow every hour." He sighed, leaning on his staff. "I'm not supposed to give you my own opinion, but you know what my hope for you is?"

I looked at him as permission to continue.

"I'm under orders to teach you to protect yourself. Some of us would see you fighting the Want. But, perhaps your role is not meant to be a punishment for the Want but to restore the balance between the two conflicting realms. You potentially could bring peace to the Want they desperately need and you could save the humans targeted in the oncoming chaos."

Again, that savior thing. I internally cringed. But I knew better than to say that to Raf, so I said, "I understand."

"Good." He lifted the long wooden staff and tossed it to me to catch. "Now that we understand who we are coming up against and why they fight, we need tactics to win. As Kyrios, we use hand-to-hand combat and wielding our Vis at the same time. Only Vis energy itself can cut down another Vis creature." He materialized a new staff and stretched it over his head, allowing the definition of his abs to show through his body suit. "We don't have a lot of time to teach you theories, so we are gonna do it the new-fashioned way. You need to learn to bring up your Vis purposefully instead of instinctively. Use that staff as a guide for your power." He said this with a glint in his eye.

I gulped. "What's the new-fashioned way?"

"Practice. You know, they say that the strongest among us have the capability to actually speak to our Vis."

"What, like a conversation? Vis can talk back?"

He shrugged. "I'm not sure. It was said that the first Kyrios were able to speak to their Vis as guides. As though their energy was sentient." Raf smirked. "Hell, what do I know? I've never met them, and I've never been able to do it. But who knows, Balancer, maybe you can. Let's see if we can bring it out on purpose! I won't be as hard as I was a couple of minutes ago, but I'll definitely give you a good whack if you aren't paying attention. Raise your staff," he ordered.

"But I've never fought with a staff before!" I cried, secretly looking for an exit.

"No time like the present to learn. And don't just fight. Protect. Feel out your Vis!" Raf said, smirking.

The General charged from the left, swiping at my head. Instinctively, I raised my staff to block it. Raf held and threw his weight into pushing me back with a grin on his face. "Good, let yourself feel it out. You may have skills you never knew about."

"Last time I checked, I was a class A klutz," I grunted, trying not to fall over under Raf's weight.

With a grin, Raf jumped back. "You just haven't been in a situation where you had to be serious. Life or death should be motivation enough." His eyes hardened. "Come at me, my lady. Give me a hit right here." He pointed to his right shoulder. "Touch me here, and we will call it a day."

I frowned. "Okay." I ran towards him but Raf disappeared, just to reappear behind me.

"Too slow."

I swung hard behind me and hit dead air.

"Oh, come now. Where's that feisty spirit? You will never get anywhere with that attitude." He disappeared to the other side of the room, a thousand feet away. "Unless you have the desire to hit me, to literally take me down, there is no way you will get close to me."

I gritted my teeth. "How the hell am I supposed to hit you if you keep disappearing like that?"

He chuckled. "It's called quickstep, and you're right. If you wanted this to be a close combat exercise, you just should've asked." I raised the staff up like a sword like I had seen Gregor do, like a samurai. A sweat drop ran down my forehead.

At least he can't do any real damage with that wooden staff.

"Don't do that," Raf barked.

I looked around, puzzled. "What do you mean? I didn't do anything."

"You just let your guard down. Essentially, you just shouted to me, 'I don't think you can hurt me with that staff,' right?"

I gaped. "How did you...?"

Raf shook his head. "Battle experience, my lady. I can read your body entirely. And I wouldn't be so sure about your theory." He lifted his staff to mirror my stance. "One of the benefits of controlling my Vis is that I can make anything into a weapon." With that annoying smirk, Raf simply flicked his staff downward. His staff glowed purple and his razor-sharp Vis blade hit the floor, splitting it down until the widening crack stopped at my feet. My eyes bulged in fear as Raf slowly walked toward me with dangerous purpose in his eyes.

Move, come on, girl, move! If you don't move, you'll be in pieces like the floor. Move, dammit! But I was paralyzed with fear. I wanted to run and protect myself from the slow-coming madman. But all I could sense in the room was the powerful and intimating Vis rolling off Raf in waves. Every bone in my body vibrated painfully, as if an immense and heavy pressure was being pushed down on me, demanding that I lay down on the ground to ease my suffering. The only thing I could smell was the sweat rolling down my face as my body fought to keep standing straight and not bow from exertion.
Why do you insist on doing this alone? Just ask for help. the tingling said.

Oh my God, was Raf right? *Um, right. So, hey. A little help?*

A soft sensation ebbed into me that made me feel a more light-hearted, even as I was being crushed by Raf's energy. Was my Vis chuckling?

Close your eyes and just focus on me. I did as I was told. **Your own fear hinders you, Katya. It is not his Vis you should bow to. But he should bow to yours.** A deep sense of pride I didn't recognize started to swell inside of me. **It's time to remind that soul who you are. Raise your staff with both hands towards the end.**

Like this?

That's right. That pride you feel? Feel it build and spread all over you. It's a pride that won't be silenced by Raf's repressive energy. Just do not falter. I will help you. Swing your staff now!

Opening my eyes, I found Raf now only a few feet away, his energy still pressing down but now only affecting me minutely. I took a step back and swung my staff vertically. The prideful swell erupted, travelled down my arm, and through the wooden staff. The Vis erupted into a wall of energy, splitting the entire room in half and engulfing it in a bright blue light.

It was over as soon as it happened.

Well done.

I dropped to my knees, exhausted and unable to see anything before me. Did I hit Raf? *OMG, did I kill him?* As the light faded, I made out a shadow about fifty feet ahead of me. It was Raf with his arms crossed over his chest and head tucked in. He was surrounded by a shield, unharmed. He released his stance and his shield shattered into glass pieces and disappeared. "I didn't expect that from you yet."

"Neither did I," I panted.

The General closed the gap between us and knelt down to my level. "My lady, you're exhausted because you've never used your Vis like that. It's like running—gotta build up endurance." He smirked. "But you should feel accomplished. You nicked me." Just below his shoulder on his arm, a small cut glared back at me.

I smirked at my instructor. "I almost thought I killed you."

He guffawed. "Not yet, my lady. We'll get there soon. Before we know it, you'll be able to create a Vis dome as big as this training space."

22

"General Raf," a quiet Jae said behind us with an easy smile. "Ms. Katya."

"Ah, Young Jae. Right on time. My lady, until next time." General Raf bowed and exited into a portal.

The young Lieutenant turned his attention to me. "Did your session go well?"

His eagerness to please was too endearing. "Yeah, it did. I am starving, though."

Young Jae extended his arm. "Then let us return to your chambers for a scrumptious lunch, shall we?" Unable to resist the charming smile, I took his arm and we paraded back to Towers in high spirits. Jae regaled me with funny stories of some of the Kyrios working there. ("Sean over there? He blew up his barrack trying to manipulate his Vis his first day.")

I arrived at my chambers with a large smile on my face. "Jae, you are so different from everyone I've met here. I thought Kyrios were very serious. Very doom and gloom."

Jae grinned. "Not all of us, Katya. We did live once. We know how to have fun once in a while."

That brought back something Gregor said about his family. "So, you guys did all live before, like as actual humans?"

He gave me an amused but puzzled look. "Of course. Where did you think we came from?"

Before I could answer, my room door suddenly swung open and Gregor strolled forward with a tray in his hand. His eyes took in the close proximity Jae and I inhabited, and his blue eyes immediately cooled. "Lieutenant Young Jae. You're still here. I hope everything is in order."

Jae quickly saluted his superior. "Of course, sir. I was simply ensuring that Lady Katya had returned safely to her room, sir."

Gregor looked between the two of us with a calculating eye. "I am sure that once she enters the room, she is safe. You may return to your duties."

Jae quickly nodded, but he returned his sights to me. "Until tomorrow then, Ms. Katya," he murmured quietly.

I gave him a small smile. "I look forward to it."

With a sly wink, Lieutenant Young Jae was out the door.

I smiled to myself. *At least I have one friendly face here.* I could feel Gregor's displeasure as he placed the tray on the desk. "I hope you made inroads with training," he said quietly.

"Eh, I was able to surprise General Raf and nick him on the shoulder. I think that's making inroads, don't you?"

I saw him smirk out of the corner of my eye as I made my way to the lunch tray. The food looked good enough—soup with sandwiches and some fruit. *Man, what I wouldn't give for a piece of chocolate, though!* Gregor stood off to the side and watched me eat. But not much else was said. The silence made me a bit twitchy, so I asked, "Where did you get the food from? I thought you said Kyrios don't need food."

Gregor barely removed his sight from the floor. "Human food. This is different."

"How different?"

"Is the food inedible?"

I started. "No, not at all. It's actually quite good."

"Then you shouldn't worry yourself about it." I got the hint and ceased any more attempts at idle chatter. The moment I was done, Gregor finally moved from his corner. "Are you ready to begin our training, my lady?"
Resisting the urge to roll my eyes, I nodded.

The Scot looked me over and then said, "Please sit on the floor. Are you familiar with yoga?"

I nodded again. Gregor instructed me to begin deep breathing for about three minutes and try to calm every nerve in the body. By the end of the three minutes, the tension within the room had oddly dissipated. I cracked open an eye to see that Gregor too was doing some deep breathing. He must have felt my eyes because his own immediately opened.

Silently, we both surveyed each other for several seconds. I didn't want to go through this tension. I wanted to tell him that

I would ignore whatever I was feeling if he would just return to normal. Just return to the man that I'd met, only a handful of days ago now, but who was already becoming my closest confidant.

But he'd made himself very clear. I could not become a distraction for him. But if only he would just talk about it, maybe we could reach some middle ground.

His blue eyes pierced into me and somehow his gaze reflected everything swirling inside of me: hurt, caution, displeasure, yearning. The Kyrios cleared his throat. "I'm going to continue your Vis training and control. We're going into your soulscape to find your Havadar."

"Soulscape? Hava-what?"

Gregor sighed. "Your soulscape is where your soul resides and where your inner Vis is stored. And it's also where most of your dreams take place. Not those nonsensical ones where you dream about flying fish or deep-sea giraffes. It's that place where your soul connects with your mind and communicates. Most people can't really see their actual soulscape, since it's shrouded by the mind's visual stimulation, but the soulscape is the true home of your soul and Vis."

Seeing my baffled expression, a ghost of a smile flitted across his face. "You'll see. And a Havadar is this." In a familiar blue flash, a sword rested on his lap. From the point to the hilt, the entire sword was a coppery color with the occasional silver diamond decorating it, embedded down the middle of the blade. "This is Dusk, my Havadar. Every Kyrios is able to wield a weapon created from their inner Vis. We also call it a heart protector because it's forged from within the heart of the wielder. The Havadar only responds to the wielder and cannot be wielded by anyone else." His sword hummed quietly before disappearing again. "Because you wielded weapons during that Wrecker episode, the Generals think you are able to call a Havadar. We are going to find out. If you do, it could help you gain better control of your Vis."

"Does my having a Havadar make me Kyrios?"

Something indiscernible flittered across his face. "No, you're just a complicated living human being with some extraordinary abilities." He cleared his throat again.

"I'm going have you lay down on the floor and have you continue your deep breathing." He adjusted my position to ensure that I was somewhat in the middle of the floor. As I closed my eyes and continued my breathing, the Scot said softly, "I'm going to push you into your soulscape. Fair warning, it's not going to feel pleasant."

Keeping my eyes closed, I began to ask, "What do you—" The words died on my lips as I suddenly felt enormous pressure on my chest. I had heard the expression "an elephant sitting your chest" before. I never had one sit on mine, but I think what I was experiencing would be pretty close to the same. As I gasped for air, I could hear Gregor whisper in my ear, "Do not fight it. Close into yourself. You need to relax."

Sure pal, easier said than done. But I tried to ignore the immense discomfort and allowed my mind to shut down and tried to relax. It actually came much easier than I realized, and soon the discomfort was gone. My eyes remained closed as I tried to listen for Gregor but heard nothing. I cracked open one eye to find that the floor underneath me had changed from the wood of my bedroom to a smooth dark marble. I raised my head slightly to find that I was in an opulent room filled with doors. The walls were covered in sand-colored granite, with several torches lit and mounted on the walls. The doors were of dark mahogany, but none of them had knobs. I looked to each end of the room to find that there was no end. It was an endless hallway of doors. And silent. Not even the flames from the torches made a sound.

And the Twilight Zone begins.

Something shifted behind me and I yelped in surprise. Gregor groaned softly and propped himself up from the ground. "Ouch, that entrance was a bit harder than I thought. Your soulscape was putting up a fight there."

I said nothing as he rose from the ground and stretched his arms. I couldn't say anything because my mouth had gone bone dry at the sight of the Scot in a toga. Yes, a toga! It wasn't the first time that I had seen his chiseled chest, but to see him in a toga that ended at his knees gave me a better look at the fit specimen he was.

Realizing I was staring, I cleared my throat and looked down the endless hallway. "Why are you wearing a toga?" I asked out loud.

The Scot looked down at himself and chuckled. "Your old soul is dating itself, though we already knew it's much older than that. Eh, be thankful we aren't naked, then!"

I pursed my lips, desperately trying to get the image of a naked Gregor out of my head. It wasn't until I looked down that I realized that my clothes had changed into a toga too. The more I thought about it, I did feel slightly different as well. I rose from the floor, sighing. "I wish I had a mirror to look at myself."

No sooner had I said it did a mirror materialize out of thin air. I whirled around and sputtered, "H-h-how did that just happen?"

The Kyrios simply smiled, "You are forgetting that this is your soulscape. It does answer your desires."

Ha! Right, soulscape. We are in the world that my soul created for itself. Simple enough, right? I returned to the mirror to find that I had indeed changed. Not only did the one-shoulder floor-length toga fit my body perfectly, but my skin had a slight otherworldly shimmer and my hair went way past my back. My ephemeral image kinda freaked me out. Sensing my discomfort, the mirror vanished. Running a hand through my hair, I returned my attention to the Scot who had been watching me.

"What now?"

Gregor sighed and rolled his shoulders. "We are here so you can find your Havadar. So you tell me, where do you feel like we should go?"

"Where do I feel like going? What kind of question is that?"

"Just be still. The answer will come."

I copied Gregor's actions and rolled my shoulders to relax. I began the deep breathing exercises and hoped that something would come up it. I remembered my earlier training and the tingling's words about asking for help. *Hey...um it's me again. Not really sure where I should be going. Some direction, please?*

I didn't hear an immediate response and thought perhaps I couldn't speak with the tingling in the soulscape. However, after a few seconds, I felt my heart rate slow down considerably and something within me just clicked. A flash of heat shivered through my body from head to toe and I could feel myself stand erect, at full attention. A slight beep blipped at my center and with each beep, the sound continued to grow, like a pulse reverberating outward from within my core. The pulse thinned as it became a sonar, sending out signals throughout the entire soulscape. For several moments, I stood erect, waiting for the answering call back. For something to echo back to me. It soon found its mark.

"There." I pointed down to the left corridor. "We need to go this way." I didn't bother to wait for Gregor's response. My feet led me way down the endless hallway. As we passed the doors, sounds could be heard from behind the endless doors that decorated the hall. Sounds of laughter, tears, anger, and sorrow.

"What are behind these doors?" I asked the Kyrios, my first question in about fifteen minutes.

Gregor eyed me carefully. "These are your memories."

I blinked. "My memories? If I open a door, I can see my memories?" Curious, I approached a door where loud laughter could be heard behind it. Before I could reach for the handle, Gregor grabbed my hand.

"The moment you open the memory door, it will be very hard to get out of it. I suggest that you stay on your current quest."

I dropped my hand, realizing that it had been the first time since our argument that we'd had any kind of contact. I didn't realize until that moment how much we'd touched before, not held by these new barriers. Not liking the way his hand left a slight ache within me, I focused on the echo. "Fine. Let's go."

We continued to walk down the hallway, the pulse rapidly sending out signals the closer we got. Finally the pulse could not stop lurching within me as we approached a door. The door was very similar to others we had passed by. Except it was completely silent.

"This is it." I looked at the Kyrios, a bit apprehensive. "What do I do now?"

A small smile graced his features. "What do you want to do?"

I want answers. I resumed my deep breathing to figure out what I had to do when the tingling voice spoke out to me, clearer than ever before.

Hello, Katya.

23

I opened my eyes to find that I was at the lake I had visited in my dreams a few nights before. Just like in my dreams, I was floating a few feet above the large rock in the middle of the beautiful, scenic lake. The familiar mist came in as I remembered, but it felt different. A presence from within the mist could be felt everywhere. Oppressive but comforting all at once. Someone was here with me.

"Hello?" I called out. "Anyone there?"

You know I am here. Why do you question that? the voice said everywhere.

I looked wildly around, but no one came into view. "Because I can't see you."

Would you feel better if you could see something?

I nodded, not particularly trusting my voice.

Suddenly, a gale of wind surrounded the rock I floated over, forcing me to crash down onto the rock itself. The wind was such a force that I ducked down, hoping not to get pushed over into the water. When the wind died out, I opened my eyes to find my complete carbon copy standing in front of me. I quickly stood up in alarm. At first I thought I had subconsciously performed the mirror trick again, so I moved slightly to see if the figure would move too. It didn't.

"Does this satisfy you?" my copy asked. Other than our vague outward appearance, the resemblance to me ended, particularly with the eyes. They were old, all-knowing and wise. It felt like I was staring at the beginning of time, where wisdom was first born and all understanding stemmed from.

Finding my voice, I asked, "Who are you?"

Mirror-Me slightly smiled. "I am you. But I am not all of you."

Resisting the urge to roll my eyes, I said, "That doesn't make sense."

"There are many things that you will not be able to fully understand. That is why you will always question what exactly is front of you."

"But what do I call you?"

Mirror-Me looked at me for a moment. "You may call me Mika."

I was surprised at the simple name. "Okay, Mika. Now can we get to the real reason why I am here? I've heard you speak to me before; several times now. Are you my Havadar?"

A serene look fell over Mika's face. "Yes and no. Right now, I am simply your guide to your purpose, a gateway to your Vis.

You were chosen to be the Balancer, a power that would awaken when the Living Realm would fall into great peril."

All types of alarms went off in my head. "What do you mean 'would fall'?"

Mika shook her head. "That cannot be revealed to you yet. You will learn about it in time."

"I don't understand. Why did you choose me? I am not anything special!"

Mika approached me and placed a hand on my shoulder. "Why are any of us here? This is what you were created for, your purpose. The sooner you come to accept this, the easier it will be for you." Mika then grazed her hand down my cheek. "I am a part of you, don't forget. I know all that goes through you. But I can only go as far as you want me to. All the tools have been provided to you. It is up to you to begin the work and up to you to finish it."

I simply stared at the calm mirror image of myself. "Mika, I don't know about this. This is more than I bargained for. All I ever wanted was to be normal. This isn't normal."

Mika simply smiled. "Normal is really in the eye of the beholder. Your normal isn't everyone else's. It will all come to you. Eventually. As for your Havadar, it is not here. For your protection, it was made separate from you. You will need to go back home to find it. Additionally, you need to make a choice about your family."

"What do you mean?"

"Before you came here to Ager, the Wanters had been surveying you, trying to understand what you are. Needless to say, they are not happy that the Kyrios have you. It is more than likely that they are awaiting your return to the Live Realm. They could be using your mother as bait to make you yield to them."

"You mean absorb me," I said, fighting back the panic.

She nodded. "You yielding to them could put the Live Realm in jeopardy. But you could possibly free your mother from harm. You have not completed your training, so perfect Vis usage may not be a possibility for you, even with me guiding you. If it comes to this, what will you do?"

My face twisted in confusion. "What is there to choose? I'm going back for Mom."

"Even though your presence could put millions of souls at stake? What of the men, women, and children you are meant to protect and to save? Is it fair to subject them to harm for one person?" She looked at me, still calm, but I could feel her probing.

"I…" I stopped, realizing she had a point. Could I really put everyone in harm's way for one person? My mother? My thoughts raced beyond comprehension at the decision in front of me. I looked up at Mika, searching her wise eyes for some answer, some indication of what I should do. "Can't I save both? Can't I keep people and my mother safe?"

She returned my gaze, looking sympathetic. "Are you really asking me? Or do you just want me to endorse the decision you have already made?" She suddenly looked up to the sky. The mist began to clear, allowing me to see that the landscape was slowly disappearing around us. "I believe that your mate is getting anxious about you. It is time I send you back. And Katya? Remember, everything that happens, happens for a reason."

Just as I was about to ask her what the heck she was talking about, Mika suddenly sent a palm thrust to my chest, sending me to the ground. I bolted up from the ground, gasping for breath when I realized that I was back in my room in Ager.

Gregor was kneeling over me, looking at me with great concern. "Are you all right?"

I coughed, trying to fill up my lungs. "What happened?"

"When we were at the door, you went into your deep breathing, and then you suddenly collapsed. I thought that the stress of being in the soulscape was too much for you so I brought you back to your body. When you still didn't respond, I was about to start some emergency measures when you came back up."

I wiped my brow, now dripping with sweat. "Man, that was intense."

Gregor lifted my face and searched my eyes. "Where did you go?"

"I spoke to my soul? She never really said what she was except that she was my guide and gateway to my Vis."

"What did she say?"

"She was as clear as the rest of you. Spoke in riddles and said don't fight it."

The Kyrios chuckled and tucked a strand of hair behind my ear. "Sounds like she knows what she is talking about."

"Says the king of confusion and mixed signals," I joked softly. But my barb only reminded him of his proximity and he quickly rectified it.

"Well," he said, clearing his throat, "I'm glad that you made contact. Now we can move forward in your training."

I shook my head. "Not yet. She said my Havadar isn't inside of me. For my protection or something. She also said that my mom might be in danger."

His eyes widened in surprise. "Wait, what? Not inside of you? Did she say why she's in danger?"

"All she said was the Wanters might be using her as bait. How many days have passed since we've been here?"

The Scot rubbed his chin for a moment before saying, "Hmm, it's been about twenty-hours here so three days have passed in the Live Realm."

"Mom might be back home at this point. And she's probably freaking out about my email to her."

Gregor grunted, "What did you tell her?"

"Because she couldn't come home in time, I was going to go on vacation without her to Scotland and that I found a Scottish guy to hang out with," I looked at him purposefully so he could not misunderstand who that male companion was intended to be.

He chuckled in disbelief. "If you were my daughter, I don't think I'd take that news very well."

"I know that!" I said flippantly. "I need her to be angry with me rather than freaking out about my safety. Now that I really think about it, she's my mom. She's gonna freak out regardless." I took a deep breath, knowing my mom had a whupping with my name on it at home. "Gregor," I started, "I know the stakes, especially with my energy going nuts at times. But I need to go home to see whether my mom is safe. Can we do something to make sure that we can keep everyone safe? Without sacrificing anyone?"

The Scot shook his head. "Katya, I understand, but I'm sorry. I can't authorize your leaving."

"I know you can't. But the Generals can. Can we speak to them? Besides, you guys want me to get my Havadar, and apparently it's back in the Live Realm. Leaving it there could also be a problem." I got up from the from the floor and offered a hand to Gregor to join me. "I know what's stake here, Gregor. If we figure out a plan together, no one has to get hurt."

Our eyes locked on each other and a battle of wills ensued. For several minutes, we said nothing, sizing each other up, searching for the other's commitment to the overall mission. Finally, Gregor blinked, grabbed my hand, and stood up. "Okay, Katya. I think I know of a way to appease both sides."

Hope flared inside of me and I couldn't keep the upbeat tone out of my voice. "What's your idea?"

He grimaced, "Let me think it through first before I tell you. The rest of the afternoon is yours to rest. I will escort you to dinner later. It just so happens that the Generals have requested your company tonight." And then he was out the door.

24

I woke up with a start later on that afternoon, realizing I'd fallen asleep—on my bed this time—from exhaustion. Slightly dazed, I trudged out of bed to answer the knock that had awakened me. Gregor stood on the other side, still aloof as ever. "Lady Katya, I am here to take you to Central Tower." He looked me over and said, "Do you want a minute to freshen up?"

I looked down to find that my bodysuit had unzipped in the front, showing quite a bit of revealed skin. I quickly adjusted it and stepped out of the doorway. "I'll be out in a minute." I quickly closed the door, finger combed my hair, and adjusted it back into a firm ponytail.

I stepped out of my room to find Gregor already walking down the hallway. "Let's go to dinner, shall we?" I hustled to reach him and finally caught up at the base of the tower. We walked in silence to Central Tower, though I did risk a couple of glances Gregor's way. If he saw them, he never acknowledged them.

"Are you going to tell me what the plan is?" I asked softly as we walked through the courtyard.

His jaw clenched. "I'm going to ask them to put you in a soulbind."

I stopped short. "A soulbind? What the heck is that? And why do you look so tense?"

Gregor stopped as well, still trying to avoid my gaze. "It's the only solution that can work. I'm sure the Generals, if they allow you to do this, will come to the same conclusion."

I slowly moved closer to the Scot, lightly touching his arm. "Can you please look at me and explain what it is and why you look so tense?" Gregor cleared his throat before turning towards me. Even as the sky darkened, his eyes shone brightly with worry and trepidation. "A soulbind is essentially a Kyrios prison. If a Kyrios changes sides or becomes a liability, a soulbind is the soul's version of handcuffs. It's normally meant for those who have lost all control and who have begun to change into the Want."

I could feel my brows arch high into my hairline. "Kyrios can change into the Want?"

"Any spiritual creature can." Gregor's eyes bore into mine, quietly conveying something to me. "Becoming a Want creature is simply a matter of choice, of where your loyalties lie. To change your loyalties from peaceful interaction to absolute destruction is not tolerated, especially by those who have pledged themselves to the fight. The Vis bind can be a horrible device used to cause immense pain. After several hours, the soul can only take so much."

Horror-struck, I demanded, "And you want to put that on me?"

"No!" Gregor shook his head. "I hate that I've even come to this conclusion at all. But I know how the Generals think. Their concern is not your mother but the entire Live Realm. They need to protect all humans from not just the Want, but from you too." Gregor inched closer to me, looking desperate. "I know said it's painful, but there are several levels to a Vis bind and it won't be as nearly destructive as it could be if you were a Wanter. At most, you would feel pressure inside of you. Not crippling pressure, but you will feel it. But anything longer than three hours could be damaging."

His jaw clenched and I could feel the anxiety rolling off of him. "Katya, I am concerned about this. I have a feeling that something could go wrong and since I have...taken you under my protection, I am advising you not to do this. I can send someone else to collect your mother and put her in a safe place under our protection. You don't have to go personally. We will figure out something, but we need to keep you safe."

I wanted to cry. It was the most emotion I had seen from Gregor since we met. I also understood why there were measures in place to remove any distractions. Here was the proud Scot, filled with anxiety because of me. Because he was worried about me. What would they do to him if they found out our...relationship? Would they put this soulbind on him? I steeled myself for what I was about to say and hoped that he wouldn't take it to heart too much.

"Gregor," I said, steeping back from him. "If the soulbind is the recommended step, then that's what we'll do. You will just do your job to ensure that I'm kept safe. You should only concern yourself about my security. Anything else is unnecessary." I walked away from him, keeping my gaze towards the tower so I could now avoid his reaction. No further words were exchanged, and the only contact he made with me was when he dutifully gathered me in his arms and jumped to the top floor where the Generals were waiting for our arrival.

We found the Generals in a room across from the conference room we had visited before. This round room appeared similar, except for the round table and the one table setting where I assumed I would be sitting. *Looks like I am eating by myself.* The Generals stood from the chairs and gave me slight nods.

"Lady Katya, so glad you could join us," Nabil called out with an easy smile on his face. The others murmured similar greetings, although Raf's smile was a bit more genuine. I answered with a small smile and took my place at the table setting.

Once the Generals took their place, I noticed that Gregor still stood by the doorway. He stood rigid at the door, as if waiting for a command. When Nabil noticed where my attention was directed, he called out, "Gregor, my boy, please sit down. You are welcomed at this table as well. This is to be an informal meeting."

Gregor curtly nodded and sat at the opposite side of me. I felt the Generals watching me as I watched Gregor get settled. They were apparently waiting for me to say something, so I didn't disappoint. "What is the occasion for this meeting?"

Nabil glanced at Ref and began, "My lady, we just wanted to touch base with you. He nodded towards Raf. "Raf reported that you did well today in training. But we are a bit concerned about your session with Gregor today. Not to have your Havadar inside of you is quite alarming. It means that your training will be much harder from this point on. We wanted to stress that your continued cooperation is necessary. We simply want you to succeed. The fate of the entire Live Realm is resting on your shoulders." He looked at me with hooded eyes, but I could feel something underneath his statement. Something not particularly sincere.

I cleared my throat, wishing to clear my head at the same time. "Actually, there is something I want to say."

Michiko, sitting two chairs away from me, looked at me kindly. "Speak, child."

I nervously looked at the other Generals and made eye contact with Gregor, who conveyed nothing in return. I sat back in the chair, hoping that I expressed confidence in my relaxed pose. "I will be making a short trip back to the Live Realm to collect my mother and to determine where my Havadar is. I will be gone several hours to collect my mother and place her out of harm's way. My internal guide advised me that I would find my Havadar once I returned."

Nabil rose from his seat, the anger coming off in waves. "Have we not made it clear," he said softly, "that is unsafe for you to return until you have mastered your power? So that you will not put others in danger?" The room suddenly became stifling. His anger became more than just a feeling, but a physical force that pressed against me. A quick look around the room told me that the other Generals felt it too, but they didn't nearly feel as oppressed as I did.

I could the control on my temper slipping. My Vis spread all throughout my body, strengthening me with self-righteous anger that wasn't all me but a bit of Mika as well. I rose from the table as well, matching his soft tone. "And have I not made it clear that I must return? I did not come here for permission; I came here to discuss my plans. I am going to collect my mother and my Havadar. I am the Balancer, and I must do what must be done. I do not take this lightly and have taken those lives into consideration when making my decision. Please refrain from throwing your energy at me." My voice took on a more unearthly tone and my body vibrated with anger and a blue light shone around my body.

I sensed the Generals and Gregor's shock, but my sights were set on Nabil and his oppressive power. "Stand down, General Nabil. This is no way to conduct a meeting amongst equals." I could feel the raw authority coming from my throat.

Nabil's eyes narrowed for a second, as if assessing the situation. He lowered himself down in his seat, his eyes never leaving mine. Once he was fully in his chair, I could feel the power receding within me, leaving me slightly drained. I held on to the table to keep my balance as I sat back down. "Now General, like I said, I understand your concern. But we have a solution that should make you happy. Gregor?"

"If I may, General Nabil?"

Nabil finally broke eye contact with me and nodded.

"I've spoken to Lady Katya, and she agrees to a soulbind for the duration of her Live Realm visit. I believe three hours should be sufficient."

Raf looked at Gregor sharply. "Is this really necessary? I'm sure Lady Katya should be able to handle the visit. What of the dangers to her?"
Gregor nodded. "I understand. However, if only done for a limited amount of time, it would allow Lady Katya to find the missing piece of her Havadar and to place her mother out of harm's way."

Lamar spoke up. "Nabil, there is a security threat concerning her Havadar. The Havadar is essentially an extension of herself, her Vis. We don't know what form this has taken or where it could be, for that matter. If her Vis guide says that it is in the Live Realm with her family being the key, it is imperative that we collect it. Imagine the strength the Want could display if they somehow get a hold of and absorb the entity holding the Havadar."

I frowned. "I thought a Havadar couldn't be wielded by anyone else."

The Security General spoke gently. "Yes, if it maintains contact with you and resides in you, that is true. We don't know the effect of having it outside of you will do. Theoretically, without you controlling it, the Havadar may have formed its own personality, state of mind, etc. It could be converted into a Wanter."

I bit my lip. "I don't like the idea of someone using a piece of me against me."

"None of us do, Lady Katya," Raf said gruffly. "Nabil, we need to get it before they do. If Gregor is escorting Lady Katya, I don't think it will be a problem. Besides, I think she can protect herself." He grinned, looking at me.

Victor simply nodded his consent. Michiko eyed me closely before saying, "I don't see much harm in her returning for a few hours. Let her go. We have more to lose if she stays."

Lamar crossed his arms across his chest, looking down at his forearm. "As long as Lady Katya understands the dangers she will face with the Vis bind and accepts it, I agree to let her go."

I nodded. "I have already spoken to Gregor at length and I agree this is may be the only way to save everyone."

Nabil looked as if he wanted to say something else, but held his tongue. "Looks like the majority rules on this matter. You shall leave at first light in the morning. You have three hours to return or suffer the consequences." He stood abruptly from his chair. "Excuse my rudeness, but there are preparations for this departure I must see to." He nodded towards my plate setting. "Sophia shall bring you your dinner now. This meeting is adjourned."

Without another word, he was gone.

As if sensing my uneasiness at Nabil's departure, Raf grunted, "Don't worry about him. He's used to getting his way since he's been here the longest." He grinned. "Now only if you could wield your Vis like that all the time, I'd be a happy soul."

I grinned as well. "Well, piss me off enough and I just might."

The rest of the Generals laughed heartily and the tension was lifted. As the laughter died down, Victor rose from his seat, "My Lady," he purred, "I am sorry that you have still not eaten. Your dinner should have already arrived. Sophia!"

Footsteps could be heard from outside in the main room and they softly made their way inside. A tall blond with pale skin entered, holding several plates in one hand and a pitcher in the other. I studied her a bit, feeling that I had seen her before.

Victor remained standing before the table. "My lady, this is Sophia. She works with myself and General Lamar as a floater. She will be serving you tonight." He then quickly spoke some rapid French that sent the blonde quickly to me. On closer inspection, I realized that this was the same laughing woman I had seen Gregor with, earlier in the courtyard. I quickly looked away, not wanting to catch her eye.

"Generals, will you join me? I understand you don't need food, but I'm told you can enjoy it," I asked brightly.

The Generals all shook their heads no. Lamar also stood, "We simply stayed to ensure that you had settled with your dinner.

We shall leave you in Gregor's capable hands." Lamar looked to Gregor. "I shall meet you at the gate in the morning, Gregor. I want to ensure that all goes well."

Gregor stood from his chair and gave his salute. "I shall see you in the morning, sir."

With that, the Generals stood and made their way out, murmuring their goodbyes and goodnights. I nodded and smiled at each, appreciating their support.

As I turned my attention back to my food, Sophia bent over slightly to pour water into my cup. Feeling completely uneasy, I turned to her, giving her a winning smile. Her gray eyes reflected complete hatred. Taken aback, I returned my attention back to my plate and fiddled with my utensils.

Sophia straightened and turned to Gregor, "Is there anything else I can do for you, sir?"

Gregor looked at me and then back to Sophia, "No, Sophia. You are dismissed."

Sophia bowed and left the room. I could still feel her heated stare at my back. *What was that about?* Finally feeling hungry, I tucked into the food set before me. I could feel Gregor's gaze on me as I ate.

Unable to stand it, I finally said, "I hope you understand my point earlier."

The Scot said nothing, simply sat back in his chair. "Clearly."

His one word answer pained me as much as our earlier exchange. But I knew I had to stay stronger, no matter how much I wanted to hug him and caress the worry lines out of his forehead. I quietly ate my food, and as I took my last bite, I sighed and said, "Tomorrow is a big day. I guess I should head back and rest, huh?" I stood up from the table and started to walk towards door, noticing that I was alone. Gregor was still at the table, looking pensively down.

"Gregor? Are you coming?"

Gregor's eyes snapped up and was doubly surprised to find my concerned gaze directed at him. His eyes warmed and he stood up slowly. "My lady, wherever you may go, Live Realm or Ager, or anything else in between, I will always be coming."

25

Gregor escorted me quietly back to my room. Though nothing was said, I could already feel his walls were back up. *It's for the best, Katya. It's for the best.*

Outside my door, the Scot finally said, "Your training will have a slight adjustment tomorrow, presumably to accommodate the successful location of your Havadar. You will not train with General Raf in the morning, but in the evening. We will resume our training session the next day."

I nodded and reached for my doorknob when I stopped and said, "Gregor, I probably should say this more often, but I really do appreciate all that you do. I know I'm not easy to deal with but," I made eye contact with him, "it does make this whole thing a lot easier to deal with when you're around."

For several moments, the Scot stared at me. He opened his mouth to say something but shut it abruptly. "I'll see you in the morning, my lady." With a curt nod, he was gone.

Still feeling the fatigue from the adventure in my soulscape, I plopped down on my bed of pillows and stared at the ceiling above me. The last coherent thought I had was whether it was possible to get the drop on a Kyrios for pissing you off royally.

I'm suddenly in a city. Smack dab in the middle of the street, within what looked like a financial district. Towering buildings with imposing windows stretch as far as the eye can see. But instead of maple trees, the streets are lined with palm trees. Is this Florida or California? *I wonder.*

My eyes dart side to side, looking for some action. I run down the street, looking for someone, a cart vendor, a businessman on his phone, a cabbie searching for fares. Nothing, not a soul. In a blind panic, I suddenly dart to the corner. But I stop short. I finally find someone, about fifty yards before me.

She's a Kyrios—a tall blond with immensely cold eyes. Sophia. She stares me down, considers me carefully, and then smirks. She saunters towards me with a carefree ease. I, on the other hand, feel like lead, unable to move an inch. She extends her right hand and materializes a long thin blade and hilt, both black as her bodysuit. Her Havadar. The freezing glint and the murderous intent in her eye tells me everything I need to know. I look frantically around for someone, anyone, to stop this mad woman.

Gregor finally appears, walking from another intersection towards us. Sophia must sense his presence because she stops and looks at him expectantly. I try to speak, but my mouth won't move. I pray that my eyes convey the sense of panic and gratitude I feel now that he is here to save me.

Yet the closer he gets, the more I can see the unforgiving line in his jaw, the cold nature of his eyes. Eyes that glitter dangerously red. Eyes of the Want.

Bewildered, I open my mouth to say something, but fall mute once again. Gregor doesn't break my stare until he is shoulder to shoulder with Sophia. He grabs her by the hair and roughly pulls her to his lips for a punishing but passionate kiss.

My heart races to the pit of my stomach and sends my knees crashing to the ground. As the two Kyrios release each other, Sophia turns gleefully in my direction, her eyes now glittering red. Within seconds, she's launched herself into the air with her Havadar above her head, intending to send my head in the opposite direction from the rest of my body.

I awoke from my dream with a scream that would've shaken the dead. Sweat poured from my brow and heavy steps were heard outside my door. To my surprise and relief Young Jae burst through the door.

"Ms. Katya! Are you all right?" He sat down at the edge of my bed with concern in his eyes. Jae looked me over anxiously as I caught my breath. All of the shock, anger, and exhaustion hit me in the gut, and tears began to stream down my face.

"Oh, my lady," Jae crooned. "What has upset you so?"

I shook my head, gulping for air, grasping at the blanket covering me. "I'm just emotional because the weight of the world is on my shoulder and I am just trying to be strong. I... Don't you wish you had complete control of your life? That you could be living how you want and not how the universe planned?" I whispered brokenly.

For several minutes, only my hiccups and sobbing could be heard. Jae inched closer to me and said softly, "May I speak frankly, Miss Katya?" I raised my eyes to find him staring at me intently.

"I would prefer it."

The young lieutenant studied my face, gauging my emotional state before he out a breath. "When I was a kid in South Korea, I was groomed to take over my father's business. Every day, I was reminded by my father that I was next in line and that I needed to make him proud. But all I wanted to do was hang out in the fields behind our house and stare up at clouds and write stories. And whenever I got caught goofing off and got punished, I swore to myself that I would find a way to get to my own happiness, my own life. Not the life my father set out for me."

"Did you?" I asked softly.

Jae gave me a sad smile. "No, I never had a chance to. But sometimes I think about what it would have been like if I had focused on being the best version of my father's dream? Maybe something in between—completing what was expected of me but still able to do it in my own way? I believe that you are in the same place, Ms. Katya. Find a middle ground that makes you happy but still fulfills your purpose. Follow your instincts. Or your dreams."

I raised my eyes to find his eyes glittered mysteriously.

He continued. "They will not steer you wrong." He laid his hand on mine, his eyes never leaving my own. His hand closed around me, instantly filling me with warmth along with slight trepidation.

"Thank you, Jae." I gave him a slight squeeze, but quickly released it. The young Kyrios continued to look at me earnestly. "Ms. Katya, I think what you lack is someone looking out for you. A friend."

A friend? I thought Kyrios shouldn't have human friends. I gave Young Jae a crooked smile. "You are right. But I don't think Nabil will be offering friendship anytime soon."

Jae chuckled, giving me a rueful smile. "No, Nabil is not one to make any friends. Enemies, yes. Friends, no." He leaned even closer and said softly, "If at any time you need any help or have any questions, don't hesitate. Just simply come to me and ask."

"I think I might take you up on your offer."

The Kyrios beamed and I was again taken by how attractive I found him. He rose from my bed and gave me a sweeping bow. "To think I should serve such a beautiful lady. My afterlife is finally complete."

I rolled my eyes but laughed softly. His words reminded me of an earlier conversation we had. "Jae, I do actually have a question."

"Of course. What is it?"

I suddenly felt a bit odd asking—felt like a personal question. But my curiosity won. "How does a person become a Kyrios?"

Jae stiffened and suddenly looked uneasy. "The formation of a Kyrios is not an easy explanation. The beginning is different for everyone, but in the end, it's all the same. The epitome of internal warfare."

Before I could ask him to elaborate, the door suddenly burst open and Gregor charged in with his eyes blazing. "Lieutenant Young Jae, what are you doing in her chambers?"

Jae instantly stood to attention and said promptly, "Sir, while I took over your watch, the Lady was experiencing a nightmare and was giving off copious amounts of energy. I came to investigate and to ensure the Lady's safety."

Gregor glanced me over, checking Jae's story out. With the nightmare I'd just had, and remembering our necessary distance, I avoided making eye contact and instead busied myself with the blanket covering me. His relentless stare just made me feel more uncomfortable.

Finally, Gregor's attention returned to Jae. "Very well. You are dismissed, Lieutenant."

Young Jae nodded. He then turned to me and gave a curt bow. Right before he returned to his full height, he gave me a slight wink and walked out the door.

Gregor remained at the entrance, his brow furrowed. "Are you all right?" he asked softly.

I smoothed my hair down and fluffed my pillow. "Yes, I'm fine," I said curtly.

"Do you want to talk about it?" he asked slowly. The soft husk of his voice made me want to melt into his arms and continue to cry, but Jae's words about the middle ground helped me stand firm.

"Thank you, Gregor. But it's probably best that I go back to sleep. We can talk later, soldier."

He nodded, and as he made to leave, I softly said, "I wouldn't mind someone keeping me company while I fell asleep, though."

Wordlessly, the Scot grabbed the stool nearby the window, set it by the door, and watched on as I eased back to sleep.

26

The next morning, a soft rapping on the door awoke me from my uneasy sleep.

"My lady, we are scheduled to leave within an hour for the Live Realm." Gregor's soft brogue carried through the closed door. "Are you awake?"

"Yes," I said groggily. "Give me a couple of minutes. I'll be out in a little bit." The ensuing silence was my answer. I dragged myself out of bed and made for the basin and the mirror. A quick glance in the mirror showed a beat-up face lacking sleep. After a couple of splashes of water, I felt a bit more awake. Not completely awake, just more awake.

I took off my jumpsuit and got dressed in my original clothes. When I was satisfied with my outward appearance, I opened the door to find Gregor standing there without protest, waiting for me. The image of him, handsome but dutiful, started my own internal dialogue.

Is Jae right? Should I pay attention to that dream? Could Gregor betray me?

That can't be right. He did kiss me.

He was just caught up in being human. You know that, Katya.

But he's been looking out for me too. To his own possible detriment. Why risk putting me in a soulbind if he was going to betray me?

As my internal battle ensued, I was staring at Gregor with utmost intensity. When it went on longer than necessary, the Kyrios cleared his throat. "Lady Katya? Are we ready to go?"

Snapped back to reality, I cleared my throat, hiding my embarrassment. "Yes. Sorry." I quickly made for the stairs, not waiting for him to answer. He caught up with me easily and in silence we made our way to the main gate.

"Are you sure you are all right?"

"Of course," I said with false cheerfulness. "Let's hurry. Wouldn't want to keep General Lamar waiting now!" Sure enough, General Lamar was waiting for us at the gate. The General nodded in our direction, while Gregor gave him a salute.

"Good. You're here. Let's get down to business." He looked me over carefully and then continued. "The Vis bind, as explained, will in a sense be imprisoning you. Think of it as a cage, trapping your energy. You have three hours before the Vis bind begins to affect you more severely." He stepped closer to the both of us. "I cannot stress the risk that you are facing. There is no telling how your soul will react to this. Gregor, any sign that the Vis bind is at its limit, you will need to bring her back immediately to me so that I can remove it. My lady, I give you one command. You must stay calm. While your control is getting better, your Vis is still linked to your emotions, your adrenaline. Any bump to your

Vis could bring thousands of Wanters searching for that power, devouring and destroying anything in their path."

Fear and trepidation must have shown on my face, because Lamar gave me a slight smile. "Don't worry. The entire Kyrios force is here to protect you. Besides," he shot a knowing look to Gregor, "I know Gregor would give his life force to protect you. Isn't that right?"

Gregor's facial expression betrayed nothing, but his eyes widened slightly. "Of course, sir."

Lamar's smile grew. "Good. Let us begin then." He closed his eyes and pressed his palms together, sending huge amounts of power to his hands. Soon a bright yellow light streamed through his fingers, giving his dark face an eerie glow. He then separated his hands, stretching the yellow light until it formed a sphere in his right hand. Then, without warning, he thrust the sphere into my center, leaving me gasping for air. The elephant feeling returned again, but this time I felt completely numb. I could still feel physical sensations: the coldness of the ground, the warmth of Gregor's hand as he helped me back up. But I felt numb. Like I was in shock from the serious loss of someone special. Not being able to feel Mika within me felt like no other loss I had ever experienced.

"The bind holds. You have three hours. Good luck, my lady." Lamar gave a quick nod and left for Central Tower. Still feeling a bit shaken, Gregor led me through the gate and to the portal point.

Gregor studied me as we walked further away from the main gate. "How do you feel?"

"Like I lost my best friend," I said quietly. "I don't like this, Gregor."

The Scot grimaced and walked a bit more quickly. "Then let's get this done quickly so your best friend can be returned to you."

With a quick snap of his fingers, the blue portal opened. Five seconds later, we were standing outside, a block down from my house, in an alley behind a bodega. The air felt different. Perhaps it was because I had been in a different realm, but the air itself felt like it was lacking Vis. The air wasn't the only thing different. My neighborhood was riddled with cracks in the pavement. Some homes looked lopsided, with foundations crumbling. In the distance, I could hear a myriad of sirens addressing people who must have been causing mischief due to the uncertainty. *The Wanters have been very busy.* I shook my head free. My mother first.

I asked, "Why didn't we appear inside of the house?"

"I checked it before I opened the portal on this side. There were a handful of souls throughout the entire house."

Feeling a sense of dread, I bolted down the street and toward the house. Yellow police tape greeted me, covering the door. A small crowd of the neighbors parked themselves on the lawn, quietly murmuring to themselves. Just by the door, we saw three uniformed men walking around the foyer, brushing the walls, looking for prints.

I couldn't see Cynthia, but I could hear her bawling uncontrollably. "She never does this. I just know something bad has happened to her. I can feel it." A quick look at the driveway revealed my mother's car parked at an angle. As if she had pulled in quickly and bolted inside of the house.

"Um, Gregor, remind me how many days have passed?"

"As of now, four and half days."

I looked back at the Kyrios beside me, who looked equally concerned. We walked over the police tape, past the three occupied police officers, and into the house. We found Cynthia sitting beside my mother on the family room couch, saying something softly to her. My mother was hunched over with her head in her hands. Her dark hair looked frazzled, like it hadn't been combed in days. Both of them looked exhausted and bedraggled. My mother was still wearing her work suit, something she never keeps on once she gets home after a trip. I looked around, not knowing what to do or what to say.

Before I could ask Gregor for advice on what to do, I heard my mother say, "Katya?"

Every single head swiveled to the middle of the foyer. I could only squeak out, "Oh, hey Mom."

I quietly stepped forward as the police officers, Cynthia, and my mother stared at me. I cleared the ball of anxiety from my throat and tried to chuckle. "What's going on? Did someone die or something?"

"Did someone die?" my mother repeated hoarsely. "Did someone die?" Her voice rose in pitch. "Do you have any idea what you have put me through these four days? Where in the hell have you been?"

"I told you, Mom. Traveling with my friend here," I explained, attempting to sound nonchalant. If I started stuttering like an idiot, the whole story was going to be blown. I looked back to Gregor, who was as still as a statue.

My mother saw where my attention went and stood up from the couch. "Who the heck is this?"

Cynthia suddenly found her voice and screeched, "That's him. That's the guy she was last with!"

"Everyone calm down now," a voice said behind us. I swiveled around to find a blond man wearing a black bowler hat and suit. His dark gaze never left mine as he came from the upstairs, and it made my skin crawl. Something in the back of my mind told me that I had seen this man before.

But making sure my mother didn't commit murder—of me—was my first priority. The bowler hat man said, "My name is Detective Sloan, and I'm in charge of this investigation. Are you Katya Stevens?"

I gulped. "Yes, sir."

He crossed his arms and arched his eyebrows. "You have been gone for four days with this man?"

"Yes, that's true—"

"What's your relationship with this man?"

"He kidnapped her!" Cynthia yelled. "He made her write those emails to her mom and me because he kidnapped her."

I rolled my eyes and threw my arms up in frustration "Cyn, does that make any sense to you? I'm right here. I left on my own. And I came back on my own. Gregor is not my kidnapper."

"Okay then." My mother was suddenly behind me, with her eyes blazing with anger. "Answer my question. Who the heck is he?"

I stepped back closer to Gregor, looking over all people in the room. "I would tell you if you would just give me a minute," I said crossly, in hopes of trying to buy time, "I would gladly tell you who Gregor is."

What I hoped to be a dramatic pause only ended up ticking off my mother. "Get on with it, young lady!"

"Gregor is—"

A warm hand encased mine, and I found Gregor looking down at me with loving intensity. "What Katya is trying to say is that I am her husband."

27

The silence that fell over the room lasted an eternity. In actuality, it only lasted for about five seconds before my mother and Cynthia erupted in unison. "WHAT?"

I quickly schooled my features and tried to channel a blushing bride. "Yes, we got married in New Hampshire three days ago."

The room continued to erupt with my mother's angry shouts and Cynthia's shrill shrieks. All the while I kept my mouth shut, knowing that if I even tried to engage them in a conversation, I would explode. Literally. The bind on my Vis felt a bit snug. Gregor sensed my battle and gave me a squeeze. Detective Sloan had enough of the noise and whistled loudly with two fingers.

"Okay! Let's get to the bottom of this. Everyone in the living room now." Cynthia and my mother reluctantly shuffled into the next room, their eyes never leaving Gregor or me. They both sat in the armchairs, leaving Gregor and me with the couch.

As we sat down on the couch, Gregor gently raised our joined hands and kissed them. My heart began to pound painfully against my chest as his eyes warmed. Behind the sweet gesture, however, there was a silent message to me. *Take my lead.*

Detective Sloan stood the middle of the room. "Ms. Stevens, your mother and your friend called us two days ago, after you had been missing for several days. One note to each stating why you left, which was apparently out of character for you." He sat on the coffee table directly in front of me. I really didn't like the weird glint his eyes gave off. "After four whole days, you now show up with a husband? This is not even the guy your mother said you were dating." He pulled out a notebook and glanced at it. "Roger Simmons ring any bells?"

"Roger and I broke up over a week ago." I said quickly. "You can ask him that."

"We did, and he said the same thing. He also said that you were with an old friend from school. From an exchange program. Your mother said you never had any friends like that."

Gregor gave a small smile. "Detective Sloan, I'm that old friend. Before you continue to berate my wife with questions, I think it is best to begin at the beginning, don't you think?"

Detective Sloan didn't immediately look away from me. If anything, he seemed annoyed that his attention was called elsewhere. He gave Gregor a terse look. I think he wanted to tell Gregor to shove it, but said, "All right, start from the top."

"I have been in love with Katya since the first time I met her, ten years ago. She befriended me when no one else would. She was such a sweet girl and treated me so well that I never forgot about her when my family moved back to Scotland," Gregor said, so earnest I almost forgot none of it was true. "For many years, though, I thought of her often, and I never had the courage to tell her how I felt. So when my family moved back to the States,

I took the opportunity to tell her I loved her." Gregor turned to me, his eyes shining brightly. "I just never thought that she felt the same about me." He squeezed my hand gently to prompt me to say something.

"Yes," I said breathlessly. "I also had a soft spot for him since way back, but when he moved back to Scotland, I thought I would never see him again. Gregor coming back into my life was simply a miracle. And I just didn't want to let him go again." Right on cue, Gregor leaned in and gave me a soft kiss. Polite enough for public view, but it stoked fires in me and tugged on my bind.

Cynthia's eyes narrowed, and I could tell that she wasn't buying what we were saying.

I guess neither was my mother.

"I'm not going to even bring up the fact that you are only eighteen, in high school, and shouldn't have even thought about getting married," my mother said through her gritted teeth, "but why did you write that email?" She bust out of her chair, her anger still raging. "You leave home, leave me to go traveling with a man who I don't believe for a second you met at eight years old! Damn it! I want the truth! Where the hell have you been?" she screamed.

I could feel tears itching the corner of my eyes and a slight tugging at my core from the bind hitched my breath. I had hoped that no one noticed it, but Cynthia was watching me a bit too closely. "What's the matter, Kat?"

"Mrs. Stevens, I strongly urge you to take a deep breath and sit down," Gregor said quietly but authoritatively. My mother wasn't ready to release the daggers in her eyes and looked for some clink in the armor Gregor had erected to catch my eye.

But I refused to look up. The floor and my hands were much more captivating. Besides, I knew the moment I looked at her, she'd see right through me.

"Mrs. Stevens, please. While I understand you are upset, screaming does not help the situation, does it?" Gregor asked carefully, as one would when trying to talk down an enraged dog or a toddler. For several minutes, Mom remained silent and standing. Her lack of movement began to unnerve me, so I slowly picked my eyes off the floor to find that she was staring through me, rather than at me. A sudden chill danced on my back, but no one took notice of the involuntary action or the sudden shift in my mother's eyes.

"Mrs. Stevens?" Cynthia asked quietly. "Are you going to sit down?"

"Oh… Um, yes. Yes, I will." Mom quickly sat in her chair, as if standing had suddenly burned her. I quickly averted my eyes to Detective Sloan, who had been watching all of us. He suddenly seemed excited about something. He gave an eerie smile and caught me in his stare.

"I don't think you're necessary any longer, sir," I said, addressing him directly. "I think my mother's reaction is proof enough why I did what I did. And Cynthia," I rounded to face my best friend, "you've would've tried to convince me to stay or would've done something to make me forget about Gregor completely. You haven't kept it a secret that you don't like Gregor! Why would I have told you anything?"

Cynthia chewed on her bottom lip, looking somewhat contrite. "Kat, I act the way I do so I can protect you. And I guess I was right, then! Married?" She spit the word with venom. "This isn't right, nor was this planned for you!"

I smiled sadly, looking down at my hands, hoping I looked sorry. "I understand everyone is upset, but I love him, and I just wanted to make my own choices about this." I made a show of clutching Gregor's hand to my chest. "I just want to live my life with my husband."

Gregor's eyes softened, his free hand caressing my face. "I love you, too." His following kiss was purely perfunctory, but even the slight brush of our lips sent an intense stirring within me, tapping into a bed of desire. It also caused a slight twinge through my bonded energy. I hid my discomfort behind a smile, but Gregor wasn't fooled.

I turned back to Detective Sloan, who seemed disgusted with our open displays of affection. "Like I said, we no longer need your services. I'm of age and we eloped in New Hampshire. Nothing more to discuss. At least with you, anyway."

Detective Sloan gave me a funny look and then smirked. "Of course, I tried to explain that to your mother." He turned to my mother and said, "The missing person just didn't want to be found. Your daughter has disregarded any feelings she had for you and has tied herself this man." He paused. "Mr...?"

"MacGregor." Gregor growled.

"Gregor MacGregor?" He asked dubiously.

Gregor's chest puffed up slightly. "Aye. All of Scotland knows about us. The clan of the MacGregors is one not be trifled with." His brogue came in a bit stronger than normal.

Detective Sloan simply smirked and returned to address my mother, who oddly hadn't said a word. "Kids your age gets into all sorts of mischief. But they always return home. Always. Mrs. Stevens, I leave your daughter's fate in your hands. Do your motherly duty." My mother simply nodded. I didn't appreciate the way her eyes looked blank or the way that Detective Sloan was telling her to be a mother.

He actually commanded her to be a mother. What the hell was that about?

Gregor and I shared a look. The clock was ticking, and the detective need to go. The Kyrios rose from the couch and put out his hand for a handshake. "I'll walk you to the door, Detective." The two men left the room, leaving me with my very quiet mother and my flushed best friend.

I decided to try the flushed best friend first. "Cyn?" I asked carefully. "Say something."

The redhead pouted. "What can I say, Mrs. MacGregor? Apparently I can't be trusted."

I rubbed my temples, trying to keep calm. "Cyn, please. Let's not do this. I cannot lose my cool right now. I didn't come back for this. I came back to explain—"

"Explain why you left that sorry-assed email, right!" She screamed at me, tears streaming down her face. "I thought I lost my best friend! I have every right to lose my cool!"

"Listen, I finally have a chance to explain it to you both, but we can't do it here. We have to get my mom out and in a safe place. Cyn, just stop acting crazy for a second and listen!"

"I'm crazy? This whole thing is insane! Right, Mrs. Stevens?" Cynthia turned to Mom, who still sat unnervingly quiet in her chair. "Mrs. Stevens?"

Mom snapped out of her stupor—her eyes finally focused. "Yes,

Cynthia, it is insane." She rose from her seat and grabbed my arm. "Katya, can I talk to you in your room? Now?" The pressure at my elbow told me there wasn't much room for discussion. I nodded and we briskly made for my room. Gregor was nowhere to be found.

Mom closed the door, but she didn't immediately face me. With her back turned, she said, "Okay, where have you been really?"

My heart dropped to my toes. "What do you mean, Mom? We just went over—"

She whirled, her eyes widened in anger. "Stop it!" she hissed. "I raised you, Katya Elizabeth Stevens. I know all your tricks. Do you think I don't know when you are lying?"

"Mom," I pleaded, feeling the discomfort grow. "I need you to let this go. Please. There are more important things to discuss, but we can't do it here." Forget the discomfort. A full-blown headache was coming on.

"Tell me now, Katya," her voice dangerously low. "Where have you been? Who have you been with? What have they taught you?"

Been with? Taught me? Alarm bells going off, I said, "Mom, really. Can you just stop? We don't have time for this." Irritated, I turned away. But turning my back to her was one of the worst things I could have done. She grabbed me by my shoulders and turned me around, her fingernails digging into my skin. Her grip tightened enough to make me yelp out in pain. But it was her visibly calm face that freaked me out the most. "So you refuse to tell your own mother what you are up to?"

I shook my head, not trusting my voice. Her eyes studied my face, as if memorizing it. Then, almost like a cartoon, she broke into a large grin, her eyes glittering with hatred and mischief. "So be it then." My mother grabbed me by the neck and slammed me into the hardwood floor. Wood splinters flew everywhere as the force of her blow created a body-sized hole in the middle of my room.

I felt Mika slamming into the bind barriers, internally screaming to be freed to protect me. But the Vis bind held, causing me just as much pain internally as my mother on the outside. My mother's eyes glittered, taking on a familiar red look I had seen before. Like the creatures that had chased after me in downtown Boston. The same creatures that terrorized others all over the world.

"Mom," I managed to gasp. "S-s-stop it!" But her inhuman strength kept me in the crater, forcing me down, closing my breathing pipes.

"I'm afraid I can't do that, Balancer." Her voice changed from her normal tone to a high-pitched, cold laughter. The type of voice you imagined in your worst nightmare. "You have been tied with a Vis bind and sent into my grasp. I'd be a fool not to take a full advantage of this."

My survival instincts began to kick in, and I immediately started kicking and squirming, hoping that I could shake her off, but it just ended with me being in more pain and the she-devil sounding highly amused. "You are weak! The General was worried for nothing! I never thought I would have the honor of destroying the Balancer. My masters will be so pleased. To be rid of the threat to everything we've worked for!"

"Where's my mother?" I hissed, desperately gulping for air.

The she-devil's grin became even larger, cutting into my mother's cheeks and distorting her face completely. "She's right here, sweetie, don't you see her?" It raised my mother's hand, which was growing impossibly long nails, poised to strike me in the chest.

Tears pooled and streamed to the floor. I tried to kick my way out, but "my mother" managed to evade each one of my kicks or ignore them all together. The headache continued to build and Mika tried to rattle the bars holding her prisoner. With the edges of consciousness slipping, I clung to the last thought before my eyes completely shut.

"Gregor..." I whispered.

You know that pivotal moment where the damsel in distress just about loses hope that she'll get rescued, but then the dashing hero comes in at the nick of time? It actually happened. I was vaguely aware of my bedroom door being blasted away from its wooden post and of a distant scream that sounded like Cynthia. My savior stormed into the room, his eyes blazing blue.

I gripped at consciousness, forcing my eyes open, tears still streaming from the pain—both physical and spiritual. When our eyes connected, it only fanned the fire of his anger. "Release her, Poser," he demanded, his voice dangerously low. My mother sneered, but she didn't move her hand from my neck or drop her raised claws.

"I will do no such thing. I will have the glory of terminating the destroyer of our plans."

Unconsciousness was getting closer—my eyes could no longer stay open. Seconds later, an enormous spiritual pressure spread throughout the room and the Poser screamed and let go of my neck.

Coughing spasms took over, revitalizing my breath. Mika was

still pressing against the bind, rattling her cage. It made me feel even sicker. The screeching wouldn't stop, but Gregor didn't move. As a matter of fact, he stood unmoving with his hand raised, his eyes still a blinding blue, staring at the source of the screeching. Following his gaze, I found my mom pinned to the wall, slithering around, unable to move anything but her head.

"Gregor," I gasped. "Please don't hurt...my mom..."

The Scot glanced at me for a second, still unmoving. "Come out of the body, Poser."

My mother crackled. "Why would I do that? You wouldn't dare harm this body. To remain here means to remain safe." Whatever force pinning the Poser down must have increased because the screeching became louder.

"Gregor, stop!" I screamed.

"Shut up, Katya! Leave the body, Poser! If I need to destroy the body to be rid of you, I will do it. And you know what happens if you don't leave a dead body. I hope you are prepared to remain there forever."

My mother gave a loud growl, thinking over its options. No one moved. I fearfully looked between Gregor and my mother's pinned body. Would he really kill my mother? The Poser suddenly grinned widely, stretching my mother's face beyond what a human could do.

"You win, Kyrios." The Poser closed its eyes, and Mom's body started to convulse. I looked on in horror as I watch my remaining parent go through a series of violent seizures. And I had no idea what to do.

A small creature slowly emerged from her chest. It looked

similar to the Cravers that chased me downtown but it had a tail three times longer than its own body. It had wings just as long as its tail. Its beady eyes stared at me as it rose up, its red pupils peering into my Vis bind. It opened its mouth and a small green sphere shot out and through the window. Gregor cursed loudly and raised his free hand. Within seconds, a bright blue light emanated from the center of his palm. From the light, Gregor's Havadar emerged and he slashed the Poser in half. The Poser's cackling laugh and its body disintegrated into nothing.

28

I expelled the breath I forgot I was holding. My mom was still pinned to the wall by the invisible force, but her features returned to normal. She looked like she was sleeping.

"Is my mom okay?" I asked, my voice breaking.

Gregor released the hold and carried her to my bed. "She's unconscious, but other than that she's fine. She won't remember the attack."

"Katya! Katya, are you all right?" Cynthia cried out, crashing into the rubble that was my bedroom. She immediately cradled my face, staring into my eyes. "Are you okay?"

I nodded. "I'm fine." A complete lie. *This is not how I planned to explain my new role in life.* I looked at Gregor, searching for some answers, but his eyes never left Cynthia.

Satisfied, Cynthia's eyes narrowed on Gregor. With three steps, she stood in front of the Kyrios, gave him a once-over and then punched him straight in the face. Gregor's face snapped to the side and I could only stare.

Wait a second. Gregor is stronger than anyone. How did Cynthia do that?

Cynthia crossed her eyes and said coldly, "When I gave you my charge to protect, Kyrios, I expect it to be done thoroughly. How in the world did a Poser enter into this home?"

Gregor looked at her, puzzled. He massaged his chin and chuckled darkly. "You've got to be kidding me. Your energy is... I can't believe I missed it completely. Are you honestly blaming me? You've been here. Haven't *you* been a little lax in letting anyone enter the house?"

Cynthia's red hair seemed to crackle with energy as it swelled with her anger. "I had no idea where the two of you had gone! Not one word, not a thing! When her mother received her email, she immediately called me, demanding an explanation. There wasn't anything I could do! Mrs. Stevens, in her hysteria, allowed herself to be taken over by the Wanter that probably had been lurking around her for the past several weeks. You would know that if you had been keeping an eye out for the ones left behind!"

Gregor sent his Havadar back to its secret place. "Does anyone else know about you? How is this possible?"

Cynthia's bravado deflated a bit. "I'm not completely sure. It's only been a couple months since I've known, and I'm still piecing things together."

Gregor guffawed. "You've been on my case since I've got here, and she doesn't even know what you are!"

"Charges aren't supposed to know until they are ready! You know that!" Cynthia hissed.

"Um," I whispered. It was loud enough for the two fighters to turn toward me. "I know that this might be a little much to ask for," I said, with my voice rising, "but could someone kindly tell me what the HELL is going on?" I grimaced, massaging my throat. I turned to my best friend and hissed, "How the hell do you know what Gregor is? How are you talking about the Want and Posers?" I turned to the Scot. "And why are you shocked by her? Why should anyone know about her?"

Mika rattled her cage causing me to wince and gasp in pain.

Both Gregor and Cynthia turned to me in concern. "Katya," Gregor said, "you need to calm down."

I shot him a dirty look. "Maybe I'd calm down if I knew what secrets were being kept from me."

Cynthia bit her lip—a clear sign she was nervous. "Well, you see Kat, this is going to sound absolutely crazy, but you have to believe me." She sighed and took a hold of my shoulders. "I'm just going to come out and say it. Sweetie, I'm really your twin in a sense. I'm actually your Havadar."

My world shifted for the second time in three days. "You're my Havadar? Like the weapon that is supposed to be inside of me that I wield on call?"
She nodded.

"You realize how crazy that sounds, right? You are essentially telling me that you are a part of my soul. My own energy."

"It's as crazy as you being with Death and not telling me anything either," she half smirked. "Why do you think we've been together all our lives? Why we have been able to read each other so well?"

She was right. My earliest memory of Cynthia was when we were five years old. I was trying to explain to my parents the Wanters I saw on TV. They'd gotten very upset and had sent me outside to play.

I was crying on my front steps when this pretty redheaded girl from next door came up to me and asked, "Why are you crying?"

"No one believes me."

She sat beside me and smiled such a sweet smile, "I'll believe in you."

That day I looked into her eyes and felt that if at least one person believed in me, I'd be okay. Now I find out that the person I considered my sister, my twin, was really a piece of my soul.

"Look, I am sorry for not telling you about Gregor. If I was honest with myself, I thought you were going to abandon me because here is Kat again, talking about weird stuff. Plus, he put some weird spell on me that forced me to keep silent. But..." I exhaled. "You've been lying to me. All our lives, you've been lying to me," I said softly, refusing to look at her.

"No Kat, you don't understand—"

I stood from the floor, purposefully accepting Gregor's hand and refusing Cynthia's. "After all that I suffered with, the images and the creatures, I pretended, NO, tricked myself into believing people were right and I was wrong. You could've seen them the entire time. You could've backed me up!" My eyes watered at the thought that I could have brought my parents some peace if Cynthia had just spoken up.

Cynthia already had tears streaming down her face. "Please, Kat, you need to listen to me. I wanted to see what you could, but

I couldn't. I was being honest. I only started to see and feel things about a couple of months ago, on our eighteenth birthday. I was having strange dreams and—"

Mika's silent screams reverberated through my body and came out of my own mouth. The pain within my soul became so unbearable I wanted to die right there. My knees buckled underneath me and I grasped at Gregor's clothing to stand upright.

"Katya!" Gregor commanded. "What's wrong? Calm down!"

"The Vis bind," I screamed hoarsely, dropping to my knees, clutching at my throbbing neck. He passed his hand over the center of my chest, his eyes widening.

"The Vis bind is at its limit. I don't understand. It hasn't been three hours yet."

"You bound her Vis energy?" Cynthia shrieked. "Are you crazy? You are crushing her soul!"

"It was the only way to keep her and everyone here safe," Gregor shouted over my sobs. "Her powers could've brought the—"

A sudden shift was in the air. A wave of several different spiritual signatures shook the atmosphere, making their way towards us. The waves weren't pleasant feelings, but pure bloodlust.

"The Want are coming," Gregor whispered. I wanted to know how they knew we were there, but the Vis bind tightened again, causing me to writhe in pain and scream at the top of my lungs. Everything just hurt, and I would have preferred to pass out.

A Craver's scream could be heard in the distance, coming closer.

Gregor picked me up and shifted me so I could piggyback. "I've got to get her back to Ager. I can't remove the Vis bind myself."

Cynthia blocked the doorway. "No! You are not taking my charge again. I must be by her side."

"Cynthia, Havadar, whatever you are, you aren't doing her any favors. She needs the Vis bind removed or she is lost."

Cynthia finally released the tears she had been holding back. Her arms fell limply at her sides and her shoulders slumped over. "Fine. But you need to take me with you."

"Mom," I whispered, "what about my mom?"

"I'll call for backup," Gregor said quickly. "We need to leave the house now." Two quick taps on his phone and two female Kyrios appeared inside of the house.

"Major Gregor, a massive fleet of Wanters are on the move here. We must evacuate the Live Realm immediately before we are overrun."

Gregor shifted me on his back. "Collins, grab the human woman and take her the safe house in South America. Put as much distance between here as possible before those Wanters arrive. I'll be taking the Balancer and her companion back to Ager." Another chalkboard scream filled the air. "Go!" The taller of the female Kyrios gently but quickly put Mom on her back. She was still out cold, but breathing.

"Please take care of her," I whispered hoarsely.

Collins gave me a small smile. "We will do our best, Balancer." They were gone.

Gregor turned to Cynthia. "Outside now." We bolted out the front door to find people running as fast as they could away from the neighborhood. They continually looked behind them, screaming in fright and running even harder. I saw Amie and her mother shoving their way through to get out of the way of the terror behind them. People were running everywhere. Homes and belongings left behind.

I wanted to call attention to Gregor, tell him to save Amie and her mom and get them out of the way. But my vocal chords failed me and I couldn't utter a word.

The three of us turned around and found the oncoming storm behind everyone's terror. What looked to be a tornado blowing through the neighborhoods of Boston was actually large numbers of Wanters. There were Cravers, Wreckers, and others I didn't recognize. And they literally destroyed everything within sight. It was at the very moment that I saw them when the bracelet given to me by General Lamar gave another zap, causing Mika to nearly explode inside of me. The blast within me was so strong that Gregor and Cynthia were thrown ten feet away from me.

That grabbed the fleet's attention.

I weakly tried to get up, but I felt my energy ebbing away. I could hear Gregor screaming for me to move, but I couldn't comply. The Cravers were going to be the first to feast.

However, Cynthia ran in front of me, facing the Wanters coming head on.

"Finally, I get to protect you, like I'm supposed to." She looked over her shoulder and smiled. "I love you, Kat. Don't be afraid. I'll be there with you."

Her last words oddly felt like a goodbye. I could only moan in the heap that I'd become, wordlessly begging her not to leave, to not doing anything foolish, to come back. On some level, I think she understood my anguish; she nodded and returned her attention to the fleet. The first Cravers exploded through my house, destroying the second floor. Wood, rubble, and debris should have covered us, but Cynthia stopped it.

How she did it, I wasn't sure. But I could only remember that my best friend glowed with power before me. I vaguely remembered Gregor grabbing me and hoisting me over his shoulder. I remembered chalkboard screams and more rubble crashing about as we vaulted into an open portal. Gregor ran through the gates over Ager, shouting commands and calling for General Lamar.

I had only made it to the courtyard when I was laid on the ground. I heard running steps coming towards us. As someone yelled for supplies, I took a hold of Gregor's hand and pointing to my convulsing wrist to show him the cause of my new pain. He took one look at the bracelet and wrenched it off with ease. Lamar's concerned face loomed over me, telling me to hold on. Nabil was beside him, standing over me, looking thoroughly displeased.

With the bit of energy I had left, I gave them both what I hoped was a smile and said softly, "Told you I'd be fine. Piece of cake."

29

"Kat. Katya, time to get up." I slowly opened my eyes to feel a familiar marble stone floor and sense of weightlessness. I sat up and looked around. I was back in the toga. I was in my soulscape.

"How did I get here?" I whispered.

"I brought you here," Cynthia said from behind me. Her hair had grown past her waist and she wore a toga similar to my own. There was a shimmer around her body that added to her ephemeral beauty. But what really struck me was how it felt right for her to be there. Like something I never knew was missing had been returned to me.

"It's really true, then," I said softly. "You are my Havadar."

She smirked at me. "Well, yeah! There is no way I could have made up something like that. Besides, who else could deal with you but yourself?"

I rolled my eyes. "Figures. I've been best friends with myself. I'm a pure narcissist."

Cynthia giggled. "There are worse things in the world to be. You could be Andrea Pana. That's a nightmare you never want to have." We both laughed, but we sobered up quickly at the thought of what everyone back in the Live Realm was going through. I wondered whether Amie and her mother made it to safety. Hell, I even worried over Roger.

Cyn closed the gap between us and squatted down to my eye level. "Kat, first please know that I love you very much. I only started to find out who I was only about a few months ago. I started to have dreams where Mika—"

"You've met Mika?"

She nodded. "She said that everything is not what is it appears to be. That things would start to change soon and that I would have to make a choice. To either begin a new life away from everything or to help you. Without a second thought, I picked you. Mika then said she knew that I would choose you. Then I started to have flashes of you even when we were apart. Like I knew when you were stressed or upset. And I couldn't say anything because I knew you would've never believed me. I know you wanted to keep that stuff from when we were kids in the past. I didn't want to drive you away."

"We really are the same. I didn't tell you about Gregor because I was afraid to drive you away. How long did you know about him?"

She bit her lip. "That day we all hung out at your house. Mika told me about the Kyrios and how they have a distinct energy about them. I'd never had a chance to be close to him until that day. I knew something was going on, but you said there was nothing to talk about." Her eyes saddened, remembering. "You didn't realize it at the time but you leaving without me was weakening our bond as wielder and Havadar. You have no idea how lost I felt without you."

I studied my hands, not sure how to respond. "Your parents?" I asked softly.

Cyn sighed and sat beside me, drawing in her knees. "My parents had a child—a baby girl who went through a hard delivery. Her lungs weren't completely formed, and for two minutes, her heart stopped."

At my horrified look, Cynthia shook her head. "It was her time. Her life was only a few moments long, but she felt the love of her parents. That's all a soul needs to feel complete—love. But my parents would've been devastated and lost since they'd tried so long to have a child. So the family that was to move next door to you was given a child. My parents were blessed and I was blessed to have them."

"I still don't understand how you could be me, but in another body."

"Your soul and Vis are immensely large—three times more than normal human standards. Your body could never hold all of it inside. In order to keep you intact and prevent a Vis explosion, your soul and Vis were split, and half of it was placed into this body. I formed my own conscience, but I am still a part of you and still your Havadar, and I will come to protect you at your call."

I thought for a minute. "That night at Nelly's, when Gregor and I disappeared, I was able to fight in a moment of panic. Was that you? Is that why you looked so exhausted?"

Cynthia nodded. "Yes, you were calling for me without really knowing it. My corporeal body was fighting against it, so it took some effort to respond to you. The same thing happened that night we were at Jillian's. You didn't nearly pull as much energy from me, but I could feel something. You were in trouble."

"Then you could see the Want this entire time?

"No. Only you had that ability, especially when we were much younger. Mika said that you were starting to attract attention, and I guess a Vis bind was put on you at eight years old."

"A Vis bind? Who put it on me? And how did it get off?"

Cynthia shrugged. "She never said who, but she did say the hold had weakened and that it was time." Cynthia paused to consider her own words. "Time for what? I'm not sure. But you gotta think…with everything that has happened…"

I shook my head, not fully believing I was having a conversation with my best friend in my soul. "Don't take this the wrong way, but did you become my friend because it was your cosmic duty?" I looked at her uncertainly.

Cynthia began gnawing on her bottom lip. "Not exactly. I still have a mind of my own. I mean, think about it. We've fought before, we have disagreed on things. I'm my own person." She smiled crookedly. "I… Just because we happen to share a soul doesn't change the fact that I chose you to be my very best friend. That I wanted to share experiences. That I am happy that we grew up together. We are truly no different than twins."

Damn, this isn't the time to cry! I took a moment to quickly wipe the offending tear and said, "You've been protecting me our entire life, haven't you? Really protecting me?"

Cynthia expelled a breath of relief and gave me a bone-crushing hug. "Yup. Since forever. Even before I even knew what I was doing. Remember that accident on your front yard?"

I nodded. Cynthia and I had been playing in my front yard one afternoon when Cynthia suddenly wanted to go inside for pudding. At first, I didn't want to go inside, but she insisted that I go with her. I had just run in after her when a truck swerved off of the road, slammed down on the concrete, and skidded right into the front steps. The truck took out the front yard, the front steps, and a quarter of the front of the house. Right where we had been playing.

Cynthia turned to face me. "Mika told me that I could feel The Want causing havoc internally, even if I couldn't see them. They caused that crash, along with...other accidents."

"What other accidents?"

Cynthia's eyes became impossibly sad. She took both of my hands into hers and expelled a deep breath. "Kat, um...there is something I have to tell you. Mika told me this but I think you should know too. The truth about your dad—"

I looked her, puzzled. "What about him? Cyn, he's been dead for ten years. What does he have to do with this?"

"Kat, please just listen for a second."

I shook my head. "Look, there's already so much to deal with. Please don't drop something else on me. Seriously, stop looking at me like that. My dad has nothing to do with this!" I attempted to walk away, but my Havadar firmly pulled me back me and pinned my arms to my sides.

"The Want killed your father, Katya."

I shook my head. "Come on, that's not true. My dad died saving me and his coworker in an accident. That's it."

Cynthia shook her head.

"Cyn, it was a freak accident. Everyone said so. Mom, the police. It was an ACCIDENT!" I screamed.

Cynthia shook her head again, tears streaming down her face. "I'm sorry, Kat."

An intense bubble started to build right next to my heart, and I continued to shake my head in denial. I wrenched myself free and my feet started to run down the hall, searching for the answer. The bubble spread throughout my body and into my head. The tears couldn't be stopped nor could my cries of anguish.

I need to find it. If what Cynthia says is true, I need to see it for myself.

My frayed senses spread out, looking for the correct door. I heard Cynthia running after me, but I couldn't care less. I was going to prove her wrong. She had no idea what she was talking about. My feet suddenly stopped in front of a nondescript door. The sounds behind it were muffled, as if someone had lowered the voices impossibly low. Not silent, but they were definitely hard to hear.

Cynthia's sandals slapping against the marble floor became louder as she caught up to me. "Katya, don't! You can get lost in your memories," she gasped out.

"Be my Havadar and protect me. Pull me out," I said snidely.

Her reproachful eyes caused an annoying pang of guilt. I tried again. "Please, Cyn. I need to see this."

Annoyed, she threw up her hands. "You stay, getting me into trouble! Fine! But your full body can't go in. Stick your head through the door. I'll hold your waist and pull you back out. Remember, you cannot go inside."

I nodded, bracing my hands against the door post. Cynthia took such a tight hold of my waist that if this had been my actual body, I'm sure she would've left bruises. She spread her feet wide and assumed a strong footing.

"Ready?" I nodded again. "Go ahead."

Taking a deep breath, I dunked my head into the wood. I half expected my head to collide and bounce back but the wood became fluid and I was immediately transported.

My head floated in the ether as I watched my eight-year-old self skip down the sidewalk with my father in tow. My heart momentarily faltered at the sight of him. A tall man with deep brown eyes that reflected the kindness he had for people. I watched as he and Mini-Me made for his car, as he secured her in the backseat, and drove away from the after-school daycare I frequented.

While driving home, he remembered that he had left an important file at work. He looked at Mini-Me sitting in the back seat through his rearview mirror.

"How about a trip downtown with Daddy, Kitty-Kat? That sound okay?"

Mini-Me bounced in her seat excitedly. "Yeah! Let's go, Daddy!"

Alone time with Dad was the best. He purposely took the time to be more fun than Mom. The best moments were when he would put me on his shoulders or sneak me extra candy without Mom knowing. I could see the hope for ice cream plastered all over my little face. My mom would always get super mad when she found out, but I loved it anyway.

The trip downtown was quick. They parked without difficulty in front of the historic Franklin building where Dad worked. Dad was an engineer and at the time, many engineering companies in Boston used historic buildings that they had restored themselves for offices. The old brick building stuck out in particular because every other building surrounding it was built with concrete and glass, making it the oldest building for several blocks.

With the sunset bleeding red over the old building, everything seemed normal. I looked on as my father and Mini-Me entered the building, passing through security and upstairs to Dad's office. He quickly grabbed a file sitting on the corner of this desk, turned to Mini-Me, and hoisted her on his shoulders, making her giggle. "Kitty Kat, since we are already out, let's say we get some dessert for dinner tonight? What would you like?"

Mini-Me pretended to think hard and propped her chin on Daddy's head. "Yes! Chocolate ice cream!"

Daddy held on to her legs and galloped through the empty hallway, earning shrieks from his rider. "Ice cream? You got it, princess!" I couldn't help but smile at his antics.

As they exited the building, Dad ran into his coworker Matt outside of the building. He set Mini-Me on down on the ground and talked for a few minutes.

Even within the memory, I felt an odd tingle at my core. I could feel something flying over our heads. I lifted my head and held in the scream I wanted to release. Three Wanters flew into the building through an open window. These looked like miniature Wreckers, with wings made out of bones. One remained perched on the top of the building, staring down at the three of us, releasing a terrible screech.

And Mini-Me saw everything I did. She looked up at my father, hoping that he felt it, that he knew there was trouble. But he simply continued to talk to Matt. Mini-Me's eyes darted around, suddenly very nervous. It wasn't that I could see what caused her discomfort but a familiar pit lurched in me. We could both sense something was going to happen.

Mini-Me then unknowingly gave off a flare of energy, born of her fear and agitation. Not particularly strong, but slightly more intense than any other human could emit. And the remaining miniature Wrecker noticed. It gave a particularly loud screech and released from its mouth a bright orb into the air, just like the Poser in my bedroom, and it veered left up the street against the incoming traffic. It was calling for backup. Mini-Me instinctively wanted to go elsewhere but was rooted by Dad's hand holding hers.

My own panic started to rise, as I now knew what a message orb could do. I wanted to yell out and scream to them to get off the sidewalk, to get out of the way and hide. I didn't need to be there anymore; I remembered what was coming. I remembered the pain that I was about to endure but I was completely powerless to stop it. So I stayed. I remained nothing more than a mirage, reliving the deepest horror life can offer.

At the intersection, less than half a mile away, a car suddenly turned sharply, cutting off traffic, and drove onto the sidewalk. Screams of panic rose as pedestrians ran for cover in between cars, sprinting into buildings or angling their bodies in between the skyscrapers around them. Those who were less lucky found themselves clipped, hit, or dusted aside by the accelerating vehicle.

Dad must have seen the car first as both Mini-Me and his coworker were facing the opposite direction. With a strength that I didn't know he possessed, he pushed Mini-Me and Matt out towards the building entrance's alcove yelling, "Get out of the way!" After pushing us, he attempted to follow, but it was too late. The speeding car clipped his left side, breaking his hip. The momentum then sent him careening unto the car's windshield, shattering it into pieces and sending his body over the hood of the car. He crashed into the concrete below on the top of his head.

The car would continue for at least for another half a mile before crashing into a newspaper stand. Later on, we would find out that the driver had claimed that he heard voices demanding that he drive on the sidewalk. He was also a horrible drunk.

It all happened within one minute.

Stunned at the sudden push, my eight-year-old self winced at the scratches on her elbow and knee. When she noticed that only Matt sat beside her, she began to scream, "Dad? Daddy? Where are you?" Sirens could be heard in the distance, other hurt pedestrians yelling for help. But nothing from Dad. Mini-Me did eventually find him, several feet away, bleeding on the sidewalk, looking broken. She attempted to run to him but Matt stopped her. She fought with all that she had to get to her father, but the grip on her was relentless.

Mini-Me's view was obstructed by Matt's shoulder as he hoisted her up into his arms. But she did see a flurry of small Want creatures flying down from the top of building, thoroughly distracted now by the carnage. It would be the last time in she would see a Wanter for many years.

I understood why the door was muted. If painful memories remained as loud as the joyful ones, there was no way we could possibly move on. And as I watched Mini-Me release sorrowful screams, I was tempted to stay and cry along with her. To not leave my father alone. To acknowledge the pain that I had been burying for so long. But the tug at my waist reminded me of my anchor and my chain in the present.

Cynthia's tugs became more insistent, so I reluctantly exited. She looked absolutely relieved, but quite worn out. "Thank goodness you're all right."

I said nothing as I slid down the wall, bringing my knees in. "They caused that accident that killed Dad. I think it was because of me. I gave off some energy and one of them noticed. But they never got me—they got more energy with the accident itself than they bargained for." I sighed, fighting back the tears. "Dad really was a hero."

I felt Cynthia's hand smoothing my hair. "His love for you gave him the strength to go against his own sense of self-preservation to save you." She pulled me into a tight hug. "Your dad's sacrifice allowed you to be here and now. To allow you to claim the destiny set before you. We have work to do to save the others out there. Amie, our friends from school…even those jerks Roger and Pana."

I chuckled under my tears.

Cynthia smiled weakly. "But you have a choice. No matter what they say to you. Nothing is forced on you. Whatever you decide, I am with you." Cynthia's knees suddenly gave out, sending her to the ground.

"Cyn, what's wrong?" I moved her hair behind her ears to find that her skin looked transparent. As if she was losing her form in the soulscape.

She grimaced. "I've weakened myself quite a bit here. I don't have much time."

"Time? "

"We need to make this quick. Kat, are you sure about the Kyrios?"

"What?"

Cynthia's body suddenly flicked like a dimming light bulb. She gasped in pain, "Are you sure about them? You trust them?"

I hesitated but said, "I think I can trust Gregor. If I am being honest with myself, I do care for him. And I think he does care for me as well. You saw him out there today. I trust him with my life."

Though in pain, she searched my eyes for any sign of uncertainty. She nodded. "Let's hope your faith in them is not in vain. I need you to say out loud, 'I need you by my side, my protector, my Havadar Diantha. Say it quickly!"

I grasped her opaque hand tightly. "I need you by my side, my protector, my Havadar Diantha."

A large white glowing orb left her chest and soared into mine. Every bit of me felt electrified, which I thought was impossible in soulscape. She shuddered, her body become more and more invisible. "I gave you enough of your soul back so you can fight," she smiled weakly. "It's not everything—Mika said it's not time yet." Cynthia gave another weak whimper. "Tell absolutely no one that I am your Havadar. Gregor already knows to keep quiet. I'm sending you back. Just remember—be strong, sis."

"Cyn, wait—" Her palm caught me in the middle of my chest, emptying my lungs of air and sending me out of the soulscape.

30

When I opened my eyes, I was surrounded by a number of pillows, silk sheets, and a warm hand enveloping my own. Gregor sat by my bedside, his eyes closed in sleep. Never had I seen the Scot in such a deep but peaceful state. He always said Kyrios didn't need sleep unless they were completely empty of Vis. I guess the attack had tired him out too. It gave me a chance to really appreciate the Kyrios's chiseled face. I knew the power that he had and it tugged at my heart to see him unguarded and unreserved.

I closed my eyes in concentration, delving into myself. Searching to confirm everything was in order.

I'm here.

I nodded, knowing Mika wouldn't see, but would understand anyway. My mind whirled with the information that I'd learned about my father and the current state of my home. I internally sighed and asked, *What happens now?*

I could feel Mika give me a small smile. **That is entirely up to you. You know that.**

Well, a little bit of guidance wouldn't hurt, you know! I said, annoyed, rolling my eyes. Her response was silence. Sighing now outwardly, I opened my eyes to Gregor staring intently back at me. Not a word was said. But his blue eyes were as expressive as an orchestra performing a symphony that spoke of regret, misery, concern, and longing.

Not knowing how to respond, I said, "What—"

He effectively silenced me when he grabbed the back of my head and descended on my lips. The intensity of the kiss was enough to take my breath away, warm me to the tips of my toes, and place the same symphony within my heart. The sweep of his tongue and the firm pressure of his lips robbed me of my sanity. When breathing became an issue, he released me, keeping little distance between us.

"I almost lost you there," he said against my lips.

"Meh, it wasn't that bad. Just a typical soul-crushing afternoon," I said with a smile.

He chuckled, his eyes relaxed. "You constantly get in trouble, don't you?"

"Apparently so." I pulled away and sat up. Not wanting to call attention to that enjoyable-but-unsanctioned kiss, I asked, "What happened?"

Whether Gregor noticed the change in my tone, he didn't say. He moved so that he sat on the bed. "By the time we got to the gate, your soul was getting the life squeezed out of it. General Lamar almost didn't make it in time to take it off. You've been out of it for about two days here, so about a week or so in the Live Realm."

"That long?" I started to get out of bed to only have Gregor hold me back by my shoulders. "What about my mom or Cynthia? Cynthia said she was weakened?"

His eyebrows furrowed. "How did you know that?"

I explained everything, including my trip down memory lane. He slowly pulled away and sat back in his chair. I could feel him changing back from the concerned kisser to hard-core Major.

"So the Want killed your father." He shook his head. "It's not your fault. The Want has been causing destruction even before you were born," he said fiercely. Gregor then shifted in his seat and glanced down at the floor. "Their destruction has touched everyone."

I returned to my original question. "What happened to my mother?"

He looked at me carefully and propped himself on his knees. "Your mother is safe. Collins took her down to Buenos Aires. There hasn't been the same intensity of destruction there yet, so we thought it would be best. Your home has been essentially destroyed, so she's been placed in a safe house with guards from one of our units. General Nabil was concerned that she would become another target. At most, what she knows is that the 'police' have placed her in protective custody in response to the terrorist attack that occurred in your neighborhood and throughout Boston. She demanded to see you, but we assured her that you are safe and at another location."

A small smile broke through my face. "Kinda crappy about my house, but thank heaven she's all right."

Gregor rolled his eyes and smirked. "That's certainly true."

I pulled the sheets off and attempted to get out of bed. Gregor intercepted me a second time. "Where do you think you are going?"

I tried to shrug him off. "I want to find Cynthia. She said she was nearby. By the way, she said you are not supposed to tell you anyone about her being my Havadar."

Gregor's aloof demeanor slipped. "Katya, about—"

"Look, whatever debriefing you are about to do can wait." I tried to push past him, but the Kyrios grabbed me by my waist in an unforgiving grip. I tried to push him away, but he wouldn't budge.

"What's wrong with you," I huffed. "I need to find Cynthia!"

His large body had initially blocked my view of the rest of my room in the tower. But in our struggle I was now able to look past his shoulder and notice another bed in the corner by my window. In the bed, there was a body.

Completely still, I asked, "Gregor, who is that by the window?"

His shoulders sagged in defeat. His blue eyes sought me, begging me to stay calm. "Katya—"

"Who is that?" I yelled. He allowed me to push past him to see a battered Cynthia looking close to dead. Cuts and bruises covered her once-lovely face, making it almost unidentifiable. Her once-long red hair was singed and uneven. Her skin was deathly pale and looked impossibly cold. I fell down to my knees, tears pooling on the floor. I tried to reach for her, but was stopped by an invisible shield that covered her entirely.

"No," I whispered. "Come on, Kat. Wake up. This is a dream. This has to be a dream." I barely registered Gregor's presence behind me.

"Katya, listen to me."

"No!" I screamed. "This isn't real. This can't be real." I turned, clutching at Gregor's shirt. "Please, Gregor," I begged, unable to see through my tears. "Don't let this be real."

Before my legs could give out underneath me, Gregor tucked his arm underneath my knees and held me close to his chest. He brought me back to my bed and sat me down on his lap. His hand rubbed at my back, keeping the numbness from settling in.

"Katya," he said softly. "Cynthia isn't gone. She's alive."

I glanced at his face. "She's alive?"

He nodded. "She's near spirit depletion. As we escaped, she must have gone against something quite massive to use up most of her spirit energy. We are still trying to piece together the details, but that fleet was incredible. Not only did it take out your house, but your entire neighborhood and three others nearby. She'll recover, but it's hard to tell how long it will take."

"What does Cynthia need?"

"Her Vis is dangerously low, as if it almost vanished. We've had to force-feed her energy through that field to keep her consciousness here, but there's something...off."

"What do you mean?"

"She's been given energy for as long as you have been

recovering. But she's not recovering. It's almost like a coma. She's not getting better or worse."

I thought of the orb that had left her and went into my chest. *You stupid girl.* I asked quietly, "Is it because she came into my soulscape?"

Gregor grimaced. "It wouldn't have been easy for her, but there's something more at play."

"Foul play?" I whispered. I almost hesitated in saying my next words but I meant what I said to Cynthia—I did trust Gregor with my life, and nothing so far from his actions proved me wrong. "Gregor, about that security bracelet...that was the second time that it caused me to lose control."

He rubbed the shadow on his chin. "I know. I asked General Lamar about that. He was puzzled about the malfunction as well. He said that the bracelet had been checked over by their security team before they gave it to him. He said he would look into whether there was anything going on with their team and others.

"Which brings me back to Cynthia. It's like something is siphoning her energy away and we can't determine who is doing it. I hate to think that one of our own Kyrios is working against us, but that fleet knew where you and Cynthia were. It's possible that the Poser felt that Cynthia was giving off the same Vis signature as you and told the fleet to get the both of you. But it was too close, too quick in my opinion." His jaw clenched. "In a way, it's my fault too."

My heart softened at the grief-stricken look on the Scot's face. I gently touched his shoulder. "What do you mean it's your fault? You had nothing to do with this. Those rat bastards did this."

"I should've destroyed that message sphere the Poser sent out."

He palmed his face. "But I was more concerned about keeping your mother safe."

I thought back to Cynthia's intense question about the Kyrios and wondered if she knew something. I looked back at her comatose body. "And we have no idea who's taking her energy?"

His answer was his hand rubbing my lower back to comfort me. I eased my head into the crook of Gregor's neck, taking a moment to try to let the dust of the past few days settle. I knew I had to stop being timid about my role here.

"Gregor?" I said quietly. His hand stilled, acknowledging he'd heard me. "Do you think I can do this? Be this savior of the Live Realm?"

He wordlessly caressed my tear-stained face, bringing me to a calm peace. "Katya, your best friend risked her soul because she believes in you and your abilities. And not just because you're the Balancer. Because you can see clearly. Because I think you've seen the beauty and ugliness of humanity. That's what we need now. For you to be our eyes and to provide us with a vision to move forward. I don't have a doubt that you are more than capable." He smiled softly. "You can end it all. But it's up to you." He released my face for my shoulders. "What do you choose?"

The question of the hour. I closed my eyes, reviewing everything that had happened so far.

"What if..." I started. "What if I just wanted out? What if I just can't handle all this?" I locked in on my favorite set of blue eyes. "What if I can't handle this with you? I would be lying if I said I don't care about you, Gregor. But I know we can't move forward as I wish we could. I do not want to put you at risk."

For a moment, his eyes reflected a bit of shock and pain, but he quickly concealed it by releasing me, setting me on my feet and standing back. "If that was your honest wish, I'd request that you be released. The Generals, while upset, wouldn't want to keep a soldier here who didn't want to fight. But you couldn't go back to the Live Realm as you are. We'd have to find a measure to make your Vis less threatening…but then perhaps you could go back to normal."

Normal. Something I've always wanted. I stared at the floor, already knowing my answer, but I had to ask one more question. "Do you want me to stay?"

"My answer shouldn't influence you."

I crossed my arms over my chest. "I already have my answer. Whatever you have to say won't change it."

Refusing to look at me, he said, "In my opinion as Major—"

I shook my head, closing the space between us. "No, you don't get to do that. I don't want the Major. I want Gregor to answer my question."

Gregor lifted his eyes from the floor and met mine. He studied my face, spending a few moments at my lips, sending tingles down my spine.

"I don't want you to fight," he said quietly.

I swallowed down my disappointment.

I nodded and made to move past him when he grabbed my wrist. "You didn't let me finish."

Sighing deeply, I turned back to him, giving my full attention. He let go, running a hand through his already-tousled hair. I had a feeling he had done that same movement countless times since we'd returned to Ager. "No, I don't want you anywhere near the fight, the violence, or the ugliness of this war. War is vicious, Katya, and I don't want it to change you. I want you to stay just the way you are." He picked back up my hand and threaded his fingers with mine. "Sweet, innocent, caring, feisty, and clumsy." He chuckled when I hit him on the arm. "So no, I don't want you to fight. But against my better judgment, against all the Kyrios protocols, even against my deepest wish to keep you out of harm's way, I very much want you to stay. Here with me."

The Scot's hand warmed me to my core. With ease, he'd burrowed his way past my defenses and rendered me speechless. So I acted. My arms curled around his neck, and on the tips of my toes, my lips greeted his with all the bottled-up passion I had in me. He met me with equal fervor, his hands clutching the small of my back and pressing me closer.

We kissed for several glorious moments, and then I pulled away, studying him as he studied me.

"Are you sure about this? What about me being an anchor for you?"

"The way I see it, you're not in the Live Realm. You're here with me in Ager, fighting beside me. Our goals are the same. Therefore, it's a loophole. But at the same time, let's not particularly broadcast it."

"But Gregor—"

He kissed my forehead and clutched me a bit closer. "Katya, take it from someone who knows. These moments of happiness are so fleeting and few and far between. In life and in death. Can't we just enjoy each other while we can?"

I had other concerns on the tip of my tongue, but I remained silent. I knew I would eventually have to return to the Live Realm. Maybe enjoying the here and now was the best solution for us for now. With one last perfunctory kiss, I sighed happily and said, "Bye, Gregor," and started for the door.

"Katya?" he said, confused.

I stopped at the door and said over my shoulder, "Or do you want to come with me? No, actually, I need you to come with me."

"What do you mean?"

I smirked. "I can't get up Central Tower by myself! Someone needs to tell the Generals that the Balancer is ready to do some intensive training."

31

While Gregor's dazzling smile showed his relief in my choice, he told me (demanded, really) that I stay in bed and said that he would bring the Generals to me.

As I lay in bed, watching Cynthia flicker from time to time, I thought about our time together in the soulscape. Both my parents had been attacked because of the Want. Because of stupid, power-hungry creatures wanting to wreak havoc and devour my Mika and Cynthia. Seemed like everyone wanted a piece of my world-ending power, and I didn't even know how to fully use it. That was going to change.

A knock at the door brought me out of my musings. "Come in!"

A cautious Jae stepped in and took a look around. When he spotted me among the pillows, his eyes lit up like it was Christmas morning. "Ms. Katya! You're all right! You gave us such a scare."

"I'm sorry I caused you to worry."

He shook his head earnestly, striding forward. "Please don't be. You couldn't have helped it even if you wanted to." He took Gregor's seat. "Major Gregor asked me to watch over you while he alerts the Generals. How are you?"

"I'm resolved, Jae." I looked at him closely. "Can I ask you a question?"

"Of course," he said with an easy smile. "I wish you would."

I took a moment to adjust myself in my bed and sat directly in front of him, debating how much I wanted to tell him. "How does one train with their Havadar? You know, to really fight?"

His eyebrows quirked up. "You found your Havadar?"

I nodded, resisting the impulse to say anything else.

Jae nodded happily. "That's fantastic news. I assume that's why the Generals are coming."

I nodded again. "What kind of training should I expect when working with my Havadar? I want to be able to understand what I'm in for before I tell the Generals what I want. I would've have asked Gregor, but I doubt he would be excited to teach me how to fight."

"No, I suppose he wouldn't be," Jae said quietly, gauging my reaction.

I blinked. "Why is that?"

Jae sat back in his chair and shrugged. "Major Gregor has a reputation of being particularly hard on female Kyrios because he doesn't want to fight them. That is, everyone but Sophia."

I could feel my gut tighten with a familiar hot feeling. "Sophia?" *That blond Kyrios that gave me the dirty look?*

"She's another Lieutenant on the Southern European squad. She's quite exceptional with the sword. Gregor enjoys spending time with her. There were rumors that they were together, but that could just be baseless gossip." At the sick look on my face, Jae asked, concerned, "Are you getting tired?"

I smiled weakly. "No, just a slight dizzy spell. It will pass." *Maybe my dream about them was a really a vision?* Clearing my throat, I asked, "How are your skills, Jae?"

He propped himself on his knees. "I'd like to think of myself as exceptional with my sword." With his palm up, a sword appeared in his grip. The very thin sword was pure silver from tip to grip.

"It's beautiful."

He grinned. "Thanks. This is Slumber. His name coincides with my ability to put humans to sleep. We sometimes take passing souls through their dreams while they sleep."

I massaged my chin, thinking. "Could you get me into the dream of a normal person?" Funny how I didn't fit in that category anymore—I was becoming more and more comfortable with that fact.

He nodded. "Yes, but why would you need to do that? The only other time we go into a human's dreams is to wipe out the memory of a Poser invasion."

The thought of the Poser's assault on my mother made my heart ache for her. I took a hold of Jae's hands and looked at him earnestly. "I want to talk to my mother and let her know I'm okay. I didn't know that visiting her in her dreams was an option, but if it is, I'd like to use it. Going to the Live Realm now is out of the question."

Jae chuckled. "More than you realize. But I think we might be able to do something. Let me ask General Lamar's permission. As security, he'll have to give clearance."

I nodded. *Better to have Lamar decide than Nabil.* Loud steps could be heard from downstairs, marking the Generals' arrival.

Jae quickly stood up. "I must go. I do my best to convince General Lamar of your wish."

"Thank you, Jae."

His eyes became unreadable but he said, "Just remember, sometimes help comes from the oddest of places." And with that he was behind the door.

I didn't have a chance to think about what Jae said before I heard voices approaching. Gregor stepped in with General Lamar and Nabil in tow. Lamar looked pleased to see my progress. Nabil just looked guarded and a bit sour. With a sweeping and mocking bow, he said, "Lady Katya, so good to see you up and about. You had us worried there."

I rolled my eyes—something about him just annoyed me. "So I've heard." I rose from my bed, not wishing to look sick in front of them, let alone Nabil. "Generals, after receiving some new information, I've decided to make a slight change." I stopped for a dramatic pause. Lamar took the bait.

"Which is?"

Nabil stepped forward, silencing my answer. "Before you answer, Lady Katya, might I take this opportunity to show you the new developments in the Live Realm." He nodded to Gregor, who pulled a small green glowing sphere out of an air sliver. The light from the sphere pulsed.

Curious, I stepped forward. "What is it?"

Gregor cleared his throat. "This is our version of message sphere, like the Poser's sphere you saw before. It's able to record messages from anything and be sent out to whomever we wish. Well, those who have Vis energy." He gave me a grim look. "We just recorded several news stations from your area."

"Why do I need to see Boston news?"

"It's not just Boston news. It's news from around the United States."

He waved his hand over the sphere that projected a small image of an anchorman on a news telecast. "Small tremors for the second week in a row. These quakes are not yet life-threatening, but scientists are baffled at as to why New York City would have any tremors at all. As far as scientists can tell, there is no reason for these small quakes whatsoever, but research is ongoing—"

A new image of an anchorman with a Southern accent appeared. "We're already five days into a record-breaking heat wave and there's no sign of reprieve for the people of the Southern states. Remember to stay cool and keep out of the midday sun. We've already had four fatalities this week, and authorities expect several more among the most vulnerable population due to heat stroke and other heat-related illness."

A new team of anchors began another newscast. "John," the woman stated. "It seems that Southern California might experience its first tsunami? Tell us more about this impending threat."

The man nodded. "That's right, Heather. Due to the earthquake that struck Japan last night, high waves are making their way towards the West Coast. Scientist believe that the waves will diminish before reaching the coast, but officials have evacuation plans ready just in case—"

The sphere went dark.

"There are similar reports coming from all corners of the world," Gregor said quietly.

A knot grew in the pit of my stomach. "What's going on? What's happening?"

Gregor returned the sphere to his air locker. "We were right when we thought the Want were up to something. All of the tremors and heat are clear indications that their efforts are intensifying. We think it could be because you've been named the Balancer. Our intelligence is still trying to determine what they are planning and what the reason behind these gate openings could be. Our original plan is now more important—the Los Angeles gate has already gotten a few inches bigger. Still not big enough for a level-three Wrecker, but it's still causing some harm. If they are planning a major attack on the Live Realm, we think they might try to get their heaviest hitters out that gate." He shook his head in disbelief. "We must find a way to close that gate and frustrate their efforts."

I could feel Nabil watching me the entire time throughout the explanation. "This is what you are up against, Lady Katya. The task before us is daunting, but it will get done. It is a matter of deciding where you are going to be. If you don't wish to be here, say so now. You know this, but the Want will stop at nothing to get your Vis. To devour you would be a clear testament that no power in existence can rule them. That humans are their playthings and that they have always owned the Live Realm." He crossed his arms and continued to watch my face looking for some hint I was backing out. "If you wish to leave, simply say the word."

I gave Nabil a look. *He just wants me to go, doesn't he?* Mika shifted within me and it only brought on a sense of pride within me. If God supposedly gave me this gift, no one in existence was going to stop me.

I narrowed my eyes at the Head General and said in a clear voice, "I've decided to stay and continue my training here to take my place as the Balancer." Their reactions were predictable. Lamar with a smile. Nabil with a curt nod, though there was a slight jerk of his head. As if his attention wasn't completely on me.

"I'll alert the other Generals of the good news," Nabil said quietly. He turned for the door when I called him back.

"Generals, I do have a question."

"There always is one, isn't there, my lady?" Nabil sneered.

"I'd like to train with my Havadar immediately. I want to fight." Both Generals looked at each other.

"The point of the mission was to collect your Havadar and get it away from the Want. We never intended for you to train with your sword, nor did we think you'd want to train for battle with your Havadar. Your lessons were aimed at you gaining control of your Vis. You said you only wanted to help to close the gates. What has brought about this change?" Nabil asked slowly.

"Does it really matter? I am now able fight at full strength."

"It matters entirely. Why?"

I gripped my hands hard, digging my nails into my fists. "Because the Want are vermin. Disgusting vermin that need to be wiped out. They have hurt my mother. They killed my father, and they placed my best friend in a comatose state. They have destroyed the only home I've ever known, and my friends are scattered in the wind. I intend to eradicate anything remotely Want from the Live Realm and this world." I stepped forward to Nabil right under his chin. "If the Want are itching for a fight, fine! The sooner the better, so I can return to my life. That explanation good enough for you?"

The three men stared at me with mixed reactions. Lamar looked genuinely pleased and had a broad smile on his face, but Nabil and Gregor looked troubled. Lamar stepped forward and palmed my shoulders. "I think training with your Havadar is a fantastic idea. I'll see to your training at once, Balancer. I must say, your Vis is deliciously surging."

I smirked and looked at the enthusiastic General. "Considered me fired up and ready to go. Thank you, General." He lingered at my shoulders before releasing me.

Nabil cleared his throat and stepped between Lamar and me. "I will allow you to commence your Havadar training, however, I'll provide you with a full protection guard."

Lamar narrowed his eyes. "Is that really necessary?"

Nabil's eyebrows arched smugly. "Of course. Havadar training can be quite difficult. Unknown discharges of energy should be maintained and so they don't become a liability. I shall pick some men to be in Lady Katya's entourage."

Lamar and Nabil locked eyes silently. Clearly a war of wills was taking place, and I wasn't sure why. Lamar relented and returned to me with an easy smile. "I will depart now, my lady." With a quick bow, he was gone.

Nabil remained, his arms now locked behind his back. "My lady, this was not the road I intended for you. The Kyrios force was intended to fight and protect you as you did your part in closing the gates. I will ask you again, are you sure this is what you want?"

I gritted my teeth, holding back the string of curses I wanted to throw at him. "General, I want to fight for myself and rid the world of these monsters. This last trip outside into the Live Realm has just shown me how much I need to learn so I can do my part. That includes fighting and using my power to its fullest."

Nabil smirked. "Oh yes. However, I don't believe that was God's original intention in creating you." He inched closer. "I will do as you ask, Balancer. However, let me reiterate this. You must listen to every command given while in Ager—no questions asked. No arguments, is that understood?" He looked me down, assessing me. "Be careful or you might find yourself in grave danger, splitting yourself from your Vis forever," he said softly.

A chill swept up and down my back. Nabil studied me once more before nodding. He turned to Gregor, who was watching our exchange carefully. "Gregor," he barked, "come to Central Command shortly to discuss the new detail." Gregor saluted and the head General exited. Gregor closed the door and gave me a suspicious look.

"What was that about?"

"That's what I want to know."

"Katya, why are you talking like this? When we were just talking about you fighting, I thought you meant closing the gates, not blazing into battle with your Havadar in hand."

I huffed, sitting back on the bed. I was starting to feel dizzy. "Gregor, it's not really up to you."

Gregor followed me towards the bed and sat back in his chair. "Your welfare is my concern, though. While you are the Balancer, my job is to keep you safe. Havadar training is one thing, and I get you want to protect yourself. But to fight against the Want is completely different. Your role here is just to close the open gates."

Angrily, I stalked over to my window. "Don't you get it? The Want have been a destructive force for my entire life. I've had people call me crazy since I was child. You know why I have a weird relationship with God? My own overzealous religious grandparents thought I was possessed. They used to keep me locked up in their prayer room—which was a closet—for hours, trying to pray out the demons out of me. I would cry and beg to be let out and they would just thump me with their bibles. I couldn't go to sleep whenever my grandparents visited because I was petrified that they would take me from my room and lock me into the prayer room again. All because of the Want. I had to change schools because other parents didn't want their children to play with me. Because I saw the Want. And their destruction. And their anger and jealousy. Because those pathetic dead souls simply can't let go of what they can never have. They have caused too many humans pain. How many more have to suffer?" I looked back at the Scot, who was looking stonily back at me. "The world will be better off if I can figure out a way to get rid of all the Wanters in existence. The Want will pay. Every type, every size, whatever."

His jaw clenched before he responded. "Revenge is a very

dangerous path, Katya. You have no idea what it does to your soul."

I rolled my eyes. "Before you start your 'good' angel mambo—"

"I am NOT an angel," he hissed angrily. My eyes widened at his outburst. Catching himself, Gregor stepped back, clenching his jaw. "You know what, fine. You'll get your wish." He stalked toward the door and reached for the knob but turned back to me. "Just remember, your title is the Balancer, not the Destroyer. We already have one—his name is Drachen."

32

Gregor didn't return for the rest of the day. A random Kyrios came in wordlessly and brought my dinner. I refused to ask where he was.

This war between the Want and humans had started many lifetimes ago, and it felt like my family was suffering casualties for no reason. A war just because God liked us better and the Want is jealous of the life that they can't have anymore? My nails dug into my palms. *Anything Want will fall. No mercy, right, Mika?*

My answer was dead silence. *Mika?*

If you hadn't noticed, these are the moments where I let you decide for yourself.

What are you talking about? I've already made my decision.

Again, silence. *Great, first Gregor, now you. Whatever, you two will come around. I'm just embracing the true potential of my role now.*

Still dead silence. I hope she sensed my massive eye roll because I took my time doing it.

Before you give me the complete silent treatment, can you tell me what Cynthia did in the soulscape? What was that orb?

The Kyrios was right. She is currently under attack and cannot sustain her body's full functionality. There was something trying to siphon her remaining energy. But before the attack could take all of your Vis energy from her, she gave it back a portion of it to you. Diantha has been returned to her wielder.

I swallowed. *You mean Cynthia is inside of me?*

She has simply returned home for the time being. She is unable to speak to you right now, but you will be able to wield her once you have mastered your heart.

What does that mean?

Again, silence. For an inner Vis guide, Mika had a lot of attitude.

*   *   *

The next morning, a soft knock awoke me. "My lady?"

Jae's voice travelled through the mahogany door. "Your presence is requested in the training sphere. I'm here to escort you." With a quick splash of water, some dental hygiene, and a change of clothes, I was out the door within ten minutes. The Lieutenant and I walked at an easy pace to the training dome. As I adjusted my high ponytail, I noticed the vast silence around us. Not a Kyrios in sight.

"Hey, what happened to everyone?"

Jae looked down at the ground. "Squads are running drills in their respective barracks. It makes traveling around here all the better, right? Nobody to run into."

I frowned. "Running into anyone was never an issue before. Was the courtyard cleared because of me?"

He chuckled quickly, but he took a firm hold of my elbow, ignoring my question. "We'll be late. Come on." We entered the dome to find several people awaiting our arrival. All of them had the required drop-dead gorgeous Kyrios physique and look. I recognized Lamar, Nabil, and the pouting Gregor, but the other four people I hadn't had the pleasure of meeting to this point.

"Lady Katya," Nabil nodded. "Nice to see you up and about. Let's hope there aren't any more accidents."

I had such a good comeback, but I decided against it. I simply nodded and said, "Reporting for training, General."

"General Raf is currently dealing with the open gate situation in the Live Realm, so I have decided to ask Gregor to take over your lessons. As for these people, they are a part of your own squad. The Quad. An elite crew, handpicked by me to fight alongside you, but most of all to protect you."

All four, two men and two women, took a knee and said in one voice, "At your service, Lady Katya."

Feeling slightly intimidated, I managed a quiet, "Thank you."

Nabil adjusted his long black coat and closed it around his broad chest. "I shall leave you to the training. Gregor, as we discussed." As he turned, he beckoned to the tallest of the Quad. "Demetrius, a moment." Nabil took him aside. I wanted to try to read their lips, but Jae distracted me.

"Miss Katya." He lowered his voice. "I've spoken to General Lamar about your dream request, and he believes that he can work something out. I'll fetch you later. But do not tell anyone. It's a bit unauthorized."

I sneaked a peak at Gregor, who was standing to the side, speaking to the other three in the guard. "I'll pretend I know nothing."

Jae gave me wink before exiting with General Lamar. The Quad stood by Gregor, looking expectantly at me. The shortest of them, a woman with olive skin, dark curly hair, and hazel eyes stepped forward with a sweeping bow and a cheeky smile. "I am Zenobia, my lady. I am overjoyed that we have the privilege of protecting you. Should you ever need anything, please let me know."

I noticed the three others rolled their eyes, but they stepped forward in turn. The dark-haired man with fair skin that had spoken with Nabil bowed slightly. "I'm Demetrius, my lady." The next man, with long blond hair that was almost white and brown eyes, got down on one knee. "I am Sebastian, my lady." The last was a dark-skinned woman with the lightest brown eyes I had ever seen. She too got down on one knee and said, "I'm Adedoja, my lady. But you may call me Addy."

Feeling very uncomfortable, I said, "Guys, please stand. I'm not one for formalities. Just call me Katya." As they looked at each other, I added, "If you want to serve me, please call me Katya." They seemed to accept that and rose to their feet.

Gregor clasped Sebastian and Addy on their shoulders. "These four are considered your royal guard, my lady." He earned a scowl from me. "They will be with you everywhere, especially during our raids into the Live Realm." *Babysitters, great.* "But the reason they are here now is to erect a barrier around the dome. We wouldn't want any stray energy to leave the dome and cause damage to Ager." With a nod, the four disappeared. Or it seemed that they did. They were actually in their respective corners, sitting down with their eyes closed.

"Quickstep?"

Gregor smirked. "Yes. Guess General Raf showed you a bit of it. Perhaps you'll get there too. But that's for later." He checked each corner before shouting, "Begin!"

The four guards slapped their hands together and began to yell. It reminded me of how martial artists groan when they are about to punch someone's face in. But I've never seen a martial artist glow and send a beam of energy up in the air to meet in the middle with other energy beams to create a net. Nope, couldn't say I've seen *anything* like that before. I looked on in amazement, feeling the buzz of energy in the air and watching as each of the four quietly sat down, meditating. "How are they doing that?"

"Vis manipulation. When you have full control of your Vis, you can be just like that," Gregor said behind me. I turned to say something smart, but seeing Gregor's naked torso left me dull and dumb. It felt like an eternity since we were just at my house and he was walking around without a shirt, ticking off Roger. Gregor must have guessed my train of thought, for he smiled predatorily. "Are you ready?"

Before I could answer, he disappeared. "As you know, this is the speed," he said to my left, "average Wanters can move." I swirled around to see him leisurely standing around. "At most, this is what the General showed you. But the higher-ranked Wanters—" He disappeared again and then appeared further out before me. "They can go three times faster. Tell me Katya—" He began to appear and disappear in several places at once, blurring around me until it seemed that there were several Gregors surrounding me.

"Can you even try to follow me?"

The Gregors continued to swirl around and a slight panic set in. *How the heck am I supposed to do that?* The cold touch of steel at my neck froze me. A quick look down confirmed that Gregor was pressed behind me with his sword hovering over my aorta.

"In the time you took to figure out what was going on, I could've killed you twice over," he whispered in my ear. As angry as I was for falling for his ploy, I couldn't help the butterflies in my stomach and the liquid pool running through my veins at Gregor's closeness. Gregor didn't step back, but instead pressed himself a bit closer, his sword closer to my neck.

"Well?"

I swallowed down my attraction and held on to my resolve. "I guess we have our work cut out for us then." I glared at him, giving him a clear message: I'm not backing down.

His eyes narrowed, but he chuckled, stepping back and releasing me. "Indeed, there is much work to do." His sword disappeared as quickly it appeared. He pulled a cloth from his pocket and threw it at me. "Might want to wipe your neck."

A quick wipe showed that he had drawn blood. *The moment I can fight decently...* Taking several steps back, Gregor widened his stance. "The first thing you need to learn is how to control the strength of your ability. Your Vis reserves are vast, but right now they only react when you get emotional. You need to be able to draw on them with a clear head and communicate with your Vis. Have you done this before?"

I hesitated, but nodded. "I've done it only once. I created a blast of Vis, but it was hardly controlled."

Gregor crossed his arm, his eyebrows arched. "Then you can do it again. Show me by bringing energy to your hands."

Crap. I raised my hand and breathed deeply. I could sense Mika moving, but she was not moving in the direction of my hand. *Help me out here, Mika. Don't make me look stupid.* If Mika was an actual person, she would've stood in front of me, waited for several minutes, and then eventually smirked and given me what I asked for. I opened my eyes to find my open palm glowing blue. I fought the grin that wanted to burst out.

"Good," Gregor barked. "Now, I want you to create a sphere of energy in your palm, like this." He set out his hand and effortlessly got his hand glowing. "Imagine there is a dot in the middle of your hand. This dot can be filled with your energy. Focus your energy on filling that dot until you get a sphere as big as this." I watched as a sphere quickly grew out of his hand to the size of a basketball.

I did as he said and imagined the dot. Inwardly I sought out Mika. *Can you just let me have full reign, please?* Mika shrugged and let go of the control. I was immediately taken aback by how much she'd held back from me. Every extremity swelled with Vis, and I could've created a thousand basketballs. And still with all that, I could feel Mika holding back. My teeth ground together as I tried to concentrate. It was like being thrown into a raging river with waves slapping you as you came up for air. I could feel that my body was humming with power, shaking with energy.

"Control it, Katya!"

I closed my eyes as I tried to tamp everything down. I could feel heat building at my temple from exertion. After several excruciating minutes, I pushed the beast back into its cage and got control. Expelling a breath, I focused on sending energy to that stupid dot. A small sphere started to grow, filling me with intense satisfaction. I stole a glance at the Scot, who had his arms crossed, looking unimpressed and even angered. Which only released my own ire. *Why does he look at me like that? It's taking a lot of me to do this, and I'm doing my best!*

"Katya?"

I mean, what's the big deal that I want to fight? I have every right to avenge my father's death!

"Katya, stop!" I brought my attention back to my hand to find the sphere had grown to a large beach ball. *Oops.* Not knowing what to do, I simply dropped my hand, cutting off its supply. When the floating sphere began to lose its shape and vibrate, I quickly learned that letting go wasn't the smartest thing to do.

"Back up, Katya!" Gregor yelled. I took three steps back before the sphere shattered like glass, causing a massive explosion. I was immediately thrown backward, screaming, knowing I was about to hit the wall at fifty miles an hour. Just before impact, a broad chest came in between me and the concrete. The force of the explosion still crashed us into the wall. My catcher grunted, but he held tight onto to me. We descended gracefully from the crater in the wall, about sixty feet off the ground.

When our feet touched the ground, Demetrius's smirking face met my own surprised one. "It's amazing that all that power is in that small body," he said softly, but his eyes were slightly mocking.

"Don't judge what you don't know. I'm capable of a lot more, guard," I shot back, not taking a liking to him.

Gregor quickstepped next to us, looking frazzled. "Are you two all right? Katya?"

Demetrius nodded. "We're fine. My back took the hit. The lady is whole. Not very good, is she?"

It's official. I don't like this guy.

Gregor frowned. "Maybe you're right."

I rolled my eyes. "Look, it's my first day. I'll do better. Come on, let's do it again."

He sighed. "Fine. Let's go."

As I followed Gregor back to the center of the floor, Demetrius's taunting voice called out. "I'll be watching you, my lady." I nodded in acknowledgement but was more determined to swipe that smirk off.

The rest of the training session went a whole lot more smoothly. With my focus solely on the task at hand, I was able to form the basketball-sized sphere, first with one hand and then with both hands. After doing it several times and completing a number of drills meant to help me practice focusing and controlling my Vis, I was pretty wiped. It felt like hours had passed.

When my knees started to shake, Gregor finally took pity on me. "I think that's enough for today."

"Fantastic," I muttered. I retracted the last Vis sphere, and my ankle gave out and I crashed to the floor. Thoroughly embarrassed, I tried to summon the energy to get up. But my body was on strike. I looked up through my eyelashes. "Just a... give me a second here. I need a moment," I huffed.

The moment lasted for another minute. With a heavy sigh, Gregor stooped down and picked me up, bridal style. The Quad rose from their corner and met us in the middle.

Zenobia gave me a sympathetic smile. "What are your orders, sir?" she asked Gregor.

"Take the night. I'll escort the lady to her chambers and keep watch. Be here by the sunrise." With curt nods and a sideways glance from Demetrius, the Quad departed. Demetrius's words still bugged me.

"Well," Gregor said, bringing me back to the present. "Shall we head back?" He walked at a leisurely pace over to the tower, and I took the chance to look at the man holding me. A day hadn't gone by where I hadn't marveled at his good looks. But it wasn't just the looks, but the ease I felt around him. I had never let anyone get so close to me so quickly, and he'd accomplished such a level of intimacy with me in just a matter of days. Maybe it was the way he acted that intrigued me. Sometimes his boyish tease would come out when we were alone. But with others, he could be cold and efficient. Harsh, but to the point.

"Do you like doing this?" I asked suddenly. "Being a death keeper?" He gave me a look that clearly said, *That's a random question.* I shrugged. "I don't know how to peg you. At one point you are Mister Military. Other times you're 'sweet, hold your hand, kiss the pain away' man. Which one is the real you?"

Gregor stopped, studying me, debating internally what to say. "I want to take you somewhere. Are you up for it?"

I sat up straighter. "Of course. Let's go."

33

Gregor held on to me tight and then jumped high into the air.

We jumped from tower to tower until we reached the highest one in Ager. What lay below us was the back of the fortress city. It was shrouded in clouds. A horizon was set in between the clouds in the sky and the dark clouds on the ground, painting the pristine white towers gold, orange, and purple. It was an amazing sight to behold.

Gregor sat down, keeping me in his arms, and gazed out to the light-changing horizon. "It seems odd in this realm that we would have sunsets. I would like to think that Ager was created like this to remind us that time is still running and very fluid. While time runs differently here, it's still felt by everything—human or not." He sighed. "Or maybe it's just a cruel reminder that life moves on with or without you."

"Does that bother you? That life moves on with you?"

He gave me a small smile. "Sometimes, it does. Sometimes it doesn't. And to answer your question, why can't I be both? Serious but charismatic? Dutiful and debonair?

With a smile, I said, "I don't remember adding all that."

He chuckled and gave me a soft smile. "I know my job is important. We bring souls to their final destination. We protect the living. Nabil is very serious about this and wants to make sure we never lose sight of our mission. Saving souls from destruction is our purpose. You know, Nabil says the Archs don't think much of us because we are not angels. But we are only ones in all of the realms that maintain order in the everyday lives of humans in the Live Realm."

"If the Archs think they are so good, can they do what you do?"

He frowned. "No, it's not their role. Nor do I think they have the capacity. Archs don't have a shred of humanity. I think our human pasts help us understand what it takes to keep the destructive evil at bay. That part of the job, protecting people, is important to me."

"Yes, the spirit police."

Gregor's laugh warmed my insides. "Aye, something like that." We sat in comfortable silence when he said, "You know I'm not happy about you fighting."

"Really? I hadn't noticed. You seemed so carefree about it."

He ignored me. "I really hoped you'd reconsider. It isn't as simple as it looks, and to draw out your Havadar is difficult and strenuous—"

"Do you want to cripple me? Why shouldn't I be able to fight effectively? Lethally?" I challenged.

Gregor looked out to the horizon, his jaw tense. "We should

protect you. Your role should be more peaceful. And I am not saying that you shouldn't be able to protect yourself. You have been gifted with the ability, and I'd be a fool not to see it. But your reasons for fighting are coming from a wrong place."

Wishing I had more energy to argue, I said quietly, "I need this, Gregor. I need to feel like I'm standing up for my family, my friends, and myself. I need to fight back on their behalf."

"Are you willing to die for it?"

I met his eyes. "I have no intention of dying."

The tension in his shoulders eased a bit, but he held me closer. "I'm just worried about the dangers. Worried about what you'll find out there."

I snorted. "I'll be fine. That's what I have you for, right?"

"Oh, now I'm just a convenience," Gregor smirked.

I wrapped my arms around his neck and brought his face closer. "You're my favorite convenience."

"Indeed." Feeling the now-familiar lurch in my belly as I stared into my favorite blue eyes, we closed the gap between us and allowed our lips to meet. Gregor's met mine with a slight hesitancy, but he brought my face closer, clashing with my tongue with vigor. Cravers could've been flying around, bombing us with nuclear warheads, and I would've only been aware of how his hand caressed my face, the feeling of his fingers tangled in my hair, and the sound of his low groan as I brought my own hand into his hair.

The moment only lasted for a few seconds, but it meant a lifetime to me. He released my lips and nuzzled my nose. "Let's get you back. I know you're exhausted." Gregor grinned wickedly. "Wouldn't be fair to keep my student out past her curfew."

I couldn't help but chuckle and snuggle closer into his shoulder. "Jerk face," I muttered, yawning. As he sailed through the air to our tower, I could have sworn that I had seen a moving shadow in the corner of my eye.

"Gregor, did you—" Before I could finish, the shadow was already gone.

"Did you say something, Katya?" Gregor asked, still moving swiftly through the air.

Chalking it up to exhaustion, I shook my head no and passed into dreamland.

*   *   *

The next morning, a persistent knocking brought me out of a very pleasant dream. What it was exactly I couldn't remember. The last fleeting remnant was Young Jae with his arms wide open and huge smile on his face. I couldn't help the wave of good feelings the dream evoked and I woke with a goofy smile too. After several moments of choosing to ignore the raps on the door, my persistent knocker finally came into the room. Jae seemed annoyed, but relieved.

"Miss Katya, you are running behind schedule. Major Gregor is waiting for us."

Groaning, I sat up, stretching to shake the sleep from my eyes. Jae's eyes widened as he took one look at me. I yawned, "Oh gosh, sorry. My hair must be a mess right now, huh?"

The young Lieutenant quickly turned around, facing the wall. "Um, no, my lady," he stammered. "That is not to say that your hair isn't a mess. But I do like it. It's really nice. Not to say that it's not normally nice—"

"OMG, Jae! Spit it out!"

"You are n-naked!" he stuttered.

With my feel-good-sleep fog dissipating, I noticed the certain breeziness in the air. One look down confirmed I was in fact naked. And I had just given Jae a free peep show. I started screaming and clutched the blanket to my chest.

"My lady, please do not scream! You'll alert the entire guard. I'm sorry! I shouldn't have come in. I'll wait for you outside." He made for the door, still taking a sideways glance at me as he exited. Mortified, I wished I hadn't sleepily stripped to the bare after Gregor brought me back to my room. I quickly found my training clothes on the floor next to the bed and dressed quickly.

When I did leave my room, poor Jae refused to look up from the floor. "We better get a move on, my lady."

The awkward silence continued down to the courtyard until I stopped him and said, "Jae, let's just forget about what happened. It's not that big of a deal. It's just…normal body stuff."

He looked at me incredulously. "You don't have a problem with me looking at…you?"

"I wouldn't exactly put it like that." I shrugged. "The way it happened was definitely embarrassing. But we're both adults. We can be cool about this."

A small smile crept up his face, which I returned. But he turned away and continued to walk to the training sphere, turning serious. "My lady, you forgot about our meeting with General Lamar. I was supposed to meet you after your training was complete."

I smacked my forehead. "Oh crap, I'm sorry. I was completely knocked out yesterday from training. Can we meet today?"

His jaw tightened, but he spoke kindly. "Yes, the General assumed something like that had happened. I've been given permission to collect you from your training session early."

I nodded. A quick look around the courtyard showed it empty again. "Are the squads doing drills still?"

"Yes," Jae said briskly. "Under General Nabil's orders."

Since I'd been here, the Kyrios had always been milling around the courtyard, even when they had things to do. Something felt off about it and I couldn't stop my next question.

"Jae, is there anything that's being kept from me?"

He froze. His green eyes widened in surprise and consternation. "Why would you think that?"

"Call it a hunch. It just seems off to me that everyone just disappeared. Is there something going on in the Live Realm I should know about?"

Jae relaxed a bit, and he took a hold of my arm and brought me closer to him. "Yes, something is going on, but I don't think I have any new information that you already don't have," he said very quietly. "When you first arrived, General Nabil said the Kyrios shouldn't be milling about and that we should provide you with a good example."

"Example of what?"

"I believe he said something about the goodness of the Kyrios. I didn't understand it at the time and I still don't. Either way, the Kyrios have been kept very busy."

That still didn't feel right to me at all, and I was about to ask more questions when Jae brought me closer and whispered, "Say nothing else—I know you have questions. I believe General Lamar might be the only one who will answer them for you. We will speak to him tonight."

"All right, I'll to speak to Lamar. I just feel like something is off."

He gave me a small smile. "You wouldn't be the Balancer if you weren't able to rely on your instincts. I only want to help you as much as I can, Katya."

I gnawed at my bottom lip, fighting back a chuckle. "You know, I had a dream about you," I teased.

His eyebrows danced on his forehead. "Oh really? What about?"

"I don't really remember it." I said nonchalantly. "I just remember feeling really happy."

Jae shrugged but he couldn't keep the growing smile off his face. "Like I said, the Balancer should rely on her instincts. Maybe your instincts are telling you something. To stay happy and stay near happy people."

An incredulous laugh escaped my lips. "Lieutenant, your Havadar wouldn't have anything to do with that dream, would it?"

"My Havadar and I only serve at your pleasure, Katya," was his only response.

34

When we finally got to the training dome, the Quad were in their corners and in the center stood Gregor, who had on his "I'm not pleased" face.

"You're late."

"Sorry," I muttered. "Good morning, everyone!" I called out. The Quad left their corners and met me in the center.

"Good morning, my lady," Sebastian said, bowing with a flourish. The rest of the four bowed in response. I looked to Gregor, who was having a heated discussion with Jae off to the side. Not wanting to seem nosy, I turned to the Quad and said, "I guess we can start without Gregor. Shall we?"

Addy looked uneasy. "Perhaps we should wait."

I frowned, "Oh come on, guys, they'll only be a minute. I want to get started." The guards shared a look and bowed down. "As you wish, my lady."

Groaning, I said, "Guys, look at me and read my lips. Stop.

Calling. Me. Lady. Just call me Katya. If we are going to be with each other all the time, we might as well get comfortable with each other. And if you are my guard, then I order you to treat me like everyone else."

They all gave me a knowing smile. "So," Addy started, "you want to be treated like we treat each other?"

"Yes! That's exactly what I want. As a matter of fact, I'd rather be with everyone else in the barracks. I want to around everyone else. How else are we supposed to be, as Raf would say, 'comrades-in-arms'?"

Their smiles turned mischievous. "Then you'll join us tonight at the barracks for a bit?" Zenobia asked, her hazel eyes glittering.

I returned their mischievous smile. "If you guys have a plan to get me there, I'm all ears. Can I even go to the barracks?"

Sebastian put his arm around my shoulders. "We so happen have to watch a certain person tonight while Gregor runs out to the Live Realm to relieve one of the squad leaders for a couple of hours."

I looked back on the two Kyrios, still in a heated exchange. "General Lamar has asked to see me this afternoon. Can we do it after?"
Demetrius's easy smile disappeared. "Wait, you're going to see Lamar?"

"Yes. Is there a problem?" I said carefully. Demetrius didn't reply and didn't seem happy. As a matter of fact, he looked like Gregor had looked only a few moments ago. Before I could repeat my question, Gregor left Jae behind, who was staring at me fiercely. Gregor stood in front of me, his eyes still on Jae.

"Because you've been summoned by General Lamar this afternoon, our session will be cut short. So, I'm going to be a bit harder on you today to make up for the lost time. You don't mind, do you?" His arm snaked around my waist, bringing me closer.

It would've been a nice moment if the Quad weren't surrounding us. They suddenly looked around, clearly very uncomfortable, and Gregor was still shooting daggers at the Lieutenant behind me with his eyes. "Lieutenant, I believe I dismissed you."

Jae didn't say a word, but he departed silently from the sphere.

I moved out of Gregor's embrace and asked softly, "What you are you doing? What happened to being careful?"

Gregor ignored my question and returned the questioning stare the Quad gave him with a testy clip. "What are you all looking at? We are running on a tight schedule. To your positions."

For the rest of the session, Gregor had me alternate forming spheres in either hand as fast as I was able. When I was able to interchange them at faster speeds, he had me do laps, barking out orders to form spheres while running. He was not joking—he was tough and a bit mean about it too.

So you can imagine how excited I was when Jae showed up and interrupted. "I've come to fetch Lady Katya, Major," Jae said briskly.

"One minute," Gregor said, equally brisk. Again somehow I ended up with my back to Jae and with Gregor looking behind me. He lowered his eyes to mine and smirked, "Is it just me or are you happy to be rid of me?"

I smirked back at him, "I'd be lying if I said no."

He chuckled softly. "I have to run down to the Live Realm tonight. I'll be a couple of hours. Sebastian will be escorting you back to your room after your meeting with General Lamar."

I nodded and began to turn away when the Scot grabbed my wrist. "Katya," he said suddenly, his eyes searching mine.

When he didn't finish, I prompted him. "Yes?"

After a moment, he released me. His face became guarded. "Stay with the Quad. They'll protect you."

I gave him a funny look. "You're acting like I'm leaving Ager. I'll be here when you get back." I turned and looked for Jae, who hadn't moved from his spot. It might have been just my imagination, but the look on Jae's face showed complete rage. However, a blink of an eye later, his face was relatively blank, nonchalant. As I neared him, he broke out into his easy smile. "Miss Katya, are you ready?"

I cocked my head to the side, "Yes, I am very eager to speak the General."

Jae shrugged with a smile. ""Come on, the General has some news for you." With one nod goodbye to the guards, I followed Jae out the sphere and past several prominent towers to a series of Towers that were similar to my own but styled for each General's position. Nabil's tower was the largest and housed Central Command. Michiko's tower housed the archives and smelled of just old books and paper. Lamar's particular tower had a series of satellites attached at the tower's peak. Through Lamar's main door, a long staircase spiraled to the top.

"Please don't tell me he's at the top."

He grinned. "All right, I won't."

My head fell back on my shoulders with a groan. "I don't have the energy to go up these stairs right now."

Jae shyly scratched the back of his head. "If you don't mind, I could take you up." His face desperately tried not to turn red. I, on the other hand, was ecstatic. I quickly moved into his arms, grinning at him.

"Jae, you are the best!" Young Jae adjusted me, bringing me closer to his chest. His eyes softened and he gave me a sweet smile. "Anytime, Katya. Anytime."

My smile grew as I took in his good looks. "Man, you must have many broken hearts when you were alive."

He sighed deeply. "It is the burden that I bear. These looks and this dazzling smile did quite the damage to the female population back in Korea."

"Okay, okay. Enough of that. One compliment and your head grows to the size of the earth."

He chuckled as he sprang into the air, taking several flights of stairs at a time. In no time, we reached the top floor. We lifted our hand to knock on the door when we heard, "Come on in, you two."

Puzzled, I looked at Jae, who shrugged. "He's security. He sees everything."

35

We walked into a room filled with television screens.

From the ceiling to the floor, there were screens showing different places in the world: New York, Los Angeles, London, Paris, Cairo, Rio de Janeiro, Tokyo, etc. And on each screen, it showed the viewer what each Kyrios unit was currently doing. In New York, I watched some members of Gregor's squad stand atop of the Brooklyn Bridge, monitoring for any activity. In London, a group of Kyrios had cornered several wandering souls in an alley off the main road nearby Westminster Abbey to send them to the Room of Apofasi. In Cairo, a group of ten Kyrios were in formation, attacking a very large Wanter that had entered the Live Realm several feet in front of the Pyramids, causing some tourists to scatter, fearing the tremors they could feel. In Paris and Tokyo, their respective iconic towers had a few Kyrios resting at their peaks, talking and laughing. Nearby Rio, a Kyrios was monitoring a human walking through a street of a *favela*, assessing whether or not the human was being influenced by a Poser. And in Los Angeles, the city I was to head to in order to close the first gate, a number of small Wanters were chasing two children's souls. I couldn't hear anything, but I had to assume that they were screaming in terror.

General Lamar had been sitting in a chair, watching the screens when we walked in. He turned around to see with an easy smile on his face. "Lady Katya," he said. "I hear you have some questions for me and a request to speak to your mother." He offered me a seat beside him at his desk.

I took it immediately, still needing a moment to fully recover from training. "General, if I ask you something, will you be completely honest with me?"

Lamar nodded and waved his hand, effectively shutting off the screens. "What is on your mind?"

"Why do I have this feeling that you guys are hiding something from me? And why do I have a feeling that I am constantly pissing off General Nabil? I'm not trying to on purpose, but it seems that anytime I want to do something or understand something more fully, it's the biggest inconvenience."

Lamar shared a look with Jae before saying carefully, "I will not treat you like a fool, my lady. I have told Nabil to be honest with you, but he seems to think his ways are best. Being Lead General for hundreds of years will do that—makes you obstinate. But I believe that everyone should be aware of the truth about the man leading us." He raised his hand, showing a familiar branding. "I am bound to secrecy on some matters, so I cannot divulge too much, but whatever I can give you I will tell you."

Lamar leaned back in his chair. "How well do you know about our rivalry with the Archs?"

"That they are archangels, never human, do not like the Kyrios. Though not sure why."

He massaged his chin. "The Archs are considered a level over us. While we handle most of the skirmishes, the Archs deal with the major battles. They don't give us much respect. If anything, they revile us."

"Why is that?"

He shrugged. "It's been that way for as long as I can remember. And I have been here for a very long time. Just as long as General Nabil. Our first encounter with the Archs was over five millennia ago. It was because of an uprising caused by Drachen's minions in the Abyss that we could not contain on our own—the Archs learned of it and descended down from their perch to dole out their justice.

"I've never paid too much attention to the Archs. At the time I was a Lieutenant, and I followed my commanding officer Major Sherene to the meeting to discuss the Archs' plan. Nabil, a Major at the time, was so excited to finally meet the fabled winged angels that he'd heard about. But that meeting shattered many of his delusions about the system and our place in it. Since then, General Nabil has always been insanely jealous of the reverence that the Archs get, while humans fear us and view us as the Grim Reaper. He has been searching for a way to show how powerful we Kyrios can be and to show how much the Archs need us."

A rock fell into the pit of my stomach. "He means to use me."

General Lamar propped himself on knees, leaning towards me. "That is my suspicion. You beside us will be a show of force to them. The Balancer—God's own drop of power—would be with the very things they hate. When we first found you, he was very pleased. But since your relationship with him has not been on the best terms and now, because you wish to actually exert your own free will, he has been reluctant to make you any stronger. I believe that he wants you to rely on us to protect you, to be your warriors, while you complete whatever tasks are in front of you.

It took a show of solidarity from the other Generals including myself to get you to train for your Havadar."

My eyebrows continued to dance on my forehead, trying to figure out Lamar's words. "So he wants to keep me strong enough to close gates but weak enough to need the Kyrios against any real threat. But why has he cleared out all the Kyrios from the courtyard?"

The General smirked. "You have noticed that? For that, I can only speculate, my lady. While there have been orders for all squads to be at the ready in their prospective areas in the Live Realm, Nabil has also ordered that they only enter and exit the courtyard when necessary. He has asked them not to dawdle. My guess is he wants to keep you close to those he has chosen for you, who won't speak ill of him. So that you will see his good side and work well with him. Either way, we'll keep an eye on him. And I will do my best to keep you informed about what is going on."

"Thank you, General." The first chance I could, I was going to test Lamar's theory with the Quad. I didn't want lackeys around me with any hidden motives. "How about my mom?"

Lamar nodded towards Jae. "Lieutenant here tells me that you want to visit your mother in a dream."

"Yes. I'm worried about her. Gregor said that you have put her in a safe house in South America, but I need to know that she is definitely safe." Tears prickled at the corner of my eyes. "I just want to give her peace of mind that I'll be home soon."

Lamar cocked his head to the side. "Not to diminish Young Jae's abilities, but dreamwalking is not a practice that we do very often—only in instances where a Poser's interference expands longer than a few days. There is a large chain of command to authorize it. If we were to go through normal protocols, I'm afraid that you would be denied."

The dark-skinned General smirked. "Which is why we are going to do it anyway."

I grinned and took his hand. "Thank you, General!" He held on tight and seemed reluctant to let go of me.

"You know, you remind me much of Sherene."

"Your Major?"

His gaze drifted over my face, almost wistful. "Even in the face of danger, she was such a spitfire. She never backed down from any challenge and could never take no for an answer. Much like yourself." For several moments, Lamar's mind seemed to replay memories unseen to either myself or Jae. Uncomfortable, I softly pulled away from his grasp, bringing Lamar back to the present.

"Yes, well, we should get started!" he said happily.

"You won't get into trouble for this?"

He gave out a hearty laugh. "My dear, I'm head of security. Who is going to tell on me?" He slapped his knee and with a pep in his step, jumped out of his seat. "Let's get started, shall we?" He and Jae moved the chairs and cleared a space on the floor. "I've been monitoring your mother. Luckily, she is currently sleeping and dreaming. We'll need to move quickly. I need you to lie on the floor beside Jae. He'll be your guide through this." I lay down on the floor, shoulder to shoulder with Jae. "Take his hand. This is very important—you must never release his hand. Navigating dreams is very complicated. Just like the mind has many doors, there are enough paths in dreams that can get you lost forever.

You could even find yourself in the Abyss if you're not careful where you step."

I nodded, feeling the pit of nervousness. Why did everything have to be so dangerous? Why couldn't an explanation start off with "This should be a walk in the park for you"? I took a hold of Jae, who gave me a reassuring squeeze. I gave him a weak smile and closed my eyes. I heard Lamar move about the room, flipping on switches before his footsteps were close to my head.

"Since I don't have time to teach you the mechanics of dreamwalking, I'm going to force you in, like you might have experienced while visiting your soulscape. Jae's already there waiting for you."

Before I could mutter, "Oh goody," an immense but familiar pressure pressed down on my chest and my head. When I felt a hand on my forehead, I shot up suddenly, feeling completely confused and disorientated.

Jae knelt before me, gripping my hand. "Shh, it's all right. We're here."

"Where's here?" It looked like we were in the middle of downtown Boston. But it was empty. The normal bustle of shoppers was missing. There was not one teenager heading to the music store in sight. Not one car, bus, or homeless man on the corner. Not a soul in sight. It was just like my dream of Los Angeles.

Jae helped me up, not once releasing my hand. "We're in your mother's dream. She's about to show up in a few seconds." I searched up and down the street for some sign of life. But there was nothing. Even the Commons seemed desolate without its normal infestation of pigeons.

"Are you sure this—" I began, but I stopped when I heard my name. "Katya? Katya, where are you?"

"Mom," I cried. "Mom! I'm here!" Jae held tight to me. "Don't move from this spot. Let her come."

Sure enough, coming from a nearby street, my mother came around the corner and stopped dead in her tracks. "Katya?"

"Mom," I choked.

She rushed over, crying, "My beautiful baby girl!" I couldn't hold back the stream either. I was finally able to see my mother, even it was only a dream. Sobbing, she ran into my arms and said, "Oh my Lord, I thought I'd never find you again."

"I'm sorry I disappeared, Mom. It's just that there's so much going on right now."

"Shh, you'll have all the time in the world to tell me when we get home." She took a hold of my hand and turned to leave when I pulled back.

"No, Mom. You don't understand. This isn't real. This is a dream." When my mom's face fell, I said quickly, "I had to let you know I'm okay, but this only way I can come to you."

"So..." She looked around, taking in the empty metropolis. "This isn't real."

I shook my head. "But us talking is real. I was able to convince them to let me do this because I didn't want you to worry."

Mom took a quick glance at Jae. "Who is this and why are his hands all over you?"

I rolled my eyes. "Wow, Mom, freak out much? I'm trying to explain that to you."

Mom crossed her arms, but shrugged. "Okay. What's going on? I'm told our house got blown up due to some sinister plot that they can't tell me about. I'm in witness protection and stuck in a house in the jungle with three men I don't know, while my only daughter is supposed to be in a different location. But I can't know what that location is either. So first, tell me, how are you even able to talk to me in my dream and what do you have to do with any of this?"

I gnawed at my lip, suddenly feeling very uncertain. This was not going to be easy. "Jae, can I tell her everything?"

Jae gave me another squeeze and nodded. "The speech bind that Major Gregor put on you doesn't affect you in your sleep. You can tell her."

I exhaled loudly, "Mom, don't say a word until I'm finished, okay?"

Then I told her the abridged version of everything with Jae's help. Well, except the parts about Cynthia being my Havadar, Gregor and me kissing, and Jae seeing me naked. I watched as her eyes and her lips thinned as the story got more and more fantastic.

When I was finished, she looked between Jae and myself. "So you expect me to believe that you are God's drop of power that's supposed to save everyone, you work with a bunch of angels—"

"Death guards," I interjected.

"Your father was killed by invisible, dead humans-turned-monsters, and you're going to stop and maybe fight these same monsters? And you tell me all this in my dream?"

I winced. "Look, I know it seems a bit crazy—"

She gave a short laugh. "You think? Gosh, I really need to lay off those sleeping pills."

I took a hold of her shoulder, shaking it a bit. "Mom, please! This is all true." I looked to Jae. "A little help here?"

He frowned, but said, "Mrs. Stevens, if I may?" Mom eyed him cautiously but nodded. Jae held out his free hand and focused his Vis to it. A blue energy swirled furiously around until it crystallized in the middle of his palm. A closer glance showed it to be a flower that pulsed lightly. *I definitely want to learn how to do that.*

"This is a lotus made from my Vis energy. Take it. There is enough energy in it that it will transfer over to real life. It will last for twenty-four hours. When you wake up and find this with you, you will know that this is all true." Mom gently took the flower and gingerly put in her pocket. She quietly said, "It's beautiful. Thank you."

A beeping noise suddenly emerged from inside Jae's uniform. He cursed. "We have five minutes before the General will pull us back."

"W-wait, please Kat. Baby, don't go," Mom said tearfully. "You're the only one I have left."

I put the bravest face I had. "Mom, I'm just going to take care of some business. I'll be home soon."

She bit her lip and smoothed down my hair. "You promise?"

she whispered. I had never seen my mother look so lost, other than when my dad died. I felt a tear slip down as I nodded.

"Promise. I love you, Mom."

Mom began to full-out sob, and she pulled me into an awkward hug. "I love you too, pumpkin. So much." I leaned into her shoulder, hugging her the best I could with one arm. I was suddenly struck with the strangest feeling, that this would be the last time I would see her. When she started to step back from me, I wrenched my hand out of Jae's hand, closed the distance between us, and gave my mother a bear hug.

"Katya," Jae cried. "Don't move!" The two of us froze. "Why in the world did you let go of my hand?"

"I wanted to give my mother a proper hug," I said into my mother's shoulder.

I could hear him huff indignantly. "Well, now any sudden movement could open another door to who knows where."

Crap. "What do I do?" I said frantically.

"Don't move. I'm going to carefully move over to you and grab your shoulder, okay?"

"Okay," I whimpered.

Mom whispered, "Don't move, sweetie." However, her whispering moved her hair just enough that it rested underneath my nose.

I wiggled my nose, but it just made it worse. "Jae, hurry. Mom's hair is tickling my nose."

I heard a shuffling behind me. "I can't move too quickly either. Hold on." I tried to shift away from the hair, but it seemed to go further up my nose. I began to whimper louder, feeling the sneeze coming on.

"Katya, please," Mom urged.

"I'm almost there, Katya. Don't—"

The sneeze wouldn't listen and came out forcefully. The floor underneath me suddenly disappeared, sending me spiraling down. Sheer terror rocked through me as I found myself dangling over a dark and cloudy area that bled cold, evil energy. The clouds churned and clashed together with flashes of lightning that would have destroyed me. The only thing that kept me falling into the chasm beneath me was my mother's grasp on my wrist.

"Hang on, Katya!" she cried. There was some shouting between her and Jae, but I was too concerned with the dark cloud that had engulfed the entire space underneath my feet. A powerful energy emerged from it that reminded me of Mika. But it wasn't pure at all. It was…gunk. Just plain nasty. Every possible dark and depressing thought I'd ever had had come up to the surface and left a cold bite in my heart.

Then I suddenly felt like I wasn't alone in the hole. Whatever was there could sense my fear. It was laughing.

A second hand grabbed my arm, and I was pulled back onto stable dream concrete. I clung to Mom and Jae, trying to banish the murky feeling from me.

"Are you all right?" Mom questioned me from the heap of our bodies.

"Yeah," I said shakily. "Just caught off guard."

Jae caught a hold of my face and studied my eyes. Whatever he was looking for, he didn't say. But he looked satisfied. "We have a minute left. Mrs. Stevens, remember the flower. It will confirm everything."

Mom grabbed Jae's arm and said unflinchingly, "I'm entrusting you with my only daughter. See that no harm comes to her."

The Lieutenant swallowed, but nodded. We stood up and I gave my mother a final kiss. "I'll be seeing you, Momma."

Tears streamed down her face. "I'll see you later, Kitty." Our hands were still gripping each other when she disappeared. The entire Boston dreamscape faded to black.

And once again I sat back up with a gasp, disorientated. Jae and General Lamar kneeled beside me.

"Was it successful?" the General asked.

Tears again couldn't be stopped. "Yes," I said brokenly. "Yes, thank you."

Lamar smiled kindly and patted my shoulder, his hand lingering. "What wouldn't I do for the Balancer?" He rose to his full height. "Young Jae, I believe in the ten minutes you were gone, Lady Katya's bodyguards have come for her. See that she is returned to them safely."

"Of course, General."

Lamar bowed slightly. "Until next time, my lady."

"Thank you again, General."

As we exited the room. Jae scooped me up but didn't immediately leap down. He studied my face for a moment and asked, "Are you all right?"

I put on a brave smile. "I'm just happy to have seen her. Thank you for today." I tightened my grip on his neck to bring him closer and kissed him on the cheek. The young Lieutenant's cheeks flared red, but he smiled softly.

With a smirk, he said, "What wouldn't I do for the Balancer?"

36

Just as we exited the tower, four imposing figures made a beeline for us at the entrance.

"I trust everything is well," Demetrius said first, his eyes on Young Jae.

Jae quickly nodded. "Yes, sir. I was just about to escort the Lady into your care."

Demetrius gave him a glare, but he nodded as well. "You may take your leave."

Jae saluted the Quad and then turned to me. "Have a pleasant evening, my lady," he said solemnly. He bowed, and his glittering eyes betrayed him.

I rolled my eyes, but followed his lead by returning the bow, "Goodnight, Lieutenant."

The four lead me away from the Generals' towers and towards the back, where the barracks were located. "Are you really going to let me see what goes on there?"

Zenobia grinned, stretching and cracking vertebrae in her back. "Sure, just as long as we get you back to your room on time. I don't know about you, but I could use a little fun. We'll be fine."

Demetrius didn't look convinced. "If General Nabil ever found out…"

"Pssh, when has Old Man General Nabil ever been down to the barracks for some fun? Don't worry," Sebastian cut him off. "We're not going to tell. She's certainly not going to tell. And the fellas aren't going to tell."

"The fellas?" I asked.

Addy simply grinned. "We could explain, but why don't you meet them yourself?"

As we walked around several dome-shaped barracks, I snuck at a look at the Quad. "So General Nabil isn't a fan of barracks life?"

Addy snorted. "Our Lead General is too good to be down there. As if he was never a lower-ranking Kyrios."

"So we're not fans of him?"

They all made various noises that I understood as "Meh." So much for Lamar's guess about Nabil's plans.

Sebastian smirked, "He's an old man, Katya. He was taught that high-ranking officials must know their place. Old men forget their origins."

"I heard he has been here for over five thousand years," I chimed in. "It kinds means sense if you think about it. My granddad used to hate me trying to change the channel whenever he was over our house. Nabil's crankiness is just like an old man who wants to keep the TV on, but not for the sake of watching."

The others laughed at my analogy—even Demetrius, who seemed chagrined at himself at his inability to control his own chuckle.

We had just arrived outside a dome-shaped barrack with five slashes above the door post. A look around showed that the other similar domes had different numbers slashed above their door. Addy threw the barrack door open and announced in a loud voice, "My lady, meet the men of Troop Five!"

There were several people seated throughout the covered hangout—about fourteen all together. All who heard the booming voice turned their attention to the door. And I suddenly felt quite nervous. Sebastian nudged me inside. I looked at the Kyrios surrounding me, all looking much beefier this close up. I managed a soft, "Hello guys."

The soldiers continued to stare at me until a voice from the back said, "Might I remind you, Addy, that there is one less sausage around here?" Stepping from behind a very tall Kyrios came a woman who was barely five feet tall. She was dressed in Kyrios fashion but with a familiar platinum blond haircut that framed silver and steel-gray eyes.

Sebastien sighed loudly. "Yes, we know, sis. You are a woman. Keep your panties on."

The petite woman scowled. In a flash, she was directly in front of Sebastian and she flat out kicked him in the jaw. I could feel my jaw brush the floor as Sebastian dropped to the floor. "Damn it, Jaya!" he yelled, clutching his face. "What the Abyss is wrong with you?"

Jaya ignored him and turned to me, grinning widely. "Hello, my lady! I'm Jaya. Very nice to meet you!" She grasped my hand and led me forward toward the rest of the slack-jawed Kyrios. A glance behind me showed Zenobia, Demetrius, and Addy exasperated but amused. Jaya squeezed my hand, gaining my attention again. "My lady, let me just say this: don't be intimidated by this group. Like my brother just demonstrated, they are a bunch of softies."

"Sure. And call me Katya. I'm not big on titles."

Jaya began to bounce on her toes like a five-year-old. "Really? Come and sit down with us." She led me to the table where the rest of the men were seated and she placed me at the head.

I noticed the men were still standing around and said, "Guys, please, sit down too. No ceremony here, okay? I'm not General Nabil."

The men chuckled, looked at each other, and looked at the Quad, who nodded their consent. There was a sudden mad dash to grab chairs, almost coming to blows to get the chairs closest to me. To say I was confused and shocked would've been an understatement. They all looked at me eagerly, awaiting their chance to talk.

I smiled widely. "This is so great. I've been waiting for my chance to come and meet you all."

"And we as well, my lady," a voice said towards the back. The rest of the men murmured in agreement.

I guess I hadn't been the only one told to stay away. The male who'd won the coveted seat next to me said eagerly, "My lady—

"Guys, please, no more of this 'lady' stuff. Just call me Katya." I said sternly. "And that's an order!"

They seemed to accept this, for they all grinned widely and answered together, "Yes, miss!"

The man closest to me cleared his throat and introduced himself as Santiago. "I think that I speak for all of us when I say that we are pleased that you are here. We all have wanted to meet the fabled Balancer."

I rolled my eyes. "I'm nothing special, trust me. And I've wanted to interact with you since I started training, but every time I step out now, there's not a soul outside." I made a show of sighing deeply. "I guess Nabil is really working your tails off."

I noticed the some of the men looked at each other with odd looks, but Santiago pulled my attention away. "There have been several orders, but we all were really curious about you. We've never had someone here in Ager that was not a Kyrios."

"How old are you?" someone called out.

"I turned eighteen a couple of months ago."

The Kyrios looked shocked.

Quiet murmurs filled the room. "She's just a child."

"Why they are sending someone so young into battle?"

"Do the Generals realize how young she is?"

I eyed one of the men who said loudly, "Nothing but a baby!" He was a tall auburn-haired man who didn't seem much older than twenty-two himself.

I stood from my chair. "My position has nothing to do with my age." I made a point to bring my power to the surface and glowed blue from head to toe. I was pleased to see some of the men impressed. "I can take care of myself." I turned to the yeller. "And you don't seem that much older than me anyway, Babyface!"

He smiled as the rest of the Kyrios guffawed at my point. "I'm five hundred and eighty-three years old, Miss Katya."

I paused. "What?"

Auburn-Haired Man laughed. "I'm five hundred and eighty-three years old!" I took another look around and realized that the Kyrios were mixed in age. Some looked as young as me. Others looked old enough to be my father.

I looked at one particular gray-templed man. "How old are you?"

"One hundred and fifty-three."

And to a freckled young boy, I asked the same question. "Four hundred and twelve."

I arched an eyebrow. "I'm guessing your mismatching ages has to do with the time that you became a Kyrios." I turned to the Four. "What about you guys?"

Zenobia frowned. "I think I'm seven hundred and sixty-four, last time I checked."

"Nine hundred and forty-two, my lady," Addy answered.

"Six hundred and ten," said Sebastian.

Demetrius said with a proud grin, "I'm one thousand and five years old, my lady."

I shook my head. "You guys are ancient!" The men laughed at that.

Santiago spoke up again. "What Kevon meant," he pointed to Auburn-Haired Man, "was that, compared to us, you are like a child. We have been around for quite some time."

I nodded, but a thought came to mind: *Yes, they were all alive at one point. But what does it take to be a Kyrios?* Not sure I wanted to bring that question to the group at large, I moved on to something else.

"You said it's rare for others to come to Ager?"

"Extremely," Santiago said excitedly. "I can't think of a time that someone has been here without passing on. The other troops will be furious when they find out you've been here. They'll just feel your footprint and be instantly jealous."

I looked blankly at him. "My footprint?"

"You leak Vis like a running faucet," Jaya said beside me.

I looked at her, puzzled, but then laughed. "Actually, now that I think about it, when I first met Gregor, he told me that I leak energy so much it was amazing I went on unnoticed."

Jaya nodded in agreement. "He is very right. I noticed you the first time you walked through the East Gate. You have so much Vis that it just runs out of you constantly. Your training has helped, but you still have a bit of drip still going. Any strong spiritual entity could find you quite quickly."

I frowned and turned to the Quad. "Why haven't we addressed this yet? Isn't it going to be important to move about undetected?"

Addy said, "I think Gregor's been more focused on getting you to bring out your Vis and communicate better. I'm sure he will add stealth if he finds it appropriate."

Jaya turned to her brother and gave him a dirty look. "When is stealth not appropriate? What are you teaching her in the dome? How to hold her breath?"

Sebastian rolled his eyes. "We don't teach her. We're just there as containment shields. Plus, what would you know about teaching anything to anyone, midget?"

She growled, rolling up her sleeves. "I'll teach you something right now, you son of bitch!"

"She was your mother too, idiot," he replied.

Jaya gave a loud howl and tackled him to the ground, trading blows. I looked at Zenobia and mouthed, *Are they serious?*

Zenobia looked bored. "They always do this. It'll be over soon." He was right. Jaya had successfully pinned her brother down with him screaming, "Okay! Uncle! Uncle!"

The petite blond laughed triumphantly, giving Sebastian a parting kick. She repositioned herself beside me again and said gleefully, "I think this just proves that I should be Katya's bodyguard instead."

Kevon shot out of his seat. "Are you kidding me? This comes from the girl who hightailed it out of her first battle, leaving a puddle behind!"

The men guffawed, and I caught myself giggling, giving an apologetic look to Jaya. Kevon threw me a wink.

Jaya jumped up on the table and stomped in front of Kevon. "Last time I checked, someone couldn't stop weeping after *his* first battle!" She patted his head condescendingly. "Poor baby needed his bottle?"

The way Kevon's face matched his hair got me giggling harder and gasping for air.

Kevon stood from his chair, now eye to eye with Jaya. "At least I got on Squad Five by my own merits, not because my brother pulled some strings, you bitch." The men suddenly got eerily quiet. The atmosphere immediately changed. And if the crackling energy around Jaya wasn't any indication of something wrong, it would've been the men's nervous sideway glances for an exit.

Jaya grabbed Kevon's collar, bringing him inches away from her face. "What did you call me?" she asked, dangerously soft.

"Jaya, why don't you calm down?" Sebastian said quickly, looking at me, concerned.

"Shut up!" she yelled, her eyes never leaving Kevon. "This one thinks I'm weak. Why don't I just show him now how weak I am?" Angrily, her eyes flashed both red and blue in tandem, reminding me of Gregor's face in the alley, so long ago now.

I couldn't even ask what was going on when the Quad began shouting for Jaya to calm down. Kevon seemed ready to have it out. The rest of the squad began to back up, getting ready to dash out of the way.

But all of it didn't matter. The door burst open and a furious Gregor stepped inside.

"Where is Lady Katya?" Gregor thundered. All eyes swirled to where I was seated—at the head of the calamity. Jaya and Kevon froze in their battle stances, with the rest of the barrack looking on as the Quad surrounded the fighting pair. It probably looked like I had ordered them to fight for my entertainment!

I gulped and slowly raised my hand. "Um, hey Gregor! You're back! Have a nice trip?"

Gregor took in the scene before him and didn't say a word. He simply quickstepped beside me, scooped me up, and flashed out the door. He paused in the doorway and said over his shoulder, "I'll come talk to you lot after I take care of this one." He slammed the door behind us and stalked towards my tower.

The silence was deafening so I said, "Hey buddy, want to talk about it?"

His eyes narrowed down on me. "Not now, Katya. Not now." I took the hint and shut up. The tense silence continued when we made it to my bedroom, and he stood there staring at the floor.

The longer the silence went on for, the more horrible I felt. "Will you just say something?" I begged. "Please, it's killing me."

"Killing you?" he asked incredulous. "Killing you? How do you think I felt when I was supposed to find you protected and guarded in your room but to find it completely empty? Not an ounce of energy in the room?"

"Actually we need to talk about that leaking—" He shot me a sharp look and I realized that I could bring it up later.

Gregor ran a hand through his tousled hair. "And where do I find you? In the middle of the fourth-strongest Kyrios group with a brawl about to break out! Are you that thick?"

Thick? As in stupid? Feeling my own anger rising, I said, "They didn't fight! The Quad had it under control...somewhat." I sighed, realizing he was right. "Look, I asked the Quad to take me to meet some other Kyrios. I mean, aren't they my fellow fighters against the Want? Why shouldn't I get to know them better?"

Gregor just looked more frustrated. "Katya, there are things I don't think you are ready to face yet."

"What does that even mean? If you would just be honest about what's going on, maybe I'd listen. Or does this have to do with them being stronger than me? Oh, those scary Kyrios, whatever will I do?" I scoffed. "What do I have to do to prove that I can handle this? You said Squad Five is the fourth strongest? Maybe I should just go to wherever Squad Two is and—"

"No!" he ground out. "You—" he beseeched me for some understanding, but I didn't get his point. Gregor shook his head. "Never mind. Just please stay away from the barracks. The men there are a bit too rowdy for my taste. You might get caught up in something."

I frowned. "Can't we meet in the middle? I don't want to be put on a pedestal. I believe someone told me when we first arrived here that he was no better than anyone else and preferred to be with his troop. Maybe I'm just taking his lead."

He gave me a stern look. "Let me think about it."

He turned for the door, but I called him back. "You aren't going to tell Nabil about the Quad taking me there, are you?"

Gregor's blank stare turned into a smirk. "No, but they don't know that yet." With that, he bid me goodnight and closed the door behind him.

37

Three weeks.

It had been three Live Realm weeks since I'd said goodbye to my mother. A full seven days in Ager.
Gregor had been absolutely relentless. It was boot camp for Vis fighters. Any questions I asked that weren't directly about training were met with a running penalty. I planned a murder every day that week.

The Scot had the Quad sweat it out too. For three days after our excursion to the barracks, they did whatever he wanted, including training along with me. The worst part about it was they went completely formal on me, refusing to look me in the eye. When I refused to speak to Gregor until he came clean with them, he told them he would not tell Nabil about our trip. They got comfortable with me again shortly after.

And I had to give Gregor credit. After the first couple of trainings, I'd gained better control over my Vis—we'd even taken care of the leaky Vis situation, so I could now move about Ager relatively undetected. After that, Gregor then taught me how to increase my speed by sending Vis to my feet and increasing my stamina. I wasn't at full quickstep yet, but I was definitely faster than the fastest human in the Live Realm.

Once I could run, we moved to hand-to-hand combat. Throwing punches at Gregor while he barked orders at me was the highlight of my session. I had gotten better control. Just not perfect. In one hand-to-hand session, I was just about able to bring up a barrier around me at will, and I got so excited that I lost focus and caused another explosion. Oops.

After convincing Gregor that was I able to bring up my barrier without accidental explosions, Gregor told me it was time to pull out my Havadar.

"It's time?" I asked nervously.

The Scot nodded and had me focus all of energy into my right hand. "Do you feel pressure behind your hand?" Gregor barked from behind me.

"Yes," I grunted, trying to hold my focus, anchoring my glowing hand with my left.

Gregor moved to stand in front of me. I almost lost my focus with his broad, naked torso now in my view. "I want you to push that pressure to the tips of your fingers."

"What?"

"Come on, you can do it."

I grunted, trying to focus hard on my fingertips. Sweat was pouring down my face. When a yellow glow came from my fingertips, Gregor met my eyes with a hard stare and asked, "Why do you want to fight?"

"To get back at the Want for making my life miserable, for my father's death," I said through gritted teeth, closing my eyes.

I could sense Gregor shaking his head. "That's not good enough. Why do you want to fight?"

"To make the Want pay—"

"No!" he barked. "Why do you want to fight, Katya? What makes you do this? Why are you in Ager? Why did you take this role?"

My body vibrated painfully from exertion and my desperate focus on the Vis while trying to think at the same time. *What brought me here? They ruined my home! They attacked my mother! They put my best friend in a spiritual coma. Amie and my other friends from school are in danger. I need—*

"I need to protect my family!" I cried out. "I want to protect my friends. I don't want others to suffer. I don't want to experience pain anymore. I want to protect my world."

An immensely hot feeling covered my hand, and I felt a weight drop into the palm of my hand. I felt my fingers close around a cold leather handle with tassels attached at the end. I opened my eyes to see a beautiful silver sword. The handle was wrapped in silver leather with stray leather tassels at the end. The blade was light in weight, thin but long, the length of my arm and then some. Diantha had come forth.

It was awesome.

"Is this what Mika meant? Did I just master my heart?"

Gregor grinned. "Do you understand now? That's the real reason, the heart of your mission. A Havadar couldn't have come out unless it came from a place and purpose to protect. Your anger and revenge towards the Want had only clouded your true warrior heart. Congratulations. You are officially a Vis warrior." He showed me how to return the Havadar back to my body.

After showing him that I could pull it out a couple of times at will, he pulled out his own.

At his battle stance, my eyes widened. "What are you doing?"

The Scot's eyebrow arched up. "Taking a page out of General Raf's book. Getting you ready for battle. What do you think?" he said innocently. "Let's see how you do!"

I mimicked his stance with trepidation. "B-b-but I just pulled my sword out. Let's take a break, huh?" I faked a yawn for good measure. "Man, am I tired!"

Girl, don't be such a baby! You have more attitude than that! Cynthia's voice filled my head.

I stared at the sword, incredulous. *Cynthia?*

Who else would it be? And about time too. I've been waiting for you to get control over yourself. Finally, I can come out to play.

"Hey!" Gregor called out, getting my attention, grinning widely. "If you don't lift that sword, I'm going to scar that pretty little face of yours."

"Wait!" I shouted as he charged at me. He stopped and gave me an exasperated look. Not having anything else to say, I batted my eyes. "You think I'm pretty?" Yeah, it didn't work.

He came at me anyway, and I had to lift my Vis sword up to protect myself—just in time.

We then focused on just battling over and over again to the point I had difficulty lifting my arms. But with every fight, I knew I was improving significantly. Cynthia, or Diantha, rather, coached me as well. At times, moves just came to me, as if I had always known them. Hacking, feints, defensive poses, kicks, punches, you name it. Every time I fought, I was able to get a better handle on Diantha.

When I was finally able to maneuver Gregor into a compromising position, he simply grinned and said, "That's my girl."

That night, I went to my room with a huge smile. I didn't share with Gregor that I was able to speak Cynthia at will now, without wielding Diantha. While I stared at my best friend's body, still encased in her sphere, I conversed with her and continue to understand more techniques and how to better manipulate my Vis into different things.

Cynthia said, *The Kyrios have their methods for how to get you ready, but we need to get to the next level. You, me, and Mika.*

I'm not sure whether Gregor sensed anything off at night, but he never said a word.

*   *   *

The next day, when Jae escorted me to the sphere, he looked odd. Like he had swallowed a lemon.

"What's with the face, Jae?" I swung my arm around his neck. An easy friendship had formed between us over the past week. Jae had become the older brother I never had. It felt so easy to be open with him, to complain about everything, and to just be myself. At times, he allowed himself the same luxury, but there were times he would seem put off or angry. He never explained it and I chose not to pry.

But the look on his face this morning had prompted the question before I could catch it.

Oddly enough, he answered readily. "I have a mission on my mind, and it's a bit hard to wrap my head around it."

"Are you going to the Live Realm too?" I asked worriedly. No one would tell me outright, but I knew the situation in the Los Angeles was starting to get even more bothersome. The day's upcoming training was to show Nabil that I was ready to head out and begin closing gates. I looked Jae over and gave him a brave smile. "Whatever it is, I know you can do it. You're one of the best people here. Whatever the mission is, I'm sure you'll do your best."

His smile looked forced. "Of course, Katya. Thank you." As I was about to step into the sphere, he held me back. "Katya?"

"Hmm?"

He opened his mouth to speak, but then fell silent. I felt an eyebrow arch in response. "Jae?"

Jae's forced smile appeared again. "Good fighting today, okay?"

I rolled my eyes and chuckled. "Of course. I wanna get out of Ager! Let's keep our fingers crossed that Gregor isn't successful in killing me today." I waved goodbye and entered the dome to find a number of people awaiting my arrival. I approached Gregor, who was talking quietly to Generals Nabil, Lamar, and Victor, Raf (his first return in days) plus a female who I wasn't particularly excited to see. The Quad was absent.

"Lady Katya, I think we've all been waiting for this day," Nabil said.

I bowed my head in mock reverence. "General, I for one can't wait to pass this test and get a change of scenery and people."

Raf guffawed. "Seems like my time away has done nothing to my lady's sass."

Nabil's eyes narrowed, but he didn't remark on my tone. "Gregor has reported to us your success with your training. As you know, the largest gate thus far in Los Angeles has been growing, and a high-level Wanter could force their way through at any time now. Such a breach of the fabric between the realms would leave a gaping hole that we can't have. The sooner we can patch up that tear, the better. So with today's training, we need you to do and show your best."

My ears perked. "Will you be staying to watch, General Nabil?"

Nabil shook his head. "Unfortunately, no. Raf has returned with intel that the Generals and I must review and apply to our, well, really your, next raid. While we trust Gregor's abilities, we decided the best way to test your abilities is to give you a new sparring partner."

General Lamar interjected before Nabil could continue. "Nabil, perhaps we should—"

"Lamar!" he said sharply. "We've all already decided."

The dark-skinned General's lips became thin with displeasure. Nabil cleared his throat. "As I was saying, we have decided that you should have a different sparring partner, someone other than Gregor."

He motioned for Sophia to move forward. "I'm not sure you've met Sophia yet."

The tall female bowed. "I haven't had the pleasure." Her smile wouldn't have fooled anyone. She clearly did not like me.

I couldn't help but look her up and down and say, "Wait, didn't you serve me my food that one time?"

Her smile faltered and her eyes turned into daggers. I simply smiled.

Nabil looked at the both of us, giving a warning look to me especially. "Sophia will assess your skills and provide us a report. Please abide by her instructions. Gregor, we'll leave you with this." Gregor had his "I'm not happy" look on. I think he wasn't sure who he was angry with—me, Sophia, or the Generals. I gave him a shrug. *I didn't ask Ms. Pinch-Face to join us. Blame Nabil for everything. That's what I do.*

As soon as the General exited the dome, the Scot went into trainer mode. "Get into your stances, ladies."

I pulled out my sword and stepped into the stance Gregor had taught me. But Sophia got into a different stance, one I had never seen. "Oh crap," I muttered.

"Begin!"

38

Sophia charged at me. Hard.

The clanging of our Havadars echoed through the sphere. Cynthia murmured within me, *She is going for blood. Be careful.* My opponent threw her weight behind her attack, but I could hold up. We didn't move, wanting to see who would break first.

"Hmm, seems like my Gregor has taught the Balancer well," she smirked.

"Your Gregor?" I grunted.

Her smirk widened. "Oh yes, he is mine. Always has been. We came to Ager at the same time, as part of the same training class. We've always had each other's back." She jumped back and charged again, this time slashing at me. The extra sessions with Cynthia were paying off. I could counter every time. She began to speed up, forcing me to dodge. I tapped into Mika for a bit more speed to keep up.

"Hmm, that's funny," I said loud enough as our swords met in a deadlock again. "He never mentioned you once."

She snarled and aimed a kick at my midsection. It connected. I yelped in pain, but still managed to block another blow. Sophia's eyes became hooded as she sent a flurry of kicks and sword thrusts at me. Somehow I withstood it, though I was clearly wearing out faster than she was.

She suddenly flipped back, watching me gasping from exertion. "This is the savior of the Live Realm? I knew she couldn't handle it. Gregor, I thought I told you to get rid of her."

Excuse me, what?

"Enough with the talking, Sophia!" Gregor barked from the far corner. "Focus on the sparring."

I put on my best smile. "Gregor doesn't respond to whining, Sophia. Besides, last time I checked, he wanted me to stay."

Sophia's eyes narrowed. "What did you say?"

I leaned on my sword, studying my nails. "Now was that before we kissed in my room, or after?" I said soft enough for Gregor not to hear. "Or was it that wonderful time we spent on the roof together?"

Ouch! Good one! Cynthia snickered.

"When did this become tea time?" Gregor yelled from his corner. "I said *spar!*"

"Gregor kissed you?" she whispered, her frame shaking.

I chuckled, lifting my sword and pointing it at her. "Yes. Not really yours, is he?" I readied my stance again. "You know what? General Nabil was right about this. This was a great idea!"

"He has never... Even when I ..." Sophia had a wild look that immediately put me on edge. "You think this is funny? I'll show you funny, little girl."

She returned to her initial stance and gave a guttural shout. Her energy spiked and the entire room's temperature rose. **Up your guard, Kat. She's changing!**

Mika, changing into what? When Sophia returned her sights on me, blood-red pupils stared back at me. The bloodcurdling screech she uttered struck a chord in me.

"You're a *Wanter*."

"Sophia!" Gregor shouted. "Stop it!"

Sophia's transformation wasn't complete. Her once-beautiful face became stretched and deformed. Her brows lowered and her nose flattened on her face. Her smile broadened, showing more pointy teeth. The energy radiating from her was almost stifling. It took tapping into my extra reserves to stay firm on my feet. With her transformation complete, she stood tall, changing her stance again. "Oh, that feels much better. Balancer," her voice now guttural and disturbing, "let's have some fun."

She charged at me faster than I had ever seen someone move, so fast that I could barely keep track of her. The only thing keeping me from being cut down was Diantha; I threw the sword up as a defense against her as she slashed, banged, and thrashed her sword at me.

Judging from the pain I was feeling, she was winning. I moved to defend and slipped on my own blood. *Where did that come from?*

Gregor quickstepped in between us, throwing his arms in front of me. "Sophia, stand down now!"

That only seemed to infuriate Sophia further. "Get out of my way!" She smacked Gregor in the face, sending him to the other side of the sphere, where he crashed into the wall.

"Gregor!" I cried.

Sophia sent a slash in my direction that forced me to jump back. "Mind yourself, Balancer. I'm sick and tired of everyone talking about you. A weak, pathetic human child to save us? Is this what the Kyrios have turned into? A bunch of bedwetters. I did not sign up for this!"

She ran in circles around me, at an impossible speed, continuing to torture me with cuts to my body.

"You can barely protect yourself against me! What will you do when you come across a level-three Wrecker or Stuffer?" She laughed gleefully. "They'll treat you like play food." With another hard blow, my Havadar clanged to the opposite side of the room, close to where Gregor landed. The blow also left my right arm utterly useless. I tried to call Diantha back to me, but I was absolutely shattered.

She was right. I just got totally owned.

I dropped to my knees, clutching my bleeding arm. The blond Wanter smirked, showing all her ragged teeth. Sophia raised her sword over her head. "Think of this a mercy kill. You simply take up space."

Mika, shield!

Sophia's sword banged against the sudden barrier erected

around me. The deformed Kyrios rolled her eyes and gave the barrier a swift kick. "How long do you think you can keep this up? You're bleeding out. Once you lose consciousness, your barrier will be gone too." It was getting harder to keep my eyes open. But I stared back at her defiantly.

She leaned in, her eyes looking mischievous. "Let me let you in a little secret. I heard that you want to destroy anything that is Want. It's your little revenge, is it? I have a question then, Balancer. How are you going to destroy an entire Kyrios army?

"What the hell are you playing at, Sophia?

She gave a guttural laugh that sounded more like rumbling growl. "Kyrios and Wanters? One and the same. Oh, yes, you are helping Wanters. Every single one of us. And you are simply a means to end against our competition with the Archs. General Nabil hates that Archs revile us so much. You are our ticket to one up them." She laughed.

"Let me share another little secret with you, Balancer. The true purpose of this fight was to figure out whether you could take me out or not. To see if you really could be a threat to us. Since you aren't, we will just have to use you as a battery." She grinned, baring her teeth. "But we won't kill you, sweetheart. You will be alive the entire time. Feeling the excruciating pain of having your energy sucked from you for the rest of your existence."

A crack appeared in the barrier, an unfortunate sign of my slipping away. Smirking, Sophia lifted her hand and a red, crackling sphere formed in her palm.

At the confusion splashed across my face, she chuckled, "Gregor must've kept this Wanter power from you—along with many other things. Must keep the precious Balancer happy and unsuspecting, after all. This is called a Seizure Sphere. This little sphere has the force of three earthquakes." She bared her teeth again at the fear in my eyes. "But here is the good news for you. I don't want you here at all. I don't care that they want to keep you alive. I want you dead. Trust me, I'm doing you a favor."

I knew I didn't have the type of energy to withstand that. Clutching my bleeding arm, I closed my eyes and silently prayed.

But the blow never came. I cracked an eye open to see Sophia in a headlock. Gregor had grabbed her from behind.

"Enough, Sophia!" he bellowed. She struggled at first, but Gregor quickly pressed two fingers to her neck, sending an electrical charge through her body and knocking her out completely. Her limp form crashed to the ground, and her face returned to normal—whatever that even meant anymore. I wished I was pleased. I wished I could've jumped up for joy at Gregor's rescue. I wish I could've said something.

I couldn't.

Because the guy who I had just been fighting over, the guy who had me hungry for his kiss, the guy who I'd trusted the most in Ager and in all of the Live Realm was staring back at me with blood-red eyes, distorted facial features, and white pointy teeth.

39

"No," I whispered. "No."

Gregor's face returned to normal, with my favorite blue eyes staring back at me. But all I could see was red.

"No!" I screamed.

Gregor rushed towards me. "Katya, let me explain—"

"Stay away from me!" I tried to get to my feet but fell back to my knees.

The Scot looked distraught. "Please, let me help you!"

"Stay away from me," I gasped in pain. He tried to come closer, but my shield remained intact and zapped him back in the process.

The Scot grimaced, but he tried to reason with me. "Katya, you are bleeding!"

"Just stay away from me," I bit out. *Mika, give me some energy.*

I need to get back to my room. Now. Without interference. Like a shot of caffeine, energy returned to my legs, and I stood back up. Without a glance to Gregor, I walked out of the training dome with my shaky shield intact, clutching my bleeding arm. Every step was painful reminder of everything I had just witnessed.

I had never felt so stupid in my life. I'd noticed the signs. I knew something was off. And Gregor had lied to me the second time we'd ever met. The more that I thought about it, the angrier I got. Just a few feet away from my tower, the Quad appeared behind me.

Addy gasped, "Katya! What happened? We felt your energy in our barracks and—"

The Quad stopped in their tracks at the hard, angry stare that I gave them. Demetrius opened his mouth to ask another question but I never gave him the chance. Sending Vis to my feet, I ran quickly to my tower, into my room, and slammed the door. The moment the door was closed, my shield shattered, and I slumped to the floor in pain.

I heard Cynthia's voice in my ear. *Kat, your arm. It's not broken but we gotta treat it.*

I don't want anyone touching me right now. We'll do it ourselves.

By the time I was finally able to rip some of the satin sheets into strips and wrap them tightly around my biceps using my hand and my teeth, I wanted to sleep deeply. But my mind was still racing.

They were all Wanters. I was supposed to destroy Wanters, right? How could I fight alongside the same monsters that I was supposed to eliminate?

But how they can be human? Is this why Nabil didn't want me to get close to any of them? Because he was afraid that I would bail on them if I knew their ugly truth?

And didn't I ask Gregor information about his life? Why didn't I push more? Why didn't I demand answers? How could I been so stupid?

I'm not sure how long I sat slumped against the door, but I must have dozed off. I was startled awake by a knocking on the door.

"Katya, please. Can I come in?"

I almost said, *"Go to hell. Oh that's right—that's your home."*

But Mika interjected, **You won't get any answers to your questions if you hide yourself away. You won't gain anything unless you let him in.** Rolling my eyes at her sound logic, I stood up from the hard floor, noticing that my arm hurt much less than it had before. **Your Vis is helping you heal**.

I nodded and opened the door to find the Scot more disheveled than I had ever seen him before. His black bodysuit was still covered in dust from the earlier fight, and his dark hair looked like he had run his hand through it a million times. I wordlessly let him into the room and closed the door. I made it a point to set the bedroom chair at the furthest point in the room away from my bed.

"You sit over there."

He sighed and sat in the chair as instructed. "Katya, first I want to say I'm sorry. I never meant to keep this from you, but it's more complicated than it seems. It was for your protection."

"My protection?" I chucked darkly. "Let's not bullshit each other here, Kyrios. You didn't tell me you were a Wanter because you wanted me on your side so you could use me in Nabil's vendetta against the Archs. My only question is why didn't you guys just come clean? Why didn't you, Gregor, just be honest with me? I asked you after that incident in that alley what you were. And you said the changes in your face was your armor." I chuckled again, shaking my head. "And I believed you. You were the first person...if that's what you are, a person. I don't know anymore. I confided in you. I let you into places only two people in the world have ever known. And you *lied* to me."

Gregor looked at me imploringly. "Katya, I didn't want to scare you away. Every story you told me about your experiences with the Want have been nothing but painful. I didn't want to give you a reason not to trust me or the Kyrios."

"And you think this method is better? Everything you have ever told me—I don't know whether it's true or not. Was this a setup from the beginning? Am I really closing Abyss gates? Am I really protecting people? Do you really send souls to the Room of Apofasi? Or maybe you just devour them and their Vis like the other Wanters do!

"No!" Gregor exploded out of his chair. "I am not like that! Yes, I am part Wanter, but I am still human. I made a choice a long time ago to be Kyrios."

"What do you mean, you made a choice?"

He plopped back in his chair, staring at the ground. "The only way you're going to understand is if I tell you about my past. After six hundred years, I still struggle with it, so please bear with me."

The Kyrios sighed, agitated and visibly exhausted. "I had a life once. In Scotland, a long time ago. I came from the clan of the MacGregors."

"Wait, your name is really Gregor MacGregor?"

He looked indignant. "Yes, and it's a powerful name, thank you. We MacGregors held the most beautiful land in all of Scotland, and many people tried to take it from us. Not to mention, our clan was wealthy. We were gifted by the first Scottish king with a treasure called the Isle Pearl. One of the largest pearls anyone had ever known in Scotland. It was said that our clan had been the keepers of the Pearl for hundreds of years. There was an old tale that said the continued prosperity of the Highlands depended on a MacGregor keeping watch over the Pearl. It didn't stop other rival clans from attempting to take it. No one had ever been successful until…"

"Until?"

He shifted uncomfortably, as if the memory burned inside of him. "A cousin clan, the MacCollins, fell in favor with the then-English king, a man we didn't recognize as ruler of Scotland. As punishment for our disobedience and treason, the English king decided that we couldn't own our lands any longer, and the MacCollins were named rulers of our area. We were stripped of everything—title, money, land, everything. The one thing they didn't get was the Pearl. The last thing my Dah told me was where it was buried and he had me swear on my life to never reveal it. I was seventeen when it happened.

"Then my Dah was captured by the English army, given a sham of a trial, and beheaded as a traitor, making me laird of our clan. We were sent into the trees, exiled, and forced to watch vermin inhabit our land and eat our food.

"But we survived, those of us who hadn't fled to neighborhood villages. My remaining clansmen made their way as mercenaries. It wasn't the best work nor honorable but it kept food in our bellies. It was during an assignment that I met my wife Eleanor. We got married and I left the mercenary work to my clansmen and became a trader. We slowly and quietly began to rebuild our lives, making sure that we didn't call attention to ourselves as the MacCollins were still looking for me. Eleanor brought a peace to my life I never thought I could get again. We had a son, Aiden. They were both the center of my world."

When I didn't say a word, he continued. "We lived quietly in a small village for four years. I wasn't a great trader, but my clan looked after each other in any way they could. Stealing and raiding the MacCollins for provisions was their favorite way. One night, a group of the raiders came to my home, begging for help. Their scouter was sick and they needed someone to do some research for their next raid. Against my better judgement, I agreed to help. I thought I would be safe, as I was to just watch their guards and making notes about breaks and changing of shifts. I made a grave mistake and got caught. When those bastards figured out that I was the last laird of the MacGregors, they beat me half to death trying to get information from me, about where my clan and the Pearl was. I never spoke. I thought that since they couldn't get anything from me, they would soon kill me and destroy the only other competition. I wish they had." He scoffed, his eyes now glossy.

"After weeks of beatings, they decided to get inventive, punishing me for my indiscretion, for my refusal to talk. They caught my wife and son. They tortured my son in front of me. He screamed for me to save him, but I could do nothing but watch in anguish. He was four years old. Then they forcibly violated my wife in front of me and beat her until she couldn't scream anymore. I broke and told them everything.

"Then my cousin Edwin, the leader of the MacCollins, came in.

He promised a swift death for me, but not before he killed my family before me. Edwin first paraded my remaining clansmen in front of me and killed them one by one. He then beheaded my son and wife before he did the same to me."

I wanted to throw up.

Gregor looked at me with a searingly fierce look. "Remember how I told you how the Want are formed? Either they stay behind and become bitter or they are so enraged at death that they become one? I turned into a Wanter at death. I wanted everyone and everything to pay for the pain they caused me, my family, and my clan. I wanted revenge, and every last soul on earth was going to suffer. How could I not turn into a Wrecker?

"My soul felt like it was torn as I changed. Within the first six hours of my change, I caused so much havoc, I essentially destroyed the MacCollins clan. But it wasn't enough. I hated everything. I wanted *everything* gone, no matter what it was.

"But there was a part of me wanted the pain and the grief to go away. It was with that awareness that I met Nabil and Demetrius. They told me that I had a choice: to continue living with the pain that I was suffering from and become part of the problem or to let my anger go and be part of the solution. I only had a few hours to decide, before I would remain a Wrecker forever.

"I don't know how they did it, but they showed me what I had become and it scared me. I didn't want that body. I didn't want that future. And I began to change back into who you see now. But my old life was gone. My old body was gone.

"Nabil told me I was now a Kyrios—part Wanter, part human. By holding on to my humanity, reclaiming it after the grave, I'm not really dead, but I'm not really alive either. I'm just a…death guard.

"When we need to increase our strength, we change into a mixed form with the red eyes and deformed face, calling on the wrath inside of us to protect what was made sacred with our choice. So, in a way, it is like my armor." Gregor looked at me, searching for understanding. "Each Kyrios went through an ordeal and a change like this, but we all made the decision not to continue to be a destructive force like the ones that took our lives. I've been grappling with that anger and hatred ever since."

I bit my lip in thought. "What about your wife and your son?"

He studied his hand. "They crossed over. Last I heard they are in Paradiso."

I looked over to Cynthia's body, which was still encased the dome. She had specifically asked me whether I trusted them. If she were to ask me the same question now, I couldn't give her a straight answer. "So was it pure coincidence that you all decided not to tell me you were part Wanters?"

Gregor grimaced. "After your run-in with Cravers downtown, General Nabil thought it would be best if we concealed it for a while, until you got used to us. But your pent-up revenge on anything Want made us wary. The Generals decided, for everyone's sake, that it would best to keep it a secret for a bit longer until we worked together in the Live Realm and you could see that we are on the side of the living. That our purpose truly is to protect the souls."

"But Gregor, I thought we were closer than this. Even if I may not have liked what I heard, I would have accepted it if you just told me the truth about you from the very beginning!"

"Katya, try to understand! It's how I died—the lowest moment of my existence. I died, not once, but twice. In flesh and in soul.

It's not something you just open up and talk about over dinner. I wanted to tell you. I really did. But it was just hard."

I rolled my eyes. "That is such a cop-out. You had no issue pulling out my darkest secrets within several hours of meeting me. Why couldn't I have had that same opportunity? And what about the stuff that Sophia said? That Nabil's purpose for keeping me is so that he could have a one-up over the Archs?"

"What are you talking about?"

I threw the closest thing I had at him, which was a pillow. "Stop playing dumb! Sophia isn't the only one who has told me all about Nabil's plan to show up the Archs because the fabled Balancer is on the Kyrios's side. That there wasn't a plan to make me stronger but keep me in damsel-in-distress mode so I'd have to rely on the Kyrios's power. Is that why you didn't want me fighting?"

Tears slowly streamed down my face. "I didn't want to believe it. And that's why I am so angry. I'm angry at myself for letting it get this far."

The crestfallen look on Gregor's face broke my heart further. "Katya, hear me out. It isn't a secret that Nabil has issues with the Archs. Everyone knows that. But I swear I have never heard of any plan to showboat your power or to keep you weak on purpose. My honest concern was—and still is—you getting hurt, just like today."

He stood up to get closer to me, but I immediately backed away.

His jaw clenched. "And you have to know. The reason why we are cautioned against having relationships with the living is because our human side wars with our Wanter side. Humanity craves connection, while the Wanter craves isolation. Every moment with you, I resist the Wanter side so I can be with you to protect you. So I can feel more of my humanity again. If after all this, you can't accept the dark parts of me, I will do as you wish. Whatever it may be."

"I need time, Gregor." I answered tiredly. "I'm not saying no. I just need time to sort everything out."

Gregor looked like he wanted to say more. He rethought it and then nodded. "I have to let the Generals know that you aren't seriously hurt, but that's all I will tell them." And he left.

After the door closed, I couldn't say how long I cried, but I must have fallen asleep. I awoke to darkness. I slowly crept over to my best friend and leaned against her cot.

Cyn, you were warning me, weren't you?

Kat, I wasn't sure of anything at that time. It's just that I knew that something was off about their energy. I didn't know exactly it was.

Mika began nudging at me. I tried to ignore her, but she was insistent. *Look, Mika, I don't even want to talk to you right now. You probably knew about this the entire time!*

She ignored my attempts to fight with her. **There is something for you on your bed**.

A note had been laid at the corner of my bedspread. No one here had ever written to me, so I was a bit surprised to see the small, neat writing that belonged to Gregor:

Katya,

I know you need time, but I just needed to say one more thing. Being with you, I actually feel like my twenty-three-year-old self. You make me laugh. You tick me off, but I want to kiss your tears away anytime I see them. I admire your fire, but I want to keep you safe too. I feel alive again because of you.

Kat, I realize that there is a lot of misinformation swirling around you. I understand. But I don't want to lose you because of this. We need to talk. Come to my chambers when you're ready.

Gregor

"What am I supposed to do?" I whispered out loud. Now that I had a chance to cool down, I felt like understood Gregor a bit better. But I couldn't completely let go of what Sophia had said either, especially because she was right in some ways. Could I really trust them? A clipped knock at the door startled me out of my thoughts.

"I'm not ready to talk, Gregor," I called out.

"Katya? It's Jae. I must speak with you."

I stared at the door hesitantly. He did give me hints earlier today that something wasn't right. I opened the door a crack. "What is it, Young Jae?"

"I have news from General Lamar," he whispered. "He has a way for you and your friend to leave quietly." I grabbed him and hauled him inside my room.

"What are you talking about?"

Jae didn't immediately speak. His eyes roamed my face, looking very troubled. "Katya, are you all right?"

That one simple question threatened to open the floodgates again. "I just…" I said unevenly. "I don't know anything anymore. You tried to tell me that something was…but I wouldn't listen…"

Jae embraced me, speaking soothing words in my ear. "Don't cry, Katya. Please don't cry." I clung to his shoulder, searching for warmth for my cold insides. "I wanted to tell you everything about us, but they wouldn't let me. We were all under gag order."

"I know," I whispered. I pulled back to give him a small smile. "I know you tried." Several different emotions flitted across through his face. Anger, sadness, regret, and hope.

He took my hands into his and brought them to his chest. With intense eyes boring into mine, he said softly, "Run away with me."

I briefly forgot how to breathe. "What did you say?"

His grip tightened around my hands. "I know a way out of here, where we can leave undetected. You don't have to be in fear of anything. We can hide out in the Live Realm. We can be together," he said quietly. One of his hands travelled to my face, wiping away a stray tear. "I know it's a lot to take in, and I know you are upset about Sophia and Gregor, but give me the word, just one word and you will become my entire world. One word and I will give you everything I have and more."

When I just stared back at him, not knowing what to say, Jae moved in for a soft kiss. When I didn't immediately pull away, both his hands became entangled in my hair and he deepened the kiss. I began to get lost in the feelings the kiss brought out—the desire to escape from all the madness was rich inside of me. I'd never acknowledged it, but deep down I knew Young Jae had feelings for me.

And in that lost and broken moment, I wanted to cling to the possibility of freedom.

I was about to lift my hand to bring him closer when I felt something crinkle underneath my foot. The letter. *Gregor.*

The illusion Jae had created was shattered, and I dropped back into reality.

I slowly pulled away, tapping his chest to stop. "I can't," I whispered. I took a step back, keeping my eyes down. "Oh, God, I'm all over the place. I can't, Jae. I'm sorry. We shouldn't have done that."

His arms fell listlessly to his sides. "They'll probably keep lying to you, you know. He'll keep lying to you." he said harshly. I cringed, knowing who he meant by "he."

"I've got to give it a chance. I'm in too deep."

His face and his body went rigid. "So you won't change your mind?"

I shook my head. Jae's normally warm brown eyes went cold. In that moment, I could tell he couldn't stand the sight of me. He turned away, reaching for the knob. He stopped at the door and said over his shoulder. "Let's just go the General's tower. He's expecting you."

Before I could ask again for his forgiveness, Jae whirled around and marched straight out the door. I floundered to run after him.

He never looked back.

40

We wordlessly met at the base of Lamar's tower.

Jae grabbed me roughly into his arms, leapt to the top, and entered the security room. The room was oddly dark—not one monitor was on. As though my touch burned him, he dropped me to the floor, where I landed on my still-healing bicep.

"Hey!" I said. Jae wordlessly stalked away, taking a position in the far corner.

"Are you all right, my dear?"

I groaned, trying to adjust my eyes.

"Is that you, General? I can't see you." One monitor flickered on, showing a blank white screen. It was just enough light to illuminate Lamar sitting his chair, facing me. But the shadows that remained put me on a bit on edge.

"Is this better, my lady?"

"A few more monitors would be appreciated, General."

He shrugged and a few more monitors came to life, dimly lighting up the room. Lamar left his seat and crouched down in front of me, looking concerned. "You are not seriously hurt, are you?"

I massaged my bicep. "I've been healing quickly, although I'm still not completely better. But for the most part, I think I'm okay."

He beamed. "Fantastic. Time to continue." With a snap of his fingers, a chair emerged underneath me, like a bad spy movie with cuffs holding my ankles and wrists down.

"What the hell? General Lamar, what are you doing?"

General Lamar smiled widely and took a deep breath in. "Oh, I do enjoy it when your power flares. It adds a wonderful crispness to the air." He licked his lips. "Such pure energy..." His hand hovered over my head and he seemed intent on touching me, but he pulled himself back.

"No, we mustn't touch other's belongings," he muttered to himself. "He'll be upset with me."

I struggled against the cuffs. "What the hell is going on? Young Jae! I thought we were friends! What's the meaning of this?"

Lamar snapped his fingers again, tightening the cuffs around me. "My dear, he never really was your friend to begin with. He was following orders from me."

I craned my neck to get a good look at Lamar. "You? I don't understand. Why would you do this to me?"

The General looked at a gadget in his hands and rubbed his

chin thoughtfully. "We have a few minutes before he arrives, so a small explanation wouldn't hurt."

"He? Who is he?"

The General snapped his fingers again and a small chair emerged from the floor. He sat with such flourish that I imagined he was very much enjoying himself. "Patience is not your strong suit, is it? Now, if you would allow me, I'll start from the beginning. How do humans start a story again? Oh yes.

"Once upon a time, there was a sweet Kyrios major named Sherene.

"Sherene was one of the most powerful majors that the Kyrios force had ever seen. She could have been a general, but she turned down the position when a seat became available after an untimely death. I was Sherene's deputy, and I could not have been happier. We were in love. And Sherene had such a soft touch with dealing with souls turning into Wanters. If she was able to get there in time, she was able to talk them down with only a few words, sending them to Apofasi or convincing them to join our ranks. I was satisfied to stay with her for eternity.

"Until Nabil sent her to an assignment by herself, to deal with a soul turning. Nabil says that she insisted she go alone. I know she wouldn't have left me behind. But she did. And she was caught by surprise during the turning. It was a particularly vicious death, resulting in a particularly vicious Wanter, and she couldn't handle it by herself. She was able to gut him, but she expired as well.

"And I never had a chance to say goodbye.

"Since then, I've began to ask myself, why do we do this? What is the point? For protection? What has our protection accomplished? The Living have become increasingly weak, constantly susceptible to the prodding of the Want. One mere suggestion and they are ready to hate, harm others, and burn everything in sight to the ground. Most of the time, the Want have already left them, and they still don't have the capability to be good." His face turned to rage. "We have spent eons protecting something that has always been rotten to the core. Kyrios lives lost! Friends devoured!" he growled out. "And for what? Because we chose this? Because we are looking for redemption? Why bend over backwards for people who don't deserve it?

"I decided to move up in the ranks and show others the truth behind this mask called Ager: that it is a sham and that we shouldn't deny ourselves the power of what we are."

"What are you saying? That you've been working against the Kyrios?"

He grinned sinisterly. "That's exactly what I'm saying. And what better way to do that than as the head of security? It unfortunately required the death of the previous general, but overall I think it was a good plan, don't you?"

"That's sick!" I said, starting to pull against the cuffs, realizing the true danger I was in.

"Hmm, I suppose. Now back to my story. For many years, I have been sending information out to the Want Generals, giving our team here a hard time. But you, my dear, after your first visit to Ager, I knew you would be the key to my ultimate goal. Your energy is something out of legends, incredible even to those who have been around for thousands of years. When we found out who you were, I had you come back to be under our 'protection.'

"Michiko was easy to manipulate. I was able to convince her that we needed to monitor you for scientific research. Raf wanted the opportunity to train you. Most of all, Nabil wanted the Balancer within our ranks."

"So," I said through gritted teeth, "that part about Nabil is true?"

Lamar gave me an exasperated look. "Didn't I say patience? Anyway, the Want Generals wanted you stronger than you were when you arrived. Someone like you doesn't come around every day, so why absorb you before you were ripe, so to speak? When they did absorb you, they wanted their growth to be instantaneous. So training was introduced, over Nabil's concern that you could learn to overpower us.

"When you requested permission to leave Ager and find your Havadar, I created the opportunity to give my comrades a chance to devour you and your Havadar."

I could feel Mika humming with my rising anger. "You told them where we were."

He nodded with a smirk. "Oh, and much more." He pulled out the silver bracelet he had given me from his pocket and snapped it back onto my wrist. It gave me such a horrible jolt that I screamed. Lamar sniffed the air with relish. "I will never get enough of that. Your Vis is impossibly good. As you can see, the bracelet was made to force you to react, making your Vis flare out violently. That first bracelet was a test to see how many Wanters you could attract. But your visit home was a perfect opportunity to weaken you and capture you.

"Which reminds me, how was it that your friend had enough Vis energy to throw back an entire Want fleet?" Lamar gave me a calculating look.

Remember, keep quiet. Cynthia murmured.

I looked at Lamar defiantly. "I'm learning as you do, you prick."

Lamar didn't take kindly to that name and gave me another jolt. "Well, no matter. She was an unknown liability, so I put her in a coma. No energy to move or think. It was bit risky bringing her here and keeping her weak. But so far my calculations have been correct. Especially since the experience spurred your training and increased your Vis reserves even further." He leaned in and sniffed at my neck. Sighing deeply, he said, "Just the smell of your Vis makes me want to devour you right now and make you a part of me."

I cringed away.

Lamar sat back in his chair, despondent. "Since you are at the end of your training, my fun and manipulation has come to end. Nabil wants you out in the Live Realm closing gates. And we can't have that. Which is why Sophia made such a show for you today, to effectively burst your bubble. So you can see the ugly truth about us. Jae has been instrumental in setting this all up, hasn't he?"

He shot Jae look of pride. "Jae has also been hurt by the decisions of this pseudo-soul saving group. He lost his twin brother. They died together, but they are now separated forever. Because of this blasted system. Such a shame." He shook his head. "Like I said, all this has to come to an end. His Lordship thought it best that we make it look like you had cut your ties with the Kyrios after finding out that we are part Wanters. You know, to make your disappearance look purposeful rather than sinister."

"What do you—" There was a sudden loud banging at the door. Lamar smiled widely and made for the door. "That must be his Lordship. He's been dying to see you again."

See me again? The door opened to reveal Sophia with her signature smirk. She gave me a wink and stood by the door next to Jae.

But my attention was on the strange man that had walked in beside her. In a full gray suit, he sauntered in gracefully with his attention solely on me. His slicked-back blond hair was hidden by the black bowler hat he wore. He grinned as the recognition showed on my face.

"Detective Sloan?"

He walked slowly towards me, still grinning. "Katya, in the few weeks you've been away, you certainly have grown. Ager has been good to you."

I struggled against my restraints, not liking the looks of this. "How are you here?"

He wagged his finger dismissively. "I couldn't stand to be away from you. You know, I met you earlier than that missing person investigation. Lamar had just given me some information, and I had to find you myself. I bumped into you on a bus a number of weeks ago. As soon as I felt your Vis energy, I knew I had to absorb you. I alerted Lamar immediately, asking him to keep track of you and bring you in.

"And to top it off, you were the fabled Balancer. A leftover over gift from God for times of trouble for humanity. Ha." He walked around me, watching me squirm. "When you returned home, I couldn't talk freely like I wanted, not with that Kyrios major tied to your hip. But Lamar was so good to arrange this little meeting for us!"

"You're a Want General?" I asked slowly.

The man in the bowler hat chuckled. "I suppose this humanoid form confuses you." He edged closer to me. "Yes. My name is General Krenlin of Want Fleet Five, and you are about to send me into history." He smirked and turned to Lamar. "Is she ready?"

General Lamar nodded eagerly. "Yes. Her Vis reserves have grown exponentially since she has started her training. Just smell the air, sir."

"Hey, assholes! Stop talking about me like I am not here!" I yelled.

Krenlin flashed in front of me, slamming his hands on the back of my chair. Hovering over me, his dark blue eyes gleamed angrily. "You are in a precarious situation, little one. I will not be addressed as such. I am more powerful than you can imagine. I gave the order that caused your mother's mental anguish, had her infiltrated by my Poser foot soldier, sent the attack on your friends and family in the area, and destroyed anything that was remotely important to you."

Krenlin smiled smugly. "Here's a fact you may not know. As a Wanter, the more powerful you are, the more readily able you are to assume the image of the souls you absorb. This next form is my absolute favorite." His form began to shimmer and melt down into a mousy-looking girl with large glasses and flat brown hair. Her large brown eyes, which normally shined with ready tears, had a distinct coldness.

Amie stood over me and smiled deviously.

Cynthia's internal sobs turned into my own. "Amie," I whispered brokenly. "You...you..."

"This one was a fighter. I believe that she might have been seeking you or searching the rubble that was your home.

Unfortunately, she was pinned down by shifting debris. She held on to dear life, crying out for anyone to save her, underneath rubble near your home. She cried for anyone to find her—her mother, you, your friend Cynthia, even her bullies at school. Her voice finally went hoarse and she withered away after several hours. Internal bleeding. By the time anyone found her, she was dead." He shimmered again and morphed into himself. "Your sweet friend Amie died because of you, because she was looking for you," Krenlin's voice said. "But I have to thank you for her soul and her Vis, Balancer. Couldn't have done it without you."

Pain. Anguish. I was flooded with all the emotions that accompanied grief. But it was rage that turned my body impossibly hot. My power flared violently. "I will destroy you!" I screamed. Every nerve in my body was on fire and wanted to explode. But the cuffs stopped me cold, absorbing the massive power flare.

Krenlin took a deep breath of the air. "Oh, yes, you were right, Lamar. She is ready for absorption. Just being near her, I can feel the pure Vis rolling off her body." I struggled against the cuff, hoping that they would melt from the heat I was giving off. Krenlin shook his head, chuckling at my feeble attempts. "Oh, don't worry, sweetie. You'll join your friend soon enough."

He clapped his hands in delight. "When I absorb you, your absolute power will become mine. My brethren will praise me as the destroyer of the Balancer. Master Drachen will have to take me seriously, and this war and the entire Live Realm will be won over." Krenlin looked at me like I was a piece of gum on his shoe. "There's no happy ending, no reunion in Paradiso for you. Simply darkness."

In one last attempt at reason, I turned to Jae, who remained stony in the corner. "How could you do this to me? I thought you were my friend. You promised my mother you would protect me!"

My last shout moved him from the door to the front of my chair. He bent over until he was eye level and said softly, "I gave you a chance. I guess you're really 'in too deep' now." Never had I seen his eyes so cold and expressionless, so un-Jae like.

I felt my tears burn in the corners of my eyes. "I'm sorry, Young Jae," I whispered brokenly. He didn't say a word. He simply turned around and returned to the door.

Krenlin smiled, amused at my despondency. "Now that all that is out of the way, can we get started?"

Lamar, with a devious smile, lifted his hand over my chest. "This might hurt a bit."

A purple sphere emerged out of his hand and was thrust into my core. The room was soon filled with my screams as he tried to extract my soul and Vis from my body. It was nothing like any pain I'd experienced before—not the Vis bind, not the feeling of fighting with Sophia. Every fiber of my body was on fire and attempted to fight back against the extraction, but I desperately wanted the pain to just stop.

It felt like an eternity had passed when it finally did.

The room was now filled with an odd beeping that caught everyone's attention. "What is that, Lamar?" Krenlin demanded.

"The shield around the tower is being attacked. Someone knows where we are," Lamar answered tersely.

"What—argh!" Krenlin was suddenly thrown to the wall by a red blast of energy. Lamar and Sophia met the same fate, sending them into the wall and knocking them out. I looked around to find Jae dropping his hands, still glowing red.

"Why did you...?"

Jae rushed for me. "We don't have time. Krenlin and Lamar are too strong to be stunned for long." He easily pried open the cuffs, and I finally found myself free from the chair. He took a hold of my arm. "Come on, we need to get you out of here."

"Wait, what about you?"

He gave me a small smile. "I'm making my peace with you. I made a promise to you and your mother. Now come on, we've got—"

He paused. I stilled as well, too afraid as to why he'd stopped.

"Jae?"

The Lieutenant's eyes glowed blue and he gently touched my face. "I love you, Katya." I stood in shock as his eyes turned violently bright and he grabbed me by my shirt and threw me out the nearby window.

In slow motion, with glass shattering around me, I found myself falling through the air, facing Jae, whose eyes had returned to normal, pleased and content. But any light in his eyes soon disappeared and the small smile he wore slipped away as a hand, crackling with red energy, protruded out from the middle of his chest.

41

Jae's body crumpled beyond the windowsill and out of my sight as I continued plummeting to the ground.

All I could do is stare at the cloudy sky above me as it rapidly pulled away from me. All I could think was *Jae's dead. Jae's dead*, as I hurled to the ground. I barely noticed the two arms slipping underneath me in midair and cradling me close to a broad chest.

A familiar brogue said, "Katya! Are you all right?" As we descended slowly down to the ground, my eyes sought out the best darn blue eyes I'd ever seen.

"Gregor," I said brokenly. "He's dead."

Gregor looked at me strangely. "Who are you—" BOOM! An explosion sent us careening to the ground. Gregor took the brunt of the force and slammed into the concrete. Shouts surrounded us as the troops emerged out of their barracks, responding to the noises. The ceiling and roof of the security tower had been blasted clear off, leaving only the top floor. Among the debris raining through the air stood Krenlin, Lamar, and Sophia with bored expressions.

"Well," Krenlin said in a loud voice, "looks like the Balancer is in the arms of her beloved protector. Poor Young Jae." He picked up Jae's lifeless body by the head. "Looks like he loved in vain. Poor sod." Krenlin threw the body to the ground below. But the body never made to the earth below. It glowed eerily until it evaporated. Green particles floated into the air, leaving Jae's clothes to flutter to the bottom.

"Lamar, you bastard!" Nabil cried furiously, making his entrance. "What is the meaning of this?"

Lamar laughed heartily. "As if you didn't have some inkling! I've made some new friends and shifted around some priorities." I could hear murmuring from the Kyrios troops. Every face mirrored the same confusion and anger.

"Lamar, think about what you are doing. You made a choice many years ago! Don't throw everything away in vain," Nabil tried.

"And where has that decision led me? Led us? More battles? More causalities with the living who do not appreciate our sacrifices? More souls are turning Want every day. If they are going to change and continue to change at this rate, what is the point of all this?"

"Because it's an outcome worth fighting for," Michiko shouted back. The other Generals, Raf excluded, appeared behind Nabil, looking just as furious.

Lamar snorted. "Maybe for you. But I think it's time I take a new direction." He took off his black coat and threw his General medallion to the ground. He gestured to Krenlin. "Lord Krenlin has a wonderful crusade I couldn't help but join." He then clasped hands with Krenlin and began to change. Spikes made of bone emerged at his elbows and shoulders. His plain black pants and shirt changed into the same suit Krenlin wore. Lastly, the former General's brown eyes went completely red. Sophia went through a similar transformation, with spikes protruding out of her chin and her navel. Her clothes shifted into a red, fitted gown with long slits along her sides.

Gregor tightened his hold on me. "What is Krenlin doing in Ager?" I felt power spikes from the rest of the Kyrios around me. It seemed that everyone knew exactly who Krenlin was.

Krenlin came forward and bowed with a smirk. "Long time, no see Nabil! I don't think we've ever met outside of the Live Realm before."

Nabil's power surge shook the ground underneath us. A blue sphere, humming with electric currents, grew to the size of a beach ball in his hands. "Do not call me 'friend.'" Several other Kyrios reacted as well and soon the courtyard glowed blue with numerous powerful spheres.

Krenlin shook his head in mirth. "Sophia and Lamar, I think we've worn out our welcome. It's time to go. I believe we are needed in the Abyss."

"Do not let them escape!" Nabil shouted. "I want those traitors in custody now!" Several Kyrios leapt into the air to be met by a large barrier protecting the three, who were now floating in the air.

Sophia laughed loudly at their attempts to crash through the barrier. "I'm afraid I'm never coming back, Generals. But I'm sure I will see you all again in the Live Realm." Her eyes bore into mine, taking in Gregor clutching me to his chest. "Especially you, Balancer," she said bitingly.

"Sophie!" Krenlin chided. "Hands off now." He waved to me. "Katya is my one and only. No one can touch her but me." I couldn't help the shiver that travelled down my spine. Gregor felt it and tightened his grip further.

"Well," Krenlin said, bored. "Plan A didn't work. Now on to Plan B!" With a snap of his fingers, a black hole emerged over their head. All three leapt in and it closed right after them. No one made a sound—everyone was in shock that a well-liked General had suddenly gone AWOL with a high-ranking Wanter at that.

Nabil snapped out of it first. "Men, our security has been compromised. Those in the security unit, if your loyalty is true, I want you to reconfigure and reinforce the wards and barriers as best as you can. I want all exits sealed now.

"Victor, take a unit to block the main entrance. Michiko, send a message to all units in the Live Realm about the closure. Everyone else, remain in your quadrants and stand guard. They may launch an attack on Ager at any time. Go!"

Bodies flew, Kyrios running everywhere. Gregor had just put me down when Nabil turned to us. "I want you two to follow me to Central Command." We arrived there in silence and entered a small room to the side, where Michiko and several others were furiously working the controls, sending messages out. Nabil closed the door behind us and gestured for me to sit down.

"All right, Lady Katya. Tell me what happened."

I robotically relayed the details, including what had happened in my room and Jae's sacrifice. I could see Gregor's jaw tightening as I described the kissing. But I didn't have the chance to react to the flash of jealousy. I just felt horrible. Amie and Jae were gone forever, and I hadn't been able to help them. At the end of my explanation, both men looked down pensively. I couldn't help but whisper, "I'm sorry."

"No," Nabil said tiredly. "I'm sorry. I have failed you, my lady."

"What are you talking about?"

Nabil suddenly aged before my eyes, looking like a man of more than five thousand years old rather his typical appearance of around thirty-five. "I have suspected Lamar for some time now. I just wasn't able to prove it. Nothing concrete. When word of you came, he immediately took an interest. Lingered in places you once were. Now we know he was taking in your residual Vis energy.

"When you came back, nearly soul-crushed, he said that your power had fought the soul bind. I suspected he might have been behind it. And I am sorry I couldn't spare you from this."

He attempted to massage the fatigue away from his face. "There is something you need to know that very few do. Gregor, I expect your utmost confidence in this. It must stay in this room."

We both nodded. "Lamar was correct about one thing. Yes, I did want you and your allegiance with us. I will not make excuses for that. I thoroughly believe your role is simply to close gates. But my desire for your allegiance was not about flexing our newly attained Balancer in front of the Archs. It was to keep them from finding out about you."

"I don't understand."

Nabil sighed. "In the same records that General Michiko found, it said that once the Archs find out that you've awakened, they are to take the sky and descend upon the Live Realm with you as their leader. If you were to team with the Archs, it would mean that it was time for the world to end. And you would end it."

I felt faint. "So you are saying I'm not actually the savior, but that I end everyone's life? End the entire world?"

Nabil shook his head. "The records are vague at best, but that's certainly how the Archs will take it. And with you training, they might take it as gospel. That you were preparing for them. We are lucky—because they are so high above everything, they haven't found out about the Want's current onslaught or kept track of who you are. I swore Michiko to secrecy so that this news would not travel by gossip. It's probably where the rumor you heard came from. Michiko must have used it to explain my actions to someone who was less conscientious than they should have been."

A sharp knock at the door interrupted us. Michiko stuck her head in. "Nabil, Gregor, you need to see this." Her face was grim.

We returned to central command to see a screen with General Raf featured in the center. In a word, Raf looked rough. The General's white-hair was now peppered black, showing the dirt and grime from the last few hours in the Live Realm. Scratches and cuts plagued his upper body. A bleeding gash over his left eye forced him to squint and wipe the blood away from his vision periodically.

"General Raf, what news?" Nabil asked.

"The situation is at a critical stage. More small Wanters have attempted to overrun the Los Angeles Abyss gate. The ensuing accidents caused by the Cravers and Posers have reached an all-time high. The gate over Los Angeles has grown exponentially in the last twelve hours. The Wanters are overly excited, chanting that their own Balancer is awakening."

"Huh?" I asked. But a withering look from Gregor shut me up quickly.

Not missing a beat, Raf continued. "There also has been a huge surge of negative Vis energy coming from the LA gate. And the Want has become particularly concentrated there. Five large tremors have occurred in the last two days."

I could only imagine the panic down in California.

"General Nabil, the situation cannot wait any longer. We need the Balancer to close the rift here so that we can clear the Want."

Everyone at Central Command froze and turned to stare at me. My stomach dropped to my toes. Nabil rubbed his temples in fatigue. "Raf, stand by for further instruction." The screen went blank. Nabil eyed me, gauging my reaction. "What do you think, Balancer?" he asked softly.

I wanted to scream, *No! It's chaotic out there! Gregor was right. I'm in way over my head, and I quit.* Just as I was about to open my mouth, I remembered Amie and how I hadn't been there to help. So many others were like her in the Live Realm, and while I didn't know what was going on with the Archs and what my work in the Live Realm might mean to them, I couldn't abandon everyone in the Live Realm either. Even if I wanted to run and hide. My mom used to say to me, "Women can be emotional and broken people, but never in the face of what needs to be done."

"I can do this," I said out loud, surprising everyone. "We must do this." As I took in their faces, a new sense of determination fell over me as well. I was still scared as heck, but I felt Mika spread through my body and strengthen me. Nabil scrutinized me from head to toe, and whatever he found, he was satisfied. He turned to a technician at the control. "Get General Raf back on. Tell him to expect a squad with the Balancer within two Live Realm hours."

I exhaled the breath I was holding as I watched the scurry of movement in response to the order. The Kyrios seemed to move with more purpose. With more fervor than before. And with the furtive glances I was receiving, I was pretty sure I was the cause of it.

Nabil looked to Gregor and me. "Prepare to leave from the east gate in two Live Realm hours. Gregor, set her up with some armor. Lady Katya," he said quietly, "we are putting all our faith in the idea of the Balancer. Let us hope our faith is not misplaced." I simply nodded and followed Gregor out the door.

Our trip to our tower was a quiet one, save for the sound of squads shouting and marching about, carrying out their orders. We made a beeline for my bedroom and closed the door. My body was flattened against the wall as soon as the lock clicked shut. Gregor's body covered me completely, his lips devouring me with desperation. His hands were everywhere, as if memorizing every curve, every inch of me. My own hands were in his hair, over the flat planes of his chest and stroking his hard-lined jaw. Despite everything: the pressure, the lies, the destiny, the war, I was extremely pleased to be pressed against the man who taken every inch of my heart.

After several moments, Gregor pulled away, resting his forehead against mine.

"I desperately don't want you to go."

"Gregor—" I started.

"But at the same time, I know you have to do this. After our talk with Nabil, it's even more important now."

I gnawed on my bottom lip. "What if I really the end the world?"

He shook his head. "One battle at a time, Kat. Let's deal with the immediate crisis first. Before anything else happens, I want you to know I am proud of you."

My insides turned to mush. "Really?"

He cradled my face and searched my eyes, seeking something. He said, "There is one thing I want you to promise me. Stay alive. Stay by my side. I don't want you to join me over on this side just yet."

I gave him a small smile. "I'll promise to do that if you do me one thing for me. Well, actually two."

"What is it?"

I inched as close as possible and gave him a soft kiss, filled with everything I was feeling but couldn't voice. I think he understood because his eyes softened with a smile as we separated.

"Hold on to that kiss for me. I'll want it back later."

A grin lit up his face. "Well, what if I don't want to give it back?"

"There is a 'must return' policy on that kiss. Think of it as a loan."

Gregor chuckled. "Okay, fine. What's the second thing?"

I felt my smile dim slightly. "Could you hold me until I have to leave?" I asked in a small voice.

Gregor pulled me into his arms and kissed me on my forehead. "I'm not leaving your side." We laid on my bed, his chest to my back. Being held close stopped the jitters and the shock of Nabil's news from overtaking me. Could I really be the end of the world? If the Archs found me, would they try to convince me of their vision? What if this all turned into something I didn't want? Could I be my own version of the Balancer?

I'm not sure how long we rested there, enjoying the contact, but it felt like it was over too soon. Gregor said, "It is time to get ready." He disappeared into his room and returned with a box. He gave me a wan smile and stepped outside again. Inside were several black pieces of armor for my chest, arms, and knees. And each piece fit me perfectly, snapping over my black Kyrios bodysuit.

I took one look at a mirror in the corner of the room and realized I looked like every bit the Kyrios fighters I had seen in Ager. The bags under my eyes did not diminish the look of fear and determination I wore as I adjusted my kinky, curly hair. I chuckled to myself. Just weeks ago, the only concern I had was whether I should flat iron my hair or keep it curly. Or if I should cut my hair or maintain the long hard-fought length I had. Life can be funny that way.

When I finished, I stepped outside my room to find Gregor dressed in a similar fashion. He checked that each piece was in place and said, "Are you ready?"

I nodded. Gregor opened his mouth to say something, but decided not to. He simply nodded. "Let's go."

42

We traveled in silence to the East Gate to find General Nabil, the Quad, Jaya, Kevon, and Santiago waiting for us.

"I've taken the liberty to increase your number of guards, my lady. I'm told you have already met these individuals," he motioned to Jaya, Kevon, and Santiago. "It is my hope that despite everything, you all can work together." He gave me a meaningful look.

I cleared my throat. "While I don't appreciate the secrets that have been kept from me, in some ways I can understand. Many people back home don't know about my past because of my fear of rejection." I made sure to look at all of them in the eye, including Gregor. "I am willing to put all of that aside. We have work to do. Together."

The relief and grins on their faces were clear and they answered, "Yes, miss!"

A ghost of a smile flitted across Nabil's face. "Your mission is clear, Kyrios. Get the Balancer to the rift and give her the necessary cover to get the job done by any means necessary."

They all nodded. I guess that meant they were going half-Want. I began to coach myself. *Don't freak out. Don't freak. Do. Not. Freak.*

General Nabil took another look at us, looking grim but determined. "We wait for your return. Depart."

The Kyrios saluted him and we began to move quickly out of the gate. They formed a small circle around me with Gregor to my left and Demetrius to my right. We headed far out enough outside the gates that Zenobia could open a portal large enough for all of us to walk through at once.

On the other side, we arrived in what looked like the middle of downtown LA. Night had just fallen and the area was relatively deserted, save a few cars that looked like they had been abandoned. I guess they hadn't been kidding about the increasing number of accidents. As much I wanted to marvel at finally making it to California, the presence of the otherworldly guard dampened my thrill.

The group ushered me to a nearby alley where we found a disheveled General Raf with several injured Kyrios resting against the buildings' walls.
"General Raf—" Demetrius started.

"Shh," Raf said.

All of us fell silent. A loud screech could be heard about a mile away, quickly fading. When Raf felt it was safe, he said, "We've been reduced to hiding out here until you all arrived. As you can see," he said bitingly, "we've gotten a couple of scratches." Some of the Kyrios looked like they were about to keel over from exhaustion and their injuries.

"General Raf," Gregor interjected. "What's the plan to get to the gate?"

The general grimaced. "The Wanters have drastically increased their numbers in the past couple of hours." He held out his hand and manipulated a ball of energy until it looked like a map of the city. "The gate is about one and a half miles east, towards the Arts District. We are here." He pointed to a large building directly in front of the gate. "Between us and the gate, we are looking at more than a hundred Wanters, ranking from the lowest to level-three Stuffers and Wreckers. We have two other Kyrios groups in a building to the east and west, ready to strike with us." He pointed to a smaller building standing directly to the rift's right.

"And the living?" Demetrius asked.

Raf shook his head. "Anyone living around here has been avoiding the area entirely." He pointed to the middle ground between us and the gate. "This is all a mess due to our fighting. Much of it is just debris from the buildings that were clipped or craters that have formed in the street. Before the hard fighting occurred, the skirmishes alone were freaking the living out and the place was evacuated. Now rumors have been flying that this place is either the epicenter of the tremors or just plain cursed. Either way, those in charge in the Live Realm figured out a way to explain away what they can't understand. As usual. It's just us and the Wanters here."

"What's your plan to move us, General?" Gregor asked.

He sighed. "We'll move forward and engage the Want from the west and the east, pressing them into the middle. Gregor, Demetrius, and Jaya, you will take Lady Katya around the fighting from the west and get to the gate. We'll close the Want in a circle long enough to close the rift." He turned to me. "How long do you need?"

Everyone looked at me. I inwardly turned to Mika. *Well?*

A pause. **Seven minutes**.

"Seven minutes," I repeated.

General Raf nodded. "Then we'll do our best to give you that. Gregor, Demetrius, and Jaya, you three stay with Lady Katya. The rest of you come with me. We'll alert the others of the plan. Move out in fifteen." Zenobia, Addy, and Sebastian turned to me and bowed deeply, their right hand over their hearts. "It has been a pleasure to serve you, my lady." Santiago and Kevon joined them on their knees.

I desperately held back the tears that wanted to fall. "I expect to see all of you when I get back. There are more gates to close." They each gave me a smile and left, following after General Raf.

I took a deep breath, stealing a glance at Demetrius and Jaya. Their expressions were passive, but both of their bodies looked rigid. I guessed they were getting themselves ready. Gregor's body looked rigid as well, but his focus was on me, looking very grim.

I was about to ask what was wrong, when I felt Mika prodding me. I moved to a corner, sat on the floor, and closed my eyes. I hoped it looked like I was meditating and that no one would bother me.

Mika? I asked.

Katya. Her voice was calm as usual. **The three of us need to talk**.

Yeah, we do. How are we going to do this?

You are not capable of bringing forth the power to close the rift. You're not ready yet.

What? If I can't do this, then why did you let me say we could?

We can do it, together. But you need to do exactly what I tell you. Diantha, you will need to listen well. This concerns you too.

What is it I have to do? Cynthia asked.

Katya, you need to die.

I screamed in my head, *Are you crazy?* Cynthia just sputtered in the background, not believing her orders.

Quite sane, thank you.

This is no time for jokes, Mika! I can't do that. Not willingly!

Katya! Her voice almost boomed within me. **There are very few instances where I will insist on something. This is one of those times. The choice is always yours. But if you don't close this particular gate, things are going to get much more difficult for everyone. This is your role and your responsibility. This is the first crucial step.**

I couldn't answer. I didn't know what to say. But Mika knew that. She felt my acceptance.

Cynthia was still sputtering. *This is going to the hardest thing I have ever done. To just let Katya die?*

Mika's calm voice answered. **You can, Diantha and you will. Katya, I will tell you when it is time.**

"Katya, we need to move out."

I opened my eyes to find Gregor, Demetrius, and Jaya with their Havadars out. I pulled Diantha out as well. Knowing it was my best friend, it oddly felt comforting in my hands. We all moved out the entrance to find Raf's team moving toward the west. Raf grinned at me. "We'll meet again, my lady."

I nodded. With that, he was gone. Gregor led us a bit further down the middle to a deserted street. We waited in silence for the General's signal. It was several moments before we saw blue sparks glowing in the sky.

"Move!" Gregor shouted. We ran down the street, looping around pieces of debris and cars to return to the middle. We heard clangs of fighting in the background as we sprinted to the gate. Being in front of the gate was an entirely different experience than seeing it from central command. The gate was easily one hundred feet tall and another two hundred feet wide. It was just a massive dark hole, sucking the life out of the area and pouring out dark energy. There wasn't even any concrete to suck up anymore. Just dirt, slowly getting sucked into the gate.

It sent chills up and down my spine, raising the hair on my neck. It was the same turbulent energy I'd felt in my mother's dream. But the worst part was, from deep inside the tear itself, a loud, deep breathing could be heard.

"What is that?" Jaya asked.

"No idea, and I'd rather not find out. Lady Katya?" Demetrius said.

I gulped. "Right." I tried to summon my own energy, but it felt like nothing would come up. Being next to the dark rift had blocked the Vis reserves I had. "Something is off. I can't bring up my power!" I panicked.

"Lady Katya, you are just delaying the inevitable." Hovering over our heads were Lamar, Sophia, and two other men I didn't recognize. At least they looked like men. At a closer look at their claws, their jagged teeth, and their horns protruding from their backs and their red eyes, I realized they were Wanters.

"Oh great," Jaya muttered. "The Thirsty. Level three too."

Lamar grinned down at us. "The power you feel from the gate is the future. This realm's new awakening. Even after all that training, I think this is a bit too much for our precious Balancer to handle," he sneered.

Gregor stepped forward in front of me. "Think about what you are doing, Lamar! Sophia!"

"We didn't come here to talk," Sophia laughed. "We came to end this—and her."

"Over my dead body," Gregor growled, his eyes glowing blue.

"That can be arranged!" Lamar shouted. The traitors charged at us. Our swords clashed against our opponents. My combatant was the lovely Sophia.

"Look like we get to pick up where we left off, Balancer!" Sophia grinned; her face glowed with wicked pleasure. Our Havadars sang as we met blow for blow.

"Why are you doing this, Sophia?" I yelled. "You are turning against everyone because of me?"

Sophia snorted. "My reasons are none of your concern. I'd

worry about that dark face of yours first!" She swung hard, sending my knees buckling under the weight. I landed down hard on the ground with my free hand, trying to break my fall. I instantly knew I'd broken my wrist. Sophia must have heard it snap because she grinned widely. "Already? I told Krenlin that I wouldn't need to do much to send you into pieces.

I managed to push her back with my Havadar, mustering some energy to get some space to breathe. I got up gingerly, holding my hand to my body.

Cyn, can you help out a bit here? I sensed her grin.

Let's try out some of that extra training!

I smirked at Sophia. "You caught me off guard once, Sophia. Not again." With a flash, Diantha reformed into two new, short blades, while the hilt wrapped with cloth that shimmied up my wrist to my elbow. The new weapon reinforced my broken wrist, and I was able to tap into some of my previously blocked energy. I quickly used some of the energy to mend my wrist. It was a short-term solution that Cynthia had taught me, but the moment I relaxed, it would be rendered useless again. "Besides, I thought Krenlin wanted me for himself."

Sophia didn't look impressed. Shrugging, she said, "Right now, I don't care what he wants. I want you dead now." She attacked again, but the two blades gave me some advantage. Our Havadars sang and clanged, blow by blow. I could only imagine how we looked, fighting and quickstepping as fast as we were.

Frustrated, Sophia leapt back. "Let's see how you do with this, little girl." Her eyes glittered as she lifted her free hand and formed a small black hole the size of a bowling ball. The black hole began to suck in all the air around us, taking in everything nearby—trees, dirt, even a car or two. After sliding towards her about fifty feet, I slammed my blades into the dirt and held on for dear life. The sucking suddenly stopped, but Sophia's eyes remained gleeful. She slammed the sphere into the ground, causing all the wind and debris sucked in to explode out into a mighty gale storm, solely aimed at me.

"Mika!" An enormous shield formed around my body, blocking the heavy metal debris from hitting me. I could hear someone calling my name, but I couldn't lose focus now. By the time the gale-force winds stopped, I was exhausted. Mika had used the majority of my available energy to protect me. Diantha returned to her original form. My wrist hurt like hell. My shield cracked and shattered into pieces. I barely had the strength to stand up.

Sophia was right. Mika was right. I wasn't ready for this.

I watched Sophia approach me, in no particular hurry. She could tell I didn't have anything else up my sleeve.

Katya and Diantha, Mika said softly. **It's time**.

"Okay," I whispered. I leaned on my Havadar and tried to look bored. "Nice trick, Sophia. Got any more?" I yawned. "You're kinda boring me here."

She stopped dead in her tracks. "What?"

I rolled my eyes. "I mean, if you were really trying to rough me up, take a page out of Gregor's book. Gregor has shown me better tricks than that and we've been together..." I counted my finger, "a handful of times now. And let me tell you, the man does not disappoint. He is such an animal!" I winked at her.

Her expression was pure rage, her eyes bleeding red. With her sword raised, she quickly charged at me with murderous intent. And I did nothing as her Havadar ran through my stomach.

43

Dying really sucked.

Forget the pain licking at your body like fire. Forget the "my-life-flashed-before-my-eyes" montage. What got me was the slow motion. I never thought that my end would feel like one of those cheesy "slo-mo" moments where time moved as fast as a snail.

It took an eternity for my body to crash to the ground.

I remembered being very aware of everything around me. Clashes of power, screams of rage, and cries for mercy. The wonderful cacophony of a battle winding up to its pinnacle. The players' faces were not clear, but each sound was heard distinctly. It's amazing how your ears seem to hit their peak as life leaks out. Almost like a light bulb getting brighter and brighter before it explodes.

I remembered someone calling my name and saw how his quick movements sent him zipping to my side. His cries reverberated through me, making me wish that I had enough strength to lift my hand and brush it against his cheek. It made me wish that I could say his name one more time. To tell him how much he pisses me off. To say how much he drives me crazy. To say how, in the short time we'd known each other, he'd become the most important person to me.

To say that I was sorry.

I remembered his cries became more incessant, urging me to hold on. But there was nothing else I could hold on to. I had to let go. The sounds became mumbles, buzzing in the background. My eyelids became heavier.

Are you ready? Mika asked softly.

If I could have nodded, my head would have bobbed up and down. But she understood. She knew my agony, my pain.

As my eyes closed on the scene before it, on the most beautiful set of blue eyes I had ever seen, I felt the light within me dim, as if it too was dying out.

My heart completely stopped. And then the light erupted.

It was suddenly like Mika and I had switched places. I could see right through my own eyes, but didn't have the controls anymore. It was odd seeing my body rise up on its own, seeing Gregor's tear-stricken face respond with confusion. But it was awesome seeing Sophia's shocked and angered face. She made to charge at me, but Mika lifted our hand and sent out our own gale wind, careening the traitor into a nearby building.

"Katya," Gregor whispered.

I felt myself smile. "Everything will be fine now, Gregor," Mika said. I think Gregor instantly knew it wasn't me talking but someone else. Mika didn't wait for a response and began to walk towards the rift. Through Mika, I could feel everyone's individual energy. Demetrius's fierce aura. Jaya's prideful energy. Gregor's apprehension. Even the Wanters that fought against us. It was overwhelming, but normal at the same time. Mika stopped about fifty feet in front of the gate and raised our hand.

Our body rose in the air until we hovered in front of the gate. She clapped our hands together and closed our eyes to focus, building a ridiculous amount of Vis though our body and channeling it into our hands. It was almost like she was synching us with the energy within the Live Realm and borrowing it.

"I really wish I had absorbed you when I had the chance."

We opened our eyes to find Krenlin floating fifty feet away, looking fascinated and ticked off. "I'm afraid I can't let you do this. The gate must remain open. The new Master insists on it."

As if on cue, the horrible dark energy surged. We could see a huge pair of eyes from deep within, staring out at us. We didn't hear a word, but a distinct roar could be heard from the dark energy.

Krenlin smirked. "He says hello."

Mika hadn't moved an inch since Krenlin's arrival. She simply said, "What must be done will be done."

The Want General sighed. "I'm not even talking to Lady Katya now, am I?" He shook his head. "It's truly a pity. You and I could have been together forever. Now, I have to destroy you." He took off his bowler hat and revealed a long boney spike at the top of his head. With a loud grunt, he pulled the spike out of his head, wielding his own long sword. Just as he readied himself to pounce, a red sphere shot Krenlin in the face, sending him to the ground below. We turned to see Gregor in his own battle stance, his Havadar pointing at the Wanter, who was struggling to get up. The Kyrios had already transformed to his half Want form.

"Your battle is with me, Krenlin," he said in an unearthly tone.

Krenlin stood from the ground, touching his bruised face. "Do you know how many souls I had to devour and absorb to get this face?" he screeched.

Gregor smirked. "Wait till you see what I'm going to do it." The two met head on, and the force of their energies clashed and sent tremors into the earth. Mika returned to gathering positive Vis energy into our body. The "new Master" watched from inside the rift and sent enough ripples through it that we couldn't help but tremble from the dark energy that moved around us.

What is that? I asked Mika.

Something that should've never been created.

Mika finally moved. **We have enough energy**. Speaking in a loud voice, speaking in another language I couldn't understand, Mika directed the energy in our hands toward the top of the rift. The seam between the realms began to slowly close—like a huge zipper pulling together two pieces of fabric. Our body became increasingly hot from the Vis energy from the earth, but we stuck to our task. One inch at a time, working to return this part of the world back to normal.

Our dark voyeur from inside the rift fought against the closing with each inch. It became a battle of wills. Dark versus light. When we couldn't move it any further, the zipper stuck half way down, Mika said to me, **Katya, remember what I said. We need to do this together**.

What do you want me to do?

Think about this world. The world you love. Think about love, and peace, and everything that the Want hates.

What I love? My mother, the parent who gave up everything for me, who was patiently waiting for me to return. I wanted to see my mom's proud smile as I got my high school diploma and my college degree.

My best friend, my Havadar, waiting to be freed from her coma prison. Waiting to return to her body.

And Gregor. I loved him. He was my protector, my friend. And I didn't want to leave his side ever.

That's it, Katya. Think about everyone you love. Gregor.

I thought of the first time I had seen him, at Amie's party. Him in the alley. Him telling me what he was. Our adventures with my friends. Our falling out after I learned who I was. Faking at husband and wife. Us training together. Him holding me before the battle, telling me how he cared.

The rift closed with every thought I had about my family, my friends, and Gregor. We could feel the "new Master's" frustration when he only had five feet left.

We sank to the ground to close the remaining space when a humanoid hand shot out of the rift and closed around our neck. A low and rumbling voice spoke. "Do not think you have won here. Your Vis will be mine."

Our body began to convulse from the lack of air, and I could tell Mika was beginning to lose control. The hand tightened its grip and started to siphon off our power. With everything within us, taking whatever energy we had left, I pushed from inside and yelled, *You are not getting her*!

A burst of energy engulfed us completely, burning up our body so hot that the hand released us and retreated as the rift completely closed. Our body continued to burn like fire as I continued to chant, *No one is getting you.* The ground shook as we became a beacon of light, releasing all the Vis energy we had gathered into the ground and air.

At the last second, I felt something major depart from my body before the controls were returned to me and my limp body fell to the ground.

The last thing I heard was Mika saying, **It is done.**

44

And now for the top story worldwide. The whole planet has released a sigh of relief—for over seventy-two hours, there have been no reported tremors. Experts warn that this may simply be the eye of the storm, but they are hopeful that we might still find an answer to the source of these quakes. The President of the United States, after declaring a state of emergency for the entire nation, has directed supplies and medical help to shelters and hospitals as needed.

The President reminds us that now is not that time to panic, but to remain calm and vigilant...

*   *   *

I felt someone running their hand across my cheek, pausing to trace a small scar that had formed on the corner of my eye when I was eight years old. Only one person in the world would know that scar. I cracked open my eyes to find my mother gently caressing my face with tears in her eyes. "My Kitty Kat."

"Mom," I said hoarsely. "Where am I?"

"Argentina, sweetie. You're at my safe house."

A look around showed she was right. A small room with the bare necessities. A window opened wide, showing palm trees, tropical plants, and a toucan sitting on a branch. I could hear Spanish being yelled down below.

Before I could ask another question, a pair of footsteps thundered down the hallway until they came to a stop at my door. Cynthia, in her redheaded glory, grinned widely as our eyes met.

"Kat!"

"Cynthia," I said tearfully. She looked like she wanted to give me a bear hug, but opted to sit down at the foot of my bed instead. "You're back to normal—" I darted a look at my mother. "How are you feeling?"

My mother smirked at me. "You don't have to watch your words around me, silly. I remembered the dream, and Cynthia gave me a refresher. You can ask Cynthia how she got back into her body."

With a huge grin, I asked, "Um…okay! How did you get back into your body, Cyn?"

She waved her hand flippantly. "Eh, it was nothing. Once the Kyrios figured out that Lamar had placed a soul bind on me, they removed it, and I got the ol' strength back." She grinned. "But don't be confused. Just because some of our energy has returned to this body, it doesn't mean you don't have the other bits of me still inside you. Besides, we need more training. Sophia got to you way too easy!"

I cringed, remembering. "Hmm, maybe I'll want a different trainer."

"Sorry, honey. There are certain things Gregor can't teach you about me. Anyway, this is a girls' club. No boy Kyrios allowed!"

My smile died at the mention of the dark-haired Kyrios's name. "Where is he?"

"Right here." Leaning against the door was the most beautiful man I had ever seen. His blue eyes never left mine. Out of the corner of my eye, I saw Mom and Cynthia share a look. I checked him over from head to toe—nothing out of place. Still perfect as usual.

"Hi," I said breathlessly.

"Hi, yourself." He sauntered into the room with an easy smile.

Mom cleared her throat. "Why don't we leave the two of you to sort things out?" She stood and ushered Cynthia out. She gave me a knowing look before closing the door. Gregor sat at my side, his eyes roaming over my face. "How do you feel?"

"Just exhausted. What happened?"

He sighed. "When you closed the rift, a huge shaking stopped all of us from fighting. When the Want realized that the rift was closed, they immediately retreated. Krenlin's parting words were, 'This is only the beginning.'"

My eyes dropped to my fidgeting hands. "How many gates are there?" I said quietly.

Gregor lifted my chin up. "At last count, about fourteen. Yes, this is the beginning, but we will make it to the end."

"What about what Nabil said?" I said uneasily. "If I continue doing what I do, what about the Archs finding me?"

"We deal with it when the times comes. We'll just focus on the gates. As soon as you get better, we'll close the rest of the open gates and try to move as quietly as possible." He smiled. "Fancy taking that trip around the world?"

The corners of my mouth quirked up. "I've always wanted to see the world. But wait, did anyone else get hurt?"

His eyes saddened a bit. "We did lose a few men in the fight."

I held my breath. "Anyone I know?"

Gregor shook his head. "No. Your guards suffered some injuries, but they'll recover."

I sighed happily. "Thank God."

The dark-haired Kyrios folded his arms over his chest. "But I have a bone to pick with you. I thought you promised me you weren't going to die."

"I'm not dead," I smiled sheepishly. I waved my arms and hands, noting my left wrist was healed. "See, I'm fine."

He shook his head, "I distinctly felt you die. You broke your promise." I could see the remnants of the ache from seeing my lifeless body in his eyes.

I took his hand in mine. "I'm sorry you had to see that, but I had to. Mika said—" I stopped short, sensing something was off.

Gregor looked at me puzzled. "What did Mika say?"

I ignored him and searched deeper and deeper. Found nothing. "Mika's gone," I whispered.

"What?"

"Mika's gone, Gregor! Where is she?" I panicked. I was about to get out of bed when Gregor held me down.

"Katya, calm down. She may have gone dormant again. You released all of your Vis in that blast. She may be within your soulscape again."

I relaxed a bit, but I wasn't completely convinced. "Are you sure?"

"I still sense a lot of Vis energy in you. She has to be there somewhere. Where else could she be?"

I nodded, hoping he was right.

Gregor took my hand into his again. "Even though you broke your promise for a moment, I'm very glad you kept it in the end." He tucked a loose strand of hair behind my ear.

I remembered my last thought before I died. "Gregor." I looked down at our joined hands. "Sometimes you annoy the bejesus out of me."

He chuckled. "Okay?"

"Hold on, let me get this all out." I took a deep breath. "You can tick me off within seconds, but make me want to kiss your face in the same amount of time. As my heart was stopping, I realized that I never told you how much your smile means to me or how much I enjoy the feeling of your arms around me. Or how you have my favorite pair of eyes. And I know I'm human and you're not...completely human."

I took a deep breath. "But I told myself before I died that, if I ever got the chance, I would tell you that I love—"

I couldn't finish. My lips became preoccupied. The same passion and urgency I'd felt expressing myself to him was returned as Gregor encased me in his arms, driving me insane with the movement of his lips and tongue. My own hands found themselves gripping his shoulders, moving to massage his scalp, earning a groan.

He pulled away, leaving a trail of kisses on my face. "Silly girl. I think I fell in love with you the moment I saw you. This beautiful lass staring me down sent enough shivers down my body to remind me I even had a body."

I laughed and rested my head on his shoulders. "So, we love each other. Now what?"

"We'll break the rules together. Not sure how Nabil will take this, but right now, I don't care."

I smirked at him. "Hey, that's your beloved mentor there. Be careful, Kyrios." I eased back into my pillow, letting my hand linger in his. "When will I see the others?"

He smirked. "Funny you should mention the others. Because of your upcoming work, General Nabil decided that you should have a full guard with you during this world tour. The Quad, Jaya, Santiago, and Kevon have been designated as your personal guards and they will be stationed here."

"Nice! That's the best news I've heard all day."

As the sun streamed into my room, Gregor paused to take another look at me, painting me with a serene look that warmed me to the core. He arched an eyebrow, as if waiting for something.

I rolled my eyes, but was unable to keep the smile off my face. "What is it?"

"Aren't you going to ask?"

"Ask what?"

Both his eyebrows rose. "If you're not going to ask, then I'll just keep it." He made to leave but I pulled him back down.

"What are you talking about?"

His eyes warmed over and he tweaked my nose. "I kept *my* promises."

Giggling, I threw my arms around his neck. I asked sweetly, "Can I have my kiss back, please?"

"Gladly."

As our lips met for a sweet and soft kiss, I decided to let go of all of my worries about Mika and what the Want was planning next. Just for a moment, I decided to let go of the imminent threat of the Archs finding out about me. Just for a moment, I even let go of my worries about closing the gates for the next couple of months.

For that moment, I decided to take Gregor's advice: Enjoy the sweet moments while you can, for you're never promised another.

ACKNOWLEDGEMENTS

It's never how you start but it's how you finish. It's taken me five years to get here. And, what a journey it has been!

First, I want to thank my husband Everett for being my rock, my cheerleader and pushing my butt out the door to get to work. I couldn't have done this without you. No one else but you.

I want to thank my editor Brenda Peregrine for being my partner in crime with this book. I know I must have pissed you off plenty of times but I want to thank you for being so patient with me and hanging in there through it all.

I want to thank my Editorial Board crew over at SugarCane Publishing. You guys answered the call when no one else would and you have stuck it out. To the first of many! To friends who have encouraged me along the way, my little brother – the original partner in crime and to my parents, thank you for giving me the space to be me.

Father, thank you for providing me the intelligence and imagination to complete this book. We have so many more to complete and I can't wait to complete the journey with you by my side.

All my love,
K. T.

ABOUT K. T. CONTE

K.T. Conte is a lover of books, people and all things wild and crazy. She received her B.A. in English from Boston College and her law degree from Suffolk University Law School. While she has and continues to be a licensed attorney, her first love has always been books from the tender age of two. Originally from Massachusetts, K.T. currently lives in New York City with the monsters in the closet, her husband Everett, a couple of building fairies, two squirrels living outside her apartment she swears are evil incarnate and her dog, Champ.

www.ktconte.com

CPSIA information can be obtained
at www.ICGtesting.com
Printed in the USA
LVOW03s0207091117
555586LV00004B/259/P